# Under The Nail Polish

# Under The Nail Polish

## Tina Griffith

**To order additional copies of this book, contact:**
Xlibris
1-888-795-4274
www.Xlibris.com
Orders@Xlibris.com
757625

Many thanks, to Gordon Sauck, Mechelle Tait, and Grant Greening for their excellent editing skills.

The inspiration for this book came from Stephanie Blake and Corrina Caseley.

# Chapter 1

It was 1:00pm, on May 27, 1965, and the weather outside was perfect - sunny and warm, with not a cloud in the sky. There was a slight breeze fanning any exposed skin, which gave you the illusion that you were somewhere in the tropics.

Inside the perfectly squared courtroom of the Court of Queen's Bench, the air was musty, and filled with smells from the thousands of people who had been part of the proceedings, long before today. The ambience had gone completely silent in the last minute or two, and all eyes were now fixed on the grey-haired man sitting behind the large desk.

During the trial, the Honorable Judge Gordon had looked long and hard at the handsome defendant. The judge had specifically noted the apparent lack of emotion and attention, which the younger man had been displaying throughout the duration of the trial. Everyone in the courtroom had found it difficult to concentrate, with the way that the man was constantly adjusting his clothing, as if that was the most important thing on his mind; every elaborate move was theatrical and quite distracting.

Over the past three days, the highly-esteemed judge had tried to listen intently, and felt that he had heard all of the testimony that had been presented to him by the prosecution and the defence team. He had secretly wished that this particular hearing had been conducted with a jury rather than as a bench trial, so that his decision would not be the only one needed in order to make the final verdict.

From the beginning, Judge Gordon had an inkling that something wasn't right. In the end, all things had pointed to the fact that Andrea's death was not her husband's fault. To the outside world, this was an open and shut case without any complications. To the learned man, who had been presiding behind the large bench for over 20 years, there was an unsettling stirring in his stomach that he couldn't quite put his finger on. But, regardless of how he felt, the judge knew that he needed to make a decision.

The 66-year old judge let his weathered eyes gaze back to the papers, which lay haphazardly in front of him, and he could feel the anxious hush of all those in the courtroom as they waited for his ruling. He was not 100% convinced that the man in question was not guilty, but the judge felt somewhat satisfied that all the facts had added up to only one possible answer. With this in mind, the distinguished man in the flowing black robe, gazed at the mesmerized onlookers and then at the two men who were seated behind the prosecution desk. And in a gradual and methodical movement, the man who held the final vote, shifted his furrowed eyes past those in the defendant's area. Seconds later, these same old eyes rested firmly upon the handsome respondent, who was mindlessly fidgeting with his expensive clothing.

Judge Gordon was growing impatient and cleared his throat repeatedly, which ultimately made Nico look up. Now that he finally had the defendant's attention, the man in authority lifted the gavel with his right hand, and delivered his judgement in a strong, booming voice.

"I've weighed all the evidence, and after much deliberation, this court has decided to rule in favor of the defendant." As he spoke, Judge Gordon's steely grey eyes were staring directly into the face of the alleged murderer. "Nicholas Julius Kostas", he announced sternly.

His lawyer poked him in the ribs, which made Nico stand up. "Yes, your honor?" His blank expression did not indicate compliance.

"Due to the lack of sufficient evidence to rule against you, you are hereby declared innocent in your wife's unfortunate and untimely death. You are free to go."

Like the sounds of soft waves rolling against a stony shore, a hush of stifled gasps of relief and surprise could be heard throughout the entire room.

The magistrate slammed the gavel down onto the large desk, which signified that the case before him was now closed. Judge Gordon then stood up and turned his back towards the courtroom. While moving himself to the exit, he turned to the bailiff and requested a 10-minute recess.

"All rise!" the bailiff announced loudly. The uniformed man watched with considerable interest, as the entire population in the gallery stood up as a collective unit. Together they waited, until the judge had exited the moderately-sized judicial chamber. The instant that the heavy door had shut behind him, a tamed mumbling sound erupted from the people in the closed-in area.

Twenty-five of the individuals present began rejoicing in loud whispers. They congratulated the lawyers for doing a good job, and they praised the attractive man who had just been acquitted of his wife's murder. The rest of the assembly were astounded by what they believed was the wrong verdict. They shouted their opinions and profanities towards the apathetic people in the justice system, and then left the building - either by force, or on their own volition, but all were muttering under their breath.

Nico's sensuous lips let out a heavy sigh of relief, and for the first time in a month, he gave his well-toned body permission to relax. While he bathed in the friendship and glory that was being thrown at him from all directions, his emotions suddenly took control. He wasn't sure if he wanted to laugh or cry; the adrenaline was pumping through his body at top speed, altering his better judgement.

His tanned face couldn't help but smile now that he had been declared innocent, for this was yet another victory in his long road of acquiring vast amounts of money that shouldn't belong to him.

The incredibly expensive lawyer, who had just represented Nico for the third time, noticed his client's facial appearance. In a hurried and unexpected manner, the defence attorney's hand rushed out and landed firmly on Nico's forearm. The powerful grip was meant to stop Nico from becoming lost in the moment, and it worked.

Nico turned his head to look into Mr. Kendy's face, and after interpreting the wise attorney's stern expression, he nodded with acknowledgement. No words were needed - not for a fear of being overheard, but because this was now becoming routine. Nico immediately altered his facial muscles to appear humble, and then bowed his head ever so slightly, as he looked out at all the people in the courtroom.

Nico was tired and hated how long this ordeal was taking, but he knew that he had to continue with this charade for a little while longer. Nico had been told how very important it was to show the public that he was a grieving widower, and that he was thankful that he had been acquitted of his wife's death.

Nico appeared to be relieved but sad. This was in accordance to how his expression should be seen, for the cameras and the public who would later be judging him. He knew more than anyone, that the press took hundreds of pictures at one time. He also knew that they would and could, study the many features of his face more closely and with infinitely more detail, once they returned to their offices to report this surprise verdict.

Nico prided himself on being an excellent performer, and he understood that these next few minutes needed to be acted out to perfection. In his head, he was playing the part of a man who had just lost his wife in an unfortunate accident. In reality, he had just committed another perfect murder.

Secretly, he couldn't wait to leave the very familiar, semi-dark and dreary courtroom, and he hoped for the next few interviews to go by quickly. Ten minutes later, as he was being led outside and into the cool fresh air by his lawyer, he was grateful that it was almost over.

"Over here!" shouted Leo Mafrica, the top photographer for one of the leading magazines in the country. His images were considered masterpieces, and sold in venues around the world.

Nico and his lawyer, Mr. Kendy, turned and posed for what they assumed would be the front page photo. After a few more blinding shots, they shouted their thanks to everyone for their generous time and support.

"Can we go now?" Nico whined into his lawyer's ear.

"In a minute", Mr. Kendy barked. He pushed the words out of his mouth without moving his lips, while his right hand waved in the same exact manner as the Queen of England. The 35-year old lawyer loved the adoration from the public, and since he was trying to climb up the ladder at the Mathews & Tait Law Firm, he relished all the positive exposure that he could get.

"Fine", Nico sighed. He pouted like a child who hadn't had his way in months. His attention was beginning to wander, he was slowly losing his composure, and he desperately wanted to go home.

After a strong poke in the ribs from his lawyer, Nico corrected his posture.

"Mind what you're doing!" Mr. Kendy stated sternly, while flashing his phony smile to everyone in attendance.

Nico now stood tall and behaved accordingly, until he was free to leave the growing circus of curiosity around him.

To keep his momentum going, he gave himself a small pep-talk. "A few more minutes and then I'll be home-free", Nico promised under his breath. And he knew in his heart that he could do it, for he'd had to endure this very same thing, several times before today.

*Nicholas, or Nico as his father had always called him, had literally clawed his way out of a destructive childhood. Having to contend with an abusive, alcoholic father from Valetta, Malta, and an overworked, often-absent mother* from a rough Italian neighbourhood in Brooklyn, made Nico grow up very quickly.

Both of his parents were loud and constantly at odds with one another, but they seemed to have a lot of steamy passion for the other, as well. There was never any money for childhood things like siblings, bicycles, or toy soldiers, but there always seemed to be plenty of cigarettes and booze in the house.

Up until he was 8 and 9 years old, Nico had no choice but to accept the many punishments that had been given out by his strict father. He hated almost everything about living in that home, and he wanted desperately to run away - but how and with what?

Nico soon learned that having money equals freedom and power, so he began to explore how he could get cash into his pockets. Pushing a lawn mower and scraping snow and ice off of sidewalks and driveways, was an awful lot of hard work that showed very little results. Helping old ladies with their groceries, only jingled his deep pockets with loose change.

By his 10th birthday, he was already exploring other things he could do to make some quick and easy cash. Some were legal and some were not, but at least he had a bit of money to count before he went to sleep at night.

At 14 years old, he was tall for his age and very handsome to look at. His eyelashes were dark, as were his large eyes, and his lips were full and quite welcoming. He had the swagger of someone who knew what he wanted out of life, *and the smoldering good looks of someone who knew exactly how to get it. He hung out with a rough crowd, but he was usually more of a loner.*

*A month before his 15th birthday, a woman almost twice his age, saw him lighting up a cigarette and confronted him. To her, he was intriguing, self-confident, and looked like a rugged Rock Hudson from the side. She asked him for a light, and then lured him into some friendly banter.*

*She loved his delicious accent, and how he moved his mouth when he spoke. He showed all of his teeth when he laughed, and he looked directly into her eyes when he replied to her questions. After a few minutes of sizing him up, she asked if she could spend some time with him.*

*"Why not?" he stated cheerfully. He saw no harm in chatting up this woman.*

*She took a deep breath and then asked him what he would do for a buck.*

*Nico acted tough and talked a big game, but he was a virgin. He was naïve in the ways of the heart and unsure of what she wanted him to do, but she bribed him with sweet talk and a sensuous kiss. After that, he was putty in her hands. She grabbed his arm in a familiar manner, and took him somewhere dark and unappealing. She then placed his hands exactly where she wanted them to go, and whispered further instructions.*

*Nico was surprised by how soft her skin was, how long her legs were, and how wonderful she smelled. He was shocked by how uninhibited she was acting, but this also aroused him beyond belief. Nico loved hearing her moan, and waited patiently for her next command. He actually complied quite willingly to all of her playful suggestions.*

*Carla was 40 years old, and she could tell within seconds that Nico had not had any experience with a woman before. This made their time together even more exciting for her. "Slow down", she whispered. His package was strong and rushing to get to the finish line, but she needed him to let her enjoy all that his eager 7 inches had to offer.*

*"Oh, my God", he chanted. "Oh, my God!" He couldn't believe how good this felt.*

*"Give me one more minute", she ordered softly. Carla was patient with him, and felt it was her duty to teach him to go slow when it was needed, and faster at the end. "You're a very good student, and I promise you that I have so much more to show you, if you are willing to learn and listen."*

*As if he was in a deep and unbelievable wonderful dream, the 15-year old could only nod his acceptance, for the words could not find their way to his mouth.*

*Nico was proud of the fact that he had lasted 30 minutes in total – his first orgasm exploded from his body a minute after entry, but he was ready to begin again a minute later.*

*Carla was more than delighted with all that he had delivered, and immediately gave him some money. "I know I told you a buck, but you are worth so much more."*

*He just had sex and she had paid him for it. Nico was shocked and very happy. "What's your name? Maybe I can call you sometime", he asked with the innocence of a trusting child. The boy might have the body of a stallion, but he was still a young teenager at heart.*

*The experienced woman hushed him to silence, by placing two fingers against his soft, young, eager lips. "I know where to find you, sweetheart", she whispered, and then she walked away.*

*Nico stood there all alone, and totally bewildered by all that had happened. The minute she was out of his sight, he turned and went home.*

*Nico saw her once a week for a month, before he was introduced to a few of her girlfriends. "You don't mind, do you?" Carla asked in a little girl's tone of voice.*

*He smiled and shook his head in response to her question. Two days later, he experienced his first threesome. From then on, he was involved with one or two women, a few nights every week. Word spread quickly, and soon he had a harem of women who were paying him for his favors.*

*By the time he turned 17, Nico had more money in his bank account, than all the people on his street made in a year. He was rolling in money, and all he had to do was make love, and whisper a few sincere compliments in someone's direction. "Life could not get any sweeter!" he declared with conviction. He then exhaled a long sigh of contentment.*

*Just before his 20th birthday, one of the women who Nico had spent some quality time with, died. What was more unexpected, was that she named Nico as her sole beneficiary. He ended up receiving $12,000 dollars from her will, and all he had to do was sign his name and the cheque was his. While he was sad about her death, he couldn't believe his good luck about the money. This strange experience made him wonder if it could happen again.*

*Two months later, Nico met a nice girl and they began to date. He continued to get together with a few of the women in his elite group, two or three times a week, but he no longer wanted to be as busy as he had been, out of respect to his steady girlfriend, Lucy. He told his lady friends of his plans, and they quickly expressed their sorrow. They understood his situation and agreed to his conditions, and waited patiently for their turn to come up in his schedule.*

*The summer turned to fall, and soon the snow began to cover the ground. Lucy was terribly excited, for this was her favorite season and she couldn't wait to show Nico what a good skier she was. In the same hour, on the day when the slopes were officially open, she called Nico at work and invited him to go skiing with her. After a short hesitation, she heard him agree.*

*"You won't regret it!" she screamed enthusiastically. Before they hung up the phone, Lucy added, "I can't wait to get you up there!"*

*As Nico hung up the phone, a thought occurred to him. He wasn't wishing it, but he wondered what would happen if Lucy were to die on the slopes. After analysing the situation, he decided to try an experiment.*

*Nico was not a skier, but he did know that one needed to wax their skis before using them. On the morning of November 11, he packed their gear and other things into the back of the car. He then drove to the Caseley Mountain Lodge, while his girlfriend slept in the seat beside him.*

*Unbeknownst to Lucy, Nico had applied a very generous amount of wax to the bottom of her skis – way more than what was needed. He knew very well what he had done, and was now anticipating the outcome.*

*Throughout the last few months, Lucy had grown to love Nico. She had envisioned that their lives together would one day flourish into marriage, and she hoped that at least two children would follow.*

*Lucy believed that by her sharing this experience with the man of her dreams, that she could prove to him that she was a great catch. She even expected, that if their afternoon went as well as she believed it would, the day might end with Nico proposing.*

*What the wide-eyed, beautiful young lady didn't know, was that this day would turn out to be her worst nightmare.*

*"We're here!" he called. He turned to look in her direction and his eyebrows immediately drew together, giving his face a grieving expression. Nico bumped her awake softly with his arm, and wondered if he should really go through with his plan; he enjoyed her company and he didn't want her to die to prove a point.*

*"Are we there?" she asked in a weary tone. As she stretched, she looked around.*

*Nico nodded while turning off the motor. He got out of the car and proceeded to take all of their things to the bottom of the hill.*

*"I can't wait to get up there", she confessed. The 23-year old university student was giddy, and was staring up at the top of the mountain as if it held hidden treasures. "I wish I was already up there", she announced softly.*

*Nico watched her strap up her boots and put on her mittens. "Okay, you have fun", he stated. There was a peculiar lilt in his voice as he spoke.*

*Her happy expression turned to pure shock. "Aren't you coming with me?" she questioned before he walked away. She pulled the sides of her hat down over her ears, as she waited for him to answer.*

*Nico moved his feet until he stood directly in front of her. "I have to get something from the car, but I don't want to hold you up", he suggested lovingly. "I'll be right behind you, don't worry." He leaned in and kissed her lips, and then grabbed her by the shoulders and turned her around. "Go on!" he ordered.*

*"Okay, but don't be too long", she commanded. She made sure to add a slice of humor to her voice, so it didn't sound too strict.*

*"I won't", he uttered with ease. Nico had no intention of going skiing, but he wanted to make it appear as if he would be right there with her. He took several steps towards the car, and then stopped. Once he realized that she was safely seated on the chair lift, he positioned himself in what he thought, was a perfect spot to watch her begin her run down the first-class mountain.*

*Fifteen minutes later, Lucy was in position. She slammed her poles into the ground, one on either side of her feet, and did one more adjustment to her gloves and hat. She looked around for Nico, and when she didn't see him, Lucy figured that she would catch up to him at the bottom of the hill. For now, she was excited and ready to begin her first trip down. She lifted her poles, and bent her upper body forward. With one strong push, she was on her way.*

*Adrenaline was pumping through her veins, as Lucy anticipated a perfect run down the sparkling packed powder. Because she was moving a bit faster than she would have wanted, she brought the tips of her skis together and pushed the tails apart. She then tried to apply pressure* on the skis' inside edges, but the familiar technique wasn't working. At this point, it was evident that something was seriously wrong.

Other skiers, and a member of the Ski Patrol, had noticed that someone was appearing to ski in a reckless manner. Rather than race out and possibly get themselves injured, they looked through binoculars to see if this showboating was being done on purpose.

Half of Lucy's mind was interlocked with a million options on how to stop herself from racing down the hill, while the other half had become delirious with questions as to how and why this was happening. "Get a grip!" she shouted to herself. Lucy could feel that she was on the verge of losing her sanity, and she knew that she needed to come up with a plan if she wanted to get out of this alive. With the speed that she was travelling, it was hard to stay calm. "Think!" she ordered loudly. Inside of her mind, she was screaming with fear.

After trying to slow down and finding that she couldn't, the experienced skier felt that she only had one option. If she could steer herself off of the active slope, she could slam into a bush, or something just as soft. The veteran skier did her best to maneuver herself towards the trees, while announcing to everyone in her path that they should move. "Coming through!" she shouted loudly. "Get out of my way!" She was more than scared about how this would end up.

Nico was shocked by how quickly Lucy was coasting, and he almost felt sorry for her. He had never been on a slope before, but he could see that she now lacked the proper handling of her skis and poles. Nico sat mesmerized as he watched his girlfriend try to figure out how to gain control over her current situation. With one leg crossed over the other, his entire focus was on Lucy's frightening trek down the mountain.

Nico wasn't sure if he had breathed or even blinked in the last few minutes, but he was sure to keep his eyes on the female figure that was causing so much disruption on the hill. All around him, he heard people making snide comments about the 'out of control skier', and never once did he let on that he knew what was happening.

Lucy was able to make it across the wide berth of firmly-packed snow without hitting anyone, and she sighed with relief. As she cast her eyes towards the thick evergreen trees, she noticed that there was no snow or ice on the ground under their large and heavy branches. In that split second, the beautiful young woman knew she was going to die.

"N-I-I-C-O-O!" The deathly sound echoed everywhere, and could be heard for miles around.

Nico had heard her screaming, as had everyone else, and once she disappeared into the trees, they all lost sight of her.

*BANG!* The horrible thud was deafening, and it lingered in the air for several minutes.

*Seconds later, sirens were blasting, whistles were blowing, and people were rushing everywhere. Five members of the Ski Patrol raced to find the adventurous skier, hoping that he or she would be injured but still alive. Sadly, Lucy's battered and lifeless body was found in a mangled mess, and brought down the hill on a stretcher, an hour later.*

*For the past hour, worried and crying individuals commented on how 'this kind of thing could happen'. Nico stood among the mass of curious onlookers, but he remained silent and still. He walked over when her body was close enough to touch, but they wouldn't let him near her. "But I'm her boyfriend", he stated in a mono-toned voice.*

*"We'll need you to answer some questions for us." They led him into a quiet room where two men in uniform waited, and then offered him a hot beverage. "Do you have any I.D. for yourself and for the victim?" the taller man asked.*

*Nico pulled out all the paperwork that he had, and then it hit him – Lucy had really died. He didn't feel guilty, but he did feel quite sad.*

*Minutes later, two men burst through the closed door. "We think we know what went wrong", a member of the Ski Patrol stated with confidence, and then he continued. "The bottoms of her skis appear to be super thick with wax."*

*"This caused them to move much faster across the fresh layer of snow and ice, than what is normally expected", an officer of the RCMP advised.*

*Everyone stood silent, while the men in authority nodded their heads in agreement.*

*When Nico got told that Lucy had died, he didn't have to pretend that he was surprised, because he really was upset. He was also shocked that his plan had worked! And just as he had intended, he was Lucy's beneficiary.*

*Nico received a great deal of money from the rental place, another cheque from her insurance policy, and one from the ski hill. He eventually received everything that she had once had in her possession, and all within five weeks from the date of the accident.*

*Nico couldn't believe it. He was so surprised that he could make this kind of money by hardly doing anything, that he stopped sleeping with 80% of his little harem. He kept Carla and a few of her friends on his 'to-do list', because he liked their company and it gave him something to do, but everyone else had to go.*

*Nico loved his new-found wealth, because it gave him the ability to buy and do everything that he ever wanted. But almost a year later, his money was running low, and he decided that he needed to find another steady girlfriend.*

*It didn't take him very long before he met a very nice woman, and this time, he became so infatuated with her, that he asked her to marry him. However, once he put a ring on her finger, he got scared of the heavy commitment and didn't know how to get out of it. "What did I do?" he moaned to himself at least once a day. "Why couldn't I just keep her as a girlfriend?"*

*The weeks went by and he was panicking like crazy, so he finally dropped the bomb. They had just finished their lunch when he blurted it out. "I think we need to break up." There was no build-up to that moment, or any previous warning to indicate that this might even happen.*

*"What?" Izzy was completely shocked, and it felt like her whole world had just exploded. At first, her mind couldn't think of anything to say. When she found her voice, she stumbled over silly promises – anything that would keep him in her life. "I'll give you everything I have, just don't leave", she pleaded. She was crying and desperate, and told him that she loved him to the core of her soul.*

*Nico couldn't break up with her in that condition, so he brought her close to his body and surrendered his heart to her. "I'm sorry", he began. "I didn't know what I was thinking." But a month later, when she asked him about the wedding, the same creepy feelings crawled over the skin on his body. It made him cringe with fear, and then a phone call changed everything.*

*Izzy learned that her mother had died. She never knew her father and she was an only child, so she was the sole heir to whatever her mother had left behind.*

*Nico rushed into his girlfriend's arms, and he gave her all the comfort that she needed. He ran her errands, he made sure that she ate and slept every day, and he did everything that was required, in order for her to feel that he was in her corner.*

*After the funeral, it was Nico who pushed the idea of marriage. "It's what your mother would have wanted", he said softly. He was playing on Izzy's guilt and hoped that she would fall for it. "We could even have it in her garden", he suggested. He guessed at how nice the colorful yard might be, and he could see that Izzy was about to play right into his hands.*

*"I guess."*

*"I'd love to marry you", he said with quiet emphasis.*

*Izzy decided that her mom would want her to be happy, but maybe it was too soon; she had a lot to do, what with cleaning the house and re-arranging her mother's things. She couldn't possibly put a wedding together right now, could she?*

*Nico could feel her thoughts racing around in her mind, and it made him happy to see that they she might be interested in getting married.*

*Izzy's eyes were now a bit brighter, and the ideas were beginning to percolate; the flowers, the dress, where the ceremony would take place, and when it will happen. "Give me a few months", she said after a few minutes of silence. Her face was softening at the thought of the lovely service.*

Nico sighed with great relief, for while she was planning a grand wedding, he was thinking of ways to spend her money. He didn't know how he would get it, but he felt sure that it wouldn't take too long before it fell into his hands. Nico, being a determined individual, fixated on how it could happen. Looking as happy as a kid on Christmas morning, he put his thoughts down on paper.

As the weeks went by, Nico made sure that their lives were content. Izzy was happy, a date was set for their wedding, all the arrangements were being finalized, and to the outside world, it looked like the happy couple were about to be married.

Two weeks before the wedding, was when they needed to put deposits down on the flowers, the caterers, the band, and on the reception hall. That's also the day when Nico had them add each other's names to their bank accounts, life insurance policies, RRSP's, and everything which Izzy had gotten from her mother's estate.

The plans for the next day, was for them to have some rest and relaxation. Nico and Izzy spent the morning in a tub full of lavender bubbles, while drinking slightly-cooled, pink champagne. The afternoon was spent having manicures and pedicures, and then it was off to dinner. The main item on the menu, was for them to discuss the details of their honeymoon. After desert, they spent almost two hours giving each other enormous pleasure, and then they slept the rest of the night away.

*Three days before the date of their wedding, Nico put his plan into action. He knew that Izzy would be out doing errands that afternoon, so he slipped into the home unnoticed, did what he had to, and left again - without her ever knowing he was there.*

*At 5pm, he called her with apologies that he was running late. "Sorry, honey. I'll be there soon." Unbeknownst to Izzy, Nico was actually making the shameful phone call from a nearby phone booth.*

*"You were supposed to be here already", the 26-year old woman groaned. Her tummy was rumbling and she wanted to eat, but because she knew how much Nico hated re-heated meat and vegetables, she opted to have everything hot and ready for him when he walked through the front door.*

*"I know", he sighed, trying to sound just as sad as she was. "But I'll be there as quickly as I can."*

*Izzy was feeling somewhat shaky and a little queasy, so she decided that she would snack on a few crackers and cookies to tide her over. "I can't wait for you to get home."*

*Nico could hear how unhappy she was, and advised her that he was famished. "Start cooking and I'll be home in twenty minutes", he announced. "Love you!" he added quickly. It would be the last phrase he ever said to her.*

*Izzy cooed her great admiration for him into the phone, and then she hung up. She was munching on a chocolate* chip cookie as she brought everything out of the fridge and cupboards, and then she popped a second one into her mouth. As she reached into the drawer for the book of matches, she could feel the rush of sugar fill her body with happiness. She opened the flap and ripped off one of the paper sticks. Unfortunately, before she lit the pilot light, the gas in Izzy's stove had already been on for quite a while.

## BOOM!!

The back part of the quaint house had exploded so loudly, that it shattered windows up to two blocks away. The senseless blast also took her life.

Nico was driving slowly, and could see and hear the eruption for miles away. He made sure to arrive in front of her home, at the same exact time as the police cars and the fire trucks. Again, he didn't need to pretend to be surprised when the authorities told him that his fiancé had been killed in the explosion, for he was surprised that his plan had worked. "What?" he gasped in disbelief. The color drained from his face as tears of sorrow fell down his cheeks. He even dropped to his knees, to make it seem like he was overcome by grief.

"Hey! I need someone over here to check him out!" called a police officer. After placing a warm blanket over his shoulders, they walked Nico to the ambulance. They asked him for his I.D., they asked him if there was anyone in the house, and they asked him if he had any place else to go.

*Nico answered all of their questions as best he could, and then he was driven away in the back of a police car. He was brought to the Cavalier Hotel, where he was given a room for the next week, free of charge, compliments of the manager.*

*For the next two weeks, generous donations of clothing and food were coming into fire and police stations for Nico to pick up. The house had been totally gutted by the blast and the ensuing fire, and fire officials believed it to be caused by an accidental gas leak. As the cheques began to fly into his hands, Nico's bank accounts were being restored to their fullest capacity.*

*The years went by and Nico felt no remorse for his wrongdoings. Each time he saw that his bank account was running low, he would find another woman to make him rich. He would convince her that they would be together forever, that they should share bank accounts and insurance policies, and that they should be each other's beneficiaries. When these ladies were gone from his life, Nico lived quite well off the ill-gotten money, and without a drop of guilt touching his soul.*

*Nico had been completely alone for almost three months when he met Andrea Cooper. It was the beginning of spring in 1964, and the very handsome man was standing in line to cash a cheque. He couldn't help but turn his head, when he heard her sweet voice laughing at a feeble joke from one of the customers in the bank. He was immediately drawn to her and couldn't help but stare in her direction. He loved how she looked, and then he watched how she attended to her current customer.*

*She was average looking, but she was completely captivating. The second she was free, he made a beeline for her teller station. Their eyes met and he could feel her body swoon.*

*"Hi", she sighed. "How can I help you, today?"*

*He flashed a toothy grin in her direction, which only added to his dark hair and slight Mediterranean accent. "I'd like to get cash from most of this cheque", he said in a suave manner. "And I'd like to deposit the rest into my account." He aimed his potent charm in her direction, and then he watched as she drank it all in.*

*Nico hadn't planned on having another woman in his life just yet, but he found the girl to be quite enchanting. She was plainer than the girls he had dated in the past, but there was something about her that was captivating all of his senses.*

*They instantly felt at ease with one another, and they both noticed the chemistry that flowed between them. He made her laugh, and she made him chuckle. Before she handed him his money, she quickly glanced at his name on the cheque. She decided to be bold and used it as he tucked the small fortune into his wallet. "I hope to see you again, Mr. Kostas."*

*His heart skipped a beat when he heard her say his name. He blushed slightly, and he could see that her cheeks had reddened, as well. He tapped the wooden counter in front of where she was sitting, and he told her to have a great day. He then watched her nod and smile before he walked away.*

*Andrea took a minute to recover, and then she tried to carry on with her job. She'd held that teller position for the past 5 years, but she had never experienced anything like what had happened that day.*

*The 24-year old woman thought about Mr. Kostas throughout the rest of her shift, and then all through the night. She couldn't believe it when she saw his handsome face come through the door the next day, one minute before she was told to go on her lunch break. "What are you doing here?" she whispered. She could feel the sexual magnetism that made him seem so self-confident.*

*"I came to take you for lunch." He was looking at her as if he was preserving the moment for later.*

*"I'm not able to leave the building, but you can join me in the break room." She pushed the door open and walked through, hoping that he would follow.*

*They spent the next 20 minutes firing questions back and forth. When her break was over, she made him promise to come back the next day, around the same time. She was ecstatic when he nodded and said yes.*

*Nico came back to the bank the next day and the next, and then he asked her out on an official date for coffee. They had their second date a week later, and soon after that, they were inseparable.*

*For the first few weeks, Nico truly liked Andrea. She was different than any other woman he'd ever been with, and he really liked her company. They found that they enjoyed the same things, they got along very well, and for the first time in his life, he now had hope for a real future with someone.*

*Three months later, his feelings for her had changed, and he thought about breaking up with her.*

*Andrea was at the point where she was beginning to feel secure with herself and their relationship, and she announced that she would like to take a trip with him.*

*"It takes money to travel", he suggested. Nico was in a bad mood and he spoke in a sullen voice. He hadn't lifted his head up in several minutes, nor was he very interested in continuing their conversation. Without worrying about how it looked, he very openly checked his watch and noticed that she only had a few minutes left on her break. He sighed, and wished for the time to go quicker.*

*"It's a good thing that I've been saving money since I was 10 years old." She was foolish to give him this information, but she continued. "I also have stocks and bonds locked away in a safety deposit box in the bank, and I've paid into a pension plan since my first day on the job", she announced stupidly.*

*Nico looked up with amazement stamped all over his face. Suddenly, everything about her had become very interesting.*

*"I'm worth tons!" she giggled. She spread her arms out to the sides, as if she was trying to touch the walls with her fingertips.*

*Nico's eyes shot wide open, while his mind was swirling with dollar signs. He now had to romance the hell out of her, while thinking of the many possibilities on how he could inherit her vast fortune.*

*"Oops! My break is over!" she announced loudly. They said good-bye, and each went their own way. Unbeknownst to Andrea, she had just signed her own death warrant.*

*Nico couldn't believe all that he had heard, and he knew that he had to work quickly if he wanted to get any of her money. He drove her home from work that day, and after they had dinner and he had kissed her good-night, he told her he loved her.*

*Andrea had waited so long to hear those words, and she said it right back. "I love you, too." She was giddy for hours afterwards, and it made her believe in fairy tales again.*

*As Nico drove away, he congratulated himself on taking the first step. He now knew what had to happen next.*

*Nico waited a few weeks, and then he saw the perfect opportunity. On her birthday, he got down on one knee and proposed to her.*

*"Yes!" she screamed at the top of her lungs.*

*"Because I can't wait to marry you, can we do it as soon as possible?" He batted his gorgeous eye lashes, while aiming his charms in her direction.*

*Andrea agreed, and then spent every waking moment of the next month, finding the perfect dress and the ideal spot for their wedding. She would have wanted to have a traditional, flashy wedding, but her future husband suggested that they keep the costs down. She insisted that she could pay for everything, but Nico repeatedly asked her to stop wasting her money.*

*"We should add each other onto our bank accounts, life insurance policies, properties, and all other documents that a husband and wife should share", he suggested in passing.*

*"Of course", she stated happily. Andrea couldn't wait to prove to the world that she was finally going to be a wife - complete with joint accounts and the same address.*

*Nico married the average-looking woman five weeks after he proposed - not out of love, but because of what she had to offer. There was no pre-nuptial agreement, no more than a small handful of people in attendance, two bridesmaids and two groomsmen, and hardly any flowers.*

*Without the bride's knowledge, on the day after their wedding, Nico had upped the amount on their insurance policies. He then placed the paperwork in the safety deposit box in her bank, and waited for the day when it could be presented in front of a judge.*

*As the weeks turned into months, Nico began to lose interest in doing the daily chores of being a good husband. He was not in love with Andrea, but he was in love with her money. He had found so many faults with her, but he knew he shouldn't make her unhappy. "After the winter holidays", he chanted. "That's when it will happen."*

*On January 2ⁿᵈ, Nico had finally had enough, and now he wanted to put his well-thought-out plans into action. "Let's go on a second honeymoon", he announced in a happy tone. "Valentine's Day is coming!" he stated a little too loudly.*

*"What?" She was stunned. His proposal had come totally out of the blue, and Andrea didn't think that they could afford it. Nico had put her on a budget, but he didn't know that she had spent more money at Christmas than she had planned to. For the past week or so, she had been trying to find ways to hide it from him.*

*"What do you say?" Nico pleaded. His lashes were raised as far as they could go, while he looked at her with hope. "Well?" He prayed that she would say yes.*

*Andrea was in shock, and still trying to decide how she should react to his question.*

"Honey?" Nico purposely pushed the front of his body up against the front of hers. He then placed a loving kiss on her lips, while he wrapped his arms behind her back. "What a better time for a honeymoon than on Valentine's Day?"

Andrea was stunned to learn that he meant for them to leave in six weeks. "I-I don't know if I can get away", she stammered nervously.

"I've already talked with your boss and he said yes", he announced with conviction. Nico was overjoyed to begin this quest as soon as possible, as it meant that he would be single soon, and wealthy again.

She was surprised that all of this had been done without her consent, and because she felt that she had no choice, she said yes. "I guess so."

"That's my girl!" Nico was overjoyed by the many possibilities that lay ahead of him. "Now, where shall we go?"

They both chose Disneyland - each for their own reasons. He made all the arrangements, and it wasn't long before they boarded a plane.

As they sat side-by-side on the Boeing Aircraft, he looked into her eyes, and with genuine emotion, he made this promise. "This will be a trip to remember."

She smiled and agreed, and then kissed him tenderly on the mouth.

*It was 1pm on their second day in California, and they were enjoying a small bit of lunch in their room. Andrea Kostas was talking non-stop, but Nico continued to smile through her gibberish while encouraging her to finish her food. "We have a long night ahead of us, or did you forget?" he cautioned dimly.*

*"Oh, I didn't forget." She was now blushing at the thought of what he had proposed, and wondered how she had gotten so lucky. Her husband was handsome and kind, taller than she was, and always spoke softly, even when he was angry. "Wine and a light supper on the beach", she recited.*

*He nodded his contentment, and asked her to eat the rest of her lunch so that she could go and lay down. "You'll need your rest", he informed her playfully. When he watched her push the last forkful of food into her mouth, he stood up and walked towards her. "Good girl!" he cheered.*

*Nico was still playing the doting husband, even as he was tucking her into bed. He then kissed her forehead and suggested that she have a nice long sleep.*

*"I will", she sighed. Andrea lowered her eyelids and dreamed of their upcoming romantic adventure.*

*Nico left the room and closed the door softly, and then dashed to the front lobby of the Elexus Hotel. He moved quickly, while preparing all the arrangements for her 'sudden and accidental' demise. He felt no regret as he gathered all that was needed, and he hoped that everything would go according to plan.*

Nico had scouted out the perfect area on the beach, while she had taken her nap. He noticed the two large, very colorful danger signs, which were put on display to advise people to be aware of alligators, and he ripped them out of the ground. He hid these wooden posts inside of some large bushes about a block away, and covered them up so that others would have a hard time finding them. He then hurried to get the seafood and wine, and made sure to be back in their hotel suite when she woke up.

He was sitting in a chair and pretending to read, and holding a full glass of chilled wine when she opened her eyes. "Come, my dear", Nico whispered sensually, as he offered her the other glass. "Let us get ready to have our supper on the beach." When he saw the familiar smile building on her lips, he anticipated his imminent future with total joy.

An hour later, as the sun was going down, they made their way to the gorgeous sandy shore. It was a perfect night - no clouds or people in sight.

As they sat on the blanket, that he had so lovingly spread out on the sand, Nico plied his wife full of warm seafood and strong wine, while lulling her into a false sense of security. "You are so beautiful in this moonlight, my love", he cooed.

Andrea's face blushed as she smiled shyly in his direction. She sighed lovingly from being so happy, as the words 'this must be a dream' continued to splash through her mind.

*"Eat, my love", he coaxed softly. "Half of this is for you." He hand fed her the warm seafood, knowing full-well that it would make her ill. He had also purchased one of the strongest wines in the nearby market, for when she needed to calm the ill feelings in her tummy.*

*Once he saw that his wife was beginning to feel the hostile effects of the strong alcohol and the bad food in her intestines, Nico suggested that she lay down next to him. This foolproof act helped to calm her down, and he now had full control of what she could see around her.*

*While Andrea lay close to him, Nico stroked her hair with one hand and threw bits of the rotten seafood towards the water's edge with the other. He soothed her with soft words, while keeping an eye on the mysterious shoreline. It wasn't too long before Nico thought he spotted something moving in the water. After squinting his eyes, he could verify that it was a very large alligator. He hoped that it would want to collect the tidbits of food which were laying on the sand.*

*Nico was giddy with excitement and congratulated himself. He was pleased that his plan was working, and now he needed to proceed quickly.*

*"I don't feel very well!" Andrea complained while holding her stomach. The color of her skin had gone from pale white to a sickly green, and her lips were becoming quite dry.*

*"Oh gosh, I'm sorry", he said with empathy. "I'm going to get you a cloth for your forehead, and a large glass of cool water for your tummy,"*

*"Hurry back!" she called. Her voice was filled with impatience and worry, and she could feel that her body was starting to fill with vomit and gas.*

*"I will be right back, my love." As he stood up, he purposely tossed some more food near his wife's feet, in hopes of coaxing the very large alligator to come even further out of the water.*

*Andrea was weak and closed her eyes, and she wished for the unpleasantness in her body to go away.*

*Nico took a few large steps away from his wife, and then turned around in order to catch the scaly alligator crawl out of the water and move closer to his wife's recently manicured toes. Surprisingly, but to Nico it was an added bonus, a second alligator had poked its large eyes out of the water. Nico took another ten steps towards the hotel, to get even further away from his wife.*

*The next 60 seconds were completely horrible, but went by very quickly. The alligators bolted out of the water at the same time, hoping that the large mass on the blanket was tastier than the small, smelly pieces of white meat on the shore.*

*Nico stood frozen to the spot, and watched as his wife struggled for her life. He almost felt bad for her, as he heard her screaming his name while she was being dragged into the cold lake, but he didn't do anything to help her.*

*Nico was breathless as his mind drank in all the horror that was happening. He shrieked in agony until a dozen or so people came running, but of course, by then it was too late to save her. Nico had witnesses to his wife's death, and he had played the part of a grieving widower better than any actor alive.*

*The police got involved, as did some employees and guests of the hotel, who gave their own versions of what they thought had happened. Nico was also questioned by all of the proper authorities, and then sent back to his hotel room to get some rest. He was given a free bottle of red wine to calm his nerves, and just before midnight, he began to pack up all of his belongings.*

*Nico had not intended to leave California so quickly, but he couldn't wait to inform all who needed to know, of his wife's unfortunate demise. When he went downstairs to pay his bill the next morning, the owner of the hotel offered to waive the cost of all of his bills. They even paid for a limo to take him to the airport, and Disneyland Park flew him back home free of charge.*

*He was delighted, but he couldn't show it. Instead, he kept a sorrowful look on his face, as he continued to profess how grateful he was to everyone, for all the kindness that they were giving him.*

*Two weeks later, the police in California had contacted him, to let him know that they had found her left hand. The authorities were able to identify her by her finger prints, but added that they didn't expect to find anything else.*

*Nico was quite grateful, and thanked them for all that they had done.*

*The police also advised him, that they had found the two danger signs which had been hidden in the dense bushes. "We've concluded that it must have been some teenagers, who had taken them away as a prank", the officer stated. "We're very sorry if that is what caused your wife's death."*

*Nico was shocked, but appreciated that this ordeal was soon going to be behind him. "Thank you for calling", he said, making sure to sound sad. In reality, Nico sighed with utter relief, as he had gotten away with it again.*

*Nico Kostas appeared in front of Judge Gordon three months later, and was declared innocent of any wrong doings in the death of his wife. It took several more weeks for the paperwork to be processed, and then one-by-one, the cheques began to come into his hands.*

Nico had been given the last of the money this morning - a rather large cheque from the insurance company. His only thought was to deposit it, for he couldn't wait another minute for the money to flood his bank account.

With so much happiness spilling out from every pore in his body, how could Nico possibly know that his life would change so drastically, and in the next few minutes?

# Chapter 2

It was near the end of summer, in 1965. The Rolling Stones had recorded, 'Can't Get No Satisfaction', a horrifying earthquake measuring 7.5 had almost destroyed many cities in El Salvador, and Muhammad Ali had knocked out Sonny Liston in the first round of their championship rematch. It was an exciting time to be alive, and for the bride, Monica Bellam, it was the dawn of a most exciting future.

When she opened her big brown eyes, at 6am on that beautiful Friday morning, the fresh-faced woman was more than overjoyed to welcome the first few minutes of what she believed, would be her ultimate perfect day. Little did she know that in a few short hours from that very moment, it would be by far, the worst day of her entire life.

Monica, who worked as an accountant at Shopper's World, rolled onto her side and grabbed the small pad of paper off the nightstand. Laying back onto the propped up pillows, she checked off the first item on the list of things to do – hair appointment at 9am. "Check!" she affirmed strongly. She hugged the small item close to her chest and smiled, while her mind drifted off to how she wanted the day to unfold.

In a dream-like state, the cheerful woman could see the simple wedding playing out in front of her. And then, as if she was watching the end of a romantic movie, she saw the happy couple checking into the Motel Avalon, with a full moon glowing brightly in the background.

Monica let out a soft sigh of delight, and then she realized that if she wanted to have her fairy-tale ending, she would need to get out of bed. "Eat, shower, and leave", she announced, as if it was an order. She returned the pad of paper to its original spot, and then swung her legs off the side of the bed. With a twinkle in her eye, the young woman knew why she couldn't wipe the silly grin from her radiant face, but she hadn't told a soul. 'They'll know soon enough', was her reasoning.

The bright-eyed girl stood up and walked to the bathroom, mentally preparing herself for what lay ahead. When she was ready, Monica marched out of the 4th floor apartment.

During the 20 minutes that it took for her to walk to the neighbourhood beauty parlor, the 22-year old hummed along with the song that was playing inside of her head. The sun felt warm against her freshly-moisturized skin, and when she looked up, she could see how powerful the yellow globe was shining. Sadly, she could also see that it was slowly moving in and out of the few, over-sized clouds which were hovering in the sky. Monica took a deep breath and hoped that this was not an indication of bad weather approaching.

To stop herself from dwelling on things that might not happen, the bride-to-be purposely gazed at her reflection in the store front windows. She was glowing and she knew it, and she was slightly worried that the twinkle in her eye might give away her precious secret. Although she was being distracted, Monica never slowed down her pace; she was on a strict schedule and wanted to ensure that nothing would go wrong.

The 5'7", dark haired beauty, was about to marry the love of her life. She couldn't believe that she had been so lucky as to find someone as handsome and as charming as Mr. Cayson Ross. She hadn't known him for a full year, but she knew that he was 'the one'. Suddenly, the image of his attractive face appeared in her mind. He was everything that she had ever wanted in a man, and she could tell that he loved her with all of his heart.

At last!" she cheered, as she arrived at Gisela's Beauty Shop. She pulled open the heavy glass door to the well-laid out salon, and waited for Tanya to notice her.

"You're here, and on time!" her regular hair dresser announced. "Come in, I've been waiting for you." She pointed to the middle chair as she spoke.

While her medium-length, brown hair was being curled and styled, the two women engaged in their usual banter of what was new in each of their lives. The whole process of getting her hair and make-up done, had taken 90 minutes in total, but it was well-worth the time and money.

After an unhurried inspection, Monica cooed at how beautiful she looked.

"I'm glad you like it." Tanya removed the black cape from around Monica's neck, and they walked towards the front desk.

"This is for you!" Monica stated lightheartedly. "For doing such a great job."

"You're too kind", Tanya replied. "Thank you. You have a great day, and good luck!"

"Thank you!" When Monica pushed the door open and stepped outside, she was shocked to find that the skies had clouded over. "Where's the sun?" she called to the heavens. After noticing that it had gotten cooler, she was now hoping that it wasn't about to rain. The young woman forced her feet to move quickly, and was grateful to have made it home in record time.

As she looked out of her living room window, Monica sent a prayer to the heavens for the weather to hold up until after the ceremony. "And please, God. I so want this day to be perfect", she added. She made the sign of the cross, and then attended to the other things which were on her list of things to do.

An hour later, quick flashes of bright lightening were filling Monica's entire apartment. Before too long, thunderous energy of booming sounds could be heard, igniting fear into the hearts of all those who needed to venture outside.

Monica could hear the rumblings of bad weather, but it was when she looked outside again, that she wanted to cry. Thick streaks of grey rain were now streaming down towards the earth in sheer urgency, and she hoped that it would not bring a halt to her otherwise wonderful day.

Would it stop soon, she wondered. Monica had half a mind to cancel her plans, but then she thought against it. She would not hear of it, as she had been planning this event for far too long. With a broken heart, the optimistic bride looked around at everything she had gotten accomplished so far, and she wanted to cry. She had risen especially early, and had done so much to prepare for this one special day. In an hour from now, she wanted to leave her home, in order to arrive at City Hall in time to watch her groom walk up the majestic stairs. Because of the rain, the troubled woman wondered if she should she still go ahead with her plans.

After thinking about what lay ahead of her, Monica opted to risk everything by going out. She grabbed her unflattering, black rubber boots and her large black umbrella, and began the challenging trek to downtown.

Her prospective groom, on the other hand, had foolishly slept in. Cayson Jonathan Ross had been given a small, but truly exciting bachelor party by some co-workers and good friends the night before. He had stumbled home sometime around 3am, with no recollection of how he had gotten there. He fell into bed fully clothed and wildly drunk, and in his terribly incoherent state, he promised himself that no matter what, he would not miss his own wedding.

Cayson woke up from his own snoring, checked his bedside clock, and screamed in fright when he saw the time. "What?!" He was in total disbelief. "Oh my gosh!"

He was full-out panicking as he bounced out of bed, and he began rushing around his apartment, trying to get himself ready. Off with the old clothes, on with the new ones. He got himself dressed, and didn't worry about his hair or how rough he looked. Without checking his appearance in the hall mirror, he grabbed the small velvet box which would make Monica his bride, and placed it in his front pocket. As he ran down the 3 flights of stairs to the lobby, he prayed with all his might, that he would make it to City Hall on time.

The 30-year old lawyer, who had passed the bar exam exactly 7 days ago, ripped open the front door to his apartment building with full strength, and gasped at the sight before him. "It's pouring?" he shouted in disbelief. "Are you kidding me?" He checked his watch and then tried to imagine how much time he had to get there. "Oh my gosh!" he screamed again. He was already late, and he knew that she would be furious with him.

Cayson's mind ran amuck when he realized that he would not get a taxi in this type of weather, so he decided to run to the government building as fast as he could, in order to avoid their wedding from being postponed.

Because of the torrential downpour, the minor flooding that had started to build up on all the street corners, and the traffic which had slowed down considerably in the last hour, the blond-haired man was becoming panic-stricken about failing to attend the most important moment of his life – marrying the woman who was not only carrying his child, but whom he loved more than anything else in the entire world.

Monica Marie Bellam had arrived early as she usually did, and was now waiting for the love of her life to arrive. She had carefully tucked herself under the arch, in front of the double doors, so she wouldn't get wet, but she still wanted to see in which direction Cayson was going to come to her.

In the meantime, her handsome fiancé was doing all that he could to make it there; he was already 15 minutes late, and hoped that Monica would wait for him.

Cayson was travelling by foot and was only one long block away, when the grand, 5-storey, grey-stone building, finally came into his view. The heavy drops of rain were pounding sharply against his skin, and making it very difficult for him to see anything with perfect clarity. Thankfully, he knew where he was heading, and now he wondered where his future bride might be standing.

As his wet shoes moved one in front of the other, his eyes struggled to find his beautiful fiancé. They had promised to meet each other on the sidewalk in front of City Hall, but because of the unexpected shower of rain, he hoped that she would try to stand somewhere where she would be kept dry.

The tall man in the wet dark suit, had finally arrived at the intersection of Main Street and Broadview Avenue. Because he had to stop for the red light, he used that opportunity to search for his bride. He shielded his eyes with his left hand, while he studied the entire area for any sign of her.

He then noticed the slim figure on the top of the steps and sighed with relief, for he had recognized without a doubt, that it was the future Mrs. Ross. He could see that she was wrapped in a long raincoat and wearing a large hat, and she looked like she was wondering where her missing groom was hiding. Cayson smiled when he spotted the mother of his child, and his heart began to flutter from happiness. "She came", he whispered happily. He knew she would, but a part of him had wondered if she might have changed her mind because of the weather.

Cayson brought his hands up and cupped them around his mouth. He then called out her name as loud as he could, hoping that she would be able to hear his voice through the sound of the traffic and the heavy curtain of falling rain. "Mon-i-ca!" When she didn't look in his direction, he began to move his arms in large circles. "Over here!"

he called. When it became apparent that she couldn't see him or hear him, he stopped trying to get her attention.

Cayson loved her with all of his heart, and he wanted her to know that he was only a minute away. He clearly did not anticipate, that in the next minute, someone would run over him and end his life.

An underpaid, 60-year old truck driver, was busy cursing at the faulty window wipers of his old truck, and not paying as much as attention to the road as he should have been. "Of all the days ..." he muttered with anger. The old man had one hand gripped on the steering wheel and the other rubbing vigorously against the cold window shield. The fog was collecting on the large panel of glass before him, faster than he could wipe it away. This distraction was causing him to work harder than what he was used to, and it was making him angry. It was also stealing his concentration, by preventing him from properly scanning the road through the torrent of water, which was pounding against the hood of his 17 foot delivery truck. Because the driver could hardly see anything through the thick veil of water, he did as he always did, and 'felt his way' through the other traffic on the road.

Through the driver's distorted side window, the old man could vaguely see the colors of the other vehicles moving forward. When he decided that it was safe to go, he pressed his large foot down on the gas pedal and hoped for the best. The driver was trying very hard to maneuver his large truck in a steady line with his right hand, while continuing to clear the condensation from his front window with the other. His underused muscles were now straining from the manual labor, while his oversized lips were muttering a few choice words into the stale air of the cabin.

Cayson cheered happily when the traffic light turned to green, and then stepped off the curb and straight into a puddle. SPLASH! His entire foot was saturated, right up to the ankle, but he lifted it up and tried to ignore it. Believing that she might leave if he didn't hurry up, the muscles in his athletic body went into a sprint mode. As one foot and then the other, slammed against the wet pavement, his eyes were glued to his future wife. Because there was only one thought consuming every muscle in his body, Cayson didn't notice the large delivery truck which was heading straight towards him.

"Monica!" Cayson called enthusiastically. "I'm coming!" All he could think about was her, their wedding, and their child.

In the confusion of the bad weather, the faulty windshield wipers, the traffic on the road, and the fact that the nose of the truck was quite high, the elderly gentleman didn't see the excited man rushing across the front of his vehicle.

Monica was scanning all the people in the street, and since she didn't see Cayson, this made her very nervous. Suddenly, out of the corner of her eye, she saw something out of the ordinary, and it made her hopeful. The bride-to-be narrowed her eyes, and saw what looked like a bouquet of red roses floating from one side of the road to the other. And when she heard a male voice call out her name, it registered, and nothing else mattered.

"He came!" she called out in victory. She could feel the expression on her face begin to change, when she recognized that it was Cayson who had revealed her name to the public. Her lips were spreading into a smile and her body was now able to relax. "Cayson!" she shouted very happily. She reached her hand up as high as it would go, and began to wave so he would be sure to see her.

Cayson saw her waving and this gave him even more incentive to hurry. "I'm coming!" he called.

Monica wanted to run down the stairs to meet the man who she was about to marry, but her feet suddenly stopped moving. For just then, she witnessed a large vehicle collide with the beautiful flowers, which were being held by her future husband.

In that same instant, a man had opened the heavy front door of the century-old, sandstone building, and stepped outside. He had just come out of a 1-hour, delicate meeting on the 8th floor of City Hall, and his mind was still spinning from the amount of money that he had just been given.

Nicholas Kostas was in a very happy mood as he raced out of the administration building, for he was now richer than he'd ever been before. And in that very moment, he had no other notion but to get to the bank and cash the rather large cheque. The rain took him by surprise and made him look up. Once he realized that it was more than just a simple shower, Nico stopped moving his feet. He decided to take the time to lock all of the buttons together on his long overcoat, before he ventured out any further.

Nico's gorgeous eyes were gazing mindlessly at the traffic on the road, while his hands were fumbling with the little objects on the outer layer of his clothing. It was then when Nico heard the horrible loud thuds, followed by several people screaming. His eyes quickly darted to where the sounds were coming from, and then he witnessed more of the gloomy destruction.

## *SMASH*

Cayson had been hit and dropped to the ground like a heavy sack of potatoes, but the wheels on the truck kept rolling forward.

The driver felt a hard thud against the solid steel grill on the front of his truck, and then his right tire lifted up, as if it had driven over a bump. Because of the prolonged downpour of rain, the driver was quite aware that there might be a few puddles and objects on the roadways that day, so he cursed loudly and continued to drive.

"No-o-o-o-o-o-o!" she screamed in horror. With her eyes as wide as saucers and adrenaline pulsating from every pour in her body, Monica held her breath in hopes that her future husband would stand up. She couldn't believe what had just happened, and she wondered if she had just seen a dreadful mirage through the heavy wall of rain. While she was keeping a strong vigil on the man on the ground, Monica was barely aware of the other destruction which was going on in the same area.

Had her future just disappeared before her eyes, she wondered. Monica had dreams of spending Christmases, birthdays, vacations, and everyday life with Cayson Ross, and she wasn't about to let it go. He would stand up! With everything in her body, she willed him to.

The large delivery truck was still forcing its tires to move forward, while running over whatever was in its path. On the street, it was total pandemonium. People were screaming and crying from fear, but the driver of the truck seemed to be oblivious to everything that was happening outside of his vehicle.

Out of the three people who had not seen the truck coming, two had been moderately injured; the younger man broke his collar bone and received several cuts to different parts of his body, and the older man sprained his right knee, banged the back of his head on the curb, and received several cuts to different parts of his body. But there was another person who wasn't as lucky; this man was laying quietly on the ground in his own blood.

The old man had been driving for most of his life, and he truly believed that he had hit a rough patch of road. He scrunched up his unshaven and weather beaten face, and didn't give the incident another thought. He grabbed a firmer hold on the steering wheel, pushed his foot even harder on the gas pedal, and tried his best to stay in between the white lines, as his truck continued on its way to its final destination.

Nico watched in horror as those few seconds of the accident occurred. His entire body was immediately glued to the spot with absolute disbelief, and his head began to cloud with a ton of emotions.

Monica's mind was suddenly silenced by the utter shock and terror that she had just witnessed. She felt numb and crumbled to the ground in uncontrollable tears. She sensed that Cayson was slipping away from her, and it was more heartbreaking than her mind could understand. Both of her slender hands covered her eyes, as she began to experience the beginnings of a mental breakdown. "Cay-son!" She was shrieking his name while her chin was hanging down towards her chest. She was shocked and she wanted to die along with him. "How will I live without you?" she cried, while hundreds of tears streamed down her cheeks. "Get up!" she shouted. Her grip on reality was spiraling out of control, as if she was in the scary part of a horror movie and she couldn't find a way out.

Monica wanted to go back in time and do the last 10 minutes of her life all over again. "If only I could", she chanted. She knew that she would do everything in her power to stop the love of her life from running across the street a second time. "If only I could."

Unbeknownst to everyone around him, Nico Kostas had witnessed his wife die a short while ago, and now he had just watched a man get run over by what looks like a large runaway truck. Of course, it appears that the man dying on the street had been involved in an unavoidable accident. Nico couldn't and wouldn't say the same thing about his dearly departed wife, for her death had been executed to perfection.

Monica was sobbing hysterically, and she was in total denial about what had just happened to Cayson. Her mind had become disorderly and she didn't know what was going to happen to her and their unborn child. "This was supposed to be our wedding day, and now it was going to be marked as the saddest day of my life", she exhaled with a great deal of grief.

Nico was clear minded and wanted to scurry away, but how? The police were everywhere, and vehicles were now being stopped on both sides of the street. Most people were crying, or consumed with concern and curiosity, while others were wandering around to comfort the ones who seemed lost and distraught.

Nico noticed that several people were huddling around the man who had been hit. It was hard to see if he was alive or not, but because of how fast the red puddle was growing, Nico believed that the man had been gravely injured.

Two piercingly loud sirens were now coming from behind the hill, and as they grew closer, they seemed to be beckoning for everyone to move aside so that other official vehicles could also get through.

Apprehension rushed through Nico's body, once he realized that nobody and nothing was going anywhere, anytime soon. To calm his frazzled nerves, he reached his perfectly-manicured hand into his front pants pocket, and caressed the folded cheque. Nico wanted so badly to cash it, but he wasn't sure if that was still going to be a possibility today.

# Chapter 3

As Nico stood momentarily paralyzed by the situation, from somewhere close by, he could hear a loud and endless wail of despair. He turned around to see who was crying, and immediately got down on one knee, in order to console the woman who was sprawled out on the ground behind him. He wasn't sure if there was a connection between her and the man in the street, or if she was just upset by what had happened. Regardless, he stayed close to the weeping woman, in hopes that he could help.

In the meantime, any person or vehicle that was attempting to enter or leave the intersection, was halted by the out-stretched arms of four police officers. EMS and accompanying city officials, raced with a stretcher and other equipment, to attend to the man's lifeless body. After a few long moments, the paramedics closed the dead man's eyes, and placed a large cloth over his face.

Through tears and rain that was almost blinding her vision, Monica could make out that something had been placed over Cayson's head. In a piercingly loud and deathly manner, she shrieked his name and then she could no longer control her emotions. "Cay-son!" she screamed, while extreme fear enveloped every cell of her body. Her passionate sounds were full of torment, for nothing in her soul could believe that he could truly be gone from her life. "No-o-o-o-o-o!"

Because it looked like she wanted to rush over to the scene of the accident, Nico helped the woman to stand up. He gathered her into his arms and guided the poor woman into the street.

Her heart was pumping adrenaline throughout her body at a very fast pace, which made her unable to think clearly. As she marched towards the group of concerned people in uniform, she felt stronger than normal and she wasn't about to be told no by anyone.

Nico asked people to move out of their way, as he guided the woman towards the man on the ground.

Monica was grieving and inconsolable, but quite grateful for the stranger's comfort and support. She had not yet seen the man's face, but she could feel someone strong and compassionate standing beside her.

The police were forceful while they ordered everyone to step back, but the tall stranger felt the need to speak up. "Excuse me, sir! This lady seems to know him." Nico spoke loudly, while pointing to the man in the pool of blood.

The officer nodded and waved them through, and then he continued to block everyone else from coming too close.

Monica's mind was exploding between reality and a horror movie, when she saw what was left of her fiancé's face. Nothing about that moment seemed real, but she took a deep breath and searched painstakingly for any sign of life. "Cayson!" she called, hoping that he would hear her and open his eyes. When he didn't even flinch, she wanted to faint. Her knees were buckling and her body was about to collapse, and then she felt the stranger place his strong hands under her arms to hold her up.

"Whoa!" Nico cried as he tried to catch her.

Through tears of extreme sorrow and great emotional pain, Monica blurted out some muffled words, but they were inaudible to everyone around her.

"Do you recognize him?" the ambulance driver asked, looking directly into her troubled expression.

Monica nodded sadly, as she stared into her fiancé's almost-unrecognizable, battered and bloodied face. "That's Cayson Ross", she whispered softly. She was trying to be strong, but it was no use. She turned around and buried her face against the strong chest of the stranger, who had come out of City Hall seconds before the accident had occurred.

"Thank you", the driver replied. The admission was noted and jotted down in a binder. The body had been identified, and could now be placed onto a stretcher. It was moved into the back of the ambulance, and then transported to the nearest hospital.

Because he asked, one of the police officers informed Nico where the ambulance would be taking Mr. Ross. "Would you like me to drive you there?" Nico waited for Monica to reply.

She was distraught and not thinking clearly at all. Because she didn't think she had any other choice, she graciously accepted a ride from the kind stranger. "Thank you", she said under her breath.

Ten minutes after they had arrived at the newly-renovated, Saint Rosa Hospital, they had been given the somber confirmation that Cayson had died.

Monica pushed her face in the stranger's chest again, and cried for several minutes without pause.

Nico Kostas listened as the doctor gave him the grim details of what would happen next.

"The body will be cleaned, an autopsy will be performed, and then it will be released to the funeral home."

The doctor asked the couple for a contact phone number, and because Monica was in no condition to do anything of importance, the stranger from City Hall dictated his own name and number for the doctor to use. The doctor thanked him and began to walk away.

Now that everything had quieted down, Nico suddenly realized that he and Monica were standing so close, that their bellies were touching. She had her arms wrapped around his waist, and he had his arms wrapped around her shoulders.

Nico reached his right hand up and stroked the woman's hair, hoping that that would give her some comfort. It seemed to have calmed her down a bit, and then he felt her grip loosen, as if she was moving away from him. "Do you want to sit down?" he asked quietly. He was worried that she might be feeling faint again.

Monica felt unsteady and agreed that she needed to sit down. She loosened her body from his, and using the arm which he had held out to her for support, she used it to guide herself to the nearest seat. "I just can't believe this", she repeated over and over again.

The kind man kept quiet, but wanted her to know he was there for her, and for as long as she needed him to be.

"Thank you", she said softly. "Thank you for being so kind. I'm sure that you must have other things to do than to sit here with me." While saying those words, she glanced up to see who she was talking to.

Nico examined her moistened and sad face, and recognized that her heart had just been broken into a million pieces. "No, I don't", he said with total honesty. He couldn't help but notice how truly beautiful she was, even though her make-up was now ruined and her hair was hanging in uneven, wet curls.

"By the way", he stated gently. "My name is Nico."

"I'm Monica."

"Would you like a ride back home, Monica?"

Monica lowered her eyes while she pondered her day. Her heart stopped beating for a mere second, when she realized that there was nobody in her home to comfort her. This was supposed to be her wedding day. She was going to start a new life today. This stunning revelation made her cry again. As she brought both of her hands up to her face to shield the world from seeing her fall apart, she felt Nico wrap his arms around her shoulders.

"Gosh, I'm so sorry for you", he sighed softly. Noting that the bank was now closed and he had nothing else to do, Nico made a very kind suggestion. "Come on", he said softly. "I'm going to take you to my place."

Monica was lightheaded and terribly upset, and she wasn't sure that she could leave the hospital without Cayson. "No, no I can't leave!" she insisted. "What if someone made a mistake and he didn't die. He'll need to see me right away!" She wasn't making sense, her mind was void of all excitement and joy, and her body didn't want to move.

Nico positioned his face an inch away from hers, and offered to make her a much-needed cup of tea. "We can always come back here later, if you want", he suggested. It was an obvious ploy to get her to leave, and he hoped it would work.

Monica suddenly realized that she had not eaten in a very long time. Because this wasn't good for her or her child, she solemnly agreed to go.

"Good", he rejoiced. He helped her with her things, and then he walked her out to his car.

The 20-minute ride to his home was quiet and slow. Nico opened the front door and asked her to go in first. Once they walked inside of his moderately decent home, he gave her some old clothes to change into and pointed down the hall to the bathroom. While she was getting dressed, he made her some hot tea and a simple sandwich.

Nico was quite pleased with himself, that he taken down all the reminders and pictures of his life and marriage to Andrea. His 3-bedroom home now looked like he lived alone, and that he was very equipped to do so.

Monica was in a cheerless trance, and not even rationalizing what she was doing in a stranger's home. All she could think of was her darling Cayson, and the fact that he was now gone from her life forever.

Hundreds of tears stained her face again, as she made her way into the living room area where Nico was waiting.

She thanked him for his kindness and then accepted the food which he had served her. As she held the warm mug in her cold hands, she told Nico about how different she thought this day would be ending. In an unnecessary collection of words, she began to tell him all about Cayson, their relationship, and that they were going to have a baby.

Nico's expression exploded with astonishment. When he heard the news of her pregnancy and wedding, he was surprised but not alarmed. He had concluded that they had obviously been in love, and he continued to listen to all the details of their romantic relationship.

While she spoke, Nico remained quiet and watched her as she went through a ton of different emotions. It was easy to note that she wasn't anything like Andrea, who had chatted for hours on end without taking any breaks, and she didn't care if you listened or not. Monica was gentle and spoke clearly, and her words were full of emotion. Monica's story was quite interesting, and it made you want to pay attention to every word that she said.

Nico didn't offer any advice, nor did he feel that he needed to interrupt her narrative in any way. And while he wanted to ask her what she would do, now that she was without a man in her life, all he did was remain curious.

Nico wasn't sure if he wanted to have any children of his own, let alone did he want to raise another man's child. He was a free man with a lot of money in his pocket, to do what he wanted, when he wanted. But the more he got to know Monica, the more he wanted to sacrifice what little time he could, to be by her side.

Monica was young and vibrant, and her words were composed and well-spoken. He could tell that she was the kind of woman that he would enjoy spending time with, but he wasn't quite sure that he wanted to invest in another relationship just yet.

Monica revealed lots more in the next hour, and then it was evident that she was tiring herself out. "My goodness!" she cried out, when she saw that it was just past 10pm. "Have I been keeping you captive this whole time?"

"You have, and it's ok", he chuckled lightly.

Her cheeks blushed and she lowered her eyes. "I'm terribly sorry if I've bored you, but I'm so thankful that you were here for me."

He reached for her hand before he spoke. "I have not been bored since the moment we met, and you're welcome."

Nico felt that she was ready to be on her own, so he drove her home. As they said good-night, he looked into her distraught but beautiful face, and he wondered how she would survive her first horrible night of misfortune.

Monica saw the worry in his eyes, and she was very grateful that they had met. The grieving woman kissed the tolerant man's cheek, and thanked him again, for all of his much-needed kindness. They exchanged phone numbers and agreed to talk tomorrow.

After the door closed, Monica leaned her weary body against the cold wood. She then let out a loud and exhausted sigh, while anxiety and unhappiness flooded her fragile soul. She looked around and could feel the emptiness of the nicely decorated room, and she wondered how she would get through the following week, let alone the rest of the night. She felt so lost and unsure of what to do next – a feeling which she hadn't had since her dad died. Suddenly, she felt very alone and scared. "Cayson!" she shouted in agony. Hating the fact that she would never see him again, and that this was supposed to be their wedding night, she crumpled to the hardwood floor and cried for the future that what will never be. "Cayson!" she called again and again. It was a desperate plea, as if he was lost, and if he heard her voice and followed it, they would be reunited.

Her tormented sobs could be heard throughout the building, but nobody came to her rescue. Most of the tenants heard what had happened, and they understood that she needed to be alone in order to work through the many emotions of her fiancé's upsetting demise.

An hour or so after she had gotten home, the devastated woman picked herself up from the floor and made her way to the bedroom. She wiped the tears from her flushed cheeks with the back of her hands, and decided that crying was not going to help the situation. A large part of her soul had died on that windy and rainy day, but Monica needed to stay strong for herself, and for her baby.

Monica discarded the clothes which Nico had given her to wear, and put her comfy pajamas on. They were slightly too large for her tiny frame, but they were hers and she loved them. After composing her thoughts, she called her employer and explained the entire situation.

Mr. Jensen was very surprised to receive a call from his favorite employee, but after hearing what had happened on what should have been her wedding day, he was more than sympathetic. "How about we give you two more weeks off from work?" he asked, but it was more of a friendly order.

Mr. Jensen was a family man with grandchildren, and he knew that Monica would have a lot to deal with in the next few days. "You just take care of yourself", he stated in a fatherly voice. "We'll be okay until you come back."

As tears of sadness seeped from her eyes, Monica wished that she had someone there to hug her. "Thank you", she said softly. Her voice cracked as she spoke. After another minute, he wished her well and they hung up, and then she crawled into her bed.

Monica pulled the familiar covers up until just the top of her head could be seen, and then she began to cry again. In muffled tones, she repeatedly asked why this had happened. She had lived her life as a good person, she had obeyed all of the rules that had been thrown at her, and all she wanted was to have a family. She was 'this close' to having it all, and now a huge part of it had been ripped away. "Why?" she cried, as she slammed her closed fist against the soft mattress. "Why?"

She slept very little that night, and would remain in bed for most of the next few days. She felt safe there, and only wandered out of the private pocket of warmth to use the bathroom or to search for food. Afterwards, she crawled right back into the familiar small space, and wondered what her future would hold.

On the afternoon of the second day, she thought about the kind stranger who had helped her, and decided that Nico seemed like a nice guy. Monica knew that she would be forever indebted to him for the sincere kindness which he had bestowed upon her, and then she reminded herself to call him later that day.

Nico had deposited his cheque the day after the accident, and reveled in the amount of money that was now in his bank account. With this new found wealth, his thoughts turned to what he could buy. His mind pondered about purchasing a new car, a new house, and/or maybe some new clothes. He was very happy, and never showed any signs of feeling guilty as to how he had acquired any of his ill-gotten gains.

As he was rejoicing, Nico couldn't remember the last time he had felt this good. But as happy as he was in his heart, his thoughts suddenly went to Monica. He wondered how she was doing, and hoped that she was ok.

The distraught woman had only been in his company for a few hours, but he could see that Monica was not like the other girls he had known – she was a treasure. Nico wanted to call her, but he had promised himself that he would not disturb her. He knew that she would call him when she was ready. And she did, in the evening on the third day, of the fatal accident that had torn her life apart.

Nico was delighted to hear from her, and listened intently to all that she had to say. When she was finished, he reminded her of the funeral arrangements, and then offered to go with her. Because the phone went silent, Nico decided that she might have forgotten about the appointment at 2pm the next day.

"Gosh, I did forget, but I don't want to go alone." Her voice was wobbly and hoarse, as if she had been crying for hours on end.

"And you won't have to", he replied. "But in the meantime, you stay where you're warm and comfortable, and maybe you can make a list of the things which you will need from the store. I will get them for you, and bring them to your home in a few hours."

"Thank you", she sighed. His voice and manner was so calming, and it made her feel better almost immediately. "You're being very kind to me."

Monica was quite thankful for his kindheartedness, and recited the few items which she would need for the next day or two. A minute later, she changed her mind.

"Because I only need four or five things, maybe this is the excuse I need to go and join the world again", she stated boldly. Monica then realized that she hadn't had a shower or ventured out of the house since the day that Cayson had died. "Thank you for your offer, though. I shouldn't be long, and you're still welcome to come over later."

Nico felt protective and didn't want her to overdo anything, but he decided that she needed to do whatever she wanted, in order to feel normal again. "I'd love to", he said with a smile. "Could I bring anything?" Just the idea of seeing her again, made him grin like a Cheshire cat.

"Nothing but your friendship", she replied. She was smiling for the first time in days, and it felt good to have something to look forward to. "See you around 6:30?"

"See you then." He continued on with his day, but in the back of his mind, he thought about the moment when he would get to see Monica again.

Monica was heartbroken about Cayson, but she realized that tears were not going to bring him back. In a defiant manner, she lifted her chin and marched into the bathroom. As the warm water burst through the pipes and onto her body, she began to think about the details of the funeral. When her shower was done, and she had patted her belly with the soft towel, she knew that she needed to go back to work at some point. "We'll need the money", Monica confided to her unborn child.

As she began to put her make-up on, her eyes started to tear up and she struggled to continue. "This is not going to be easy", she whispered to the image in the mirror.

Monica's mind had suddenly wandered back to the morning of her wedding, which just happened to be the last time when she had these products in her hand. "I miss you so much", she stated softly. The mascara brush slipped from her fingers and dropped to the floor, while both of her hands jumped up to cover her eyes. She was bent over the sink and sobbing again, and then she became angry. "No!" she shouted. "I can't keep doing this. He wouldn't want me to, and I don't have the energy."

It took a few minutes, but after Monica cleaned up the mess, she decided to go to the store looking how she was. Her thoughts would always stay on Cayson, but tonight she was going to say thank you to the man who had taken care of her when she needed it. She took a deep breath, held it in, and then slowly released all that she could. She would be brave for the next hour, and then, after her visit with Nico, she gave herself permission to go to bed and cry herself to sleep.

Nico was surprised when he arrived and saw how well she looked, and accepted her offer to stay for supper. They made it together, and sat at the table while they ate. They talked about his day, the weather these past few days, and what her future plans would be. It was light conversation, and when he felt that she was getting tired, Nico made an excuse and walked to her front door. "It's 9:00 and I have to get up early, but I promise to call you tomorrow." He had a good time, but he didn't want to overstay his welcome.

"That would be wonderful, thank you", she sighed. She was perfectly content to have his friendship, as long as he knew that she wasn't looking for more. She reached over and opened the door for him. "Good night, and thank you for everything!"

"Good night!" he called over his shoulder. As he continued to walk away he added, "And you're welcome."

Monica cleaned up the remains of their meal and got herself ready for bed, while Nico drove home and watched TV until midnight.

Nico arrived at her home at 1:30 the next day, and together they headed to the Trinity Funeral Hall on the other side of town. Monica was almost in tears as they walked inside the front doors of the off-white, majestic building. It had an eerie feeling and smell about it, which she presumed was death, but she didn't want to think about it. Instead, she tried to make herself be brave, and stayed quiet so she wouldn't fall apart. Absolutely everything about this ordeal was sad, but she knew it all needed to be done.

"Hello, and welcome", the director announced. His right hand was extended for shaking, while his left was showing them the way to the room where the meeting would be held.

Monica was grateful for Nico's company and leadership, and sat back while he took over some of the details. When asked about things like which coffin Cayson would be buried in, or which music should be played, Monica tried to be invisible so that Nico could answer all the questions. She trusted him, even though they hadn't known each other for very long, but she felt like he had been placed in her life to protect her.

Nico liked being in charge; it made him feel important and he acted like he knew what he was doing.

*Unbeknownst to Monica and the funeral director, Nico had just made all the same arrangements for his wife, who died a few months ago.*

An hour later, when everything had been asked and answered, Monica and Nico were free to leave. Four days later, they were back at the large stucco building, for the actual funeral.

The church had been laced with gorgeous white flowers at the end of every aisle, and the orchestral music was playing soft and mellow in the background. There were dozens of people who came up and offered their condolences to Monica, but she barely recognized even half of them. When she saw the light brown, wooden coffin at the front of the church, she couldn't help but fall apart. She put her hand inside of her purse to reach for a tissue, and then she spotted the 11 x 14" picture of Cayson, smiling to the crowd. It was placed off to the side of the podium, but everyone could clearly see it.

Nico felt Monica's knees buckle, and he grabbed her elbow for support. He then led her to the front pew, and watched her as she sobbed for a man who she would never see again. As he listened to her heart break, he wondered if he would ever feel that kind of grief.

Monica was sick with sorrow, but she was grateful for Nico's assistance and companionship. Throughout the hour-long, somber yet wonderful service, she leaned on his shoulder and stayed very close to his side. When it was all over, she exited the white building and they drove to the cemetery.

The burial was emotionally hard on her, and Monica truly hated when the coffin was lowered into the ground.

Nico placed his arm across her shoulders, but he could tell that it didn't soften the tremendous suffering which she was going through.

After the final prayer was spoken, everyone was asked to leave so that the grave could be filled in. Monica heard the words, but couldn't bring herself to walk away. She then felt a tug on her arm, and realized that she needed to go. "Bye, my darling." She uttered the words with love and great sadness. "I'll never forget you." She loved him so much, and she couldn't bear to leave him.

Nico motioned for the minister and Monica's boss, to help him guide her to the car. It was not an easy task, as she cried harder than she ever had before.

Monica's mind was reeling with tons of memories of their past, and many 'what ifs' had Cayson reached her side and they had gotten married. She was now so distraught, that she zoned out and couldn't think. Her feet weren't sure how to maneuver and she wasn't sure that she wanted to leave.

Nico, along with everyone else, could tell that she was not well. "Monica?" he called. He was trying to get her to look into his eyes, but it was like she couldn't hear him.

"Should we call a doctor?" the minister asked with deep concern. He had known Monica for ten years now, and he was worried about her current state of mind.

"No. She's just been through a tremendous ordeal and will need time to adjust", Nico advised. "I'll stay with her for a while, and if I believe that she's getting worse, I promise that I will take her to the hospital." Nico was adamant in what he was saying, as he was also worried for his new friend.

"Here!" Mr. Jensen shouted loudly. He reached into the front pocket of his pants, and dug around until he found a business card. "Call me if you or Monica need anything. I mean anything – you hear me?" It seemed like there was anger in the tone of his voice, but it was panic and worry for his favorite employee.

"I hear you, and I thank you." Nico shook hands with both the minister and Monica's boss, and then he drove his passenger home. During the entire drive, he kept watching her and hoping that she would be ok. He knew that it would take time, for this was a horrible and unexpected thing to have happened.

Nico brought Monica to her apartment and helped her to get inside. He could see that she was still very distraught, so he poured her a stiff drink and walked her to the bedroom. He pulled the covers up to her neck, and suggested that she sleep and not think about anything. He then made himself comfortable on her couch.

Throughout the night, he could hear her moaning and crying out, and several times he went to see if she was ok. It looked like she was sound asleep, but she was tossing and turning from bad dreams. Nico's body sighed with heaviness, as he knew it would be a long night.

Monica's mind kept playing back the morning of their wedding day – the rain, the flowers, and the accident. And with each performance, she tried in vain for something to change. But as hard as she tried, her attempts always ended with Cayson dying on the street. Hour after hour, her lack of success left her feeling worthless and hollow. And each time she saw him lying dead and wet on the road, she was left crying from frustration and sadness.

The next morning, Monica woke up feeling more exhausted than ever. And when she tried to remember even one of her dreams, it hit her – Cayson was not only dead, he was now buried. This reflection was more final than she would have thought, for it truly ended their time together.

Monica heard a loud snore coming from the other room, which brought her out of her grieving trance. She stood up and grabbed her housecoat, and then she tip-toed down the hall to see who was there.

She was surprised to see Nico asleep on her couch, but she was grateful that he had stayed to take care of her. To show her thanks, she moved softly towards the kitchen. She was near the end of making breakfast when he woke up, and they ate the food in front of the TV.

"Thank you for yesterday", she offered with kindness. "I truly couldn't have gotten through any of that without you."

Nico was very glad that he had been there for her. "You're welcome." She looked much better, and he hoped that she would be okay if he made his way back home. "I'll call you later, but if you need me, you call me right away."

"Will do, and thanks for everything." As she closed the door, she felt a powerful sadness that weighed heavy on her chest. She was now truly alone. As the emptiness echoed throughout her apartment, she looked up to the ceiling and began to cry. "I love you, Cayson", she sobbed. "I will love you, forever." With tears in her eyes and a deep ache in her heart, she cleaned up the dishes and crawled back into bed.

They spoke by phone the next day, and every day for the next week, and saw each other three times in between. Nico wanted to go out somewhere special, and he asked Monica to go with him. She agreed, and they met at The Olive Garden on the night before she was supposed to go back to work.

It was a simple but elegant visit, and she left the tip while he paid for the meal.

Their conversation was easy, she actually laughed at his jokes, and they made plans to meet again on the following Friday night.

"Good luck tomorrow!" he added, after they had said good-night.

"Thank you. I'll call you when I get home."

The next morning was her first day back at work, and Monica's co-workers were more than kind to her – they brought her tea and cookies, and asked her how she was feeling. Around 10:30, her boss finally put a stop to the disruptive attention and ordered everyone to go back to their desks. "What she needs is to be back in a normal environment again", he insisted strongly. As he walked away, he didn't see the many disapproving facial expressions, which his employees had made in light of his statement.

Monica chuckled at the situation, but understood what her boss was trying to do.

It wasn't until a week later, when she realized that she was now a single pregnant woman. Because she was only 3 months along and she wasn't showing, no-one knew about her condition. Because she wasn't sure that she could or even wanted to raise a baby on her own, she decided to think of other options.

She discussed this at great length with Nico, the next time that they were together. "Having this child, would be a constant reminder of Cayson", she said. "Not having it, is not an option", she added strongly. She was very confused.

"I agree", he said, although he had no real opinion one way or another.

Monica had hoped that he would give a better answer, but she understood that this needed to be her decision.

Nico was becoming fond of his new friend, but he was steadfast about not wanting to have children in his life. His philosophy was that children tied a person down, and children cost a great deal of money. Nico had taken great risks to acquire the income that he had, and he wasn't about to squander it on unappreciative children. He would though, take the time to think of other solutions for Monica's problem.

It took him a few days before he came up with what he thought was a brilliant idea, and then he suggested that they talk about it. Nico met her for lunch and delivered his suggestion. "I have a friend at work who has been trying for years to have a baby and can't. I'm sure if I talked to him and his wife, that they would be very willing to adopt this child from you. What do you think?"

"Oh, my", she sighed. All of a sudden, this situation became very real.

While he waited for Monica to think it over, Nico watched as her left hand settled lovingly on the slight bulge of her tummy. She had her face down while she pondered this momentous decision.

Several minutes later, she looked into Nico's endearing face, and with a great deal of tenderness she asked, "They will take very good care of my child, right?" Tears of extreme sadness began to glisten behind her long lashes, as she waited for him to absolutely agree.

Nico nodded and hoped that he looked sincere. "I'm sure that they will." He reached out his hand and placed it over the one which she held lovingly on her tummy. "I'll talk with him tomorrow and get back to you as soon as possible."

Monica stayed quiet and nodded her thanks in his direction.

The next day, after she got home from work, Monica paced the floor of her tiny apartment. All day long her mind had been pre-occupied with Cayson's death and the baby's future. She knew that her work was suffering, but her emotions were running high and her heart had been broken into a million pieces.

# R-I-I-I-I-NG!!

Monica got startled by the loud tone. She knew who was calling, and ran to pick it up.

"Hello?" She was full of anticipation and hoped that the answer would be a resounding yes.

"Are you in the mood for some good news?" he asked. Nico was smiling from ear-to-ear and couldn't wait to give her what she had been waiting for.

"Yes! Don't keep me in suspense!" she shouted. A part of her was eager to hear the answer, while the other part wanted to keep the child for herself.

"My friend spoke with his wife at lunchtime, and they said yes."

Monica's knees gave way with relief, and she melted onto the couch behind her. "That's wonderful news. Thank you."

"You're welcome", he replied. "Talk to you later?"

"Sure." Monica took the phone away from her ear and placed it on her lap. She gazed off into the distance as she thought about the decision which she had just made. Monica didn't want to know much about the couple who would raise her child, but she did want to know that her baby would be well taken care of. If Nico said these people would make great parents, she would have to trust him. If he told her where they lived, she knew she would be there every single day. This was going to be a tough road to travel, and she knew that she would struggle emotionally, but she hoped that both her and her baby would be okay.

Nico got off the phone with Monica, and ran to print off a bogus set of adoption papers. He then took them over to his co-worker's home, and advised the happy couple to place their signatures 'here' and 'here'.

After collecting the first payment of money, and congratulating the parents-to-be on their upcoming wonderful journey, he folded his copy of the signed papers and raced to Monica's apartment.

The adoptive parents gazed at the paperwork for a little while longer, and then they placed their copy into a brand-new, letter-sized envelope. They positioned the important document, under all of the items which laid in the bottom drawer of the dresser. They weren't sure when or if it would ever come out again, but they believed that it would be safe there.

Monica let out a long sigh of sadness, for her baby would now be someone else's to raise. The child that she had made in a night of passion with Cayson, would soon have a home without her. Though she hadn't met them, Monica hoped that those two people would be exactly what this child needed – two parents to support, protect, and love him or her. The pregnant woman sighed again, but with grief and sorrow, as this was not how it was supposed to be.

On the drive over, it occurred to Nico that he was becoming quite attached to the pregnant woman. While this is not what he would have wanted, it was what was happening; his heart was beginning to love her.

Monica's mood had now changed, and her body was drifting away from exhaustion. She thought about the fairy tale ending, and what would have happened had Cayson not been killed, and then she fell asleep.

## *Knock, Knock, Knock*

Monica got woken up by the unexpected noise, and it took a minute for her brain to figure out where it was coming from. When she looked at the time, she remembered that Nico was coming over. She got out of bed and raced to the door, and when she saw his face, she gave him the biggest hug.

Without saying a word, Nico held her body tight to his own, and he let her cry on his shoulder while they stood in the open doorway. Minutes later, she escorted him inside, where they sat on the couch and talked about the details of the adoption. "Tell me about the couple", she begged. "Not much, just what they do for a living, if they have a good marriage, if they are good people, and if you think they will give my child a happy home."

Nico's light laughter was filled with sincerity, as he tried to convince her that everything's going to be ok. As he took both of her hands into his own, he reassured her that she was doing the right thing. "Yes, Monica. My friend is a good, solid worker. He has never been late, he looks out for everyone on his shift, and he's the dad that you would want to have in your own life.

"Ok." Monica loved his answer, and then she used a full minute to absorb all that Nico had said. When the minute was up, she asked, "And his wife?"

Nico had only just met the wife today, so he knew that he had to make up a dreamy story about what a totally qualified person the woman is. "His wife is so sweet and kind, she's soft-spoken, and she loves children." He paused for effect, and then continued. "Monica, she can't wait to be someone's mother."

Monica swooned when she heard the words that immediately calmed her heart. "Thank you, so much", she sighed. She felt considerably better, so she reached for the pen. "Okay, I'm ready. Show me where my signature needs to go."

Once Monica had signed away her rights, Nico put the folded document into his pocket. "You should get their first payment in a week", he stated, referring to their deal.

*Nico had instructed Monica that there is a modest fee which the parents-to-be would have to pay for doctor's visits, medicines, clothing, or other everyday expenses. Nico told the happy couple that he expected them to give him $1,000 every month until the baby was born. Nico told Monica that the new parents are not wealthy, and could not afford to pay more than $550 dollars a month. She thought that was ok, and he smiled and pocketed the rest.*

*Nico deposited each large cheque into the bank, and took $550 out for Monica. He was very proud of himself for coming up with such an elaborate plan, for he truly believed that he was able to make everyone happy in the process.*

Nico watched her place her initial on the last small line, on the last page of the document, and then he noticed that her expression had changed. Wanting to put a smile on her sad face, Nico clapped his hands together real loud and asked, "How about if I take you out to Leroy's?"

Monica agreed, as she knew it would take her mind off her troubles. "Sure. Just give me a minute." She ran down the hall and shut the bathroom door, and braced her upper body on the sink. She then dropped her face and closed her eyes, and willed herself not to cry. After taking a few huge breaths, she emerged from the bathroom while putting a smile on her face. "I'm ready."

Nico took Monica out to dinner to celebrate, and he made sure to make her laugh on more than three different occasions. He knew that she had had a trying time these past few months, and he expected that adopting her baby out couldn't be an easy decision to make. But he felt that with his help, it was all going to work out beautifully, for everyone.

Monica tried to keep her attention on Nico and their lovely dinner out, but her thoughts were consumed with what she had just done. She wished that Cayson had lived and that they could be raising their child together. Because this was not going to happen, and she knew that she couldn't raise the baby on her own, adoption was how it had to be. Still, it was a sad situation.

# Chapter 4

As the weeks turned into months, Nico and Monica were spending a lot more time together, and had eventually become really good friends. During that same time period, they got to learn a few details about the other person. Over dinners or afternoon walks, they talked a little about their childhoods, their likes and dislikes, and how they had predicted their futures would turn out.

Monica truly enjoyed spending time with Nico. She leaned on him more than she thought she should, and she soon found herself becoming eager for his phone calls and visits.

By the time she was seven months along, Nico had fallen madly in love with her. He didn't want to, but he couldn't help it. He loved being in her company, and he understood that she was only looking for a friend. Because of this, he wondered if someday, that they might part ways.

Monica decided to stop working when she was almost eight months along; her tummy was protruding and she was embarrassed for anyone to find out her secret. She had not told anyone except Nico that she was pregnant, and it was becoming difficult to hide her situation. She knew that it would only be a matter of time before she would have to field a ton of questions, and she wasn't ready for that.

With a note from her doctor, Monica was graciously given three months off work as stress-leave. Her kind and concerned employer agreed with this decision, as he knew about Cayson's death; he had seen how sad Monica had been since that terrible day. Because she was only going to be paid a portion of her regular amount, she would be forced to live on her savings, and any money that the adopted parents were floating her way. She was very grateful that Nico had paid for all of their meals out, while she provided all of the snacks and TV shows that they watched in her apartment, for that helped her stay on budget.

By the time Monica was nine months along, Nico had become undeniably devoted to her. He hardly left her side, and when he did, he phoned her every couple of hours just to see how she was doing. He loved her voice, and he truly listened to every word she said – from how she was feeling, to what she was doing.

Nico was not a fool; he had dated other girls about twice a week, since that fateful day when Cayson had died. Some had good looks, others had money, but none could hold a candle to Monica. Some stuck around for a few weeks, while others were only there for a few hours. Nico used them for whatever he required, but always went back to Monica for his emotional needs.

Nico was delighted that Monica was going to give her baby up for adoption, and in the back of his mind, he contemplated the idea to change their best friend status to boyfriend/girlfriend. He knew she wouldn't go for it right now, but he hoped she would, sometime in the future.

Monica had grown quite fond of Nico, but she was not looking to jump into another serious relationship. She truly believed that Cayson was her one and only true love, but he had been savagely taken away from her. Soon, the baby which they had made together would also be gone from her life. The thought was sometimes too much for Monica to bear, and she thanked God for Nico's company and friendship.

It was a Wednesday afternoon and Monica was sitting on the couch. She was drinking some herbal tea while looking out of the living room window. As she stared off into the distance, Monica wondered what she would be like as a mom.

Childhood pictures flashed through her mind, as she remembered the love which her parents had had for each other. She knew that things were not always perfect for them or with them, but it was how she wanted her life to be. She had always known that she wanted a husband to love her and kids to run after, but after all the turmoil that she'd gone through this past year, she needed a moment to breathe. Maybe sometime down the road, she would be able to raise a family like her mom and dad had done – just not right now.

*Sadly, Monica was the only child born in their imperfect marriage. It was a well-known fact that Monica's parents had struggled for years to have a baby, but neither one knew why. After a while, baby-making was becoming too much of a chore, and it didn't take long before Monica's parents became less and less interested in each other. Years later, there was hardly any communication between them, let alone any intimacy.*

*Mrs. Bellam had a long-standing, socially accepted friendship with Charlie Baker, the man from the deli counter at Broback's Grocery Store. But for the past two years, there has been more banter and joking going on between them. He was tall, slightly overweight, attractive, and he could always make her laugh.*

*Charlie and his customer had begun a happy association many years ago, but when he saw her sad face more than once in the past few months, he upped his game to make her smile every time he saw her. When Mrs. Bellam started going to the store more often than usual, he made sure to have a few new jokes for her to hear. When he felt that she was ready, he asked her out for coffee.*

*Mrs. Bellam wasn't sure about going out for coffee with a man who wasn't her husband, but because he assured her that they would be going to the café where dozens of other people could see them, she decided that that would be ok.*

*Once she got there and they began to talk, she felt more at ease than ever.*

*After three more coffee dates, they spent an afternoon in the park, feeding ducks and talking about whatever came to their minds. After she disclosed all the details that led to the sadness in her life, he held her close in order to comfort her.*

*Because she hadn't felt that safe in a very long time, when he asked if they could go somewhere more private, she said yes. At the end of that meeting, Charlie kissed her on the lips. Mrs. Bellam liked it, but felt ashamed, and she rushed home. Throughout the next few days, she had decided to see Charlie again, but to explain to him why they could never be more than friends.*

*It was strange seeing him at the store, even though that's where they had met almost 7 years ago. She didn't want anyone to overhear what she had to say, so she asked if they could go somewhere to talk, and he agreed.*

*Charlie didn't want her to say that they couldn't see each other again, for he had the motel room prepared for an afternoon of adventure. "Give me ten minutes to get cleaned up!" he stated firmly. She didn't know it yet, but he was hoping to move their relationship up to the next level.*

*Twenty-five minutes later, they were in the room. "Shall we have some wine?"*

*Her heart sank. She stared at him, paying particular attention to his mouth and his hands, and she felt embarrassed. Did she never want to kiss him again? She was so confused, but she didn't want to show it. "Yes, that's a good idea", she replied, as she reached for the glass. She took a large sip of the purple liquid, and felt the warmth fill her body, almost immediately.*

*"Now", he began. "Shall we sit and talk?" He sat himself down at the foot of the bed, and patted the spot beside him with his right hand. "Come here." The stocky man reached his left hand out, and was thrilled when she took it.*

*At first she was reluctant, but because he was so persuasive, she was soon sitting next to him – so close that their clothing was touching.*

*"Now, tell me what's bothering you." His deep voice simmered with controlled passion as he spoke. He placed his arm across her shoulders and waited for her to reply. When she did, he moved his fingertips in small circles on her shoulder. They soon moved down to her collar bone, and then he spun her around and kissed her.*

*Mrs. Bellam did not stop the tender kiss from happening; she couldn't. It was the moment, how he smelled, how he touched her, and how he made her feel, that diluted her into thinking that this was ok. When her clothes came off, she grabbed for his body. They acted like wild animals that had been locked up for the past year. They were reckless and uninhibited, they let out screams of passion and they didn't care.*

*Their rendezvous ended after her unbelievable hunger had been quenched. It was by mutual consent that they had sex - an act that had not happened to her in a very long time. The unbelievable heights of sexual excitement which Charlie had brought her to, made her turn a blind eye to the guilt that she should have felt, but didn't.*

*As they both walked away that afternoon, it was with pleasure pumping through every vein in their bodies. And they knew that it would happen again.*

*That type of afternoon turned into a weekly event, and it soon developed into an improper habit – something which they enjoyed for many months. In January, when she learned that she was pregnant, everything changed.*

*At first the married woman panicked, wondering how she was going to explain this surprising situation to her husband. In a weak moment, she decided to seduce him and pass the baby off as his own. Three weeks later, Mrs. Bellam announced that she was expecting.*

*Mr. Bellam was extremely delighted by the news that a baby was coming, but he was also terribly surprised. This was what he'd wanted with all his heart and for such a long time, but something just didn't feel right about the whole situation. He had been watching his wife's face and body language while they were talking about a baby coming, and he noticed that she wasn't as happy as she should have been. 'Shouldn't she be gushing with joy?' he wondered to himself.*

*Mrs. Bellam was happy that she was pregnant, but she was embarrassed about how she had come to be that way. She knew perfectly well who the father was, so she refused to see Charlie again, or step a foot inside of the store. When she saw him on the street, she was sure to duck into any retail outlet or coffee shop, and always kept her face hidden. She gave Charlie no rhyme or reason for disappearing, and she hoped that he wouldn't take any actions to find her.*

*It had been months since Mrs. Bellam had come into the store, and this made Charlie sad. He immediately suspected that she might have gotten pregnant and that she was scared to face him. He wished that he could have confided in her, and told her that his wife and girlfriends had given birth to his eight children. But because he and Mrs. Bellam never spoke about his personal life, she never knew that he could be so fertile.*

*A month before her baby was born, Mrs. Bellam had convinced her husband to move his little family to another neighbourhood. In her mind, it ensured that her secret would never be found out. She was thrilled when her husband agreed to her idea.*

*The delivery was the easy part, and now came the hard part. For even at an hour old, Mrs. Bellam could see that the newborn little girl didn't have one single feature that reminded people of her father.*

*Mr. Bellam was fair-haired, as was his whole entire family. And he wasn't a stupid man. He'd had his suspicions about how his wife could have gotten pregnant, but he didn't know who had helped her to create this child. He could have gotten quite angry and made a big deal out of this situation, but instead of dwelling on it, he focused on being the best dad on the planet.*

*Mr. Bellam was never one to let anyone into his private thoughts. Now that he was a father, he was terrified that his little girl might be taken away from him, so he kept his fears of her origin to himself. While he hadn't known her for very long, he loved his dark-haired daughter with all of his heart, and he cared for her as if she were his very own blood and sweat.*

*Months had gone by, and Charlie decided to carry on without Mrs. Bellam's company. In the same time period, Mrs. Bellam tried to keep her secret safe from her husband, and from the rest of the world.*

*Monica Bellam had an amazing childhood; she was smart, happy, she had lots of friends, and she never wanted for anything. But in Grade 10, Monica's life became a little confusing. She had been introduced to a girl her exact age, and the other kids suspected that they were long-lost twins. Upon closer inspection, the two girls could see that they were the same height, they shared the same lips, forehead, eye and hair color, and they had the same body shape. They even had the same taste in clothing, and were wearing the exact same earrings.*

*After asking dozens of questions, Jolene and Monica found out where each of them had been born and to whom, where they had grown up, and who they were related to. As much as they had hoped that they were somehow related, there was no clear-cut evidence pointing to that fact, so they decided that all of their similarities were purely coincidental.*

*When Monica was in Grade 11, her father had become very ill. He died a year later - weeks before his little girl's graduation. Monica went to the ceremony with her mom, and while she was still wearing her cap and gown, she searched everywhere for her friend, Jolene.*

*"There she is!" she shrieked. "Jolene!" Monica grabbed her mother's arm with one hand, while waving her other arm in her friend's direction. "Over here!"*

*While the two girls hugged and said HI, Mrs. Bellam felt a little out of place. Because she was a huge fan of dogs, she involuntary turned her head when she heard one barking.*

*Jolene felt something touch her back, and then noticed that her dad was standing right behind her. "Dad! Where do you go?"*

*"I turned around and you were gone", he replied with sadness in his voice. "Because I know your love for colored scrunchies, I searched all over until I found you."*

*Jolene had spoken to her dad about 'this girl from school' for a long time, but they had never met....until now. "Dad, this is Monica Bellam. Monica, this is my dad, Charlie Baker." Jolene continued to tug at his arm until he reached out to shake Monica's hand.*

*Monica was mesmerized at how handsome Jolene's dad was. She looked into the man's face and felt as if she'd known him all of her life. She didn't know why, but he seemed awfully familiar, and his appearance flaunted a great number of features which she also had. Standing so close to him was uncanny, and she wondered why he was smiling in her direction, as if he knew her.*

*"Monica Bellam", he recited softly to himself. After one quick look, he recognized that she could be one of his children. Charlie's soul had filled with pure joy, the moment he realized who Monica Bellam was. He placed both of his hands around the one which she had intended to shake hands with, and stared directly into her eyes. "Hi, Monica", he sighed. He was truly delighted to meet her.*

*The whole thing had suddenly become very unnerving, so Monica turned her head in search of her mother. "Mom?" she called in a desperate plea. She was relieved to find that her mother was standing only a few feet away.*

*Mrs. Bellam had been down on one knee, petting and talking to a really cute Pug puppy, but turned around when she heard the awkward tone in her daughter's voice. "Yes dear?"*

*"Can you come here, please?" Monica stared into Charlie's eyes as she waited for her mom to arrive.*

*Mrs. Bellam did as she was told, and as soon as she saw his face, her lungs involuntarily sucked in a great deal of air. Her body became stiff, and she couldn't release the emotional lock which she had on his gorgeous eyes.*

*Monica grabbed her mother's hand, and very politely, introduced the man in front of them. "Mom, this is Mr. Charlie Baker – Jolene's dad."*

*Mrs. Bellam's skin color changed to a pasty white, and she suddenly felt quite ill. She wasn't sure if she was even breathing, but she wanted to die right there on that spot.*

*Charlie's heart began to pound in his chest. He had forgotten how beautiful she was, and now he understood why she had disappeared. He also realized that his heart had been aching, because he had missed her. Suddenly, thoroughly-delicious details of their meetings in the motel room, flooded his mind. He couldn't help but place a wide smile on his perfectly tanned face because of what they had done in those meetings, and the smile just happened to show all of his white teeth.*

*Charlie was getting aroused by the pictures of the two of them together, and hoped that his former lover would be able to give him even five or ten minutes of her time before the day was over. "Hi", he sighed, in a glorious, sultry manner. He decided to pull out all of his charms, in the chance that she might say yes to a short get-together.*

*He immediately placed one hand behind his back and extended his other one forward. "I'm very pleased to meet you, Mrs. Bellam", he said, hoping to captivate her. He then turned to show Mrs. Bellam that he had met their daughter. "And I'm very pleased to have had the opportunity to meet Monica."*

*Mrs. Bellam was embarrassed beyond belief. She could feel how beet red her face must be, and how tiny droplets of sweat were beginning to form on her brow and under her arms. She felt like she needed to rush away in hurry, but all she could do was stand there in fear and horrible surprise.*

*"I've heard so much about Monica from my daughter Jolene, and now I know why – the two girls are identical!" he rejoiced.*

*It wasn't in Mrs. Bellam's character to be rude, but she really needed to walk away. "Excuse me!" she begged loudly. It was the first word she had spoken in the past five minutes.*

*"Mom!" Monica shouted. She didn't know what was going on, but she hoped that her mother would apologize for being so disrespectful.*

*Mrs. Bellam twisted her body completely around, bent over, and threw up whatever had crawled from her stomach and into her throat. Being even more embarrassed than she was before, Mrs. Bellam began to run as fast as she could, in order to put as much distance as possible between her and Charlie Baker.*

*As Monica watched her mother flee from the area, she took another look at Jolene's dad. "What happened?" It was a rhetorical question, but she would accept any answers from any person for miles around.*

*Charlie beamed at Monica without saying a word. He felt that he now knew all that he needed to know, about Mrs. Bellam's sudden disappearance.*

*The dark haired girl was baffled beyond measure. She was worried for her mom, and guessed that there was something going on. "Do you guys know each other?" Monica asked. She studied the features in Charlie's handsome face while she waited for him to answer. It suddenly dawned on her, that she looked more like Charlie Baker than she did her own father. "Never mind", Monica babbled. Her head was spinning and she wanted to find her mom.*

*Charlie wanted so much to disclose that he was her father, but he couldn't. He wasn't sure how much information Mrs. Bellam had provided to Monica, so he said nothing at all.*

*Dozens of notions were whirling around in her head, and Monica couldn't think. She had been told a long time ago, that her parents had had trouble conceiving a child. She was also told in great detail, about how excited they both were when they found out that a baby was coming. She then remembered her childhood, and how much her father had loved her and doted on her. She also recalled how often her mom had tried to keep a bit of distance between the father and the daughter.*

*As Monica reflected on all of this, she whispered softly to herself. "Perhaps that was to hide a secret about where I had come from", she determined with great insight. With this assumption playing in her mind, she now had to know the truth. She searched until she spotted her mother, and then she began to run towards her.*

*"Mom!" she shouted, as she finally caught up to her. "Who is Charlie Baker to us?" she demanded. "And why did it look as if you'd seen a ghost when I introduced you to him?"*

*Mrs. Bellam was very upset, and it was clear that she had been crying. She could barely catch her breath and needed a moment to form a coherent sentence. Then, in very loud and tearful tones, the hysterical woman made Monica promise not to talk to anyone else about this disturbing conversation.*

*"I promise", she said slowly. Monica was scared of what her mother was about to tell her, but she needed to hear the words.*

*"It's true, we had trouble conceiving, and then suddenly I got pregnant." Mrs. Bellam was almost shouting as big droplets of tears fell from her eyes. "You have to know that you had a very good and kind father, who loved you with all of his heart. That's all that should matter." When she had finished her thought, she rushed to get to the car. Mrs. Bellam was still sobbing when she got home, and then ran straight to her room.*

*Monica raced behind her mother, and arrived at the house a few minutes later. Monica could hear great sobs of despair coming from inside the master bedroom, and it went on for hours. She desperately wanted to comfort the* woman who seemed to be so terribly upset, but Monica decided that it was best for them to have some time apart.

Monica went to her own room to think about the whole situation. Without knowing the full story, she began to ponder many different scenarios, but which one was right? Did Charlie rape her mother, or did they have an affair? Or maybe he had been kind to her parents, and donated his sperm so that they could have a child? "How did Charlie fit into our life?" she moaned out loud. She placed her face into her hands and wept for a few lonely minutes.

It soon became obvious that she would never know the truth without someone telling her, so Monica decided to bury all that she had seen and heard – at least for the time being. She had grown up with a wonderful set of parents, and saw no reason to continue to fuss about things that shouldn't matter. She grabbed her movie magazine and tried not think about it anymore.

For the rest of the day, Charlie couldn't do anything but think about Monica and her mother. After realizing that it was highly unlikely that he would ever get to see his daughter or her mother again, he locked the image of the two of them into a private spot in his mind, and went to be with Jolene.

Unfortunately, Mrs. Bellam died in a car accident three years later, without ever having told Monica the reason why she had panicked after seeing Charlie. Monica was angry at first, but after enough time had passed, she realized that she had been loved and protected, and she had had *an amazing life. It didn't matter how she had come to be in that family, only that she had had the good fortune to be their daughter.*

Two weeks before she was to deliver her child, Monica went through a gauntlet of strange thoughts and emotions. Somedays she was tired, cold, hot, wide awake, and cranky, and all in the same hour. On other days she was full, starving, too big, or not big enough, and she needed to pee all the time. At one point, she even began to question if she was doing the right thing by giving up her baby. "I could try to raise it", she stated in a last-ditch effort to keep it. Tears were flowing from her eyes as she thought about the little person growing inside of her – the only tie left between her and Cayson. A little treasure that she would never get to see grow up.

She began to cry as she realized that once their child was gone, the history of Cayson and Monica would also be gone – like a distant memory that fades over time. She looked down at her tummy and cried, "If I give you away, there'd be no souvenirs that our relationship had even happened." Just as she was about to go into another crying spell, she heard a knock on the door.

Nico walked in with a dozen, very colorful flowers. "How are you doing?" he asked cheerfully. He took one look at her, and he knew right away that this was one of her sad moments.

"I'm ok", she stated, through heartache and confusion. She turned away from him so he couldn't see how much she had been crying, but she couldn't hide the quiver in her voice. She very much appreciated him being there, though.

Nico hated to see her cry, but there was little that he could do for her. He knew that he could make her happy after she had the baby, but for right now, as much as it hurt, he had to let her get through this horrible transition period, herself.

Monica motioned for Nico to sit down, by patting the seat next to her. As soon as he was comfortable, Monica leaned herself into his body and stayed nestled there until she felt better.

Nico had not planned on getting so attached to her, but he believed that Monica was perfect for him. She was young, sexy, funny, and she was the type of girl that he could see himself growing old with. In essence, she was a good catch and he wanted to be the fisherman who caught her in his net.

This was an unexpected emotion for him, but having Monica that close, just felt right. Nico reached his arm out and placed it across her shoulders. Nico's face suddenly burst into a smile, which he didn't wipe off for days.

# Chapter 5

The biggest thing to hit the newsstands in 1966, according to Monica and her friends, was the release of, 'Valley Of The Dolls'. The scandalous book zoomed to the #1 spot in record time, and was made into a movie shortly afterwards. Monica was two weeks past her due date and reading the outrageous novel, when her water broke.

Nico drove her to the hospital, but because he was not the father, he was asked to wait outside the room until after the baby was born.

"No!" she shouted, over and over again. "He HAS to be in there with me!" Monica reached out and held onto Nico's shirt with all her might. "Please!" she begged. She had never wanted anything so strongly in her entire life.

She was terrified of the worsening pains and the actual delivery, so she continued to demand that she have his company. "Nico!" she screamed, when it felt like he was slipping away. "Ni-i-co!" Her voice was loud and cracking, and she didn't want to do this without him. Monica felt as if she was going to be slaughtered and she'd never see him again. "Nico, please!" she shouted.

Two nurses and an orderly argued loudly with Monica, while nearly ripping her nails from Nico's clothing. After a great deal of struggling, they were able to tear the two of them apart.

"We have protocol that we have to adhere to!" one nurse shouted. She knew her patient was not listening, but she had to make it clear why Nico couldn't come into the birthing room with her.

Nico loved that Monica was fighting so hard to keep him close, but he truly was ok not to be in the room when the baby came out. "Everything's going to be okay, honey", he confessed without really knowing if it would be or not. "And I'll be right here when it's all over."

He was suddenly free from Monica's very strong grip, but he continued to hear her shrieking, as the hospital staff wheeled her down the long hallway.

"Ni-i-i-i-co-o-o!" She was more terrified than she ever had been in her life, and she no longer wanted to give birth.

Now that he was alone, Nico took that opportunity to call the adoptive parents. After letting them know what was happening, he heard them shout with joy. Within the hour, they had arrived at the hospital, but they were told by the administrative staff, to stay in the lobby on the main floor.

Monica's labor lasted another three hours, but it felt like an entire day. It had been seriously painful, and had ended after 45 minutes of pushing.

The new mom got to hold her son for a few long minutes, immediately after he was born. "Oh my gosh", she cooed lovingly. "You are so beautiful." As she gazed into his angel-like face, she pushed aside all that she had to endure in order for him to come into the world. She opened the blanket in which he was swaddled, and fell so deeply in love with him, that she didn't feel as if she would be able to bring herself to give him away.

Meanwhile, on the next floor down, an orderly had walked into the waiting room and called out Nico's name. "Mr. Kostas?"

The startled man jumped to attention. "Yah, that's me!" he announced loudly. He was nervous and felt like a proud father, but he still didn't want to raise another man's baby.

"Come with me, please." The orderly motioned for the man to follow him, as he escorted Nico to the 4th floor.

"Oh, by the way", the orderly said with enthusiasm. "She had a baby boy."

Nico's mind drifted when he was told that Monica had a little boy. Nico would have wanted a son, but not someone else's.

Before Nico had gotten off the elevator, the heavy door to Monica's room swung open with a great amount of force.

"It's time", the nurse announced harshly, as she entered Monica's room.

*Nurse Camden was usually compassionate by nature, but she had learned to be cruel in tough times such as this; she had often seen mothers – young and old – sobbing hysterically when they were faced with the decision of keeping or giving up their newborn babies. If she played into their moments, then the child would never leave the room, and that's why she had to be tough.*

Monica gasped when she heard the gruff female voice, and looked up in horror as the imitation marine sergeant marched into the powder-green room. The new mom immediately looked down at her son's little hands and his adorable face, and everything inside of her wanted to bundle him up and run away and hide. Her heart felt like it was tearing into two pieces, as she pondered how this emotional battle would end.

"Miss Bellam, please!" Because the uniformed employee didn't have time for that kind of nonsense today, the nurse took matters into her own hands. She stretched out her arms, and ordered the patient to hand her the child. "I need to take the baby away."

Monica was holding onto her fragile bundle as if her life depended on it, but she was only able to do so for another minute. While hundreds of tears were streaming down her already flushed cheeks, she pleaded with the RN to please give her another few minutes to be with her son. "I'm begging you with everything I have!" She felt as if she was drowning emotionally, and hated that nobody in the world was coming to her rescue. "Ple-e-e-ease!" she called loudly. "I'm begging you!" Her bottom lip was quivering wildly, and her soul was breaking into the tiniest of bits.

The nurse needed to remind herself not to fall apart, so she became even more aggressive. Only then was she able to remove the tiny infant from the patient's arms.

The new mom hated that her baby was crying, and lashed out with punches to keep her child close. "No-o-o-o-o!" Monica screamed, terrified that she'll never see her son again. "I need more time to think this through!"

The RN now had the upper hand, and felt she was winning. "I'm sorry, but your time is up!"

"No-o-o-o-o!" Monica screamed, as she watched her baby being laid onto a dressing table in the far corner of the room.

The elevator doors had opened, and Nico could now hear Monica's cries from all the way down the hall. As terror gripped every part of his soul, Nico rushed into the room to see the nurse getting the baby ready for his new parents. A lump of panic formed in his throat, and he wasn't sure what he should do. He looked into Monica's face, and he could see that she was beyond grief-stricken, but he didn't know how to comfort her; the deal was for her to give her baby up for adoption. His feet were frozen to the floor, while his eyes went back and forth between the mom and her baby.

Tears of shock were streaming down Monica's cheeks, as she locked eyes with Nico. "Ple-e-e-ease!" she insisted loudly. Her red eyes were imploring him to get her baby back, while her voice was now raw and sore. "Tell her that we've changed our minds!" She felt like she was on the verge of insanity, but continued to argue with Nico to get her baby back. "Nico, please! Why aren't you helping me?"

"I'm here", he said softly, as he walked towards the bed. He stroked her hair to calm her down, but it wasn't working; she was inconsolable and not wanting to listen.

Monica stared directly into his eyes, as if she wanted him to burn in hell, and implored him to get her baby back. "Please, Nico! Please!" She was panic-stricken, and had moved the blankets away from her legs so that she could stand up. "Help me get him back!" she pleaded. "That's my baby!"

Nico used both of his hands to keep her in bed, but he used no words to reassure her that everything would be okay. The grown man had never felt so helpless in his life, but he had made a deal to adopt the baby out. Nico needed to keep his word, or give the money back. Because the last part was not an option, he had to help the nurse do her job.

"Thank you", the nurse called, as she looked in Nico's direction.

Nico didn't want her thanks. "Just get him out of here!" Nico shouted over his shoulder. He loathed himself in that moment, but knew he couldn't do anything to change what was happening.

"Why?" she screamed, as she searched his entire face for answers. The new mom was filled with a sickening disgust towards a man who had done nothing to help her. "I will never forgive you!" Monica stated harshly. The hateful words spit out of her mouth with total agony.

Nico lowered his gaze and silently agreed that he was an asshole. He was tormented to have to choose between money and what Monica was going through, but, as much as he wanted to fight against it, he felt that he had done the right thing for everyone involved. He hoped in time that Monica would agree.

Not a moment later, with empty arms and a terrible, empty ache in her heart, Monica watched as the nurse carried her beautiful baby out of the room. "No-o-o-o-o-o-o!" The deathly scream could be heard throughout the hospital's 4th floor corridors.

"I'm so sorry, Monica", Nico whispered. His own voice was now breaking as he tried not to cry.

"I hate you!" she hissed at him. Monica wasn't sure which emotion she was feeling more – a supreme loathing for Nico, or the extreme loss of her baby boy.

Nico felt a tear escape from his right eye, and hated himself for what he was putting her through. "But you know this is for the best", he stated, with less confidence than he should have used. He buried his face in the side of her neck and hoped that she would forgive him.

The adoptive couple, who had been sitting on the main floor of the hospital for the past 4.5 hours, were delighted when someone finally called their names. "Mr. and Mrs. Ryng?"

"Here!" Mr. Ryng raised his hand and stood up.

"We'll need you over here, please." After verifying their identity, the couple was instructed to go upstairs.

In that same moment, Monica was beyond consolable - she was in pain, she wanted her baby back, she hated Nico, and she didn't understand why nobody was helping her. She was suffering more than she could fathom, and she didn't think anyone cared.

Suddenly, Monica felt as if she didn't want to be part of anything anymore. With one strong motion, she pushed hard against Nico's body. After she felt free from his head on her skin, Monica reached behind her head and placed the pillow over her face, hoping to hide some of the sounds of her desperation.

Monica sobbed in a tone that was deeper than just plain grief - it was empty, and full of heartache. And it was so loud that everyone was wondering what had happened, and yet so brittle, that you would think her spirit could break with a strong sigh.

Nico could see that she was a mental and an emotional wreck, but while he didn't know how to console her, he also didn't want to leave the room. "I'm so sorry, but I'm here for you", he vowed, as he listened to her struggling. "For as long as you need me to be", he added softly. "I'll be here." He was now becoming emotional himself, and got up and walked towards the window. He stood there, everything numb, and stared out at all that he could see.

The elevator doors opened and the adoptive parents stepped out. Because they hadn't been given a room number to go to, they wandered down the halls in hope of finding someone who could help them.

In a special room down the hallway, a doctor had checked the baby out, and the newborn was given a clean bill of health. The nurse had bundled him up again, and was now carrying him to meet his new parents.

"Mr. and Mrs. Ryng?" she called.

They both looked behind them to see who was speaking. "Yes?" Mr. Ryng replied.

"I have your baby." a strong female voice stated.

"Oh, my goodness!" Mrs. Ryng breathed softly.

The door to the small hospital room must have stayed open a crack, for Monica thought she could hear people talking out in the hallway. In order to hear better, she removed the pillow from her face and perked up her ears.

"Honey, look! Look at how tiny he is", a female voice stated proudly.

Monica could only assume that that was the new mother's voice.

"Congratulations to both of you", the nurse announced cheerfully. "Here's your baby boy." The voice sounded exactly like that nurse who had taken Monica's baby away.

Monica stopped breathing and needed everything in her room to be super quiet, so that she could hear all of what was happening just outside of her door.

"He's beautiful!" the new mother exclaimed. "Look at how precious he is!" She was gushing and she didn't care.

"He sure is!" the new father agreed. The man then made cute noises to attract the baby's attention towards him.

"Have you chosen a name?" the nurse asked with an official tone in her voice. She watched them look towards each other, and then she positioned her pen to write the answer.

As the new parents bubbled with complete happiness, Monica heard the father proudly recite, "Oliver Everette Ryng".

*It was not what she would have chosen, and it deflated her ego that she was no longer in charge of her son's future.*

"Wonderful! Excellent choices", the nurse cheered. "Now I'll need you to follow me down to the nurse's station, so we can fill out the rest of the forms."

"Come on, little baby boy", a woman's voice cooed. "Let's go for a short walk."

And as quickly as the talking had begun, it had ended. "Please let me wake up and start all over again!" she shrieked. Monica began another round of crying, as she buried her face deep into her pillow. She desperately wanted time go back to the morning of her wedding. "Cayson!" she cried. "Why did you have to leave me?"

The new mom was feeling terribly disoriented, and the emotional pain was unbelievable. As she agonized about what had happened, she could feel that the muscles in her body were weakening. Monica wondered if she would ever truly recover from all the losses that she had suffered in these last 8 months.

Nico was deep in his own thoughts and worries, and hadn't heard the people out in the hallway. He eventually turned around, and it appeared as if Monica was no longer crying or moving. "Poor thing", he sighed quietly. "She must have cried herself to sleep." Nico reached out to caress her hand, and then he quietly left her room.

Over the next three days, Monica sobbed with anguish over losing the only thing that would remind her of Cayson Ross. Now that her fiancé and son were both gone, it was as if she had nothing to live for.

Nico went to the hospital every one of those days, and filled her room with roses and cards. He knew that she didn't care and never noticed what he brought with him, for her mind and heart were being consumed by other things.

Nico had never known true love before and was really worried about Monica's well-being. He had no idea that she would have taken this situation so hard, but he remained steadfast in his views, that this was truly the best thing for everyone involved.

Monica was released from the hospital on the third day at 4pm, albeit, she decided that she would never be released from the guilt of giving away her son.

The first three weeks after the baby was born, was rough, but Nico was there morning, noon, and night to take care of Monica – her sad moods, her loneliness, and her unwillingness to move forward with her life. He didn't mind sleeping on her couch, as he loved being around to dote on her and talk with her. Once Nico stopped spending as many nights with her as he had been, things changed – Monica had to fend for herself. He called her about four times a day, but he was growing confident that she was now able to cook and take care of herself.

Monica spent a lot of time daydreaming of what could have happened, had Cayson not died. In her mind's eye, she saw the three of them sharing holidays and picnics together, while laughing and having a good time. She saw them all growing old together, and then sadness set in; she realized that it can't happen that way, now that both Cayson and their son had been taken from her.

There were many moments when Monica wanted to know how her baby was doing and what he looked like, but all she could do was wonder. She often cradled an 8 x 10" picture of Cayson in her hands, and spoke to it as if Cayson could actually hear her. She constantly apologized for giving up their son, and she claimed that she couldn't have seen the boy's face on a daily basis or loved him unconditionally, without Cayson being there with them; it just didn't seem right. She hoped that he would have agreed, had he been able to communicate his feelings to her, himself.

Nico came over every evening for supper, and he made sure to do what he could, in order for Monica to feel a bit better. He got her to laugh or smile at least once per day, and he saw to it that she always ate healthy. He made sure that she had baths and got dressed every single day, and told her that it was in case he might take her out to somewhere fancy. It was his way of getting her mind back to her normal routine.

It took a while, but eventually, Monica began to feel better, and soon she was back at work. She was welcomed with open arms, and since everyone thought she had been off because of personal problems, they doted on her every whim. While she loved the attention, she longed for the day when things would calm down again; she had never been one to be made a fuss over.

It had been six months since the baby was born, and Nico found that he had fallen head-over-heels in love with his female companion. So much so, that he was actually contemplating asking her out on a date. Nico knew that Monica was in no mood for romance, and it became even more pronounced when she asked him to give her an evening off here and there.

"What would you like to eat for supper tonight?" was his usual question.

Monica would name something and he would bring it, but every once in a while she would ask him not to come over. "I just want to wash my hair and go to bed early", she said softly into the phone.

"Of course, my darling." Nico was patient and only too happy to give her all the space that she needed. During Monica's crying spells and nasty moods, Nico stayed away. When she begged him to come over for an hour, he did so with a smile upon his face. And each time she spoke the words, "I miss you", he went from despair to jovial in three seconds.

Nico knew all too well what she was going through, as he had been right there with her for almost every single second of the past year. He knew that she had been angry with him for getting the baby adopted out, but they had talked about it and now things were good between them. Overall, Nico did whatever he could do to stay on her good side, no matter what it entailed, and he delivered on every one of Monica's whims.

It was such a new role for him; usually it was Nico who was pulling the heart strings of pretty girls, but with Monica, he was the one acting like a puppy who was desperate for someone to pat its head. But Nico didn't mind; as long as he was going to win Monica's hand in the end, he felt it was all worth it.

Monica could see how much effort Nico was putting into them having a relationship, and while she loved that about him, she was not in love with him. She truly enjoyed how things were between them, but there was a line that she wasn't ready to cross.

Nico, on the other hand, hoped to cross the finish line at some point.

Nico and Monica were constant companions and really good friends, but they were not lovers – much to Nico's dismay. One day he hoped for that to change, and he promised that he would bide his time until then. For now, they were kissing hello and good-bye on the cheek, and at times he would try to place a kiss on her lips.

Because Monica felt that he was kidding when he tried to get romantic, she laughed it off, but she knew in her heart that she would be lost without him in her life.

Because he felt she was worth it, Nico respected that she wanted to take things slow. While he waited for the day when she was ready to be with a man again, he remained in her life in whatever role she wanted him to play.

# Chapter 6

With Christmas approaching, newsreels around the world were reminding everyone of the many exciting things that had happened in1966: Ronald Regan had been sworn in as Governor of California, the American Basketball Association had been founded, 'It's A Small World' had opened in Disneyland, and The Beatles had ended their U.S. tour with a concert at Candlestick Park.

To Monica, those same moments had gone by with unbelievable emotional pain. The world saw a beautiful woman wearing a forced smile, but she was pretending that she was okay. Nobody knew that inwardly, she was filled with heavy sorrow; she couldn't help but think about Cayson and their baby boy, every second of every day.

To pass the time and to keep her mind occupied, she watched a lot of TV, but she seldom caught the focus of what was happening. She spent a fortune on movie magazines, and she flipped mindlessly through the glossy pages, without really absorbing anything but the pictures.

In the darkness of her nights, Monica
ceiling, wondering why God had been so
away a man that had meant so much to hei
light glowed against her heartbreaking ex
whimpered about missing her groom and tl
usually fell asleep about an hour after she had c           into
bed, wishing for them both to be back in her life again.

A few months later, marked a full year since her baby
boy had been born. Monica continued to think about the
beautiful child who she had given up for adoption, but she
was learning to let go of the harshness of her decision.
Instead of sitting around and grieving over something
that she could no longer change, she filled her heart with
thoughts that her son was being well-taken care of, and by
wonderful parents who truly loved him. Even so, she often
wished that it was her who was raising him and watching
his day-to-day progress.

Nico was still a permanent fixture in Monica's life,
talking with her every single day, and still trying to become
her boyfriend. He was wealthy, thanks to Andrea, and was
almost ready to be in another long-term relationship. He
believed that Monica was perfect in every way possible,
and he felt that the connection he had with her, was
uncanny.

Nico didn't need her love, but he desperately wanted all
that Monica had to offer. He also didn't need to have sex
with her right now, as he got plenty of that from the many
women who looked or breathed in his direction. He didn't
want these women for any longer than a few hours, and

ᴐ came running back to Monica when he was done; ᴇ was his reason for living. He wanted to take care of her and fulfill every one of her desires, and it could not be challenged that he would wait for as long as it took, for her to allow him to be her official boyfriend.

Monica knew that Nico loved her, and it was quite evident that he was very good to her. She considered him to be handsome, she appreciated that he was very kind to her, and she even felt that she could trust him. And in some quiet tender moments, like when they were holding hands while watching a movie, she thought about opening up her heart to him.

Nico was patient, even though at times, the progress seemed to be very long and drawn out. He never gave up hope, because he knew that Monica's love was worth anything he had to go through. "One day I will become a more permanent fixture", he chanted daily. "One day she will love me with all her heart."

It was just before 8am on Saturday morning, and Monica was quietly sipping on a hot cup of decaf coffee. The TV was off, but she was being entertained; her mind was playing images of her last evening with Nico. She lowered her eyes as her lips instantly sprang into a smile, after recalling the many points where they had laughed, and ended up talking until well past midnight. They had a connection that was intimate, with sex always lingering in the background. They could banter like teenagers, but it was all in fun.

If she had to be truthful, Monica would say that she felt more than a friendship towards Nico, but she was scared of losing him to another woman, or worse. Because of Cayson, Monica guarded her heart as if it would break. At times she was so forceful about it, that she thought she could feel Nico pulling away.

A cold chill suddenly rushed up Monica's spine, at the very thought of him not being in her life. She closed her eyes in appreciation, of how attentive and loving Nico had been to her this past year. Just the thought of him leaving made her tremble, for Nico was now her whole world.

Monica opened her eyes and peered into her coffee cup, as if she was deep in thought. She recognized that sometime in the near future, there would come a day where she would either have to give Nico up, or become his girlfriend. She really hoped that when that day came, she was prepared to make the right choice.

## 'R-i-i-i-ng!'

With the shock of the loud noise startling her very existence, Monica's moment of tranquility had been broken. She ran the 5-feet across the room to answer her phone, knowing full-well who was on the other end. "Hello, Nico", she giggled like a silly teenager.

Nico's face immediately broke out into a wide smile. "Hello, my darling", he began. "How is your day going?"

Nico then listened as Monica entertained him with her cleaning plans for the morning, and her shopping plans for the afternoon. When she was done, Nico chuckled. "Sounds like you will be busy, but happy."

"I will be, but I'm looking forward to seeing you later", she gushed. She could feel herself blushing and hoped that she didn't sound like a love-sick school girl.

"I can't wait!" Nico declared. He had suddenly developed such a strong desire to hold her in his arms, that it was becoming evident to everyone around him. He was standing in a phone booth, and was now trying to hide what was happening in his pants. With his manhood growing harder as the seconds ticked away, and knowing that he would not get any relief from Monica, Nico wondered what Sasha was doing for the next hour.

"See you at 8!" Monica called into the phone. Her eyes were sparkling with anticipation of what the evening held in store.

"At 8, my love!" Nico hung up the simple black receiver, and then dialed Sasha's number.

Monica found herself smiling with enthusiasm over Nico's imminent arrival. If she was pressed to say it out loud, she would have to admit that she had fallen for him.

As she moved herself around the house, cleaning and straightening things up, she understood that she couldn't live in the past forever, but she was nervous about moving forward with their relationship. Again, she knew that at some point she would have to, or she could lose him.

Nico thanked Sasha for an amazing 65 minutes of mind-blowing pleasure, and then he made his way to Monica's apartment building.

Nico adored spending time with Monica, and lately he had noticed a huge change in her appearance and attitude. He could see that she had been smiling more, that her sad moments were becoming less and less, and he hoped that she might even be opening up to the idea of them becoming an official couple. With this in mind, he decided that the time might have arrived, when he could ask her out on a real date.

Their evening went as planned – the meal, the movie, and the company was excellent, as usual. At 11:30, they both walked to her front door. They embraced, but it felt different. Tonight he held her closer than he ever had before, so that the front of her body firmly touched the entire front of his. He then knotted his fingers together behind her back, and gazed lovingly into her flawless face.

No words passed between them, as they admired all that was offered only a few inches away. Their breathing was now changing, their pupils were dilating, and neither wanted to be the first person to speak or break the spell between them.

Monica studied the color and shape of his eyes and the fullness of his cheeks, as if she was seeing him for the very first time. As she noticed the perfect symmetry of his nose and mouth, she smiled, for she could feel herself growing warm from the very intimate moment. As she studied the perfect line of his eyebrows, she wondered why he was wearing a puzzled expression.

Nico had no idea why he felt so nervous, because he had been intimate with many women in his lifetime. But as he observed the soft expression that danced across her face, he understood that this woman was different — she was what he needed to make his life have meaning. As she pressed her body a little closer to his, Nico felt that this was the moment which he had been waiting for.

Because he had been so nervous, the contents in his stomach had rolled over a thousand times during their evening together. Nico didn't want this moment to pass by without at least trying, so he took a deep breath, bunched up his courage, and he began to speak.

"Monica?" he asked, in a voice that was cracking and a little on the quiet side. "I know that you don't want us to get serious, but I wonder if enough time has passed that I could ask you out on a real date." He had lowered his eyes during his little speech, but now his lashes were up high and his vision was dead-set on reading her thoughts. "We could take it slow, if that would help?" He hoped that it didn't sound like he was begging for anything other than a date.

Of course, she was a tiny bit surprised; the moment which she had dreaded had finally arrived. But because she felt that it was time, she happily accepted. "But only if I could pay for my own share of whatever we do!" she demanded. It was a firm statement, rather than a light request.

He grabbed her tighter because he was more than grateful, and then all of the muscles in his body instantly relaxed. "Of course!" he blurted out. He couldn't remember the last time when he had felt so fortunate.

"Okay, then." Monica also felt her body relax, for she suddenly felt happier than she had in a very long time. The deal was now done. The moment she had worried about, had now passed. She wrapped her arms around his neck, and then she placed a strong kiss in the middle of his left cheek.

Nico placed his mixed-emotioned expression into the sweet spot between her left shoulder and neck, and he hugged her even tighter. "Thank you", he cried. He was secretly praising how well their evening had ended. All that time and hard work had paid off, and he was very proud of himself for what he had accomplished.

It took a few minutes before they slowly released their embrace, and then both of them helped to shut the door, which formally ended their impressive evening together.

Monica went to bed that night, proud of how she had handled that question. "It's time, and he's a nice guy", she said, trying to convince herself. "But if us dating doesn't work out, I hope that we can still remain friends."

Nico went to bed that night with confidence in his heart. For now that she had said yes to them going out on a real date, it was unmistakable that Nico would try to kiss her full on the mouth. And once that awkward but fundamental moment was out of the way, he trusted that Monica would become more relaxed, and then the next step of their relationship could finally happen.

Monica closed her eyes, and shifted her body until she was totally covered by the two warm blankets that lay on top of her. She then drifted off to her first solid night's sleep in over a year.

Nico had tried to watch a little TV, but because his mind was entertaining some sensual thoughts about Monica, he was too distracted to really understand what was going on in the show. Just thinking about being naked with Monica in the same bed, made Nico so terribly excited, that he needed to relieve himself at two different times during the night. He woke up the next morning feeling more refreshed than he had in months. And as he moved around to begin his day, he felt elated; Nico was now looking forward to seeing how their relationship would unfold.

As the days went by, and their first official date was just around the corner, Monica decided to take extreme care to look her best. She bought some brand new make-up, had her hair cut and styled, and she applied a new coat of nail polish to her already well-groomed nails. She lifted her chin to apply a delicate spray of 'Obsession' to the front of her neck, and then moved her hand to add a little sprinkle to the nape under her hair. She then sprayed a delicate mist on her tummy and the small of her back. "Mmmm…", she sighed, as she breathed in the heavenly scent.

Monica felt mentally and physically better than she had in a very long time, and she was anxious to see what the night had in store for her. Would Nico try to give her a passionate good-night kiss? She made a bet with herself that he probably would. She tilted her head to the side as she wondered if she would let him kiss her. She wasn't sure yet - it would depend on how the evening went.

Monica leaned her body closer to the mirror, in order to inspect the coverage of the frosty-pink lipstick. She was still trying to decide if she wanted to appear alluring or playful, but she would figure that out when Nico arrived. With the baby finger on her right hand, she scooped out any access lipstick from the corners of her mouth.

Nico had also taken extra care in how he looked for their date. He bought a new suit the day before, had a facial done, and got his hair cut that very morning. He was currently standing in his bathroom, spraying his upper body with Hai Karate cologne. Nico couldn't help but admire how chiseled his muscles looked, and he hoped that Monica would get to touch them very soon. As he buttoned his wrinkle-free shirt, he realized how much he wanted everything to go perfectly; these next few hours could make or break the future status of their relationship.

Monica took a giant step backwards, in order to get a real good look at herself in the mirror over her dresser.

"Not bad", she stated with complete honesty. Monica was very pleased with how she looked, and she was surprised by how many butterflies were fluttering around in her tummy. "Why am I so nervous?" she asked to the air in the room. She shook her hands up and down by the wrists as she went from the bedroom to the living room, hoping that that would calm her nerves.

Nico arrived at the stroke of 7pm, and knocked on her door. The moment he saw her, his expression suddenly changed from nervous to sheer delight. He couldn't help but gawk, for she was the exact imagine of the perfect woman, that every man had ever dreamed of.

Monica was awestruck when she saw her date, for standing in her doorway was a well-groomed man in an expensive suit, looking every bit like he'd just walked out of a fancy magazine. And he was looking at her as if she was the most breathtaking woman in the world.

Monica felt her body go weak, and her knees gave out as she stared at him. She could swear that she had even swooned under her breath, but she didn't want him to know that. She quickly gathered her courage and pulled herself together.

"Won't you come in", she suggested. She was trying to convince him, if not herself, that her heart was not pounding, that she was not beginning to sweat, and that her face was not blushing because of the attraction she felt towards him in that moment. For how he looked, would have no bearing in how the evening would end.

Monica stepped aside and made a sweeping motion with her right hand, as if to formally entice him inside of her home.

"Thank you", he said softly, as he radiated his charm towards her. Nico locked his eyes to hers, as he extended his arm to offer her a small bouquet of flowers. When their fingers touched, he could feel the features on his face change into an even bigger smile.

"My goodness", she stated in a hush tone. Monica was blushing as she brought the colorful bouquet towards her face. She inhaled the very fragrant aroma, and the scent brought an instant smile to her frosted lips. She raised her eyes to meet his as she spoke. "Thank you. These are really beautiful."

"As are you", he countered. Now it was Nico who was blushing, for he had never been so giddy about a woman before. While this was new to him, he had to admit that he liked how it felt.

"I'll just put these in water and then we can go." Monica scurried off to the kitchen for what seemed like an eternity, but it was only for a mere 2 minutes. After putting the flowers in a clear glass vase, she took a second to catch her breath and maintain her composure. "Shall we go?" she called, as she joined her suitor at the front door.

The couple went for dinner and had a very lovely time. They felt closer than they had in all the months that they'd been together, and it truly felt like a first date. When the meal was done, they held hands as they walked 8 blocks west, and laughed and talked as usual. At the theatre, one bought the movie tickets while the other paid for the treats. Two hours later, they were standing at her front door, both anticipating the rather awkward moment of what will happen next.

Nico and Monica stood facing each other like two nervous teenagers. They both knew what was supposed to happen, so why were they so jittery? There was no talking between them, only a lot of smiling, blushing, and shuffling of feet.

"Okay, good night", Monica announced, when it didn't look like anything more was going to happen.

"Good night", Nico replied quickly. His stomach was in knots and he had trouble catching his breath, for this was the moment that he had been waiting for. But what if she didn't like the way he kissed her? This kiss was going to make or break what he had been working so hard for. If there were no sparks, if the kiss was too dry or too wet, or if there was no chemistry between them, then all of the work over the last few months would have been in vain.

As Nico looked deeply into her eyes, he knew that this needed to be done, so he decided to go for it. He stepped forward, grabbed her firmly on both shoulders, and brought his lips towards her with more passion in his soul than he thought he had.

# * SMOOCH *

Once Nico's mouth touched Monica's, there was no letting go. Their lips were pressing together and Nico's body was exploding with sheer joy. He moaned as he added a little more force to their kiss, and moved his head this way and that. When she took a step closer to his body and he felt her hands grip his back a little tighter, he could feel himself starting to get aroused. He was over the moon with happiness, as he began to believe that there was a great deal of chemistry going on between them - at least on his side there was. He now hoped that she also felt it.

Monica was actually swooning from the passion which she felt in the kiss, and she could feel herself getting carried away by her own response. His lips were soft, well-rounded, and he moved them with experience. She could hear him moan quietly while they were kissing, and it made her knees go weak. His kiss was far different from any she'd had in her lifetime before, and she felt as if she could have stayed in that position for the rest of her life.

But just as quickly as it had begun, the kiss had ended. The two bodies were slowly separating, while two sets of eyes were staring back at each other with desire for more. Fireworks were going off in their heads from the sensations of that 40-second kiss, and their hearts were speculating what would happen next.

"Wow", Nico chimed, as if that was his first kiss ever. He wanted to be proud and take all the credit for what had just happened, but the reality was that he didn't do it all by himself. "M-monica", he stammered. He didn't want to take his eyes off of her beautiful face, but slowly and very seductively, his gaze slid downward. "That was even better than I thought it would be."

The size of Monica's smile grew bigger, and her gorgeous brown eyes, which were firmly locked with Nico's, were sparkling. The skin on her face was radiant as she replied, "I agree." She hadn't been kissed in more than a year, and it felt better than she had remembered.

There was a great deal of awkward silence in the small space which they were sharing, and then they fumbled through a few verbal good-nights, which brought life back into their quiet surroundings.

"I'll call you tomorrow, okay?" Nico said, as he began to walk away. He was no longer blind to her attraction for him, and he walked away as if he had just saved the world from total destruction.

"I'll answer!" she joked, as she waved good bye to him. She felt like a breathless girl of seventeen, who had just met her movie idol.

Nico and Monica both had a hard time falling asleep that night; each wondered if this was the beginning of something special.

For Nico, he truly hoped so; he had always had a feeling that they would be dynamite together, and after that kiss, he believed that he was right.

For Monica, she was still deciding how much she wanted their relationship to change. She liked what they had and wanted to continue having him close, but she felt that she needed to make it clear to her friend that they would have to take things slow.

*Saying and doing are two different things, as we all know. While Monica spoke the words out loud, she believed them. But each time she saw his lips or she touched her own, she was reminded of the glorious kiss that they had shared.*

The next time they saw each other, Nico listened as Monica expressed in great detail, how she wanted their relationship to grow. Nico was trying to be attentive to her words and her thoughts, but he felt his gaze drop from her eyes to her shoulders, and then to her breasts. He had to admit that she was breathtaking, and worth any rules that she wanted him to abide by.

Monica couldn't help but notice his obvious examination and approval. It felt a little naughty, and it was thrilling.

"Yes!" he concurred loudly. She had finished her little speech, and Nico gladly agreed to her all of her terms.

"Thank you", she said sincerely. She was very relieved, and couldn't help but lean towards him. She then applied a lingering kiss to his perfectly shaped mouth. A second later, she was fighting an overwhelming need to be even closer to his body. She quickly ended their kiss, and then felt herself taking turns to suck her top lip into her mouth, and then the bottom. He tasted of peppermint gum and garlic sausage, and she loved it. And when she saw him staring, she tilted her head down in embarrassment.

Nico became totally entranced while he watched her lips disappear and reappear from the warm and wet opening. He could feel his excitement growing and it was almost too much for him to bear. Parts of his body were beginning to sweat, and he hoped that she wouldn't notice. His pulse was pounding at the base of his throat, as though his heart had risen from its usual place. His nostrils were flaring as his breathing was changing, and the instant she lifted her innocent eyes to meet his, he knew it was time to leave.

Nico was no fool; there was a lot riding on them being in a committed relationship. He was determined not to cross over any lines, and to do exactly as she requested. In essence, he would continue to undertake whatever it took to keep her happy and in his life.

In the meantime, Nico needed to find relief and he knew that Sherry was waiting for him to arrive. He had already advised her to be ready, and he warned her that he was ravenous.

Tonight it was Monica who took a cold shower, because it was exactly what she needed to quench her thirst.

# Chapter 7

It was April of 1968, a full year after they had had their first official date, and they were both enjoying the freedom of saying hello and good-bye with a several minute, everything touching, hands roaming, full body hug. Most nights, the embrace lasted for a good two or three minutes. They then said good-night, and Monica and Nico each went their own ways. But once a week or more, when things felt a little different, the hug became longer and way more intense. Breathing became labored, grunts and groans could be heard, bodies pushed closer together, hands roamed everywhere, and fantasies of something more rushed into their heads.

Monica was usually the one who pulled her body away from his, and yelled for him to stop. She placed a strong hand against his sculpted chest and hoped that he would comply. "Good night, Nico", she stated firmly. Her heart was usually pounding, her palms were sweating, and her insides were almost always burning with hunger for what he might have to offer. Monica wasn't innocent, and she could envision Nico's naked body joining with hers, but she couldn't risk getting hurt again.

On those nights, when he thought things might progress past a lingering kiss, Nico would try pleading. Even though he knew that kissing and hugging were the only things that Monica was willing to give up, it was in his nature to keep trying. "Please, baby", he purred softly in her ear. "Just ten minutes."

"I can't", she argued, as she struggled to get out of his arms. It was difficult for her too, but she felt she had to be strong. "Sex led to babies, which leads to marriage, and I'm not ready to go thru that kind of hurt again", she said, more than a few times in the past year.

Nico kind of understood, but this was becoming emotionally draining for him, because he ached for Monica on every level imaginable. "Okay", he whined reluctantly. He then kissed her forehead, and walked away with a forced half-smile on his lips. This was for her benefit, to imply that he was okay with her decision.

*Unbeknownst to his girlfriend, at least three times a week, Nico would seek out the naked female companionship that he was missing, and then he went home. He was usually so high after the sexual experience, that he was floating a few inches off the ground, and feeling like he was drunk with happiness.*

"Thank you!" she called, as Nico walked away from her apartment. Monica leaned against the closed door once she was alone, and tried to convince herself that she had made the right decision.

Nico wanted to have a life with Monica. But on those nights when she begged him to slow his urges down, he often wondered if they would ever be more than just two people kissing passionately, with nothing further on the horizon. And as the months dragged on, despair pulled him down, and he sometimes thought about surrendering his chase of ever having a future with her. For what has now become a full-time activity, was at times, not all that much fun anymore.

On more than one occasion he had pondered the idea that he could go back to just being her friend. But then, if he ever saw her with another man, and he was receiving the gifts that Nico had been working so hard to get, it would drive him crazy. With a heavy heart, Nico crumbled inside, as he resolved to give it 'another' few more months.

"Someday", she would add confidently, when it looked like he might be giving up on her. Whenever Nico heard that dreaded word, he lowered his head and descended into depression. He would then walk away from her apartment, trusting that 'someday' would come sooner rather than later.

On the last Wednesday in August, Monica spent a good portion of the afternoon making a lovely dinner for Nico. They said HI like normal, but it was quite obvious that he was already in a mood before he had arrived at her home. "Are you ok, honey?" she asked, almost whispering. She watched him nod and make a face, as if to question why she would ask. And then her eyes followed him as he made himself at home on her couch.

Nico's attempt to prove to her that everything was ok, was hardly enthusiastic, but his mind was totally not into their visit. He loved how everything looked and how the meal had tasted, but he ended up complaining about the recall of Ford's Torino and Mercury's Montego automobiles more than anything else. He talked so harshly on the subject, and without any breaks, that Monica couldn't get a word in edgewise.

During desert, Monica realized that Nico had only made eye contact with her three times since they said hello. It was now clear to her that something was very wrong, and because she didn't want to spend another few hours with him in this mood, she bid him an early good-night. "Call me tomorrow and we'll talk", she uttered gently, as she walked him towards the door.

Behind the scenes, a fact that Monica was not aware of, Nico had just broken up with a sweet girl named Brooke. He had been seeing her regularly for the past two years. They had been in each other's company about twice a week, and spoke on the phone almost daily.

*In the last month or so, Brooke had been hinting that she wanted to spend more time with him – go on a holiday or away for a week-end somewhere. "You must get holidays!" she demanded.*

*Nico had told her on their first date that he was a cop working 12-hour shifts, and that sometimes he had to work undercover for weeks at a time. This bought him all the time that he needed, to be with Monica, and to date other girls.*

*But lately, Brooke wanted more of his time. "Not right now", he'd replied, whenever they had this talk.*

*Brooke was a gorgeous, 22-year old redhead, and she thought they were building a relationship together. Once she recognized that Nico wasn't pushing for anything more than them just hooking up, she decided to confront him. "Will you give me a few minutes of your time to talk to me?" She watched him turn around and face her, and then she saw that his expression was empty.*

*Nico knew what was coming, as he'd been in this situation many times before. Brooke was a great girl, but she was not what he wanted for anything more than a 'quick fix'. Because he knew the drill quite well, he listened to all that she had to say.*

*Brooke was young and had a killer body. She could have any man out there, but she wanted a commitment of some sort from Nico. Despite the chance that she might lose him, she decided to give him an ultimatum. With her heart beating wildly in her chest, she tried to get her sentence out of her mouth without fainting. She took a deep breath and gathered all of her courage, and then she demanded, "Either we live together and get engaged sometime in the future, or I walk away right now."*

*Nico could see that Brooke was fighting back a bucket of tears, but he didn't love her. And because he didn't want her to walk out of his life, he cleared his throat, took a step towards her, and told her that he needed some time to think it over.*

*"At least that's something", she announced. She lowered her eyes and began to kick at an invisible stone on the carpet. She was relieved that he had heard her voice, and then decided that she would not panic until he came back with his answer. Her entire face had anxiety written all over it, and her heart was trying to stay in beat. She was breathless as she looked up at him, and she wondered if there was anything she could do or say to get him to stay in her life.*

*His gorgeous dark eyes were locked with her cat-like eyes, and Nico knew he would miss her. He couldn't let her know that, though. He was grateful that Brooke had agreed to give him some time to think, but he already knew what the outcome would be. Nico hated how scared she looked, so he took her in his arms and kissed her. When the kiss ended, he walked away.*

*"Don't take too long, honey!" she called, as he moved his body down the long sidewalk. Brooke was pretending to sound strong, but emotionally, she was as fragile as a porcelain doll. As she closed her door, the naïve girl brought her hand up to her bruised lips, as if she was trying to preserve the memory of that heated moment.*

*When their bodies had pressed together, even for that brief amount of time, Nico could feel himself lusting for her body. It was now increasing with each step that he took, and becoming harder for him to walk. His desire for her was powerful, and it tried to overrule everything that he had accomplished so far.*

"No!" he shouted into the air. He was angry with himself for wanting to give in to his urges, and scolded himself for not being stronger. He tried to push the powerful craving down, so that it didn't interfere with his decision.

Nico returned to Brooke's apartment three days later, and even though her expression looked hopeful, he made the announcement that he was officially ending their relationship.

Brooke's eyes shot wide open in total surprise. "Really?" She hoped that it was a bad joke.

Nico held her hands and he could feel her tremble. "I'm sorry, but I'm in love with someone else."

Brooke melted into an emotional mess in a matter of seconds, and began to scream and cry in a high pitched manner. "No!" she argued loudly. "You're in love with me — you said so a million times!" Nothing about this moment felt real. This was totally not how she had expected this meeting to go. Brooke suddenly felt as if she had had way too much caffeine, and that her body couldn't handle the rush.

"Let me explain....."

The young woman didn't want to hear why Nico didn't want to be with her. Instead, she continued to fight with all she had, to try to get him to change his mind. "Please!" she begged. She got down on her knees, tons of tears were now streaming down her cheeks, and her hands were placed in front of her nose in a praying position. "Please don't *leave me! Please!" Her voice was weak and shaking, but her request was forceful.*

*"Brooke, I ....."*

*"No!" With every fiber in her body, Brooke wanted him to stay in her life, and she would fight as hard as she had to, in order to make that happen.*

*It killed Nico to see her like that, but he believed that he had no choice. "I can't!" he kept chanting over and over again. He wanted to be down on the floor with her, to hold her, and to tell her that they could go on seeing each other, but he couldn't. And even though the wretched words kept pouring out of his mouth with solid conviction, he couldn't command his body to actually leave her apartment.*

*After almost an hour of insisting that he change his mind, Brooke had had enough; once she realized that it was of no use, she knew she had to let him go.*

*She was young, but she wasn't stupid. Brooke didn't want to be with a man who didn't really want to be with her.*

*She covered her face with her hands for courage, and dropped her chin to her chest. "Fine", she uttered softly. "You can go." It wasn't an order, but more of an option — one that he took.*

*Brooke moved her hands down and let them dangle at her sides. She stood tall and brave as she watched Nico leave her apartment, and then she crumbled to the ground and cried for hours.*

*Nico loved being in Brooke's company - she had a minimum paying job, she was thrifty because she could barely make ends meet, she was an okay cook, but she was amazing in bed. As he tried to put it all into prospective, he could say that Brooke was actually more than adequate in every way possible. But in truth, she was a convenience – a distraction for the times when he left Monica's apartment with something hard and irresponsible in his pants, and he didn't want to pay for it.*

*Nico focused on the sidewalk below him as he took the 25 steps to get to his car, and wondered if there was any other way that he could have done this. Breaking up with Brooke didn't make him happy, but he knew it had to be done. Suddenly, the wind picked up and a light rain began to leave tiny drops of water on his clothing and exposed skin. He shook off the wet before he got into his car, and drove away.*

*Since that day, Nico had been on the lookout to find another free-spirited girl, so that he would have someone to share his lonely moments with.*

A week after he had been asked to go home early, Nico was having dinner at Monica's home, and once again he spoke about the stupidity of the Ford Motor Company. This time, he reported that they had ordered a second recall of their vehicles, for further repairs.

Monica's head spun around with great speed, and then she glared at him in total disbelief. She had gone to a lot of trouble buying and preparing the lovely dinner before them, and she was quite confused by her boyfriend's behavior.

*As much as Nico didn't want to admit it, he was still hurting from his break-up with Brooke and he was just letting off a little steam. Deep down he was sorry because he knew he was being an ass, but he didn't know how to get past it.*

Because Monica had been rather quiet, Nico lifted his head to see what she was doing.

Nico found that he was now the victim of Monica's fierce glare. She examined the odd expression on his square face, and she could see that he seemed angry about the senselessness of the Ford situation. 'But why was he this upset about something as trivial as a recall?' she wondered.

Nico lifted his plate for a few more potatoes, and as if on auto pilot, she dished it out.

There was an odd silence in the room, and Nico felt that he needed to break it. He tried to continue with his rant, but Monica couldn't take it anymore.

With no regard for his feelings, she interrupted him with an odd piece of news.

"Guess who's dating that short guy in the mail room?" she sputtered with haste. She then stared at him to see what his reaction would be.

Nico was about to put another forkful of food into his mouth, when the uninteresting issue was shot across the table. He could not have been more shocked or embarrassed by the rude interruption, and he now felt somehow disoriented in a room that he knew quite well.

Monica could see that the question had totally shocked her dinner guest, but it turned out to be a perfect distraction.

Nico looked directly into Monica's brown eyes, and then he gently rested his hand on top of hers, in an apologetic, loving gesture. And when their skin touched, Nico realized that seeing the lovely person in front of him, was exactly who and what he needed. Undeniably, he had lost sight of her goodness and what they could have in the future; she truly was the one and only woman he wanted to have in his bed and in his home – if only she would give him the chance to prove it.

Once Monica saw the positive change come over him, she breathed a sigh of relief, and then she began to talk about other things. At one point, she even had him laughing, which made them both feel better.

Nico suddenly grasped that he had been emotionally absent – he had jumped out of her life for a while, but he was now back, and with both feet planted firmly in the ground.

"Oh, and I forgot to tell you ….."

As she spoke, Nico watched her with great interest. Monica was glowing, and she looked really happy. It made him feel genuinely sorry for how he had treated her, and he vowed that he would never take her for granted again.

But sadly, he did, and quite often. Nico continued to push up against her body, and whisper his pleas into her ear. It was always done with hope of getting what she wasn't willing to let him have. She'd laugh it off and protest, and then he'd leave her home to spend time with someone who would give him anything that he wanted.

Nico hated being pushed away from her, as it bruised his ego, but he felt that he was now getting good at hiding his dejected moments. He never gave up hope, though. He continued to give her what she wanted, when she wanted, and he listened when she spoke. He sought out female companionship whenever he felt he needed it, and he believed that Monica never suspected that he had ever cheated on her.

As much as he wanted to at times, Nico couldn't walk away from her. He wasn't sure why his soul was so powerfully drawn to her, but he chalked it up to him wanting her body and possessions more than anything else. Women were women, and he'd had a hundred of them in his life, but he'd never had anyone like Monica before.

Monica enjoyed his constant badgering and manipulative endeavors to get her into bed, but she just wasn't ready yet. There were times when she could feel herself weakening and she desperately wanted to give in to her desires, but she didn't think she could endure another round of what she had already gone through. Instead, she tried to stay strong, and refuted his advances for as long as she could.

# Chapter 8

Monica and Nico continued to date for the next four years, and for that same time period, he had been trying to get her into bed and she was still pretending to rebuff his advances.

As far as Nico was concerned, it was all about going through the motions now. Too much time had passed, and he didn't actually care if he got into her panties or not, anymore. It also no longer bruised his ego when she said no to his advances. Nico had a harem of women at his beck and call, for whenever and whatever he needed – day or night. As much as Monica wanted to think otherwise, Nico was okay to wait for when she would finally give him permission to enter the 'forbidden garden'.

There were days when this game of cat and mouse had exhausted him to the point of no return, and when he reflected on it, Nico wasn't sure why he hadn't given up by now. He suspected that it was because Monica was a habit that he just couldn't break; she fought back, she was sweet, she was strong, she needed comforting, she was disciplined, and she was an emotional wreck. He felt drawn to her for many reasons, but because she had pushed him away more times than he could remember, his affection towards her had turned into something more of a loving, protective role. The intense love that he once had for her was gone, but because of what he could gain by them becoming a couple, he swore to continue his pursuit of her.

Monica had a sense of home whenever Nico was in her company. They were as close to being a family as she had had lately, and she didn't want to give it up. She knew that Nico loved her and she wanted to give that love back, but Monica's emotional side was unwilling to give the 'forever love' another chance.

When Nico reached out for her, Monica could hear her voice telling him no, but there were plenty of evenings when she wanted to scream, "Yes!" In those moments when her lower extremities had become warm and wet, her face was flushed, her skin was glistening, and she had developed a twinkle in her eye. A shy smile would spread across her full lips, and all because her mind flirted with the possibility that she just might actually give in to his advances.

However, each time that she was within an inch of giving in to her carnal desires, panic set in, reminding her of the pain that she had gone thru, not so long ago. This kept her strong, but she wasn't sure how much longer she could hold out; she wanted his body as much as he wanted hers.

# R-i-i-i-ing!!

Nico had been out of town for the last three weeks, and he made sure to call Monica every chance that he could get. "I'll be home at 8pm, Gate A10, on Wednesday", he told her two days ago. There was a warning in his voice for her not to be late.

"I know", she answered softly, and with total confidence. She walked towards the fridge to find the note, and then continued speaking. "I wrote it down so I wouldn't forget."

"Good." He was pleased with her answer and couldn't wait to see her. "Bye for now, my love." After the receiver had been placed in the cradle of the phone, Nico turned and watched the shapely blonde with the gigantic boobs, bump and grind her way back to the bed. She then parted her shiny red lips just a little, as she slithered up the sheets towards him.

His mind was whirling by all that they had done so far, and now 'little Nico' was beginning to come to life again. The closer she moved to his body, the harder he grew; she was magnificent in every way possible. And even though they had been together for two days straight, he had trouble meeting her eyes without blushing. "You are worth every penny!" he gushed enthusiastically.

As promised, Monica picked him up from the airport on Wednesday night. "It's wonderful to see you, Nico!" she oozed with utter joy, a second after they had shared a kiss. Her eyes were twinkling as she noticed how well rested he looked. "I've missed you terribly", she cooed. She could feel her cheeks blushing.

Nico's mouth curved into a smile, for it seemed that she was excited to see him. "Thank you. I've missed you, too." He placed her left hand into the crook of his elbow, and as they walked, he hoped that she had had a change of heart. Perhaps she was now willing to move their relationship to the next level. Time will tell.

As she drove, Monica couldn't help but steal a few glances at her passenger, to watch his facial expressions as he spoke about his latest trip, and to ensure that he really was home again. "Did you get to do any sight-seeing?" she asked.

"I did." Nico described the Grand Canyon as best he could, but because he had never been there in person, he told her what he had remembered from a movie he had once seen.

"Sounds lovely", she remarked. Monica had only half-listened to his long story, but she hoped that he didn't notice. She then began to nibble on her bottom lip, as she wondered how she could tell him the thoughts that were playing in her head. She didn't want to jump into bed with him, but she did want to go beyond kissing.

Monica parked her car directly in front of his home, and they both got out. They were embracing and saying good-night on his doorstep, and tonight it was her who was leaning into his body. "Good night, my love", she sighed. The tone of her voice was Marilyn Monroe sexy, and as the four simple words lingered in the air between them, she waited for him to notice her mood.

Nico's jaw had dropped ever-so-slightly, once he realized that Monica seemed to be giving him the green light. At any other time he would have rejoiced and ripped her clothes off, but he had just spent a couple of energetic days with a boisterous, uninhibited, 19-year old prostitute, who showed him no mercy at all.

Nico desperately wanted to be naked with Monica, but he had no strength left. He realized that he shouldn't say no to her, so he decided to use every ounce of seductive charm that he had, in order to keep her in a happy mood.

As if it was being done in slow motion, Nico tilted his head to the right and brought his right hand up to her face. He then removed the wisp of hair that had somehow landed against her cheek. He leaned forward and kissed her lips so tenderly, that she almost fainted. When he pulled away, and his mouth was only an inch away from hers, he tried to negotiate. "I'm delighted that you're happy to see me, but can we meet tomorrow night to see how this ends up? I'm so tired and just want to sleep." He kissed her mouth two more times, long and hard, before she was able to breathe and respond.

"S-sure." She had been so surprised by his answer, that the sound of the word got stuck in her throat. And because that moment had become so magical, she had completely forgotten how to spell her own name. "Tomorrow night is fine." She spoke in a mono-toned voice, as if she was in a hypnotic state. As she walked away, her mind was trying to process the fact that Nico had turned her down – she was a little crushed, and now she knew how it felt.

They said good-night again, and she drove home with her eyes fixed solely on the road ahead of her. The time alone in the car seemed to clear up her head, and then she wondered what would have happened, had she gone inside of Nico's home.

In an attempt to figure it all out, her delicate state of mind suddenly broke into two parts. On one side, the couple would have moved their relationship to more than just kissing. But what if she were to become pregnant again? Would he leave her once they had had sex? The thought of it made her want to cry.

Monica tried to calm herself down, but she couldn't shake the unnerving state of fear which was crawling onto her lap. "I need to calm down", she ordered. Through her mouth, she breathed in to a count of five, and then sighed loudly as the air oozed out. *It was exactly the same sound that any teenaged girl makes, whenever you try to talk to them.*

A few minutes later, it was like she had been drunk and had now sobered up. Monica's eyes were wide open – physically and metaphorically. Her mind was sharp, she was a little angry, and she was now pleased that they had not gone any further.

Before too long, Monica had arrived at her home. She parked her car and she walked into her building. Her happy mood from an hour ago had all but disappeared, as she climbed the steps to get to her floor. Once she had gotten inside of her apartment, she turned on her TV, checked her mail, and then she began to prepare herself a little snack.

Monica was making a sandwich, when she heard the announcement that said the lottery numbers were going to be read after the next commercial. She dropped what she had in her hands, and she raced to find her tickets. She knew like everyone else, that winning was a long-shot, but she sat herself down on the edge of the couch and waited for it all to begin. When yet a fourth commercial came on, she suddenly felt very nervous - like a little child who was waiting for her turn to sit on Santa's lap.

*Because of the excitement in that moment, Monica had completely forgotten about Nico and their conversation. Her only concern in the whole world, rested with what was about to happen.*

After she heard the first two numbers being called, her heart began to thump in her chest and her eyes were as big as saucers. She was in a state of shock and had a hard time believing, that all the numbers which the host was reciting, were matching what was written on the small paper in her hand. Once she had checked the ticket a total of 5 times, she let out a scream that could wake the dead. "Oh...my...gosh!" she shouted in total disbelief. Her mind was racing with a million thoughts, and nothing was making sense. "I won!" she screamed. Monica's body jumped into the air as she continued to cheer. "Ye-e-a-ah!"

It took a few minutes, but once she had calmed down a bit, she wondered if this had really happened. She rushed to the phone with lightning speed, and ended up speaking with three different people at the lottery office. The extent of the call was 20 minutes long, and concluded with her in happy tears.

"Thank you", she said. Her voice was filled with total appreciation and a ton of excitement. After Monica's suspicions had been verified, she leaned her body backwards on the couch, and thought about how much her life was about to change. As if on cue, Nico's face sprang before her eyes, which only enhanced her giddy mood. Without hesitating, she leaned forward and picked up the receiver again, knowing full-well who she wanted to share this news with.

## R-i-i-i-ing!!

"Hello?" came the familiar male voice on the other end of the receiver.

Monica focused and tried to pull all of her drifting thoughts into check. "You will never guess what just happened to me!" she uttered. She was trying so hard to keep a strong hold on her emotions, but the excitement was a little too much for her.

Nico had just begun the process of emptying out his suitcase, and had no interest in being part of a long and drawn out conversation. But he was intrigued, and he could not imagine what she could be so excited about. "Tell me, my love." He was calm as he continued to fold and sort his things, and he was only half-listening to her news.

"I just won the lottery!" she shouted as loudly as she could. She then squeezed her eyes shut and let out a rather loud wail of delight.

All the movements from Nico's body stopped, as if he had suddenly become a cement statue. "You what?" he asked. Both of his eyebrows climbed as close to his hairline as they could possibly get, while his eyes almost popped out from their sockets.

"Well, not all of it", she added, with a little more calmness in her voice. "I just heard that a few other people have the same numbers as I do, but I won three years' worth of my own wages. Isn't that fabulous?" She was gushing and didn't know how to contain her joy.

Monica's words and excitement filled him with an unmeasurable amount of curiosity. Nico was on the other end of the line, in total shock, and he was now regretting that he had not invited her to come inside of his home. "I can't believe it", he muttered, but it was incoherent, even to himself. He was now sweating and his knees had become weak. As he stared straight ahead at nothing in particular, he tried to make sense of what all of this meant.

Monica hated that Nico was so silent. "Did you hear what I said?"

Nico needed to blink a few times in order to get the dollar bills from flashing in front of his eyes, and then he spoke. "You won that much?"

Monica was relieved that she now had his full and undivided attention. "Yep!"

"Are you planning to go on a vacation? And if so, when?" he asked with complete interest. Nico suddenly saw big shopping sprees in his near future, and he hoped for some of the money to go into his own bank account.

*The cash which he had gotten from the death of his wife was all but gone now, so this was very interesting news.*

Nico purposely dropped whatever was in his hands, and he was now sitting on the edge of his queen-sized bed. His listening skills had greatly improved, and Monica had suddenly become a very important commodity.

"How about we talk about that at dinner tomorrow night?" she asked playfully. She spoke with confidence, for she had the impression that he would not say no to her advances a second time. "Shall we say 7:00?" It wasn't a question that she posed, but a passive order, and she didn't wait for his answer. She gave him the address of the restaurant where she wanted to go, and then she instructed him to dress fancy.

Nico was stunned, as he replaced the receiver back in its spot on the phone. He sat on the bed for almost an hour, and sorted through every word of their conversation, again and again. He eventually climbed under the covers, but he couldn't sleep. As he lay there, he scolded himself for not letting her to come inside of his home. "I should have given her what she was asking for – love and attention." He slapped the palm of his hand against his forehead as a form of punishment and said, "God, I'm so stupid."

As if that had jolted something, another thought quickly rushed into his head - if she was still in a great mood tomorrow, maybe she would let him propose. When they got married, the money would be half his. His mind was now spinning with the details of how he could pull this off.

Nico took his time to roll onto his right side. He moved the covers up to protect his shoulder from the cold air, and then he began to work out a plan. As he stared mindlessly across the dark room, his thoughts raced for places where he could purchase a moderately-priced, decent ring. Once he had that figured out, his eyes closed and his mind was able to rest.

By 6:01pm the next day, Nico had left his home, and was now rushing to get to the finest jeweler in town. A minute after he had walked through the fancy front doors, he met a very attractive clerk, and decided to take up as much of her time as he could.

"Hi, I'm Koreena. Welcome to Thomas Jewelers", she said politely.

Nico smiled in her direction, and then examined all that the expensive shop had to offer. Once he had made his decision, he pulled his wallet out and purchased a yellow gold band with a relatively large stone.

The young girl with the satin smooth skin, was quite impressed by his choice. "You do realize that this ring is more than I make in six months, right?" she asked. The color of her cheeks was suddenly changing from white to pink, with fear that she might have crossed over a line.

Nico threw a sexy, half-smile in her direction, for he knew exactly what he was doing. "Is it?" he questioned with an air of innocence. "Perhaps someone has been a very naughty girl and deserves this gift?" he joked playfully.

The 19-year old clerk's cheeks were now becoming a bright red. Koreena turned and quickly walked away from the counter, completely embarrassed by the whole situation. She then rang up the sale, shoved the ring into the velvet box, and placed it into a purple bag. She walked the bag to the customer, and while trying not to look or sound nervous, she uttered the standard speech quietly. "Thank you, and have a nice day." Koreena realized that her voice had squeaked, but she hoped that he hadn't noticed.

In a bizarre fashion, Nico purposely let her dainty hand dangle in the air in front of him, and for much longer than was necessary. He understood that she felt awkward and embarrassed, and he wondered if she would want to make it up to him.

The pretty clerk jiggled the bag, and hoped that he would take it from her.

Nico couldn't help but smirk as he analyzed the current situation. He then cocked his head to the side, as he examined every detail of her unexperienced mouth. He could tell that she was young, but was she willing to comply with whatever he asked her to do?

Nico had not seen anyone else in the small but elegant store up until that moment, so when he heard a booming question shoot across the room with a vast amount of negative energy, his whole world suddenly exploded.

"Is everything ok?" a matronly female demanded sternly. Her attitude was hostile and her voice was flat and angry.

"Uh, oh!" Koreena moaned. She lowered her chin and tried to become invisible.

Nico automatically swung his head to the left, and saw an older woman marching towards them in long, strong steps. She had obviously come from the office, and was now rushing to get to the counter in record time. 'Had she been watching them all along?' he wondered.

Koreena used her eyes and facial expression to talk to her customer. 'Take the bag and run for your life!'

"Well?" the older woman barked. She raised her left eyebrow as she leaned forward. Her make-up free eyes had now shrunk into small slits that were trying to burn a hole into his soul. Her hair had been savagely pinned into a bun on the top of her head, and her pancake foundation might have been smeared on with a spatula. She had a hairy mole in the center of her left cheek, and she was covered from neck to ankle in a heavy, woolen outfit. The features on her face were distorted, she was clearly angry, and she meant business. "Is everything ok, here?" the large woman demanded loudly, as she banged her giant hands on the counter.

Before he could speak, dollar signs flashed before Nico's eyes, reminding him of what he could be losing if he didn't leave the store right away. "Yes, thank you!" he stated politely. He grabbed the bag which was still dangling in the air, and made a boy scout salute to the two ladies before him. He then turned and exited the store with great haste.

The large woman turned to the sales clerk and shouted, "And you, get back to work!"

Koreena nodded. She then watched the bigger woman march away, and hoped that she'd stay in 'her cave' until closing.

Once he had climbed into the safety of his car, Nico shoved the ring and the box it came with, into his pants pocket. As he drove away, he could feel his entire body begin to relax, for he now believed that his future was no longer in danger.

Before he had walked through the elegant front doors of 'Cinco Avenida', he could see that the restaurant was quite grand and totally out of their usual price range. This worried him, but because tonight was a special occasion, he was not going to let it bother him.

"Can I help you, sir?" a lovely female asked.

Nico had to blink several times, in order for his eyes to focus properly. It was very hard not to notice the ruby red, silicone constructed, pillow soft lips on her young face. Her shiny blonde hair was flowing just past her shoulders, and she was wearing a tight-fitting, short black dress. By the amount of cleavage that he could see, Nico could tell that she was a man-made, size 44D.

"Are you meeting someone?" she asked.

The spell had been broken, as if someone had just popped a balloon beside his head, and Nico's attention came plummeting back to earth. He cleared his throat and answered. "Yes, yes I am." He then searched the room for Monica, and saw her sitting in a booth at the back, all alone. "There she is", he stated loudly. "I'm with Monica Bellam."

The beautiful hostess stretched out her left hand in a slow sweeping motion, and then she spoke. "You can go through."

Nico bowed slightly from the waist, but he wasn't sure why he needed to do that. He figured that it was an unconscious way of saying sorry to her, for engaging with her boobs more than her face. Regardless, he all but ran across the carpeted floor, in order to get to their table as quickly as possible.

"Hi", he said as he kissed Monica's cheek, and then he took the seat directly across from her. The first thing he did was look around the room, in hopes of getting another glance at the woman at the front door. He could see that she was now busy with someone else, but his mind couldn't help but begin to devise a plan where they could meet again.

Monica cleared her throat, as she reached for her glass of a bubbly gold liquid. She could see that he was distracted, and she really wanted to have every ounce of his attention.

*Monica loved Nico as a great friend, and ever since the day after they first met, she had always wanted to properly thank him for how well he had treated her. Because of the lottery, she now could, and this was the moment.*

"I have something to say", she began. She watched as Nico reached for his own glass, and then she made her speech.

As they raised their glasses to make a toast, Monica continued her train of thought. "First off, I'm paying for dinner. It's to thank you for all that you have done for me, and with me." She pushed her glass into his, and the air resonated with a recognizable clinking sound.

Nico's lips parted ever so gently, as he wondered what was going on.

"Secondly, today I bought two tickets for the New Holland Amsterdam cruise to Alaska, and I'd like you to go with me." She took a sip and then remained quiet, so he could fully register what she had just said.

As soon as he was able to process the information, fresh energy filled him with hope of an amazing future. "Yes!" he shouted. Nico was thrilled with her offer and could hardly contain his emotions. "Thank you!" He accepted immediately, without any hesitation.

"Good!" Monica pushed her glass towards his again, and then giggled at the echoing sound. As she sucked the bubbly liquid into her mouth, she watched as her date did the same thing.

While his tongue danced from the flavor of the expensive champagne, Nico watched Monica's festive expression, and decided that this was the special moment that he had been looking for. With reckless abandonment, he placed his glass on the table, pulled the ring out of his pocket, and got down on one knee.

The instant that Monica saw what he was about to do, she jumped out of her seat. She then got down on one knee and looked him straight in the face as she spoke. "No, Nico." She reached for his hand and together they stood up. "I love you to death", she said with sincerity. "But I don't want to get married. Please say that we can remain how we are for a little while longer."

Nico's happy outlook suddenly dropped like a brick, as he searched deep into her eyes for another answer.

Her face was begging him to please forgive her, as the rest of her body remained very still.

While it killed him that he would not be able to make love to her anytime soon, Nico returned the velvet box into the jacket's silk lined pocket. He nodded a weak yes to her suggestion, and then he sat back down in his seat. Although it was one of the hardest things that he might ever have to do, he tried to be content while they enjoyed the rest of their lovely dinner.

"Thank you", she whispered. Monica knew that she had crushed him, but she wasn't prepared for the night to end with that kind of proposal.

Nico wanted to scream with frustration and run out of the room in absolute despair, but his body wouldn't let him. Instead, his head hung forward while the insult of her rejection to his proposal - before he even gave it - was still fresh on his mind.

Nico didn't know how to stop obsessing over the lady seated directly across from him. He hated dating her, if you could call it that, but he softened his stance once he realized that no other man would ever get as close to her as he had been. He was her constant companion and best friend, and he needed to be content with that, if he wanted to remain in her life. He also needed to bide his time and put on a happy face, if he ever wanted to get his hands on her money.

It took a little less than an hour, but they eventually got back to their usual selves. And when the glorious evening ended around midnight, Monica and Nico were laughing and talking like normal. After a warm embrace and a lingering kiss, they said good-night and parted ways.

Monica was very fond of Nico, and she loved how patient he had been. He was her best friend, and she hoped that he would always be there for her. Plus, he had been in her life longer than anyone ever had been before – including Cayson. She saw a future with Nico, but she didn't want her heart to get broken again.

Now that Nico knew about the lottery money, he realized that he needed to be every bit the person who Monica would want to marry. He also knew that the moment he felt that she was ready, he would definitely propose to her again.

# Chapter 9

The RMS Queen Elizabeth had been completely destroyed by a fire, in a Hong Kong harbor on January 9, 1972. Nico and Monica were shocked to hear this, but they were still looking forward to going on their trip. The Princess Cruise ship, also known as 'the love boat', set sail a few months later.

Nico and Monica were shown to adjoining cabins on the same floor, by a ship representative. While Monica relished the idea that they were only a few feet apart from one another, Nico was more than surprised by the arrangement.

Nico stared blankly at the steward, when he first realized that he and Monica would not be sharing a room. His lips thinned out with total displeasure, for he had hoped for a bit more togetherness. Without a doubt, he would work on fixing that problem, as soon as possible.

The rooms were cozy, but there was enough space for a huge bathroom and a queen sized bed. "How sweet!" Monica cooed, as she admired everything around her. She then turned to Nico, and asked him to notice the door that separated their rooms. "We won't be that far apart from each other!" she squealed with delight. "Isn't that great?"

"Ah, huh", he uttered under his breath. He was clearly not happy, but because she had made all the arrangements, he had no choice but to go along with whatever was happening. "Great."

After settling into their rooms, they met upstairs for a hot beverage. They checked out the itinerary for the week's activities, and talked about what each of them wanted to do. By 9pm, both of them were exhausted and headed off to bed.

"Night, Nico!"

"Night, Monica. Have a good sleep!"

Monica turned on the TV, and found that she could get a clear view of the front of the ship on channel 12 and the back of the ship on channel 13. "How cool!" she raved. She was mesmerized by it, and kept clicking between the two channels. In the meantime, the boat was rocking very gently, and because the music on the TV was playing elevator-type songs, Monica fell asleep sitting up.

Nico could also feel the movements of the large vessel, but it didn't lull him to sleep. Instead, it bothered him a great deal. He had seen 'Titanic' with Ernest Borgnine just a few weeks ago, and that added another strain of anxiety to the list of emotions that he was already feeling. And as much as he was trying to fight it, he could see that he wouldn't win.

The large waves outside the ship, were taunting him into believing that it wasn't just a made-up movie, but that it could really happen. Three hours later, Nico threw up for the first time in years. He knew he couldn't and shouldn't wake Monica up, so he tried to get through the next few wicked hours of distress, by himself.

Monica woke up at 7:10am, and was not surprised to find that her tummy muscles were tight; she had been told that she could experience seasickness on her first days out at sea. As she sat up, Monica could feel the bile rise in her throat, and she was thankful that she had been prepared. She had not only bought one of those things to wear around your wrist, but she had also ingested a seasickness pill every few hours, as directed. Because she had had morning sickness when she was pregnant, she reached into her suitcase and searched until she found something else that could help. She climbed back into bed and nibbled on a packet of dry crackers, while praying to feel better soon.

Nico was suffering a great deal, and it seemed that nothing was making him feel better. He had not been as prepared as Monica was, but mostly because it didn't occur to him. Now that he was sicker than a dog, he wished for a miracle.

Out of desperation, Nico called the front desk, and he was told to look out the window at the horizon. "Thanks", he muttered under his breath. He knew that he had been unpleasant to the clerk, but that was because he had hoped for a magic pill to make him feel better, and it wasn't offered. After he put the phone back in its cradle, he did what he was told to do. Strangely enough, that did work, and then he searched for the remote control. But just as quickly as he had turned away from the lovely view, the contents in his stomach felt like they wanted to jump out of his mouth. After staring out of the rounded glass window for the next ten minutes, he started to feel a bit better again.

*His brain was having a hard time understanding why the ground beneath his feet was not moving forward, while the ship was swaying side to side with the waves. But by seeing the boat moving with the swells of the water, his head was able to understand what was going on.*

About an hour after she had nibbled on her dry items, Monica was feeling somewhat better, although it took another full day before Nico had his sea legs.

"Are you up?" she called through the wall. She waited for him to respond.

"I've been up for hours", he called, not so cheerfully. He didn't want to indicate that he was not available, so he asked her to give him a few minutes, and then she could come over for tea.

They shared tea and toast for breakfast in his cabin, and when they were done, Nico decided to go back to bed for a while. "A little upset tummy", he joked.

Monica could see that he was pale and not looking very well, so she let him be.

"You have a good morning", he called as she left his room. "Come back in the afternoon to check on me."

"I will", she replied happily. "You rest and I'll see you later."

Because she was now on her own, Monica got herself ready, and decided to explore the ship. She began her excursion up on the 11th floor observation deck. There, in the many large windows, she was able to look out and saw the true beauty of what the cruise ship had to offer. As she watched the waves skipping in no direction at all, she felt strangely connected to what was happening – on the ship and outside in the water. Monica sighed and couldn't believe her luck; up until that very moment, it had truly been a very beautiful and peaceful place to be.

And then, all of a sudden, the area in which she was basking in had suddenly become alive with sound and movement. A woman stood up and screamed for everyone to see the playful whales jumping up and out of the ocean. Together, the large group of strangers, watched as one of the whale's spouted water out of its blowhole.

"Look!" someone shouted. "Over there!"

"Honey, get my camera out of my bag!" another called.

Cameras were suddenly pulled out with rapid reflex, and everyone began to take pictures. While those few moments were a bit scary at first, it turned into a magnificent experience for everyone in the room.

After a while, Monica decided to do some more exploring. She went down to the 4$^{th}$ floor and found herself in the casino, and decided to try her luck. At one point she was up as high as $350 dollars, and at another, she was down to 40 cents. In the end, she had had a lot of fun; she drank for free, talked with everyone, and moved around from one game to another.

Eventually, she went back to her cabin to check on Nico. She was grateful that he was looking and feeling better, but he was still ill. They spent the afternoon playing cards and watching TV, and then she slipped out when Nico wanted to fall asleep.

"Alone again", she sighed. Monica went up to the 9$^{th}$ floor and walked slowly past the many kiosks, trying to decide what she would have for supper. She ended up with a grand dish of spaghetti and meatballs, with a fresh salad on the side. She searched until she found a small table by the window, and then she sat down to eat. When she was finished, she went back to her room and got herself ready for bed.

Nico was feeling much better by nightfall, but he hated that the ship was still swaying. He looked out of his window when he needed to, and otherwise, he nibbled on the crackers which Monica brought back from the machines. That night he slept better, and ran to the bathroom a lot less.

When Monica opened her eyes the next morning, she stretched her finger tips as high as they could go. She then knocked on the wall to see if her cabin-mate was up. She was pleasantly surprised when Nico knocked back right away.

"See you in 20 minutes?" Monica called, loud enough for him to hear.

"That sounds good!" he replied. He ordered their breakfast and they ate in his room, where Monica was able to see that Nico was looking and feeling much better.

"We're going to dock in Juneau, today", she stated happily. She was reading the itinerary and quoting what it said, and then added "Want to go ashore with me?"

"Let's play that by ear, shall we?" Nico still wasn't feeling well, and knew he would do better if he stayed close to his cabin.

"No worries." She could see that it might take another few hours, if not a whole day, for him to be back on his feet again. "I'll check in on you later." She ruffled his hair and kissed his cheek, and then she was gone.

"Bye! Have fun!" he called. Nico felt bad that she was spending so much time alone, but he needed to concentrate on how he would get thru the current hour.

Monica had walked around the ship during the morning, and had even taken part in a long game of Bingo.

By lunchtime, when she had come back to his room, Nico was happy to report that he was feeling almost like his old self again.

Monica was very happy to see that he looked and felt better, and she became even more elated when he suggested that they go ashore for an hour. "Really?" There was an abundance of excitement in her voice. "Are you sure?" She couldn't wait to have his company, outside of their cabins.

"I'm sure", he laughed. "Give me 30 minutes and then we can leave."

They got off the ship and went into many different kinds of shops, and looked at everything that pertained to souvenirs. They held hands as they admired the lovely scenery, and they made sure to take a ton of pictures. Around 5pm, they enjoyed an early supper, and then made their way back to the ship.

By nightfall, Nico was feeling pretty good. They were in her room and had the TV on, while Monica read out the list of 'things to do' for the next day.

Skeet-shooting and playing poker was on the top of Nico's list, while Monica looked forward to sunbathing and just plain relaxing. There were many things to do on the very large ship, and they agreed to spend at least two hours apart every day. Most of their meals would be eaten on the 9$^{th}$ deck, if not in their rooms, and the rest of the time would be spent doing things together.

"Ok, I'm going to get some sleep, then." Nico stood up and got ready to give Monica a hug.

Monica stood up and embraced him, and she thanked him for a wonderful day. As she held him close to her body, she loved how they fit together so well. "Good night", she whispered softly. "Have a good sleep."

"You too!" His eyes were studying her with a curious intensity, as he watched her close the door. 'Surely this arrangement was not going to continue for the whole trip', his inner self expressed with irritation. He sat down on his bed and began to plan a strategy.

As Monica laid her head on her pillow, she couldn't help but smile. For in that brief moment, everything felt different between them. She wondered if it was because they were on the ship, or because they had spent so much time together that day. As she tried to sift through her feelings, she trusted that she was now ready to move forward in their relationship.

Nico too, felt that the dynamics of their relationship had somehow changed during the course of the day. He didn't want to push her, but he hoped that by the end of their cruise, that they would be ready to do more than just kiss and hug.

An hour later, as they each fell into a deep sleep, the large vessel continued to rock gently. This soft motion helped them both to believe, that this cruise might indeed have a fairy-tale ending.

At 7:10am, Monica was woken out of a wonderful dream, by a very loud knock on her door. The sound was brash and disturbing, and she shook her head in order for this to make sense. She wondered what time it was, and before she knew what was happening, there was another knock on her door. "Who is it?" she called. She was half-asleep and hoped that it was something important.

"Room service!" came the reply.

Thinking that she had over-slept, Monica slid out of bed and draped a housecoat over her nightie. "Just a minute!" she called, as she made her way to the door.

"Morning, sunshine!" Nico said with a great deal of enthusiasm. He looked like he had never been that happy in his whole life. "I thought we could eat in here today."

Monica was in shock, but she was glad that he was feeling better. "Sh-sure, ok."

Nico was dressed very nicely, and he smelled like he had shaved and showered in the last five minutes. He walked past her and set the tray down on the foot of her bed, and then he positioned himself to stand directly in front of her. "Good morning." He placed his hands on her shoulders and pulled her body close to his. After a quick embrace, he made himself comfortable beside the food.

Monica was still groggy from being woken up so abruptly, but as the tea was being poured, she was feeling more and more at ease. They ate and talked about what they would do that day, and then Nico gave her an hour to get ready.

The ship had docked in Skagway and there was so much to do and see. After a long train ride, they walked up and down the main street, and ducked into every store possible. After a quick lunch, they took a small bus back to the ship, and walked hand-in-hand all the way to their cabins.

That night they shared a lot of wine, and talked and laughed until midnight. Nico stayed in her bed until the morning, but all they did was kiss, cuddle, and sleep.

They spent part of the next morning trying to cure their hangovers, and then they decided to go out on the deck for some fresh air. Monica had been told when she bought the tickets that it would be cold in Glacier National Park, but she hadn't counted on the fact that it would be freezing.

Monica and Nico made sure to dress in layers, and were in complete awe at the size and colors of the majestic glaciers. They took pictures as they listened to an informed speaker talk about how these huge blocks of ice were formed, how quickly they move, and how in years to come, these glaciers would no longer be where they were right now. The many people in attendance were thrilled with the view and the knowledge, but the brisk fresh air was more than some of them had bargained for.

"Green pea soup!" an employee of the ship called. "Come and get a free cup of hot soup!"

Nico and Monica were one of the many people who headed towards the warmth of the large pot. Everyone moaned in sheer delight at how perfectly wonderful the delicious thick soup tasted. Minutes later, after placing their empty mugs on the long counter, Monica and Nico left the wet and cold deck, and dashed inside to get warm. They soon made their way to Monica's cabin, where they slipped under the very thick comforters and nodded off for a long nap.

That night, they ate supper in the elegant dining room of the 'Manhattan Restaurant'. They were dressed up in fancy clothes, and they ordered a non-alcoholic wine. They clinked their glasses together, and a toast was made for everything to stay as it was in that moment.

It all seemed so surreal to Monica and Nico – them being on the large ship, the ship being surrounded by Glacier Bay, and the passengers feeling like love was in the air.

When they went back to their cabins a few hours later, Nico hoped that tonight would be the night when she would say yes. He had been prepared for this moment, for a very long time, and he would definitely not turn her down.

As they got into the elevator, Monica wondered if she should ask Nico to spend the night. After the past few days of being in his company, she felt that the moment was right.

When they got off the elevator and began to walk to their cabins, Nico noticed a note pinned to his door. "What's this?" he asked with extreme curiosity. He reached for the paper and then read it, and the expression on his face implied that something was terribly wrong.

"Is everything ok?" Monica asked with real concern.

Nico didn't answer right away, but when he lifted his eyes to meet hers, he folded the paper and then stuck it in his pocket. "I have to use the phone, so we'll say good-night, okay?" He kissed her forehead and went to his room, throwing another kiss her way before he walked through his doorway.

Monica wondered what that was about, and hoped that everything would work out fine. "Night!" she called, and then she went into her own room. She was a little sad that the evening had not turned out how she had hoped, but the cruise wasn't over yet.

Nico called the front desk after taking his jacket off, but the clerk said he'd have to wait until morning to make a ship-to-shore call. He thanked her and went to bed, but he couldn't help but feel sad about the contents in the note.

*The note said that a dear friend of his had died, and that Nico had been named as the beneficiary in her will. Nico had to search his memory bank for who she was, and then it came to him – Constance Marroni. When he saw her face in his mind's eye, it occurred to him that she was a very pleasant girl. He then recalled how they met, and all that they had done together.*

*The gorgeous, dark-haired beauty was turning 30 years old, and didn't want to appear to have no knowledge on her wedding night. She went to a bar all by herself, and thought she would be celebrating her birthday alone. An hour after she arrived, Nico walked in. After ingesting a few too many drinks, she told him that she didn't want to be a virgin on her wedding night.*

*Nico was only too willing to teach her what she needed to know, but as long as it was understood that 'this' was going to be a casual thing.*

*"Of course!" she confirmed. Connie, her nick-name, was engaged to a burly Navy Officer and had no intention to make their 'classes' a permanent adventure.*

*"Alright, then." He pressed his shot glass against hers, and they got down to business. "Lesson One – kissing," he toasted, and chugged his drink. After slamming the glass*

onto the counter, Nico leaned his face towards Connie and he gave her a very passionate kiss. He told her what to do with her lips, and then he explained the use of the tongue. Lesson Two took them outside to his car.

There were five lessons in total, and during those long and steamy hours together, they had both learned a thing or two about the finer pleasures of first-time sex.

Connie's groom had been told that she was a virgin, and he was about to come home after being at sea for 6 months. Lester was very experienced in the ways of the world, but he'd been advised by his friends to take it easy on his bride - especially on their first night together.

Lester couldn't have been more surprised when the bride was excited to have a lot of sex on their wedding night. He tried to slow down the activities, just as his buddies had told him to do, but Connie couldn't get enough. Lester was happy and exhausted on his wedding night, and thanked his lucky stars over and over again.

Because her husband had been so pleased with her willingness and performance, and he thought that he was the reason that she liked sex, Lester made Connie's life quite blissful.

So many years have passed, but Connie never forgot Nico's kindness. Because it was the only way she knew how to thank him, she left a little something in her will for the man who was truly responsible for her liking sex.

*Life was more than wonderful for Connie and her new husband, and then everything changed. Unfortunately, Connie died giving birth to her first child, a girl. She was buried last week and the will was read today, prior to Nico and Monica having the fancy supper. The lawyer was able to track Nico down, and called the ship looking for him. Now Nico had to call him back.*

*Nico was sad to hear about Connie's death, but he couldn't help but wonder what he was going to be getting from her estate.*

Nico had a hard time sleeping, because every time he closed his eyes, his mind played the images of his dates with Connie. No details were left out, which brought him excitement several times throughout the night. By morning, he was tired but happy.

Monica knocked on the door that they shared, and asked Nico if he was up yet.

"Give me five minutes", he called from his side. He wanted to splash some water on his face, and come up with a good excuse for the note, before she asked him any questions.

A few minutes later, Monica brought a tray of goodies into his room, and they began to eat. She didn't want to ask about the note right away, because she didn't want to appear to be nosey. But when they were almost finished their breakfast, and he hadn't mentioned it, she decided to speak up.

"Oh!" he began. Because he believed that he had worked it all out in his mind, he was confident to tell the made-up story. "I was able to get that cleared up last night, right before I went to bed. The note was a message from my neighbour, who said that someone had left a package on my front door step. He wanted to know if he should take it into his own home until I get back. I called him and said, 'Yes, he should'. He thanked me, and we hung up."

Monica was intrigued, but glad it wasn't anything more important. "What do you think it is?" Her eyes were wide with curiosity, and full of hope for something wildly expensive and beautiful.

Nico had already thought of that, too. "I'm sure it's a lamp that I saw in a store about a month ago. They didn't have two of them in stock, so they had to send away for one. I'm guessing that it finally got delivered."

Monica was relieved to hear that it was something trivial, and now that that had been settled, she couldn't wait to carry on with their day.

Nico was also relieved, but because Monica had bought into his lie. He still needed to make the call, but at least now it could be done without further questions.

After breakfast, their morning was spent swimming in the indoor pool and indulging on a grand feast over the lunch hour. Afterwards, they checked the itinerary, and found that the weather was going to perfect for some R&R.

That meant sunbathing to Monica, and playing chess for Nico.

Once Monica was comfortable in her lounge chair, Nico was able to go to the 11th floor. "Will you be okay while I'm gone?" He was joking, because he could see that she was all set up for 'catching some rays', as Monica put it.

Monica smiled with true warmth in her soul. "I don't know", she mocked impishly. "How long will I have to be all alone?"

*She loved how handsome he looked, and while she wasn't sure about the feelings that were coming over her, she felt strangely attracted to him. Nico had been with her for just over 6 years, and he had certainly proved that he was worthy of her time and love. Because things didn't go as planned last night, she wondered if tonight would be the night that they would consummate their relationship. A chill ran up her spine as her mind explored the numerous improper possibilities.*

Nico loved seeing her in such a good mood, and he bent down to kiss her square on the mouth. "Not long, my love. Behave until I get back", he cautioned playfully.

"I'll try", she giggled.

Nico walked away whistling, and feeling very optimistic about how the cruise might end.

Monica knew how much he loved her, and she had to admit that she was falling for him, too. "I should stop taunting him, for the man has wanted to be more than friends for a long time", she confessed to herself. "I'm not sure what I'm waiting for."

Monica laid back and made herself comfortable in the wooden chair. She loved how the gentle breeze stroked her exposed skin, and how the slight rocking of the ship didn't seem to bother her at all, anymore. In fact, it lulled her into a light sleep.

About 30 minutes later, Monica was shocked awake by a loud bang and scraping noise. Because both had come from beside her right shoulder, she flipped up her large-brimmed, tan-colored hat, and peered in that direction. She was surprised to see a young boy, standing not quite two feet away from her chair. He was looking at her as if he had done something very wrong. "Can I help you?" she asked, in a friendly but curious tone.

"What are you doing?" The boy spoke in a soft, high pitched voice, and had the mannerisms of an apologetic, innocent child.

Monica positioned herself so that she was leaning on one elbow, in order to see the child better. He stood all of 3 feet tall, his blonde hair was rough and messy, his head was cocked to the side, and his eyes were big and bright. The beautiful little boy appeared to be bored, and was probably looking for someone to play with.

*Sometime later, Monica would learn that he had ventured out of the dining room and had seen her sitting all alone on the deck. That's why he had decided to go up to her and start up a conversation. But while he was trying to be quiet, his toe had accidently smacked against the deck chair next to hers, which made the noise, and woke her up.*

"It's called sunbathing", she replied.

*Monica had never had a full conversation with a child before, so this was very amusing.*

The child scrunched up his face, as if he had just been asked to try a food that he'd never eaten before, but he was sure that he wouldn't like.

The boy looked so cute, so she decided to keep him engaged. "Have you ever sunbathed?"

"Yeah, but it's boring", he whined. He was twisting his body from side-to-side from the waist up as he spoke. "I'm not very good at sitting still for very long."

"I can see that", Monica agreed. Both of her eyebrows had shot up, her brain was being stimulated, and she was more entertained than she could have imagined.

Suddenly, the handsome child became very animated. "Do you want to play with me, instead of just lying here?" he haggled. His body was now squirming and twitching like he wanted to start playing something right away. He became brave and took a step closer. He then placed his hands on the arm of her chair, and used his pretend-to-be-sad expression to plead for her to say yes.

It warmed her heart that the little boy wanted to be her friend. And then, as she drank in all of what made him cute, Monica noticed something familiar in the features in his face. Suddenly, an incredibly strong emotional attraction was strangely drawing her towards him. As she watched him fidget with his small hands and feet, she unconsciously began to pour all of her attention to the young child before her.

Monica swung her legs over the edge of the chair, and was now sitting straight up. "I don't know", she stated sincerely. "What do you have in mind?" She pressed her hands together and placed them in between her thighs. She then leaned forward as she waited for him to come up with a plan.

As his active mind was thinking of things which they could do, it gave her pause to really study his adorable qualities. Within seconds, she noticed that he had an angelic face, and then he flashed her with the most amazing smile ever. And in that instant, he suddenly reminded her of someone, but she couldn't imagine who it could be.

Before they were able to decide on what to do, a very nicely dressed man came barreling across the wooden boards of the deck towards them. "There you are!" he announced gently but sternly. The man appeared to be almost breathless, but Monica guessed it was more out of anxiety than how quickly he had travelled.

*The man had been looking for his son for the last fifteen minutes, and was quite relieved that he was okay.*

"You need to tell me before you run off like that", he ordered tenderly. The man waited until his son acknowledged what was being said, and then he turned his attention to the woman in the lounge chair. "I hope he wasn't too much trouble for you", he conveyed. As he delivered the words, he became distracted by her lovely eyes.

Monica laughed it off. "No, not at all." Her eyes twinkled as she gazed into the little boy's face. "He is totally delightful."

The man was very thankful – because his son was okay, and that he had not caused any trouble. "Thank you, but I know that he can be a little bit of a handful at times."

"Oh, he was no trouble at all." The sun was shining directly onto the man's back, so she was unable to see his face as clearly as she would have wanted.

"Thank you for saying so." He looked down at his son and spoke again. "I guess we'll be going now." The man placed his large hand on the child's upper back, and gently urged him to thank the lady for her time.

The boy lowered his eyelids as if he had done something wrong, and then he pronounced his appreciation exactly how he had been taught to do. "Thank you for entertaining me. I hope I get to see you again." He then reached his little hand out to shake hers.

Monica was very impressed by his manners. "Me too", she remarked, chuckling softly at how courteous the little boy was behaving. She reached out to shake his hand, but when their skin touched, it unexpectedly brought goose bumps to all parts of her body. When their hands slipped apart, Monica felt butterflies in her stomach. She sat there for a second while she wondered what had caused those strange emotions.

"Bye!" the little boy called, as he was being led away.

Because they hadn't gotten too far, Monica overheard the father shower his son with great praises. "You're a good boy, Oliver." She then watched the proud man move his hand through the boy's hair.

Just then, the hair on her own skin began to stand on end, while her senses went into complete shock. As Monica questioned why that name sounded so familiar, the muscles in her tummy tightened. Monica's mind sped very quickly through the last 6 or 7 years of memories, and it wasn't long before the information that she was looking for came to the forefront of her brain.

If Monica was not mistaken, Oliver was the name that the adoptive parents had given to her son. She had never heard the name before or after that very moment, and that's what made it unique to her.

Monica turned her head to take a peek at the little boy, who was now at the far end of the deck. This whole ordeal made her feel powerful and curious. Could it be, she wondered? Her thoughts took over and argued both sides of the entire conversation.

*She had had her baby just over six years ago – they would be about the same age. There was so much sadness and confusion attached to that part of her life, that she wasn't sure what was real and what was hearsay about that time period. But didn't she just feel a definite emotional connection between the boy and herself? Or did she just imagine that? It was all too bizarre. But what if he was her son?*

Monica turned to check, but she saw that the boy and his father had walked out of her sight. With sadness in her heart, Monica lay back down in her deck chair. Her mind was racing as it tried to sort out the strange, but very interesting last few moments. She was feeling foolish as she attempted to make sense of it all, but other than sheer coincidence, what other explanation could there be?

About an hour after Monica had had the encounter with the little boy, Nico finally returned. By this time, Monica had almost convinced herself that she had given birth to that little boy named, Oliver. She bolted into an upright position when Nico approached her chair, and could not wait to tell Nico everything that had happened while he was gone.

As the words flew out of her mouth with great speed, Monica's eyes were glistening. Her hands were flying everywhere, she stammered and squealed about how she felt, and she was more excited than he had seen her in years.

As Nico listened, fear wrapped itself into the very fiber of his being. He assumed that it would be almost impossible that the little boy was Monica's son, so he tried to make light of the situation. "Wow, that's a long-shot, Monica."

*Secretly, he had hoped to never see or hear of that baby again. If this really was the child that Monica had given birth to, they would bond, and he would totally take up all of her time and attention. If this really was her child, Nico had some work to do, to make sure that the little boy didn't come between them. First things first though - Nico had to find the parents.*

"Why?" Monica was troubled by how insensitive Nico was being, and hoped that he would at least consider the slight possibility that the boy was her son.

"I'm sorry, but I don't want you to get your hopes up." Nico was appearing to be tender and kind, but inside, he was struggling to calm down. Secretly, he wished for that little boy and his father to get off the ship at the next stop – on their own or with his help.

*Nico had worked very hard to find adoptive parents for Monica's baby, and for them to just turn up out of the blue like this, was ludicrous. There were things about the adoption which he had not told Monica; details which he never thought would ever be revealed. With a desperate situation threatening his future, Nico resolved to do what he had to, in order to make Monica believe that this was not her son. Or, he would have to devise a plan where Monica would never be able to see the father or son again.*

Nico spun his body around and looked out at the beautiful ocean that spread before him. "You and your son on the same cruise at the same time?" he jested. He stretched his arms out as far as they would reach, while he continued to speak. "That would be an amazing twist of fate, wouldn't you think?" He was trying to be logical without hurting her feelings, and he hoped that he was convincing her to laugh it off. Inside, however, Nico was filled with anxiety; what if the boy really was hers?

"Maybe", she sighed, but the woman's heart knew better. There was something about the boy and his father that struck a chord with her, and she couldn't shake it. So from that moment on, with or without Nico's help, she vowed to be on a mission to find out all that she could about them.

"Or maybe not", she whispered under her breath. In her mind, she established that if Nico didn't believe her and he wasn't willing to help her, then she would do it herself.

Nico turned back around as she spoke, and he could see the disappointment on Monica's face. Of course he didn't want her to be upset, so he swore to himself that he would make her feel better. Nico didn't want to believe that the boy was hers, and he didn't want her to buy into that story either. He wanted them to continue their lovely trip without any more drama, so he pushed the negative energy away and tried to make the moment lighter. "Come on", he implored. "What's on our agenda today?"

Monica shrugged her shoulders and decided to act dumb. "I don't know."

Nico searched his brain for anything that would take her mind off of this moment, and then he remembered her customary once-a-month routine. "Karaoke!" he shouted. He raised both of his hands high in the air, and with an abundance of energy racing through his body, he playfully roared, "I'll race you to the fourth deck, okay?" He bent down and kissed her forehead, and then he walked away quickly. He hoped that she would forgive him for being a bit uncaring, and he promised to give her a fabulous night from that moment on.

She could see that he was trying, but she needed to think. "You go ahead and I'll catch up!" she called after him. Monica waved as Nico rushed down the deck, but her heart wasn't into karaoke tonight.

"Alright, but don't be too long." Nico still had hope that she would follow him.

As Monica settled back in her chair, her mind went into overdrive. With the solitude of the water splashing against the ship, she was able to think of many ways in which she could accidentally bump into the boy and his father.

It took almost 30 minutes before Monica joined Nico in the Cherry Lounge. She ended up having a very good time, and she stayed there until 11pm.

As they walked back to their cabins, they held hands. During the last few hours, they had laughed and sang, and had a bit too much to drink. They kissed in front of Monica's door, but they went inside of their own cabins. "Night!" she called.

Nico had suspected that the night might end with him going into his room alone, but it only made him want to work harder. Tomorrow he would do all that he could, to get the man and his son off the ship.

Monica climbed into her bed and covered herself up. She then looked up at the ceiling and realized that she had been a very silly, very young woman, who had made a quick and wrong judgment. Of course she would have been able to raise a child on her own. She knew that now, but she didn't back then. How foolish she had been.

As she rolled onto her side, she realized how much she had truly enjoyed being with that little boy today. Monica adored seeing his smiling face, and feeling all of the happiness which was beaming from every pore in his body.

As the pictures of their time together flashed in her mind, she couldn't help but notice that he has a lot of the same similarities that her parents had. And the cowlick on the top right-hand side of his forehead, looked exactly like Cayson's. Or perhaps it is all just a figment of her imagination? Regardless, she hoped to run into the little boy again, and soon.

Monica got out of bed especially early the next morning, and searched the entire ship for any sign of the little boy or his father. Because Nico was by her side until noon, she could only glance here and there, without actually appearing to be looking for something or someone.

Nico was looking forward to a brand new day with Monica, a day where their minds could be solely devoted on just the two of them. He tried not to talk about the little boy around the woman he loved, but it was quite obvious that she was looking for someone. Nico knew he had to think of something to bring her mind back to them. And out the blue, the answer appeared.

When Nico spotted the captain not too far away, he excused himself for a few minutes. "I won't be gone long, sweetheart", he promised. He kissed the finger tips on her right hand, and then he kissed her mouth. "I'll be back soon."

"Don't worry; I'll be fine." Monica was thankful for the break. Because it looked like Nico was on a mission, she took that opportunity to begin another vigorous search around the entire ship.

Nico was at the captain's side within a minute, and he began to ask the high-level officer a few questions about the father and son cabin-mates. "I recognize the man from somewhere, but I don't know from where", he began. "I know you probably can't help me, but ..."

Nico played the part of a long-lost relative on the father's side to perfection, and he soon found out that Captain Stanton was Oliver's uncle on his mother's side. The captain of the mighty ship, who is a loving and dedicated father of four, became quite close to the boy and his father, after Oliver's mother had taken ill. It was the captain who suggested they take the cruise, and he paid for all of the expenses.

Once the boy's father's name had been revealed, Nico was able to confirm that the man in question was his former cell mate – Walter Ryng.

Nico's heart fell when he learned that Walter's wife had taken ill, and that she had eventually died. Nico had buried many a woman in his short life, but he had never loved any of them. Because of the insensitivity part of his personality, his sentimental mood was disappearing quickly.

Nico thanked the older man for his time and knowledge, and after a short chat about how wonderful the cruise had been so far, Nico began his journey back to Monica's side. Would he tell her anything that he had learned from Captain Stanton? Or should he keep all contents of the entire conversation a secret?

Nico decided not to let Monica know anything about the boy or his father, as that would ruin everything that he had been working so hard for. His mind was now racing with ideas on how to keep them all apart for the rest of the cruise.

Nico was deep in thought when he wandered through a doorway on the third floor. He heard everyone talking, and all at once, and it made him look up. Nico saw a crowd of seven people waiting by the elevator, but there was one person who stood out.

His breath caught hard in his throat, and he blinked more than a few times in order to really see across the hall. His heart seemed to speed up and he felt very faint. 'Could it be?' Nico wondered. This man had been a part of his past – a part that could destroy his future.

Nico was more than surprised to find that he was standing 10 feet away from his former jail mate, Walter Ryng. Nico couldn't believe it and had to adjust his eye sight again, just to make sure that it was him. Upon closer inspection, Nico noticed that his old friend looked different - haggard and quite tired. This concerned him, as Nico remembered Walter with having a lot more hair and a bit more weight on his body - not to mention a happier expression on his face. But, he had just lost his wife…

Nico's usual boyish good looks were now tainted with anxiety, as he stared at the familiar man standing a few feet away from him. Nico's eyes were quite round and he couldn't seem to blink, for fear that the image would disappear. He tried to move his feet, but they felt as if they were cemented to the floor.

Nico wondered what he should do. 'Should I go up and say hello, or should I call out to him from here? Should I make a noise and hope that he looks over, or should I continue to stand where I am and keep quiet?' His mind was asking question after question, while accessing the situation to death. But try as he might, he was not able to come up with a solid answer. Luckily for him, the elevator doors opened and Walter stepped inside.

It was as near to a miracle as there ever was, and Nico couldn't believe his great fortune. His chest expanded while taking in a very large amount of air, and while exhaling, he felt some much-needed emotional relief; he now didn't have to make a decision at all. Nevertheless, he had become very aware of the man who he had had a torrid past with, and this proved that the boy was indeed, Monica's child.

Nico lowered his head, as apprehension roared its way through his brain. He took the stairwell up to the next level and then walked down the long hallway to the right. Nico couldn't think, and watched the carpeted floor beneath his feet as he made his way back to his cabin. Once there, he laid on his bed and let his thoughts go around in circles.

# Chapter 10

When Nico closed his eyes, his mind filled with memories of all that he and Walter had done together. They had once shared the important details of their childhoods with each other, and after their lives had been so shrewdly intertwined, they had caused some negative events to happen.

How could Nico have been so blind as to think their paths would never cross again? And now, without a shadow of a doubt, the father and son were back.

In these last few minutes, it had become very clear to Nico that he would have to keep Walter and Monica apart for as long as he could – on and off the ship. For, if their lives were to brush together, Nico would be in bigger trouble than he could ever dream.

When he was a child, Walter Ryng had been a handful all through elementary school. He had behavioral problems, bad attitudes, and temper tantrums, and he had ended up in jail three times before he turned 20 years old. He blamed his parents for how he had turned out, but they firmly maintained that they had done their very best with him.

Walter was asked to leave home at 16, when it was found that his unruly behavior was causing trouble - not only in school, but also in his parent's relationship. He bounced between living with friends and on the streets for a few years, and then he met a man named, Nicholas Kostas.

Walter was 25 years old, when he had gone into 'Willy's Pub' for a drink after work one night. He became angry when he watched a man grab a woman by the back of her hair, and then he slammed her face onto the counter. Walter didn't even ask what had happened prior to that moment; he just rushed over to help break up the tension. It took four men and ten minutes before the situation had been defused, and when the police arrived, everyone was arrested and taken downtown for questioning. It was in the back of the paddy wagon when Walter asked the woman who had been assaulted, "What happened back there?"

Her eyelids dropped as the words spilled out. "I asked him to repeat his drink order", she replied softly.

Walter's lips turned into a lopsided frown, while she began to cry. He leaned in and tried to console her, but she didn't want anyone to touch her.

"Stop! I'm ok!" she shouted in anger. Her hands were moving briskly in the air, her fingers were stretched to their capacity, and everyone could see that she was trying to make a point. "It comes with the gender!" she added. "I'm a waitress, so I must be stupid. I'm a woman, so I must be weak. I get it." She then covered her face with both hands and leaned towards her lap.

Walter looked over at the drunken slob in the corner, and wondered if he even knew what he had done. The abuser was now passed out, but by how disheveled he looked, and the reek of alcohol that seemed to flow from his pores, Walter would have to assume that he did not.

After being booked and finger-printed, they all parted ways, and Walter was thrown into a small cell. He was held over-night, as it was implied from where they had picked him up and the smell of alcohol on his clothing, that he was also drunk. Because he wasn't passed out and he was co-operating, he was told that he would be released the next day.

"It's for your own protection", the senior cop expressed. "Sleep it off and you'll feel better in the morning."

"Gee, thanks", Walter muttered under his breath. It wasn't a sincere appreciation, but more of a 'thanks for nothing' kind of sentiment. Because he decided that there was nothing he could do about his current situation, he turned around and made himself comfortable.

Unbeknownst to Walter, there was another man in the cell with him. Because he had too many thoughts running wildly through his brain, Walter didn't see him.

Nicholas Kostas was up on the top bunk, his back was against the wall, and he had been watching everything from his uncomfortable perch. A full minute after Walter had sat down on the bottom bunk, Nico jumped from his bed to introduce himself. With a match stick clenched firmly in between his front teeth, Nico spoke his first words to Walter Ryng. "Well, well, well. What do we have here?" He spoke with confidence and his body language was trying to suggest intimidation.

Walter felt like his heart had jumped into his throat. He didn't want to have any problems, and he cringed when the stranger sat down beside him and threw his arm across Walter's shoulders. This felt terribly awkward, and Walter shrugged the stranger's arm off his body in anger. He'd already had quite an evening, and he was not in the mood to be someone's bed-buddy.

Walter decided to get things straightened out right away, before there was any alluding to what's going to happen. He leaped into the air, and positioned himself directly in front of the guy from the top bunk. "I'm pissed off, I'm not in the mood to make a new friend, and I'll be thankful if you back off – and I mean right now!" Walter took a step closer and bent his upper body forward.

Nico immediately placed his hands in the air as if he was surrendering, and then he stood up. He brought one of his hands down and extended it towards the new cell mate. "Sorry, pal", he began. "I didn't mean to scare you off."

They shook hands and each went to their own bunk. In the next hour, they began a conversation, and after learning how much they had in common, their 8-year history of burglary, car thefts, drugs, and peddling things that did not belong to them, began.

They were both bad boys, but they were not two peas in a pod. They were after the same thing, though – to make a quick buck, no matter how that happened. It worked well for the most part, but as soon as Walter heard that a woman had died and that Nico might have caused her death, he questioned their friendship.

Nico needed to make some money fast, so he befriended a beautiful young woman named, Sheila. Walter saw them together and automatically assumed that they were boyfriend/girlfriend. Four months later, the recently divorced woman was found dead, and Nico had to go to court to clear his name. Walter felt sorry for his friend, and sat in the courthouse every day, for emotional support.

"In conclusion, I hereby declare that the death of Sheila May Winslow be ruled as an unfortunate accident." The judge slammed his gavel onto his wooden desk with a very loud bang, and the case was over. "You are free to go", he pointed to Nico Kostas when he spoke the last sentence.

Walter felt victorious, for he had believed in his friend's innocence all along. But as they walked out of the courtroom, Walter could hear small murmurings of 'this' happening many times before.

"How does he always get away with this?" one man questioned.

"I don't know, but isn't this the fourth woman who has died while dating him?" a woman asked. There was an ugly taste in her mouth as she spit out the words.

"And now he'll inherit her money and move on to another poor, unsuspecting female", one of the lawyers was heard to say.

Walter had an unethical background, he was not young and innocent, but as much as he had done wrong in his life, he had never hurt anyone for money.

Nico always tried to be controlling and he was usually 'the brains' in most of their capers. Because of Nico's temper, Walter knew enough to stand aside and do what he was told. During their long friendship, Nico and Walter had committed a lot of crimes together and they never got caught. And during it all, not once did Walter suspect that Nico could have caused someone to die – by accident or on purpose! This current scenario was making his head swim.

"That poor woman", a man was heard to say. "She probably loved him and didn't see it coming."

Walter had heard all the testimony, and it was very possible that Sheila had died by accident. He was getting upset that everyone was insinuating that Nico had done something to cause her to die. But could he have?

Walter was shocked and in total disbelief that his friend might have committed a murder. In order to believe otherwise, he turned to face his friend. Before he could ask Nico a question, Walter had noticed his friend's relieved expression, and this caused him to worry.

'Shouldn't he be sad?' he wondered. Walter was confused; there didn't seem to be any indication that Nico was one tiny bit distraught by Sheila's death. In fact, because of how calm Nico was acting, it gave Walter the illusion that his friend was actually happy about how things had turned out.

"How about we go and get a drink to celebrate?" Nico suggested loudly. He then waited for Walter to agree.

Walter's eyes popped open with surprise when he saw that his friend didn't seem bothered by what was happening. There were no crease lines in his forehead, no worry lines around his eyes, and his lips were actually smiling. "To celebrate?" he questioned. It was almost as if Nico was thankful that he had gotten away with it.

"Of course to celebrate!" Nico laughed. A twinkle of satisfaction flickered in his eyes.

Walter was devious in a lot of ways, but he loved and respected women, and all that they stood for. He prided himself on being a lover, not a fighter, and he would proudly battle anyone who thought otherwise. Walter had never hurt a woman in his life, and he could not think of a reason to start now. 'Could Nico?' he wondered.

*As much as he wanted to include Walter in his private affairs, Nico swore that he would never divulge that he needed Sheila's money in order to survive. When asked, Nico claimed that he was having fun with her, and that they had gotten along very well.*

Nico had sworn under oath, that he was asleep when Sheila went to the kitchen to get some water, and he only woke up after he heard her scream. Therefore, he could not have been the reason that she died.

Behind closed doors though, Nico was doing what he had always done – he used her in every way possible, and would now walk away with an amazing amount of wealth.

Sheila had just been given a house, a car, all the furniture, and all the money in the bank account, in her divorce from her husband, Bradley Winslow. Because her parents had died and there were no children from their brief union, Nico's lawyers had proved beyond a shadow of a doubt, that Nico was her boyfriend and therefore, her only heir. The lawyers had also proved that Sheila had consumed too many 'White Russians' during the course of their evening – the alcohol level in her blood stream was way too high.

*That was the initial impression from the pathologist, who declared, "...according to how much alcohol Sheila had in her system when the paramedics found her, she would not have been able to think or walk on her own, let alone go down the stairs safely."*

Walter couldn't believe that his friend had gone from poor to beyond rich, in a matter of days. However, Nico seemed to be adjusting to it quite well.

Nico had been living with Sheila for about 2 months when she died, but Walter would never have suspected that the house and everything in it would someday belong to Nico; the happy couple had only known each other for 4 months.

Walter had to admit that things did move along very quickly between them, and that Nico and Sheila were inseparable after their first encounter. But after Walter had examined his friend's face, and after hearing all the suspicious gossip in and out of the courtroom that day, Walter wasn't sure what to believe anymore.

"N-no, I can't", Walter admitted. He no longer felt that he could trust Nico. He was scared for his own life, and he didn't want to be implicated should another person die. "In fact, I think I'm going to leave now."

"What? You make it sound like we're never going to see each other again", Nico replied half-heartedly. He slapped his friend playfully on the back of the shoulder before he spoke again. "Come on! What could be so important that you don't want to have a drink with your old buddy?"

Walter lowered his face and tried to explain why he no longer wanted to stay friends with a man who everyone thinks may have committed a murder. It took him a few long minutes to get all the words out, and then he said good-bye to someone he had grown quite fond of. "I hope you understand", Walter said when they were shaking hands.

Nico hated that his friend felt like he had to walk out of his life, but he kind of understood. "I'm going to miss you, Walter", he replied under his breath.

"Yep, me too. But I think I have to change my ways." Walter turned around and took his first step into his new life. He would miss Nico as much as he said he would, but he no longer wanted to live how he had been. He wasn't sure what his future held for him, but he was ready to walk against a strong wind to find out.

Nico wished his friend well, and then he reflected on his own life. He had a nice home to go to, and once the paperwork was done, he'd have a ton of money in his bank account. For now, he had nothing to complain about.

Over the next year, Nico continued to do what he'd always done – spend money and entertain the ladies.

Two years had passed, and the money was beginning to run out. Nico had to sell Sheila's possessions in order to survive, and eventually he had the sell the house. When he was looking for a new place to live, and possibly another rich woman to hang out with, he ran into someone who knew both him and Walter.

"Yah, I'd heard that Walter met a great girl and that they had just gotten married", Rudy reported. "I think her name's Evelyn. She's a nice girl, from what I hear."

Nico was shocked to learn that his old friend had changed his life so drastically. "How would I get hold of him, you know, to congratulate him?"

"Oh, I don't know", Rudy replied slowly. The unshaven man's tone was full of uncertainty, for he wasn't sure if he should be giving out any information at all. The old man peered into the bottom of his whiskey glass for almost a minute, before he said another word. "He doesn't come into the bar very often now that he's married, but I have seen him in here twice, in the past six months."

"Thanks!" Nico slapped Rudy on the back and stood up. He threw a few dollar bills down on the counter to pay for both of their drinks and added, "Well, you tell him that I was here and that I say HI to him, okay?"

Rudy was delighted that he had gotten a free drink of out their conversation, and that he didn't have to give away too much information. "You got it! And thanks for the drink!" The 5'2" tall man raised his glass into the air as Nico walked towards the front door.

"My pleasure", Nico called. "It was really nice to have seen you again, Rudy." He lifted his left hand in the air and threw a nonchalant wave behind him. He got what he needed, and for now, he had no more use for the old guy.

While Nico was happy for Walter, he was quick to note that Walter knew too much about their past. He was also aware that Walter could cause trouble for Nico, if he talked to the wrong person at the wrong time. And now that Nico knew where to find Walter, he decided to keep tabs on his old friend, in case he ever needed to call in a favor.

Several years had passed, and it was a couple of months after Nico had met Monica, when the two ex-partners would meet again. Nico had gone to the bar about once every few weeks, especially to talk with Rudy and the bartender. He made sure to keep their conversations light, to ensure that when he needed special information, that it would be supplied.

On today's visit to the bar, Nico had just learned that Walter and his wife had gone to see a fertility doctor. He couldn't have been more pleased, for this was exactly what he had been looking for.

"Is that so?" Nico stated with genuine interest. "A buddy of mine is also having trouble getting his wife pregnant."

"Yah, that's a shame", the little old man said cautiously. Rudy could feel trouble brewing, so he lowered his eyes and silently wished for Nico to go away.

"Do you happen to know the name of the doctor they're seeing? Or maybe where the building is, so I can find the doctor myself?" Nico was trying to play it cool, but anxiety was suffocating his soul. He was holding his breath while he waited for an answer, and it felt like he had pins and needles in his toes.

Rudy was very reluctant to give out any more unnecessary information. He glanced in the bartender's direction, but Charlie did not want to be involved.

The bartender threw his hands up in the air, and with an expression that clearly stated, 'Don't look at me', the bartender walked to the other end of the bar.

"I think the building's on 12th Avenue and 2nd Street", Rudy advised, but he felt like he had been forced to give it out. Without making eye contact, the old man added, "That's all I know." He was furious with himself for saying as much as he had, and chugged down all the liquid in the tall glass in front of him. When the last drop was in his throat, he banged the empty glass against the counter with an angry hand.

"Well, I hope it works out for them", Nico replied with sincerity in his voice. Now that he had this juicy piece of the puzzle, Nico finished his beer and walked to the door. "See you all later!" he called.

It didn't take long before Nico found out which building Walter and Evelyn were going to, and it took nothing for him to figure out his next move.

Nico met the receptionist 'by accident', after stating that he had stepped off the elevator on the wrong floor, thereby going into the wrong office. After chatting up the beautiful, chestnut-brown haired girl for almost ten minutes, he leaned forward and supported himself on one elbow. In a dangerously sensuous tone and manner, he offered to buy her a cup of coffee. "Because I took up so much of your valuable time", he said slowly.

The 24-year old, fresh-out-of-college woman, hoped that he hadn't noticed, but since he had walked up to her counter, she had all but swooned in clear view of all the patients in the waiting room.

*In her defense, she couldn't help but be swept away by all that this man had to offer, for he was not only extremely good looking, he had just poured all of his charm in her direction. The receptionist didn't know it, but she was looking and acting as if she had been caught in his spell.*

"Yes, please", she found herself cooing.

"I'll call you tomorrow."

Her eyes stayed fixed on his, as he thanked her and reached for the door. For the rest of the day, the receptionist couldn't hide the bright smile on her face.

After their first coffee date, Nico's appeal was too strong for her to go back to work. Over the next two weeks, the receptionist accepted another four dates from the handsome man with the dodgy character. During their short-lived affair, she answered all of his questions, and he rewarded her with the gift of his many, mind-blowing talents.

In the end, Nico had learned where Walter and Evelyn lived and worked, and that they had been trying to conceive a child since their wedding night. Because it would not seem that they could ever have a child together, this gave Nico an amazing idea.

Nico was always one to seek out new opportunities, and this time he decided to use Monica's delicate situation to put more money into his bank account. He rushed to her apartment and they talked about the idea of her giving her baby up for adoption. He even promised to find the perfect couple to raise it.

Monica was stunned with the idea of adoption, and every cell in her body cried no. But after hearing all that a loving mother and father could give to her child, Monica relented. She was still unbelievably sad about giving up her baby, but Nico made it sound like a day at Disneyland – complete with prizes.

"You won't regret this", he said when he was leaving.

"I hope not." They hugged before he left her apartment, and while she was standing there with a dozen questions whirling around her mind, his mind was already counting the money.

As soon as he was alone, Nico made a fist with his left hand and pulled it down from his face. At the same time, he had lifted his knee up to meet his elbow, as if he had just won something. "Yes!" he shouted. Nico gushed with joy as he straightened his body and skipped down the sidewalk.

The very next day, Nico parked his car outside of Walter's home. He had been sitting there for two hours, when he saw the front door open. When he watched Walter go into his car and drive away, Nico's face lit up like a Christmas tree.

Walter had never in a million years, thought that he'd see his old friend again. Their friend Rudy had mentioned that Nico had been in the bar once or twice, but nobody knew if he lived in the area or was trying to get in touch with Walter.

Walter had hoped that he'd never see Nico again, but then …

Walter was in a grocery store, minding his own business, when he looked up to see his old cell mate standing in front of him. When Nico approached him, this frightened the hell out of him, for he had no idea that Nico knew of his whereabouts.

"Hello, my old friend", he stated loud and clear. Nico loved the look on Walter's face – it was priceless, like he'd just seen a ghost.

Walter's mouth flew open in total shock, and he wasn't sure that he wanted to talk or rekindle old times. "Um, Hi!" he babbled. He then turned his back towards Nico and tried to continue his shopping. In reality, he was panicking and he wanted very desperately to run and hide.

Nico came closer and spoke quickly, while proposing the idea of Walter and his wife adopting a healthy, newborn child. Once he was finished his short speech, Walter had somewhat relaxed, and was now listening with both ears. With their sordid past being mysteriously pushed aside, they stood even closer, as Walter confessed to their fertility problems.

"Evelyn and I have tried for years to have a child together, but it hasn't been working", he began. "We truly believed that we would never have the opportunity to raise a child together, until today."

"And I can make that happen, and I will handle all of the paperwork", Nico promised. He pointed an index finger towards Walter's chest, as an added assurance to his claim.

It was too much to hope for, and Walter couldn't believe it. At first he thought it was just another one of Nico's schemes and he didn't want any part of it. But after calling his wife and telling her what was going on, they agreed to do it.

"The one stipulation is that you and Nico would not have any contact with each other, after the money and paperwork was finalized", she demanded. Evelyn was adamant and wanted this to be an unbroken promise.

Both men agreed, whole-heartedly.

While it was good to see his old friend again, Nico did not want to renew their friendship, any more than Walter did. He had a good thing going with Monica, and was working towards building a future with her. For now, all he wanted was the money that he would receive from the phony adoption.

"Then shake hands and let's do this!" Evelyn shouted through the phone.

"Really?" Walter asked. He couldn't remember the last time that he had been so happy.

"Yes!" she shouted. Glorious happiness flooded her heart, and she hoped that this was the answer to her prayers.

Walter's eyes began to glisten with salt water, as the corners of his wife's eyes crinkled with utter joy. They were going to be blessed with the baby that they'd always wanted, and they couldn't wait.

"Thanks, man!" Walter reached out to shake his friend's hand. He then leaned his head into Nico's shoulder and patted him on the back. "Really, thanks."

"Hey! I'm glad that this worked out." And Nico meant it in every way possible; Walter and his wife would finally have the baby they've always wanted, and Nico was going to have a monthly deposit in his bank account. Nico's smile was real, for he was grateful that his plan had turned out to be so easy to execute.

They walked away from each other as promised, and only had contact on the 25th of every month – the day when Nico received the money from the prospective parents for the private adoption.

Walter would have felt better if Nico hadn't been involved, but months later, when they got the phone call that told them that their baby was being born, Walter loved Nico in more ways than it was possible.

Walter and his wife rushed to the hospital, and waited for the moment when they could take their precious little bundle home. Nico was nowhere in sight when they saw their baby for the first time, and that was fine with Walter... and Evelyn.

*When she first met her future husband, Evelyn wanted to know about his past. Walter was reluctant to tell her all that he had done, but he did share a few tidbits of information about the time he had hung around with Nico. Walter also added when and why they had ended their friendship, and that's how Evelyn knew that Nico was bad news.*

There was a brand new baby in her arms, and after the last two payments were made, Evelyn hoped to never see or hear Nico's name again.

Walter adored the baby boy from the first moment he laid his eyes on him. His own dad wasn't emotionally there for him when he was a child, so he vowed to be the best father on the planet for his son.

Evelyn did not expect to fall in love with that precious baby so hard, but she did. She couldn't help but look at him, and then at her husband. They were now a family instead of a couple, and life was better than it ever had been before.

Walter loved Oliver with all his heart and soul, and never got tired of playing with his son. He was often seen getting down on his hands and knees when Oliver was learning to sit and crawl. When the boy was 2 and 3 years old, father and son colored and sang songs. They went for walks or long drives, and talked about everything that they saw. Every night at bedtime, Walter read stories while Oliver looked at the pictures. In the mornings, they ate breakfast together while watching cartoons. And then one day, their lives changed.

Walter noticed that his wife's daily routines were becoming too difficult for her to manage, so he suggested that she get checked out.

"I'm fine", she protested. "But maybe it won't hurt to see what the doctor says."

They were both devastated to hear that the doctor's findings were very grim, and that he didn't give her much more time to be on this earth.

"I'm so sorry", the doctor recited for the millionth time in his career. "If there was anything we could do …."

Walter's world was shattered, and he opted to stay home and care for Evelyn, when she could no longer walk around on her own. He thought about hiring a nurse, but that was too expensive. Plus, he wanted to be with his wife as much as possible.

Evelyn Ryng was the backbone of the family, and the person who kept the house running smoothly. When her energy levels dropped even more in the next two months, and then she developed breathing problems, she lost her will to live.

Walter worked around the clock to keep the happiness in the house going strong, but it was becoming very hard. She was his life, and he dreaded the thought of losing her. Each time when Walter walked out of the room, he made sure that his son was there to keep Evelyn company. From another room, he could hear them talking and laughing and singing, and that made him smile.

Little Oliver was by his mother's side, each and every day, to keep her entertained, and so that she could see him as much as possible. Sometimes he played near her, and his giggle would make her grin with joy.

As she lay there, Evelyn couldn't help but think about the future. It broke her heart to know that her son would grow up without her, and she hoped that he would always remember how she looked and laughed. It also broke her heart to think about Walter raising their son alone. They had not been married too long, but long enough that her husband was a huge part of her soul. She would miss Walter terribly, but she loved that he would not be completely by himself.

Walter had been home for almost two months, and his boss had been breathing down his neck the whole time. "Your work is piling up and I can't keep giving it to other people!" he fumed. "It's not fair, and I won't continue to pay you if you won't come into the office."

Walter had to say no, for his wife and young son needed his full attention. "I'm sorry that you can't understand what's going on here", he remarked in anger. "My wife was there for me when I needed her, and now I have to be here for her! She's dying, as if you didn't know!"

'Click' The other end of the line went silent.

Evelyn was the only person who Walter had ever met, who truly loved and believed in him. Yes, he had been in jail for being in trouble when he was younger, but after they met, he turned his life around and he became a better person. He wanted to be better, because of her, and for her, and he did. He would not regret being fired, if it meant that he would have to choose between getting a pay cheque and spending the last few days with his wife. It was not a hard decision emotionally, but he knew it would be hard financially. Still, he felt he had no choice.

Not surprisingly, Walter lost his job a week later. He knew life would be tough, but he didn't know to what degree. He lived off of their savings, and anything that other people gave him in the way of food or money.

A month later, when the ambulance took Evelyn's body away, Walter's neighbours and friends brought even more things to the house. While that helped fill their pantry and his bank account, when Evelyn died, she took the laughter and love out the house. No-one and nothing could replenish those items.

Walter was lost without his beautiful bride; he couldn't find his emotional balance for the first few weeks, and he went through each day on autopilot. Having Oliver with him kept things more normal, but it wasn't the same; there was a huge part of his life that was now missing.

Walter tried to raise Oliver on his own, but when the money began to run out, he had no choice but to go back to work. With his tail between his legs, Walter begged his boss to reconsider his termination.

Mr. Peters, while being very reluctant to take his employee back, was sympathetic to all that his employee had gone through, and put Walter to work the following morning. Oliver was placed in a daycare, and it didn't take long before Walter missed him and began to feel guilty.

Walter worked from 8 to 5, Tuesday to Saturday. He only got to see his son from 5:20pm until they went to bed. To make them both feel better, he made sure that they had breakfast together every morning and supper together every night, but it just wasn't the same; there was always a time factor. And because everything was being clocked, it reminded Walter of prison, and he hated that feeling.

Walter despised leaving his son with strangers, and he soon realized that it wasn't fair that his son didn't have a mother or a father with him, for so many hours in the day. "That's something that we'll have to change sometime in the near future", he noted sternly. His bottom lip suddenly sucked in between his teeth, as he thought about sharing his life with another woman. "Yah, not yet", he confirmed with confidence. "It's too soon."

It was 11 months after his wife had died, when Walter had been set up on his first blind date. It was extremely awkward and it didn't go well, but he agreed to go out again, and then again. A month later, he was becoming very frustrated, for the women who he was meeting, were definitely not suitable to be wives or even mothers.

"You're just too fussy", his co-worker grunted. It was Friday night and Walter's friend had ordered him to go out and have a drink with him. "Don't make it so complicated – have fun!" he ordered.

James was a 41-year old, dedicated bachelor, who prided himself on bedding a woman from every country in the world. "Love'em and leave'em, is my motto!" he joked.

But Walter didn't want to have a different woman in his life every week. Not only was it confusing, but he actually just wanted one person, who both he and Oliver could see on a daily basis. "Someone that I can bond with, laugh with, and grow old with", he reported. He also wanted his son to have a good mother.

"Jeez, Louise!" James shouted as he gazed across the crowded room. "Look what just walked in."

Walter turned his head to see what his friend was looking at.

Before the two women could weed out the attractive and/or available men from the losers, James had elegantly raced to their feet.

"Evening, ladies!" he stated in a slightly drunken stupor. He bowed in their presence, as if he was on stage and performing for a grand audience. "If I may bring you over here, we have a delightful table and two charming gentlemen to keep you company."

The ladies were quite flattered and agreed to join them.

"My name is James, and this is my friend, Walter." He laid his hand flat on the table, palm-side up, and moved it closer to his co-worker.

The girls said HI and introduced themselves as they sat down.

"Now, what'll you have to drink?" James inquired sincerely. He looked at one and then the other, trying to choose which one he would target.

"Rum and coke", they stated at the exact same time. Everyone laughed, which broke the tension between them.

The girls were thrilled to be getting their first two drinks paid for, and they had to admit that the company was better than they had originally assumed it would be.

James was happy to spend money on two women who looked like they were interested in having a good time, but Walter just wanted to drink and talk.

James had a knack for grasping which girls were easy, so he chose to devote his attention to Eloise. This left Arlene to get to know Walter.

"I guess you're stuck with me", he joked. Walter grabbed his glass and took a large gulp of his rum and coke, and hoped that she would have something funny to say.

"If you ask me, I think I got the better end of the deal." Arlene winked, and when she flashed her perfect smile, he had to agree.

She was about his age, very sweet, very attentive, and she was well-groomed. She didn't have to fuss with her hair, as it was short and stayed perfectly in place. Her make-up was delicate, as were her hands, and she was soft-spoken but direct. Turns out, she was a basketball enthusiast, and she could recite all the stats on the most popular players in the league.

Walter was a little surprised by her talent. "Is that the only sport you like to watch?" he asked. He found her interesting, and wanted to know a little more about her.

Arlene loved that Walter gave her his full attention. He wasn't one of those men who needed to talk loud for other people to know he was there, and he wasn't flirting with her enough to scare her away. He could talk sports, but he knew more about mechanical things and working with his hands. He seemed like a nice handsome guy, even in a dimly lit room such as this one.

Walter was having a lovely time chatting with Arlene, and he asked her out on another date.

Arlene had found him charming and said yes, without any hesitation.

It was 11pm when they all parted ways, and Arlene shouted out, "See you on Friday!"

As Walter waved good-bye, he truly believed that they had had a connection. When he drove away, Walter reminisced about all that he had learned about her - she had a warm personality, she was a first grade teacher, they seemed to have a lot in common, and she made him laugh a few times.

The days leading up to their first real date were flying by, and Walter had a happy anxiety feeling in the pit of his stomach. He worried that he was cheating on Evelyn, but then Walter realized that he needed to find a mom for his son. If he found a woman that he could be happy with in the process, he was sure that his wife would approve. At least he hoped so; it was very hard to move forward, but it was something that he knew he had to do.

Finally, it was one hour before Walter was off work and he could go to pick Arlene up. He was nervous, but happy at the prospect of seeing where this would lead.

Unfortunately, one hour into their date, they talked about their jobs and she confided that she hated being a teacher. Arlene felt it was despicable how the kids couldn't behave, how they never listened, how they constantly talked back, and how they were always getting sick.

"Before I had to be around them for 6 hours a day, I always liked kids." She spoke the words as if she had something foul tasting in her mouth. "Now I can't wait until the final bell rings, so I can go home." She glanced at the ceiling as she confessed her true feelings, and it felt as if she was relieved to finally be able to share what was in her heart.

Walter's mouth flew open in total disbelief, as he slowly shook his head from side-to-side. He didn't know what to say, so he continued to listen.

"And the summers!" she groaned, louder than she should have. Arlene was becoming too relaxed and careless, and she lost control of how much information she was giving out. "I get two months off every year, and you can bet I go somewhere where it's quiet and there are no kids."

Walter was heartbroken by what he was hearing. He couldn't believe that he had been so wrong about her. As he sat there, he was slowly becoming an emotional wreck. Inside, he was kicking himself for thinking that, because she was a teacher, she would like kids. How could he have been so wrong?

"Where do you go on your vacations?" she asked with mild interest. She sounded like she wanted to hear his answer, but her entire attention was focused on how to stab the greasy meat item, which was sliding around on her plate.

"I haven't been able to get away for a while." His voice was quiet when he spoke, and he wished for their date to be over; Walter had just about had enough. He looked down at his almost-empty platter and sulked while he ate the rest of his meal.

"Oh, that's too bad. We should plan to go away together." In her mind, Arlene could already see them as a couple, and hoped that he felt the same way. She began to list all the places that she'd already been to, and then listed all the places that she was looking forward to going to, and why.

He continued to listen to her for the next 20 minutes, but he never lifted his head. Walter was making his own list of things to do - #1 how he could leave the table without causing a scene.

Arlene had chatted non-stop for a very long time. She then noticed that her date had not contributed anything to their conversation for quite a few minutes. "Hello?" she sang towards him. When he didn't react, Arlene reached her arm over and knocked playfully on the top of his head. "Are you still here?"

Walter was now fed up, and he could no longer keep his emotions to himself. He grabbed the table with both hands, and kicked the chair out from under him with the back of his knees. "I'm sorry, but I just don't think that this is going to work out", he said as he stood up. He knew his words were harsh and his tone was filled with anger, but he didn't care. He threw several large bills onto the table, and then he turned and walked away.

Arlene was quite embarrassed and not happy to be left alone at the table. "Um, what just happened?" she asked with sincere surprise. She then watched as her date moved his body towards the front door of the restaurant. Up until that childish outburst, she thought that the evening was going very well.

Walter was livid as he walked to his car, but he drove home happy with his decision. He was disappointed that Arlene was not the woman who he thought she would be, and he was proud that he had found that out in time.

Over the next few days, every time he looked into his little boy's gorgeous face, Walter realized that he needed to keep trying to find Oliver a mom.

And one day, without even trying, that woman came into his life.

# Chapter 11

Penny Haberdash was a 21-year old, single girl, who always happened to be at the right place at the right time. The first thing that Walter noticed is that she had a wonderful sense of humor, they got along very well, and she said she loved kids. She stood just a bit shorter than he did, had a slender body shape, she was very pretty, and extremely attentive and kind. Most importantly, she had helped Walter find his smile again.

Penny met Walter, purely by accident. They were both in the same part of the grocery store at the same time, and she couldn't help but see that he looked lost. "Are you ok?" she asked innocently enough.

Without making eye contact, he replied softly, "I've been doing the shopping for a while now, but I still don't always know what I'm doing. It used to be, that when I was lost, I could ask my wife where to find things and she would tell me. Since she died, I struggle to do this by myself."

Penny's heart broke as she listened to his sad confession, as it did to the two other women who were standing within ear shot. All three ladies sighed with sadness at his loss, and all three wanted to help. But because Penny was already standing beside him, she was the one who got to assist him. "I'll help you", she offered with genuine kindness. She grabbed the thick strands of hair that hung in front of her shoulders, and moved them behind her.

Because she was curious, she peeked into his buggy and saw that the bread was laying underneath the carton of eggs. "Oops!" she gasped, which caught his attention. It was the first time that he had truly seen her face.

"Do you mind if I move a few things around?" she asked nonchalantly. Without waiting for him to reply, she reached into the shopping cart with both hands and reversed the order of a few of his groceries. "There!" she exclaimed, once it was to her liking. After she stood up again, she immediately adjusted her loose hair and her flimsy tank top.

Walter had been amazed by her candor, and now he was startled by how old he guessed her to be. Because of how smooth and wrinkle-free her skin was, he estimated her to be in her very early twenties. He hoped that she wasn't younger than that. "Thank you", he stated politely. Walter greatly approved of her decisions, and of her willingness to help him.

"You're welcome", she replied. Her voice was soft and lovely. "Now, what else do you need?" She stood directly in front of him, and studied all of the features on his handsome face. After giving him the entire once-over, she approved of the man in front of her, and decided to continue to help him.

Walter had to think. He realized that he had no lunch meat or other items to make sandwiches with, so that's where he needed to be directed to. "Do you want to help me find the best strawberry jam?" He was serious when he posed the question, and was surprised when Penny offered to walk with him.

"Sure", she giggled - like a teenager whose best friend had just asked her if she wanted to go to a movie with the hottest guy in class. Penny was content to go with Walter, and was starting to see that he was a very nice man.

They exchanged a few sentences while they strolled around, and twenty minutes later, she was walking him out to his car. After seeing that it was in decent shape and that it was well-taken care of, she decided that he was worth being nice to. As soon as everything had been placed in the trunk of his car, the pretty woman pretended to walk away. "Bye!" she called over her shoulder in a careless fashion. Penny was facing forward, but she made extra sure that her hips swayed side to side, just for his benefit.

Walter liked what he saw. He also liked having her opinion on things, and he felt strangely comfortable in her company. As she began to walk away from him, he felt a weird loss and immediately called out. "Hey!" he barked. She had helped him when he needed it, and now he wanted to do something nice for her in return.

Penny turned around, and while her eyes widened with pretend astonishment, her smile glowed with total satisfaction; her plan had worked to perfection.

Walter was very pleased that she had stopped walking. "Can I cook you dinner? I mean, as a thank you for what you've done for me today?" He hadn't counted on her saying yes, but he wanted to at least make the effort.

Penny's face spoke volumes about how she was feeling. "I'm free on Friday, if that works for you", she suggested boldly. She now waited to see if he would take the bait.

Walter knew that Oliver was going for a sleep-over on Friday night, so he agreed. He wrote down his address and they said good-bye. "See you around 7pm!" he called after her. He was smiling as he got into his car, and hoped that he was doing the right thing.

"See you then!" she called. Penny felt victorious. She could almost feel the dollar bills rushing into her hands, but she realized that she would need to play it safe – he was old, and he might be able to see through her games. Therefore, she made herself promise to be on her best behavior on Friday, to ensure that he would ask her out on a real date. After that, she would play it by ear. If all went well, she hoped to have him eating out of her hand, in no time at all.

Penny had arrived at his home on time and smelling glorious, and she had taken every opportunity to act sexy. The dinner went well, as they both hoped it would, and they ended the evening in bed. It wasn't Walter's decision to do so, but Penny had worn the right clothes and had said all the right words.

*Penny was young and willing, and she knew exactly what she was doing. When she spoke, she moved her lips in a very suggestive way, and she kept her voice soft and slow. She moved her body in a provocative manner, to accentuate certain parts more than others. She used her finger tips to touch his skin very softly, and in places where he probably hadn't been touched in years. By maintaining eye contact with him, she was guaranteed to have his full attention, and hopefully, his keen interest and anticipation of what else she had to offer. She did all of this in order to entice him into doing whatever she wanted him to do, and she had no doubt that it was working.*

Walter had not expected the evening to end up in bed, and he was extremely nervous at the mere thought of making love again. But while Penny had taken the liberty to undress him, he couldn't help but get involved.

Penny was experienced and bold, and she made sure to give him a night to remember. Her energy level was high, and she was attentive and quite experimental. She left his home the next morning, knowing full well that she had made an impression.

Walter drove to work the next morning, feeling happier than he'd been in a long time. He was beaming from ear-to-ear, and nothing had been able to wipe the smirk off his face. Not the traffic, which was backed-up for miles, not the fact that the gas tank might be too low for him to drive another ten minutes, and not the fact that he didn't have enough change to buy his coffee – he was 10 cents short. Lucky for him, the 34-year old clerk in the drive-thru window really liked him, and she giggled when she told him to keep his money. "It's on the house today."

People at work also noticed that he'd gotten his color and smile back, and they wondered what had happened. "I'm seeing someone", was all he would offer. His friends and co-workers were delighted and wished him well. "It's about time!" someone shouted.

Penny continued to see Walter on a regular basis, and she did everything in her power to make sure that he would fall in love with her.

Walter wasn't a player, and he didn't want to be with anyone but Penny. Because he didn't see any point in waiting, it didn't take him long before he asked her to 'go steady'.

Penny tilted her head while looking confused, which made Walter giggle.

"I'm asking if you would be my girl", he chuckled. He pulled her body towards his and gave her a big hug.

"Oh my gosh, yes!" she cried. With a happy heart and a huge smile, she laughed and cried at the same time.

"Thank you." Walter got down on one knee and looked up and into her eyes. He then presented her with a beautiful bracelet of moderate wealth and said, "To commemorate the moment".

Penny admired it and knew that she would treasure it forever, but she secretly had it appraised the following week. She found out that it wasn't worth as much as she had hoped it would be, but she was sure that she could get him to spend some serious cash on her, sometime in the near future. If not, she would need to step up her game, if she wanted him to marry her.

They continued to date for another month, before Walter decided that it was time to make an announcement. He didn't want to scare her away, but because he was now ready to make her a permanent part of his life, he felt that she needed to know something that he had been keeping from her.

He gathered up all of his courage and took a very deep breath. He let it out slowly, drank down a solid shot of whiskey, and then he blurted it out. "I'm sorry that I haven't told you before now, but I have a son." His voice was shaky and he stumbled over the words when he spit them out, and then he stayed quiet and studied his girlfriend's reaction.

While Penny was a bit taken back by this new crumb of information, she decided to play along. It was difficult to pretend that she was okay with him having a child, but after a few seconds of absolute surprise, she plastered a fake smile on her very pretty face, and she expressed excitement about there being a little nuisance in her plan. "Oh, my goodness!" she remarked, as happily as she could. She looked Walter straight in the eye, brought her hands up to his cheeks, pulled him closer, and kissed him square on the lips. "How wonderful! A mini-you!" she stated, when they pulled apart.

As Penny sat back, she batted her long eyelashes in Walter's direction. This gave her a few seconds to reflect on the situation. She then asked him how old the boy was, what his interests were, and where he was in that very moment.

*Unbeknownst to Penny, Walter had been talking to his son for the past few weeks, about a special woman that he had been spending a lot of time with. He wanted to see what Oliver's reaction would be, before he asked Penny and Oliver to meet. Thankfully, Oliver expressed that he was happy about someone coming over, and he hoped that she would want to play with him. Walter chuckled at Oliver's innocence, and assured his son that she just might.*

Walter answered each question in order, and was slowly feeling better and better about how she was taking the news. After he felt comfortable enough, Walter invited Penny to come over on another day, specifically to meet Oliver.

"I'd love to", she replied, in her Oscar-winning, best actress voice and manner. Penny was not good with kids, especially little boys, but she knew that this man had a lot to offer and she was not about to let him get away without a fight. "Shall we say sometime on Saturday?" She was acting sweet and coy, and desperately wanted him to believe that she was happy about him having a son. Inside though, she was seething, and her mind was overflowing with reasons why she should or shouldn't leave the situation.

"Oh, good!" Walter sighed with relief. "Saturday is perfect for me!" He was very pleased with how this conversation had ended. He had hoped that she wouldn't act irrational when he told her about his son, and because she didn't, his worries were now floating away.

Penny was not as happy as she wanted Walter to think she was, and she began to panic. She knew she couldn't keep the fake routine up for too much longer, so she pretended that the room had suddenly become too hot for her. As she fanned herself with her hands, it gave her a minute to consider her options.

Penny didn't want any of Walter's thoughts to be on his son, and she soon realized that she needed to convince her boyfriend that she was the best thing in his life. Penny changed the subject in the next breath, and then pushed all of her enthusiasm on her meal ticket.

"That's better", she sighed, making believe that the room had suddenly cooled down. "Now, let's concentrate on us", she sighed, as sensually as she knew how. She walked close enough to him, that her large breasts were pressed up against his chest. She then ran the fingers from her left hand thru his dark hair, while her other hand undid the buttons on the front of his shirt. As precise as she knew how, she placed slow and soft kisses on his lips, his neck, and his collar bone, and then all the way down his chest and tummy. The sensations from what she was doing, made another part of his body come to attention.

Walter's mouth couldn't help but release a loud moan, as his mind was suddenly diverted to grown-up activities. He loved how focused she was, and it didn't take long before his hands were beginning to undress her. Minutes later, the world and everyone in it, disappeared. And just like that, Penny had won.

The emotions on the three days leading up to the introductions, were different for everyone concerned; Walter was excited to see how his son and girlfriend would interact, and Penny was nervous about pulling off the greatest acting job of her life.

The ambience on Saturday was filled with fear, for no-one knew how the meeting would go. However, almost 30-minutes after the opening 'hellos', Walter felt like he could relax; Oliver was smiling and behaving very well and Penny seemed to like being around them both. Walter was pleasantly surprised by how well their first meeting was going.

An hour after Penny had met Walter's son, she felt that she had accomplished her best performance of all time.

And she had to, because she knew it was a sure bet that the father would not continue their relationship if Oliver did not like her. But because the boy was a real treasure, it wasn't too hard for Penny to be nice to him.

Oliver was stunningly handsome, he had a bubbly personality, he was smart, and he was also terribly inquisitive. Anyone could see that he was a handful, but Penny thought it was strange that he didn't look anything like his father. As she studied the little boy further, she noticed that he seemed to want a lot of attention, and she wondered if it would always be like that.

*Penny had done too much prep work to walk away now, and she always needed to be number one in a man's life. But if she couldn't make that happen, she would have to make a few changes in the dynamics of their little threesome.*

As Penny watched the amazing interaction between father and son, she questioned what her role would be in the house. Would she be a full-time mom with no other life beyond raising a child? Would they still have date nights, just the two of them? Or would they do everything as a family?

Penny couldn't help but see how much Walter and Oliver loved each other. They had a connection between them that might be hard for her to break. Because they acted as if they were the only two people on the planet, and Penny was the 'new kid on the block', she wondered if she would always feel like the odd man out.

Penny was young and strong, and not interested in being a mom with no actual rewards. If she decided to stay in this relationship, she knew that she would have to devise a plan where she would end up with the best of both worlds – being a wife and having a ton of money, without having to suffer with the humdrum chores of being a mom.

As Penny watched the banter between Walter and Oliver, she knew that she would have to cope with whatever was going to be thrown at her, in order to continue to be Walter's girlfriend. She appreciated how hard the days ahead might be, but if she wanted to walk away with a fistful of money, she needed to keep them both happy – father and son.

She got down on the floor beside them, and tried to be especially nice. "You sure are a cutie", she giggled, as she let her fingers move freely through the little boy's unruly hair.

Walter looked at his little family, and he loved how things were progressing. He liked how Penny and Oliver were getting along, and he appreciated how having her in his life these past few months, prevented him from wilting away. Because of her fresh energy and ultimate charms, he was kept happy, and busy enough to walk through his mourning period with some degree of contentment.

Yes, she was young, but not too young for Oliver – that was the most important part of this whole adventure. Oliver needed a mom, someone with a lot of energy to be with while Walter was at work. More importantly, Oliver seemed to like her.

Because Penny had been able to make Walter's nights more vibrant than ever, it was becoming quite clear to him, that Penny might need to become a permanent part of the family.

After Penny and Walter put Oliver to bed that night, Walter took Penny to his bedroom. This time it was Walter who took the lead, to show her his appreciation for how well the evening had turned out. An hour later, the blanket got thrown off of their sweaty bodies, and Walter asked Penny to spend the night. "Only if you want to", he added with hesitation. "You've never been here when Oliver was here — it'll be different", he promised. "But I hope you'll say yes."

Penny smiled at the thought of waking up beside him, and kissed his lips a dozen times, before giving him her answer. "Of course I will."

When Walter strolled into work the following day, he did so with a giddy expression on his face that looked like he'd won the largest lottery on record. Just thinking about how everything was working out for him and Oliver, made him so very happy.

James watched Walter saunter to his desk, and he leaped out of his own seat to ask him what was up.

With a huge grin on his face, Walter confided that he was thinking of asking Penny to marry him.

James kidded his friend for wanting to be tied down again, but even he had to agree that Penny was a very nice girl. "A keeper!" he stated more than once. "Congratulations!"

James had only met Penny on two occasions, and while he thought she was a little young for Walter, she seemed to make him happy. Since that was good enough for James, he gave Walter his blessing, with a strong, two-handed handshake.

"Thanks!" Walter was more than pleased by his friend's approval. Not that he needed someone to give it, but it was well-received. Now that both Oliver and James have supported the idea of Penny coming into the family, it was time to put a ring on her finger. After buying the beautiful, white gold band with a single diamond, Walter needed to find a romantic setting.

A family member suggested that they go on a cruise. Walter loved the idea, so the trip was booked and everything was planned. After the details had been finalized, Walter took Penny out for supper, to tell her all about the cruise.

"I'd love to go!" she assured him loudly. Penny was more than delighted about going on a trip, for it meant that she was that much closer to having his money in her hands. And just as quickly as she had gotten excited, she thought of Oliver, and her bubble burst.

Penny didn't want to become the boy's babysitter, so she fought through the next few minutes of bittersweet anxiety. She plastered an expression of gratitude on her pretty face, while her mind took the time to create a plan. And then it hit her - an idea that she knew Walter would hate, but it would bring her closer to being number one in his life. "Because we aren't married, we would need to have two separate cabins", she stated sweetly. She now waited to see how this news would be received.

Walter loved that they would be close in proximity, but he hoped that Oliver would be the one placed in the adjoining cabin, not Penny. It took him a few minutes to wrap his head around what she was saying, and then he nodded his head in agreement. "Yes, I can see that it would work better that way, as long as you are ok with this arrangement."

Penny couldn't be more okay about this, and practically shouted her answer. "Oh, yes. I'm ok with this." She hoped that after a few days on the ship, that Walter would want to switch cabin-mates, for very obvious reasons. And she would do so, in order to gain the #1 position in his heart.

"Alright! Let's do it!" he shouted.

They hugged and kissed, and then their minds went off in different directions. Penny's thoughts were now spinning with relief that she was not going to be the 24-hour-a-day mom to Walter's child. As she thought about all that the ship would have to offer, her eyes welled up with happiness.

Walter could not have thought about Oliver being anywhere else, but sharing the same room or being in the adjoining cabin, so this arrangement was perfect. And in that same moment, Walter could honestly say that he had developed a love for Penny that he didn't think would happen. Along with her other amazing qualities, he now saw her as being selfless and thoughtful – acts that made him want to show her how much he appreciated her, and how she made him feel.

Penny knew she was close to achieving what she had set out to do, and now she couldn't wait to get on the ship. Because she had been exceptionally nice to both Walter and his son these past few weeks, she hoped that Walter would foot the bill for everything and anything she wanted. It had never been clearly stated, but she was inclined to believe that he would, and she tested him every few days, just to be sure. Her short declaration was uttered in a faked innocent voice and manner, and it usually ended with, "I sure hope I have enough spending money to last me for the entire trip."

Walter would always turn to her and smile, and then he gently stroked her face or hair, with love emanating from the skin of his hand. As he locked eyes with his beautiful girlfriend, he spoke to her in a soft tone, and tried to convince her that it has all been taken care of. "You don't have to worry about that, sweetheart; your only job is to be happy."

That phrase made her relax, each and every time he said it. It also helped her to continue to do whatever she needed, in order to be thought of as another person in their family.

Five weeks later, the threesome boarded their cruise to Alaska – Penny in her cabin, and Walter and Oliver in theirs.

# *Chapter 12*

Penny had gone shopping on the Lido Deck, while Walter spent some quality time playing with Oliver. They had picked the hour when they would all meet back at the cabin, which is where Walter and Oliver were heading when Nico saw them.

Walter was waiting for the elevator and his mind was completely occupied with tomorrow's swimming date with Oliver. Walter was also on the look-out for the right place and moment to propose to Penny. So when Nico had spotted him standing a few feet away, Walter surely didn't see him.

Nico, however, was in total disbelief when he saw Walter. For in those few moments before the elevator doors had opened, Nico's heart was pounding as loud as a drum, and he couldn't even imagine the damage that would have followed, had Walter recognized him.

As soon as Walter stepped inside of the elevator, Nico released a long puff of air from his lungs, and then quickly made his way back to his cabin.

Monica had spent the last hour or so, walking around the ship. She poked her head into every venue, and wondered if she would run into the father or the little boy again. She had practiced a few opening lines in her head, but none seemed like the correct thing to say. And just when she was about to give up hope of ever finding them, she spotted a man and a child walking a little ways ahead of her.

Monica's face broke out into a smile and she picked up her pace in order to catch up to them.

Walter had gotten off on the 4$^{th}$ floor, and guided his son to cabin H4089. Penny arrived at Walter's cabin ten minutes later, and they each talked about their last two hours on the ship.

"I'm hungry", Oliver noted.

"Me too." Walter checked the time and he agreed that it was time to go and eat.

Penny made sure to give them each a kiss on their cheek, as she said good-bye and went to her own room. She then spoke softly while reminding them to be on time. "See you soon", she stated lovingly but firmly.

"In 40 minutes", Walter noted. "Promise."

"Promise", Oliver repeated, and he added a smile.

Walter placed his hand on his son's back, and urged him say good-bye. Once the door to Penny's cabin had closed, Walter made his way to the double bed and fell backwards onto the extra-thick, soft duvet.

"Daddy? Can I turn the TV on?" Oliver asked playfully. He loved being on the ship, and he loved spending so much time with his dad.

Walter had his eyes closed tightly, and muttered something which could have been mistaken for another language.

Oliver had seen that look on his father's face before, and he knew that it meant his dad wanted to be left alone for a few minutes. Oliver picked up the remote control, turned the TV on, and clicked through the channels until he found something funny to watch.

Walter's mind was jumping between being confused and clear minded, and it felt like he had butterflies going around in circles in his stomach. Up until the past few weeks, Walter had been able to cope with Penny's unusual need to have his undivided company. But lately, the time he spent with her wasn't enough. When she begged to have more and he said no, she would pout. He would then offer to buy her gifts to ease her sadness, and the more expensive the gift was, the better she would reward him. Walter wondered if Penny was jealous of the attention which Walter was giving to Oliver.

Penny was also making him spend money that he really couldn't afford to let go of. She wasn't working, and he understood that he was supporting her, but suddenly, there were more expenses than he had planned on having. Was Penny doing this to spite him for not spending as much time with her as she would like? Walter didn't know, but it worried him.

Walter let out a small groan of misery. He then covered his face with his hands and hoped that the spending would slow down after they were married.

*The day after Penny had been introduced to Oliver, she phoned around in search of a housekeeper and a babysitter. This was to ensure that those jobs would not be delegated to her in the future. Penny would keep the father happy, so that he could provide her with the things that she needed. Otherwise, the household duties were not her business.*

*Walter paid for the housekeeper to come three times a week, from 9am to 3pm. The babysitter was a live-in, and her only task was to take care of Oliver – from when he woke up until suppertime. The homely, middle-aged woman insisted on having Sundays off, which Penny was not happy about, but she agreed to, in order to keep Oliver out of her hair.*

*Next, Penny searched for camps for Oliver to go to, for whenever he had time off from school. 'No need for him to hang around the house, if he could be off playing with other kids', she decided in private.*

*After Walter had been told of Penny's ideas, he developed some emotional and financial worries about how this would all work out. Penny seduced him and promised him that it would all be okay. Since Penny was not working, she promised to be at his home as much as possible, to make sure that everything would work out smoothly.*

*But no matter how Penny manipulated the situation or Walter, the financial aspect weighed heavily on Walter's mind – too much money was going out, and not enough was coming in.*

*By day four, everyone agreed that it was a perfect arrangement – the house was spotless, Oliver was happy, and an amazing supper was on the table every single night. From 5:30 to 8pm, Walter could devote all of his attention to Oliver, and after the child went to bed, it was then Penny's turn to get Walter's complete consideration.*

*When they were alone, Penny gave Walter more happiness than he had ever bargained for, which made him feel like it was all worth it.*

*But a week later, Penny began to turn into a different woman. The 'woman-of-leisure' was no longer forced to play with Oliver, as that was the job of the babysitter. And on the odd occasion when Penny did speak with Oliver, her tone was hurried and not as soft as it had been before. Cooking and cleaning were also things that Penny was not required to do, which left her days available for manicures, hair-cuts, and/or shopping.*

*Oliver had noticed a few other changes since Penny had come to live with them, but because he had been brought up to be kind and polite, the intelligent young boy made sure to smile outwardly, whenever she was near him. What people didn't see, was that he cringed every time he heard her voice. He loved his father and he saw how happy this woman was making him, so he kept quiet and hoped that his dad would eventually find out the truth.*

*Oliver was delighted when his father announced that they were going on a cruise, but he was surprised that Penny would be going with them. His father's face was full of happiness as he delivered the details, so Oliver smiled and acted like it was going to be fun. "Great, dad!" He threw his arms around his father's neck, and squeezed him really hard. "Thanks!"*

*As Penny watched the happy moment, she stood back and plastered a fake smile on her face.*

*Walter tried to bring Penny into the embrace, but she protested. "Come on!" he declared. "This is a happy moment!" He stretched his hand out to bring her closer, but Penny walked away, explaining that she didn't want to intrude.*

*Secretly, she would show Walter her appreciation later, when they were alone. She wasn't concerned about the boy or his feelings, for he had nothing to offer. Her focus was to make the father happy, and when the time came, she would do what she has always done in the past – end things, and walk away with a ton of money.*

*It was in that moment when Penny turned her back, that Walter first noticed that something was going on. Penny's new mood and all the needless spending, was beginning to drive a wedge between them. He hoped that after they were married, that things would go back to how they were a few months ago. For now, he would put Oliver to bed and try to talk with Penny.*

*Penny knew what she was doing. She quickly apologized and Walter accepted, but even though things appeared to be better between them, underneath, Walter wondered if they really were.*

'Is that what I want?' Walter thought to himself, while examining the situation. 'Penny is so young, and she thinks money grows on trees. I want things to feel more natural, like when Evelyn was alive.' Walter paused when her name came up. 'Should I really get married so soon after burying my sweet Evelyn? Had enough time passed for me to move forward with my life?' The questions stung like bee bites, but he didn't have the answers.

"Look, dad!" Oliver's animated voice cheered. "Ha-ha-ha!" The boy had his left hand on his belly and was leaning forward in a strong laugh.

Walter raised his head, but it was not what was on the TV that caught his attention. It was when he heard his son's laughter that he knew what he had to do. The house was clean, the food was bought and cooked, and Oliver needed a mother. Penny had done all of that. What is better than a young wife who has the energy or fortitude to keep them both happy?

Walter laid his head back down on the bed again, and his thoughts drifted back to his girlfriend. He knew that it was silly to hang out with someone who was so much younger than himself, and he couldn't quite figure out what she saw in him, but they certainly seemed to enjoy spending time together. And although she was very needy and very lovely, she wasn't as hands-on with Oliver as Walter had hoped she'd be. Walter suddenly changed directions, as he realized that she was very appreciative to all that he had to offer. And in time, who knows? Maybe Penny and Oliver will be better friends.

"Dad, look!" the boy called again. *The coyote in the cartoon was being chased by a roadrunner, and the coyote was about to be crushed by a huge anvil - much to the delight of the young boy.* "Dad!" he called, as he turned around. "Are you watching?"

Walter sat up, and with the fingers on his left hand, he tousled the thick hair on his son's head. "Yes, Oliver, and I hope he doesn't get caught", he laughed.

It had been hours since Monica had seen Nico, and suddenly a cold chill had engulphed her entire body. Before she could speak, she noticed that the sun was going down. "What time is it?" she asked to no-one in particular. Monica was surprised when she checked her watch and found that it was almost suppertime. "Oh my goodness!" she muttered, as if she was scolding herself. She then raced to the nearest elevator. With a look a fear on her face, she hoped that she would make it back to her cabin in time to keep her date with Nico.

Nico was surprised when he found himself waking up from a nap. "How long did I sleep?" he asked into the air. He checked his watch, and was grateful that he would have just enough time to get ready for his date with Monica.

Penny leaned her head in closer, so that she could hear the cheerful banter that was going on in the adjoining cabin. She was only a mere doorway away from where the boy and his father were enjoying a tender moment, but it felt like they were an entire building apart. And as she listened, a small part of her wished that she was in there with them, but she knew that she had to stay strong, in order to stick with her plan.

Penny turned away from the door and checked to see how she looked in her bathroom mirror. Satisfied with what she saw, she gathered her things and left her cabin. She went out into the hall and knocked on Walter's cabin door, and then shouted loud enough for them both to hear. "Are you guys ready?" Penny was all set to go upstairs for dinner, and hoped that they were, too. "Open the door!" she called, her voice had urgency written all over it. She could hear them talking and moving around in their cabin, and a slight fear of jealously touched her soul.

Penny was relieved once the door had opened; Walter and Oliver were ready, and they both looked very handsome. The family poured their compliments all around, and then they headed to the elevators.

Monica had arrived at her cabin and was now rushing around like crazy, hoping to be ready for when Nico came to get her.

Nico took an extra-long look at himself in the mirror, and swooned at his own reflection. He was pursing his lips, moving his eyebrows up and down, and making faces and kissing sounds to his own reflection. He truly enjoyed how he looked, and he hoped that Monica would agree with his perception.

When he was able to tear himself away from the perfect image, he went next door and brought his closed fist towards the solid wood. 'Knock, knock, knock'

Monica's first thought was panic. Was she ready? She hoped so. "I'll be right there", she called. She trusted that she sounded convincing.

When she swung the door open and she saw her very handsome date standing there to greet her, all the fear left her body. Monica's eyes flew wide open with surprise, as her smile widened in approval; he had totally taken her breath away.

Nico watched as her skin began to glow, and he could tell that he had impressed her. As he looked at his date, it was obvious that she had been rushed to get ready, and he admired how everything had turned out. Because he'd seen it done in the movies, he held out his elbow for her to grab. "Shall we?"

Monica was pleased, and let out a small sigh of relief. "Yes, thank you." She could now stop worrying, and start to enjoy the rest of the evening.

As they went into the elevator and then walked towards the restaurant, Nico wondered if he should tell Monica all that he had learned about the man and his little boy. He turned towards his dinner date, and when he saw how happy Monica was, Nico decided to wait until another time to mention anything. Tonight he wanted her to be totally ecstatic, with no outside interference. Tonight it would be just the two of them.

As they entered the restaurant, Monica wondered if she would see the father and his son there. She then scolded herself, for that would be foolish; there were 14 different places where people could eat on the ship.

"Good evening", the hostess said softly. "Do you have your pass key with you?"

Monica reached into her purse, found it, and extended it forward.

"Thank you." The hostess looked on her list, and then handed the plastic card back to the owner. "You'll be sitting at the back, close to the window." The hostess motioned for someone to escort Monica and Nico to their table. "Enjoy your meal."

While Monica was being seated, Nico could see that his date was scanning the room with a purpose. Was she on the lookout for the father and his child? He hoped not. "This all looks really lovely", Nico said, in a louder voice than he should have used.

Monica was shocked by his soft outburst, but she had to agree that everything did look amazing. "Yes, it does."

At another table, not too far away, a little boy had to go to the bathroom and his father opted to walk with him. As they walked passed Monica's chair, Oliver recognized the woman, and he reached out to tug on her skirt.

Monica turned around to see what she had gotten caught on, and was pleasantly surprised to see the familiar little boy. All the features in her face had now softened, as did her voice. "Hello", she said, as she reached out for him. Monica felt a blush of happiness that they had run into each again. "And how are you enjoying the cruise?"

Nico couldn't believe this unbelievable embarrassing moment. He reached for his water glass, and while he pretended to sip from it, he made sure that it covered up as much of his face as possible.

Oliver was very happy to see the kind woman who had been sunbathing, and was only too pleased to shake her hand. "I'm very well, thank you", he said.

Monica could see that he had obviously been taught good manners.

Walter was quick to notice, that this was the same woman who had become friends with Oliver. Walter also reached out to shake her hand, much to the utter annoyance of his girlfriend, who was watching from where she was sitting. "Nice to see you again", he began. "We haven't been properly introduced. I'm Walter Ryng - Oliver's father."

Nico's heart had jumped up into his throat, causing him to spit out the few drops of water which he had in his mouth. Nico had changed since they last saw each other, and he hoped that it was enough so that Walter wouldn't recognize him.

Monica was pleased that the man had remembered her. "Hi. My name is Monica, and it's nice to see you again, too." After shaking hands with the man, she turned to Nico, and saw that he was wiping his mouth with a large white, linen cloth. "Nico, this is Walter – the little boy's dad."

Nico kept the cloth against his face with one hand, while he reached over to shake Walter's hand with the other. "Nice to meet you", he said in a low and unrecognizable tone.

"Nice to meet you", Walter responded. His eyes were suddenly pressed hard into the soul of the man who was sitting on the opposite side of the table. He was sure that they knew each other, but he couldn't be 100% certain. The name rolled around in his head, but it didn't register.

"This way, please", the waiter called out. He thought that they had gotten lost, and he wanted to make sure that they arrived at the restroom. Afterall, it was their original destination.

Walter touched his son's shoulder, and guided him away. "I'm sure we'll see each other again."

"Soon!" Oliver added, as if it was an order, and then he waved in Monica's direction.

"I hope so", Monica called. She then turned her focus back to Nico.

Nico placed the napkin back onto his lap. He was livid that Walter and his son had stopped to get introductions, but he was glad that they had now walked away. "I can't wait to begin eating; it all looks so delicious", he announced loudly. Nico was trying to divert Monica's attention, so that he would be all that she thought about tonight.

"It does", she replied. Her eyes were looking at everything that was laid out in front of her, but her mind was spinning with thoughts about the boy and his father.

"She seems like a nice lady", Walter commented as they walked towards the bathroom.

"I think so, too", he replied. Oliver secretly wished that Monica would be able to play with him the next day.

Meanwhile, the future Mrs. Ryng, who had been watching them all from a distance, was relieved that her little family had walked away from that woman's table.

'How had they all known each other?' she wondered. 'Should she go over and introduce herself? Penny decided not to, as they would never be friends anyway.

When Walter and Oliver were walking back to their table, Monica could feel that Walter was looking at her in a more-than-friendly manner. "Hi, again", he chuckled. His voice was warm and inviting, and his eyes stayed glued to hers for as long as possible.

Monica could feel herself blushing. She was embarrassed by what she was feeling towards him, but she smiled and nodded in his direction. Once he had walked past her chair and then sat down at his own table, Monica heard a woman ask him what had taken them so long. Monica's mind immediately jumped to conclusions, and she couldn't help but turn and look at the woman at the table with Oliver's dad.

Nico lifted his eyes and saw that his date was watching another man. He would have liked to say something, but instead, he watched in sorrow, as Monica's expression had changed from happiness to confusion. He would have wanted to have her full attention, but he had the feeling that it wasn't going to happen in the next couple of hours.

Nico took his own turn to glance at the other table, but he was careful not to be too obvious about what he was doing. It baffled him to see how much Walter had changed in appearance and mannerisms, and Nico was quite relieved that Walter had not recognized him.

Monica had turned herself around a few times in the next hour, and each time she hoped that she was being discreet. She wanted to see how Oliver behaved with the woman at the table. 'Was that his mother?' she wondered. 'Was she a good one?' Monica hoped so, but there didn't seem to be much interaction between them at all.

Nico felt like he was being ignored, so he cleared his throat quite loudly. "How's your food?" he asked, when she turned back around. He desperately wanted to drive her focus back to their table, but he didn't know how to keep it there.

Monica blushed at the thought of being caught, but instantly found her voice. "I haven't tried anything but the fish yet, but that was delicious." She could feel that Nico was becoming slightly annoyed by her lack of attention towards him, and she hoped that he would forgive her.

"I'm glad", he replied, but he could care less about the fish. "After this, we can go dancing, if you want." He smiled in anticipation that she would say yes, and then his mind wondered how they could avoid the boy and his family for the rest of the trip.

Nico's eyes inadvertently glanced over at Walter's table yet again, and then he spotted the beautiful young woman who was sitting with Walter and his son. She must have felt him staring at her, for she turned and looked directly into Nico's eyes. This sent goose bumps throughout Nico's body, and only when she had turned away, was he able to regain his composure.

"That sounds amazing!" Monica flashed an approving smile in Nico's direction, but inside, she was thinking of ideas on how she could spend some more time with Oliver.

Nico's attention flew back to Monica's face, the second that she looked in his direction. Once she stared down at her plate, Nico took another minute to examine the lovely woman at Walter's table; she was stunning and very sexy, and he bet that she had worked hard to look that way.

Walter glanced in Monica's direction, making a note to thank her again, for being so kind to his son.

Oliver looked at his father's date, and wished that Monica was sitting at their table instead of 'this' woman, who was currently asking for the most expensive bottle of champagne that they had onboard.

Before the champagne had arrived, Penny took a minute to scan the room. Her eyes happened to land at Monica's table, and rested there for longer than they should have. After Penny had checked the woman out, she suspected that Monica could be trouble, but she didn't know to what extent. Penny was now aware that Walter and Oliver had an attraction to that woman, and this worried her. To ensure that there would still be a wedding, Penny decided to keep her little family away from the man and the woman at that other table.

While the bubbly drink was being poured, Penny thought of something that the three of them could do together. "What do you say, if after supper, we all play a board game?" She searched both of their faces for a yes, and waited for one of them to speak.

Oliver and his dad were pleasantly surprised by the idea, and agreed at the same time. "Yeah!" they shouted with their 'inside voices'. They high-fived each other to seal the deal.

"Wonderful!" Penny stated. Her face was now wearing a supreme smirk of victory, for she had won this round. And just to make sure that she still had a strong claim on Walter, she would offer to spend some 'quality time' with her man, after Oliver goes to sleep.

Walter and his family made sure to say good-night to Monica and her dinner guest, before they exited the restaurant.

"Maybe I'll see you tomorrow?" Oliver asked. He immediately crossed two fingers on both hands, in hopes that she would say yes.

"Maybe", Monica giggled. She poked him in the chest with her index finger, and he giggled right back at her.

An hour later, Oliver was tucked away in bed, and so were Walter and Penny. The night had ended very well for them, but not so well for Nico.

Nico had taken his date to the 'White Dance Hall' on the 5th floor, because he knew how much Monica loved Latin

Music. After being seated, he made sure that Monica's glass was never empty. He also made sure to order double shots in her glass, for as long as they were dancing.

Monica's hips and feet were grooving to the beat, while the alcohol was swimming through her veins. She was feeling no pain and having a lot of fun, and for the first time in a very long time, she had no thoughts on her mind, other than dancing. At one point, Monica was asked to go up on stage and dance, which made the entire audience cheer – Nico included.

Monica was drunk and having a really good time. Her intoxicated state sent a powerful release of freedom from responsibilities and her past, throughout her entire body, with no guilt attached. She was in the moment, and singing words that sounded similar to what the actual singers were saying, and she didn't care if hers were right or wrong.

Nico loved seeing how happy she was, and he treasured having her undivided attention. When the song was over, he helped her get down from the stage, where they continued to dance among the rest of the crowd.

Because of how well the evening was going, Nico would have bet that Monica might be spending the night with him. If not in the way that he had wanted, at least he had kept her mind off of Walter and his son.

Monica had been having a great deal of fun, but when she began to feel sick, she asked Nico to take her back to her room. Once they arrived, she said good-night and went inside of her cabin, alone. She threw up after the door had closed, and then cleaned herself up and climbed into bed. After drinking half of the large glass of water which she had placed on her little nightstand, she turned off the light. She passed out mere minutes later, and didn't wake up until late the next morning...surprisingly, without much of a hang-over.

After watching Monica go into her own room, Nico stood out in the hallway feeling very sorry for himself. He felt robbed of not having her much-anticipated female companionship, but he wasn't sure what he should do about it. With a look of remorse spreading across his face, he slowly stepped inside of his cabin. "This is stupid", he groaned with misery in his voice. But a few minutes later, with a crazy look in his eyes, he decided to go back out to the dance floor.

After he got there, Nico found an empty seat at the bar. He was thoroughly enjoying himself with drinks and snack foods, and then, an hour later, he took a long time to explore the body of a curvy dark-haired woman, who wanted nothing more than to be touched all over. Nico didn't even know her name, and he didn't want to; he just wanted to get laid.

Nico arrived back at his cabin around 3am, with a smile on his face and a song in his heart. He didn't even bother to get undressed; he simply fell backwards onto his bed. Nico passed out the instant his head hit the pillow, and didn't wake up until morning.

Nico woke up around 9:30, with the image of the woman at Walter's table in his thoughts. Nico knocked lightly on their adjoining wall, but Monica didn't answer. He could understand if she wasn't feeling well after last night, so while he was eating his breakfast, he decided to venture out on his own. Nico knew that he shouldn't be so curious, but he wanted to get a better look at the woman who is on the cruise with his old friend.

By noon, Nico had covered what he thought was the entire ship, and he hadn't seen the woman nor Walter, anywhere. Nico decided that it was time to go back to see how Monica was doing.

Monica had woken up and had her breakfast brought to her room. She had just finished eating when Nico knocked on her door.

In the meantime, Penny and Walter had just come back onto the ship, after a couple of hours of walking around in the town of Ketchikan, Alaska. Oliver had been bored while walking with them, and he hated that they looked at everything, in every single store that they walked by. Once they arrived at the check-in spot on the main floor of the ship, and they were cleared to board again, Oliver ran ahead.

During his visit to Ketchikan, Oliver had been promised that if he behaved, he was allowed to go swimming when they got back. Oliver couldn't wait to go into the water, but he was most eager to find the nice lady again.

"Oliver!" Walter shouted, when his son got too far ahead of them. Without hesitating, he began to run to catch up with his only child.

Penny rolled her eyes in disgust and stamped her right foot against the ground in protest; Oliver was again, stealing her thunder. This unruly moment, only made her more determined to find new ideas to keep the boy busy, and out of their hair.

Just as Walter was coming back with his son in tow, an older couple was trying to walk past Penny. Without her knowledge, Penny had completely blocked all traffic from moving up or down the small runway.

The older woman thought that she had enough room to squeeze past Walter's girlfriend, and pushed a little too aggressively. Unfortunately, she had clearly misjudged the small space, and pissed off the woman who had been in her way.

Penny's expression went from frustration to scowling, the second that she had gotten bumped. But before anger could explode from her already-jilted attitude, Penny's skin went pale, her lower lip dropped, and her eyes sprung open very wide.

After seeing the familiar older man standing before her, Penny had become surprised and terribly embarrassed. Because she knew every detail about him, the muscles in her body froze, and she was unable to speak, think, or move.

"We're back", Walter announced loudly. He was shocked to find that she hadn't taken a step since he left.

"I'm terribly sorry", the unknown woman called. "I hope you're ok." She was speaking to Penny, whose eyes were glued on the grey-haired man in front of her.

Penny looked like she had just seen a ghost. She could hear her heart pounding from fear inside of her chest, and all she wanted to do was run and hide. She was beginning to panic, but it felt like her feet had been nailed to the floor. She couldn't scream because her throat was closing up, and she was afraid that, even if she tried, no words would be able to get out.

"Penny?" Walter was standing a few inches away from her body, and he brought his hands up and planted them firmly on her shoulders. "Can you hear me, honey?" He wanted to shake her, but she looked like she was already in shock. "Penny!" he called. He was desperately trying to get her out of the trance.

"Oh, dear!" the older woman cried. "I hope I didn't do anything to hurt her." She rested one hand on her upper chest, with worry that she had done something to harm another living soul.

Walter turned to face the female guest, and in a soft, compassionate voice, he spoke three sentences to try to assure her that everything was going to be okay. "But thank you for your obvious concern", he added. He then spun around and began to study all of the features on Penny's face.

The older man, who was clearly the companion of the female guest, took hold of his wife's arm and tried to pull her onto the ship. "Come on, Priscilla", he ordered gently. "Let's keep walking, as we're also blocking the aisle." He then looked in Walter's face. "I hope she'll be okay", he added, but anyone could see that the man had thrown the comment away, as if it didn't mean anything.

"Thanks", Walter replied. He didn't know why Penny had such an astonished look on her face, but he hoped that she hadn't gotten hurt by the older woman who had just shoved her way onboard.

Walter didn't know it, but Penny had just seen a man who she had once been involved with. The expression on her face and the fear in her heart, was because she was terrified of what would happen, if the man had recognized her and said HI. And what if he would have introduced himself to Walter? Penny wanted to die just thinking about it.

*Penny Haberdash was only 17 years old when she met 49-year old, Dr. Hugo Sauck. He had just lost his wife and 2 sons in a tragic plane crash, and he was trying to heal his broken soul. Penny was young, very pretty, extremely attentive and kind, and did odd jobs to pay her bills.*

*Dr. Hugo Sauck was attending a large party for some work colleagues, and Penny was serving some mini foods on large platters. He saw her off in the distance and was immediately smitten. When she approached, he didn't care for the finger foods which she had to offer, but he lifted one off her tray, just for the notion of being able to talk with her.*

*They got to spend a lot of time together throughout the evening, and before the night ended, he asked if she'd like to go for coffee. She agreed, and they talked up a storm for the next 3 hours.*

*Penny liked older men because of their money, but also because she felt safe with them. They wanted to protect her, and they were very appreciative for everything that she had to offer.*

*She moved in with him after their second month of dating, and their relationship held strong for the next 10 months. Their life together had turned out better than either of them could have dreamed it would be, and then came the night of an important gathering from his work.*

*Hugo arrived with Penny on his arm, and almost immediately, he could feel all the nods of disapproval from the people around them. It was then when he realized what a fool he had been, to have fallen for someone so young. She looked like his granddaughter to the outside world, but she had honestly been the best medicine for his heart and soul. Nobody voiced their comments to his face, but Hugo was able to read his colleague's expressions, and it made him feel like a dirty old man.*

*"I'm going to get some punch", Penny stated, as she let go of his arm and then glided across the room.*

*Hugo watched her shapely hips sway back and forth, and then he realized how truly young she was. It crushed him, and he didn't want her to leave his life, but he also did not want anyone to think that he was a pedophile.*

*"Here you go!" Penny placed a glass of champagne into his hand. "I brought one back for you, too."*

*Hugo took it and then looked deep into her eyes. She was extremely lovely, and he could say for certain that he had grown to love her. But was it real love, or had she been able to fill the terrible emptiness which had haunted his soul? He wasn't sure, but it felt like his world was beginning to crash around him again.*

*As they went to bed that night, Hugo watched how child-like Penny was acting, and that's when he saw the age difference between them. 'Why had he not seen it before?' he wondered. He then decided that perhaps he didn't want to.*

*As he closed his eyes, he wanted to cry, for it was now obvious that he needed to end their relationship. With Christmas only two weeks away, Hugo decided not to do anything just yet.*

*The next morning, the doctor put a smile on his face and did everything he could to make Penny happy. He even went overboard buying gifts for his young girlfriend, and took her out for an elaborate meal on Christmas Eve. After opening gifts and enjoying a wonderful breakfast on Christmas morning, Hugo told her that they needed to talk.*

*He looked into her eyes and said, "I was going to do this after the holidays, but I can't wait."*

*A smile presented itself on her pretty face, and she could feel her cheeks begin to glow. Penny's first thought was that he was going to propose, and she was thrilled. She adjusted her clothing, arranged how she was sitting, and prepared herself for the question.*

*Hugo reached for her hand and spoke tenderly, as he advised her that they needed to end their relationship. "I'm sorry", he said, while tears of great sadness ran down his cheeks.*

*Penny was devastated, and didn't hear much of anything between the first sentence and the last. She could not have been more surprised by his announcement, because up until that very moment, she had experienced the best Christmas of her entire life. "What?"*

*"I'm sorry, honey", he said softly, but he knew this had to be done.*

*It took a minute or two before the initial shock had worn off, and then tears of disbelief streamed down her face, while screams of profanity leaped from Penny's throat.*

*Hugo felt horrible, and in order to keep the peace, he presented Penny with the ultimate gift – money. She was also allowed to take each and every gift that he had given her for Christmas.*

*Penny was filled with anger about the reality of the moment, but she accepted all the material items that were being offered. She then ran to the bedroom that she had shared with her boyfriend until that day, and slammed the door as loud as she could.*

*Although his heart was heavy that their relationship was now over, he hated that she was leaving his life. Hugo really did think that this was the best thing for both of them, but he wished that their relationship could have ended differently. She was so young, and he was well-aware that she wouldn't have any trouble finding someone her own age to be with. He might also find someone else, but he hoped it would be with a woman nearer to his own age.*

*Penny had lived a simple and poor life before she met her handsome, older boyfriend, and she vowed to never live like that again. She had done everything she could to warrant a better lifestyle. But now that Hugo was trying to end their relationship, she wondered what would happen to her.*

*Penny brought her things down to the front entrance of the home, and she hoped that Hugo would say he wanted to give them another chance.*

*Hugo hated to see her looking so sad. With everything in his soul, he wanted to take her in his arms and bring her and her things back up the stairs. Because he couldn't, he hung his head in shame for hurting her. "I've called you a cab", he said quietly.*

*When Penny saw his expression, she knew it was over. But before she could reach for her bags, he made another announcement.*

*"I know that you have nowhere to go, so I found you a really nice 2-bedroom apartment in the downtown area." As he handed her the keys he added, "And I paid the next 12 months of rent, in advance." As an added bonus, he handed her a cheque. "It's a little spending money for food and anything else you might need."*

*Penny accepted it without making eye contact with him. "Thanks", she muttered under her breath. As she looked at the amount, she sighed; it wasn't as much as she had hoped for, but at least it was enough to keep her going for a while. "Bye", she called over her shoulder. She then picked up her things and walked out the front door. As she sped off in the taxi, they each waved good-bye, and both were crying.*

*Hugo was sad during his first week without Penny. He missed everything about her, but because of her, he had been able to move forward with his life again. He secretly praised the young woman for helping him to get back on his feet, and now he knew exactly what he wanted in a relationship.*

*Penny loved her new home, and she relished the idea that she wouldn't need to work for a while. But because she missed having a man in her life, it didn't take long before she landed herself another sugar daddy.*

*Hugo had been single for just over a year, before he found someone special. He met the 45-year old widow at a friend's house, and after they were introduced, Hugo asked Priscilla to go out on a date. Not surprising to everyone who knew them, they fell madly in love, and got married 14 months later. They've been happy and inseparable, ever since their honeymoon.*

Penny had gone into shock when she saw her former boyfriend again, but as soon as he and his wife had walked away, she began to feel better. While she woke up from her dream-like, horror-filled, strange trance, she found Walter staring into her eyes. His expression was that of worry, and she could see that he'd been crying; his cheeks were glistening from the few tears which had been falling down his face, possibly from the fright which he had been feeling, for her being so motionless.

Oliver had been standing a few feet away from the loud commotion, and he was confused and slightly traumatized by the whole thing. He was scared about the nature of what was happening, and he felt sorry for Penny. He had noticed her blank expression and it broke his heart. He then scolded himself for not being nicer to her when he had the chance. "I hope you'll be okay", he whispered softly into the air towards her.

"Move it along!" someone in authority shouted. The loudness of the order stirred something inside of Penny's brain, and she suddenly became more aware of everything that was going on around her.

"Come on, honey!" Walter pleaded. "Let's get you back to our room, so you can rest."

"But I still want to go swimming!" Oliver fussed, after he realized that it meant he had to stay in the room with them. His gorgeous face was now pouting, and he looked like he was ready to cry.

"Maybe we can just rest for a short while?" Walter asked gently. He didn't want to have to run after his son when he knew that Penny needed him more.

Oliver stomped his foot in protest, but when he looked into Penny's face, he changed his attitude and did as he was told. Once they arrived at the cabin, Walter and Penny laid on the bed, while Oliver turned the TV on to keep himself entertained.

Nico and Monica had enjoyed a lovely brunch, and then decided to go for a walk around the deck. As they enjoyed the perfect ambience of being on the cruise, they held hands and talked about the scenery. Meanwhile, Monica's thoughts were on the little boy and his father, while Nico was still trying to figure out how to connect with the woman who had come onboard with Walter.

An hour had passed, since they began their walk, and Monica asked to sit down. Her tummy had begun to rumble and she wanted to rest for a while. Nico made sure she was comfortable, and then he opted to go and grab her a cool drink.

"You stay here and I won't be long", Nico said softly. Using the tips of his fingers, he pushed all sides of the lap blanket around her thighs and legs, and then he kissed her forehead and walked away.

The show that he was watching had now ended, and when Oliver turned his head, he saw that both his father and Penny had fallen asleep. Because he still wanted to go swimming, he grabbed his suit and ran down to the indoor pool. As he hurried, he hoped that the kind lady would also be there. As he got closer, he couldn't believe his good luck.

Monica spotted him before he got too close. "Well, look who's here?" She was delighted to see his handsome face again, and her health instantly improved.

"Hi!" he gushed loudly. Oliver rushed up to her and hugged her with all his might.

Monica's eyes shot wide open when she felt his little arms go around her body, and she leaned in to return his hug. "It's nice to see you again", she murmured against his cheek. His tiny frame felt good in her arms.

"Wanna go swimming with me?" Oliver asked, as he pulled away from her. He changed from his regular clothes into his swim suit, while he waited for her to answer.

Monica was wearing crop pants, and decided that she could definitely roll them up a bit. "I won't go all the way into the water, but I'll sit on the edge and watch you." As she flipped the neatly tucked cover off of her lower body, she couldn't believe how high her spirits had soared since Oliver had arrived.

Oliver understood and giggled. "Okay, come on!"

Monica bent over and folded up the bottom of her short pants. "I'm coming", she called. She couldn't help but laugh at his impatience.

Oliver dashed ahead of her and jumped into the water with a big splash. He was only underwater for a quick second, before his wet hair and face emerged. "Did you see me?" he asked with joy.

Monica smiled and nodded. She sat down and was now dangling her feet into the water. "Do it again!" she called. She started laughing at his silly antics, and couldn't remember when she had had so much fun.

Walter woke up and noticed that Penny was still sleeping, but she seemed okay – her skin was a good color, she was not hot, and her breathing seemed normal. He wasn't sure what had caused her to become so statue-like, but he was glad that she appeared to be better. After pulling the blanket up to her shoulders, Walter turned around to look at his son.

The normal color of his skin drained from his face, as soon as he realized that Oliver was not on the floor watching TV. "Damn!" he swore under his breath. He was getting panicky while he checked the bathroom, and he then raced towards the door. He could feel his heart pounding as his mind began to recite their previous conversation, and then he remembered the Oliver had complained that he wanted to go swimming. Walter raced towards the indoor pool, and he was very relieved to find Monica sitting on the edge, watching Oliver play.

Walter slowed down his hurried pace while he witnessed how well they interacted. The two of them were like a family – the mom being proud of her son, and the child looking towards the mother for approval. Oliver had never acted so free and happy around Penny, but Walter was astounded by how his little boy was acting around Monica. There was more of an authentic quality about their relationship, as if they were a real mom-and-child.

Monica could feel someone watching them, so she turned to have a look. Her smiling face became even brighter, once she saw Oliver's dad standing not too far away. "Are you coming over?" she asked. She patted the spot next to hers, as a reference for where he could sit.

"Yah, come on, dad!" Oliver shouted. "The water is not cold at all!"

Monica chuckled, as that seemed to be something that Walter might have worried about. She suddenly became playful, and splashed some water towards Oliver's dad with her toe. "See? It's not cold at all", she repeated, and then laughed a little harder.

Something happened within Walter's soul, when the water on his clothes touched his skin. The thought of Penny unexpectedly left his mind, and a powerful sense of family suddenly swept in. This is how it's supposed to be, he decided – happiness, togetherness, and a feeling of everyone belonging. He's not had this kind of love around him since before Evelyn got sick. But now that he had it, how could he keep it? He was with Penny and Monica was with someone else. Wasn't she?

Walter tried to recall the face of the man who Monica was sitting with in the restaurant. A pain of misery spread through his chest, as he realized that the man did indeed look familiar. But with everything that had been going on in Walter's life lately, he didn't have the energy to recollect who the man could be. Nor did he want to; he didn't feel that it was that important. What was important, was that Oliver was happy.

# *SPLASH*

Walter was now wet from his neck to his crotch, but it didn't make him upset at all. Instead, he looked at his son with more love than he could handle, and then he leaned his body forward and fell into the pool on purpose.

Monica watched with amazement. She couldn't believe how undisturbed the man had gotten, after becoming so unbelievably wet. Her first thought was that Nico would've been totally upset, and he probably would've stormed out of the area, pouting and muttering under his breath. But here was a man who didn't expect to be soaked, and he took it in stride and made the best of the situation.

"I'm going to get you!" Walter shouted playfully. Monica watched as the father pretended to run really fast towards his son.

Oliver giggled really hard, but he didn't want his dad to catch him.

Monica began to laugh louder, when she saw Oliver being chased around the pool by his dad. "Run, Oliver!" she called. Both of her hands were cupping her mouth as she called out the order.

Walter could hear Monica cheering for his son, so he whispered something in Oliver's ear. A second later, the two of them swam towards her. Each person took one of her legs, and then they pulled her into the water.

Monica kept insisting that she didn't want to go in, but once she had been splashed so much that her entire outfit was wet, she had no choice but to join them.

They continued to play and swim for another hour, before they decided to get out and get something to eat.

Meanwhile, Nico had made two laps of the entire ship. It was a waste of his time, and he was now quite dismayed that he had not run into the woman who had been sitting at the table with Walter and his son. He checked his watch and cursed under his breath. Nico saw that he had been gone a very long time, and he still needed to bring Monica that cool drink that he had promised. He hoped that she was still sitting where he had left her. He also hoped that she was not too upset that he had taken so long.

Penny was now stirring, and she had nothing but good thoughts in her mind. When she opened her eyes, she became confused at her surroundings, and she immediately wondered where she was. As she slowly recognized a few things that belonged to Walter and Oliver, she began to remember boarding the ship and seeing Hugo. Penny's body went into complete alarm mode again, for fear that Walter would run into Hugo, and she would not be around to defend herself. What would happen if they spoke and secrets were divulged? Penny cringed at the concept, and then she leaped out of bed. After using the bathroom, she raced around the ship. She was desperately looking for Walter, while trying to avoid running into anyone who she didn't want to talk to.

Walter brought three cheeseburgers and three pops to the round table. "Enjoy!" he cheered. As they ate, Walter got to know Monica better. He asked her questions about where she lived and what she did for a living, and he listened while she told him.

Oliver then asked his own question. "Do you have any kids?" He stared at her while she thought of an answer. He had hoped that she did, so that they could all play together.

Monica could feel both Walter and Oliver's eyes on her, but she wasn't sure how to answer that question. She had been pregnant and had given birth, but she no longer held the title of being a mom to anyone. "No", she stated sadly. "But I sure would like to someday."

"You should be my mom!" Oliver insisted happily. He got up from his seat and walked over to give her a hug, much to Walter and Monica's surprise and delight.

Walter thought he had witnessed a miracle; his son seemed quite fond of this lovely woman, but he'd only known her for a couple of days. How could there be such a bond between them so soon, when Oliver had known Penny for months and they didn't have even a good connection yet?

"Thank you", Monica uttered. She had goose bumps springing up all over her body, as tears welled up in her eyes. She had suddenly developed a genuine love for the handsome little boy, but that shouldn't happen; they hardly knew each other.

Walter could tell that this woman needed to stay in their lives, so he wrote down his phone number and asked her to give him a call after the cruise ended. "I'm hoping that you would want to stay in touch with us", he added quickly. He had his own reasons for why he wanted to keep her in his life, but he needed to sort them out himself, before he could talk about them to anyone else.

Monica couldn't have been happier. As she carefully folded and then stuffed the small bit of paper into her wallet, she looked into Oliver's smiling face. "I'd really like that."

Nico was walking towards the pool, when he spotted Monica sitting with Walter and his son. Terror engulphed every part of his soul, and he began to panic from what they might be talking about.

Penny had come into the same hallway, but she stood on the opposite wall from Nico. She had also spotted Walter sitting at a table with Monica and Oliver, and it caused a great deal of concern to well up in every pore of her body.

Nico's mind was swirling with ideas on how to get Monica to walk away. As he fought with the notion of how to do it, he looked across the hallway. His lower lip dropped and his eyes grew wide, as he spotted the woman who he had been looking for. The world stood still for a very brief moment, while he debated on which woman was more important.

Although he hated having to make that decision, Monica won – Nico couldn't have his former cell-mate confess things to Monica that would be better left unsaid.

But then, Nico also didn't want to leave the woman who he had been looking for all afternoon. He locked eyes with Penny for what seemed like a lifetime, but in reality, it only lasted for 30 seconds. He spoke volumes to her from his heart, and regretted that he couldn't do it with his words or actions.

When their eyes met, Penny's soul sent thousands of tingles to every nerve in her well-endowed body. She was completely mesmerized by the gorgeous man across from her, but her mission was to get Walter to marry her. She had worked so hard to get even this close to winning the prize, and it broke her heart to turn her head away.

When their eyes unlocked, it felt like Nico was saying good-bye to her forever. With extreme anger at himself for needing to hide his past, Nico rushed to a house phone and dialed the front desk.

As the man left, Penny could feel a part of her go with him. He had touched her heart, and left it pounding deep within her chest.

"I need Monica Bellam to be paged, please. It's an emergency." He was out of breath and had lied, but he knew of no other way to get Monica away from Walter.

Not a moment later, a female voice was urging 'Miss Monica Bellam' to go to her room. "You have a call", the voice added.

When Penny heard the announcement, she turned her focus back towards the table. She then watched as Monica became frazzled by her name being called.

"I hope everything's okay", Walter stated with concern in his voice. He stood up and gave her a quick and friendly hug. "Thank you for watching Oliver until I was able to come and get him." His eyes were filled with hope that he would get to see her again.

"It was my pleasure", she sighed happily. She felt safe in his arms, but still believed that he belonged to another woman.

"Are you coming back?" Oliver pleaded. He didn't want her to go, and hoped that she wouldn't be gone too long.

As she looked into both of their faces, Monica felt like she was leaving her family behind. She hated the thought of walking away, but she knew that she couldn't stay. "I'll see you both real soon." She thanked Walter for a very lovely time, and then blew Oliver a kiss from the palm of her hand. She then she rushed to her cabin.

Penny was fascinated by all that had just happened. She continued to watch the strange exchange, until the woman began to run towards her. Penny pushed herself closer to the wall in order to become transparent. After the woman had rushed by, Penny felt free to come out of hiding.

"Hi, you guys!" she called, as she pulled the already-warmed chair away from the table. Penny had spoken with a song in her heart, while a smile spread across her well-rested face. But as she sat down, she felt dejected by the lack of welcome in their voices when they said Hi back.

"How are you feeling?" Walter asked. He placed a hand on her thigh, but it was filled with kindness, not love.

"I'm okay now." She looked towards Oliver, but he pretended to be busy. "What are you doing?"

Nico was standing at Monica's door when she arrived. "I heard the announcement and rushed to see what was going on", he said. He made sure to act worried, as if he had hurried to be there with her.

"Thank you", she declared with sincerity. Monica thought it was very nice of Nico to come to see if everything was okay. "I don't know what's going on yet, but I'm about to find out." She pressed the key into the lock and pushed the door open. She then dialed the front desk and asked them about the call.

"A gentleman was asking for you", the woman stated. Her voice was rigid and cold, and she delivered the message in a purely business manner. "We didn't get his name or room number, but he asked us to get you to your room."

Monica was in complete shock at the words that she had spoken, and then she turned to look at Nico's face. "Thank you", she uttered mindlessly into the receiver.

Nico could feel his cheeks go red, and he hoped that it wasn't noticeable. "What's going on?" he asked, making sure to add confusion and concern into his voice. *He knew full-well that the whole thing had been a scam to get her away from Walter, but he couldn't tell her that.*

Monica wasn't sure, but it looked like Nico was trying to hide something; the odd expression on his face, the color coming into his cheeks, and the over-acting was all very suspicious. "Where were you just now?" she demanded. She folded her arms across her chest and waited for him to answer.

Nico's mind was racing with excuses. "I was looking out at the ocean from the other end of the ship." His eyes were wide open, his heart was pounding, and he was trying hard not to twitch or shuffle his feet.

"Uh, huh", she said softly.

Nico's palms were beginning to perspire, and when he felt the tiny beads of sweat forming under his nose, he began to panic. He quickly brought a hand up to wipe his upper lip, and he hoped that she hadn't noticed.

Without much effort, Monica could see that something was very wrong. Had Nico seen her enjoy herself with another man and his child? She had no other choice but to believe that he had; he'd been acting strangely since they came to their supper table. Could that have brought Nico to be jealous? She hoped not, but she needed to find out.

"Did you have me called away from my lunch with Oliver?" she asked. Suspicion was crawling through her veins. Monica watched as Nico squirmed, but she wasn't sure what he was up to.

Nico wanted to confess with something romantic, like he had wanted to have her all to himself, but he wasn't sure how it would be received. "I didn't know where you were", he blurted out. He changed his expression to make himself look sad, and then continued. "It wasn't a good reason, and I'm sorry." In truth, it was the best excuse that he could come up with at such short notice.

Monica's eyebrows shot up as a hint of affection glowed on her face. Really?" she asked, as she unfolded her arms.

Nico could see that he had her attention, so he continued. "I've been searching the ship for a while, but I couldn't find you. I thought this was the best way to know where you were and that you were okay - especially after knowing that you weren't feeling well." He added the last sentence as a power-point of reassurance, hoping that the sentiment would calm her down.

Monica's anger was slowly subsiding. She could see that what he was saying wasn't the complete truth, but she loved that his heart was in the right place. She walked over to him and gave him a hug. "Thank you for worrying about me."

Nico was more than relieved at how this had turned out, for he would have thought that she would be quite angry at his deception. Instead, she seemed to be flattered.

Monica threw her arms around his neck and kissed him on the lips. "Don't do that again, though", she stated firmly, and then she ended their embrace. "You scared me." she added, with a slight giggle in the back of her throat.

Nico made a boy scouts pledge and salute, never to do that again. "Promise!" he vowed.

They both laughed, which swept all of the negative ambience out of the room. Since they were already in the quaint, tight space, Nico and Monica decided to relax with a game of cards. Nico's intention was to keep her away from the rest of the people on the ship, for as long as he could. Hers was to meet up with Walter and Oliver at dinnertime.

Penny was relieved that she had not been caught spying, and she was also grateful to be surrounded by Walter and Oliver again. And while it probably wasn't the most ideal moment to bring up the subject of marriage, she decided to do it anyway.

"Because we only have two more days left on this cruise, what do you say we have a moonlight wedding on our last night at sea?" she suggested. She now watched their faces as she held her breath.

Walter didn't want to admit it, but his feelings had changed for the young woman beside him, and now he wasn't sure if he wanted to keep her in his life. He turned to look at his son, and saw that Oliver was keeping his eyes lowered to the food on his plate.

The little boy didn't want to offer any opinions on the subject of Penny marrying his dad, and he hoped that he wouldn't be forced to give one. Now that Oliver had met Monica, he did not want Penny in his father's life. He could definitely foresee a wonderful future with the kind and fun woman, and he hoped that his dad would also have that same revelation.

Penny wondered why both Walter and his son were being quiet, so she spoke up again. "What do you say? Do you want to get married?" Her arms were out to the sides and her hands were shaking up and down, while she tried to create some interest from her little group. Her heart was breaking from them not speaking up, but she wasn't able to let this go. "Come on, guys!" Her voice became louder as she forced happiness into her words. "Isn't this what we wanted?" She looked at Walter and then at Oliver, and wondered why nobody was agreeing.

Oliver titled his head to the side and let his eyes meet his dad's. The look spoke volumes about how they were both feeling at the thought of a wedding, and when Oliver went back to focusing solely on his last bites of food, Walter knew what he had to do.

Penny had seen the deliberate glance that they had shared – it was pretty hard to miss. The fleeting look, and all the words attached to it, made her want to cry. Penny's heart had broken in half, and she now felt alone and quite lost; her future had changed its course, and it was hard to understand why.

Walter was the first to speak, but it was not what Penny wanted to hear. "We did, but maybe we should wait?" His heart was telling him that Penny was not the one that he and Oliver should be with. Now that they had fallen in love with Monica, Walter and his son felt that she was the one they wanted to be around.

Oliver pushed his plate away and asked to be excused. He didn't make eye-contact with anyone at the table, and stood up before getting permission.

"Oliver?" Penny called. She was beginning to panic, because her whole world was falling apart. "Oliver, come here!" she begged. She reached out to the little boy, and was surprised and hurt when he pulled away from her.

"No! I just want to be alone!" he shouted.

Walter wanted to snap at his son for being so rude, but he understood what was going on. "Go and play, son. I'll catch up with you in a few minutes." Walter watched as Oliver raced to the large playground in the far corner of the room. It was behind the indoor pool, and across from where Walter and Penny were sitting, but it wasn't far enough away where Oliver was ever out of sight. Once he saw that Oliver was safe and interacting with other kids, Walter turned his attention back to Penny.

"Is everything okay?" she asked. She had worry in her voice and she could feel tears building up behind her eyes. "What's going on?" Penny placed a loving hand on top of his, and tried to appear to be genuinely concerned.

Walter's opinion of Penny had definitely changed since that morning at breakfast. But if he thought about it, he was the one who had been pushing for Penny to be in his life, even though he and his son knew that she might not be right for them. Walter had to admit that Penny had some good qualities, but there was no love there. In truth, what they shared was great sex. Penny wasn't a good cook or a good housekeeper, but she was fun to have around.

When Walter thought about Monica, his heart filled with happiness and love, and his face instantly broke out into a smile. That was who he wanted to be with, and that was who Oliver wanted to be with.

Penny could definitely feel that things had changed between them. But because she had a lot riding on the outcome of this relationship, she decided to fight for the right to stay with her current boyfriend. "I'm sorry about this morning", she confessed, hoping that that was the reason why Walter seemed to be so distant. She knew in her heart that it might be the other woman on the ship, but she hoped not. "I'm better now, and I can promise you that nothing like that will ever happen again."

Walter could tell by her body language that she was trying to be sincere, and he felt sorry for her. He reached his hand out to cover hers, and then he looked into her eyes as he spoke. "It has nothing to do with this morning, Penny." He turned his entire body around so that he was completely facing her. "I just feel like things have changed for me, towards you, and I think Oliver feels the same way as I do. I'm not sure how to describe it, but I no longer think we are meant to be."

Penny's heart was bursting with fear. She had planned this out, she had worked so hard to get to this point, and all she had to do was marry him in order to get his money. If they broke up before the wedding, she wouldn't get nearly as much as she wanted.

Penny's head was spinning with thoughts on how to backtrack to a few weeks ago; they were happy then, right? She could see that Walter was trying to calm her down, but her mind was going crazy with how this will end up. As tears were spilling from her eyes, she used the back of her hand to wipe them away. "But.....", she began. He stopped her before she could say another word.

"When we get off this cruise, we could talk some more, but for now, let's take a little break and think things out." He was trying to be respectful in everything that he was saying, and he was sorry, but his heart no longer belonged to her. Walter hoped that he had not been too harsh, and he hoped that she would understand.

Penny's emotions were about to explode from her body, so she stood up and made her way back to her own cabin, as quickly as she could.

Walter felt like shit. He closed his eyes, as the air from her leaving rushed against his body, but he had to be honest. He didn't love her and Oliver never really connected with her, so why was he trying so hard to get them to become a family? He now understood that it didn't make sense to force something that shouldn't be.

In order to change his mindset, Walter turned to see where Oliver was and what he was doing. In doing so, he saw a woman who looked a lot like Monica.

All the features on Walter's face softened, as he thought about the woman who he had fallen in love with. He then remembered watching how she interacted with Oliver at the pool. And how he felt when he joined them, as if they had automatically become a family. He could recall every detail of those few moments – how she looked and the way she laughed.

Walter lowered his head, and then decided that even if Monica was dating someone else, it wasn't fair to keep Penny around when she wasn't truly wanted. She was a nice, young, vibrant woman, who would find love again - he had no doubt about that. But Monica was different; she made them feel like they had been together since time began. Monica was genuinely kind and loving, and warm and funny, and he and Oliver wanted her to be in their life.

All of a sudden, Walter remembered being 8 years old and waking up on Christmas morning with his family all around him. Everything was bright and exciting, and there was nothing but love in every corner of the room. It brought a shy smile to his full lips, for that was how it felt when he was with Monica.

Penny stormed into her room and slammed the door closed, as loudly as possible. She threw herself onto her bed and sobbed violently for the next hour. She had a huge sense of loss in her soul - not for the man and his son, but for the money and the many possessions which she was supposed to inherit once their relationship ended. If they broke up now, she would be left with close to nothing. If she wanted to walk away with even half of what she had planned to get, she needed to figure out how to save what she had worked so hard to develop.

It was almost 5pm, and Nico had gone to his own room to get ready for supper. He absolutely loved that he had been able to spend a quiet and fun afternoon, playing cards and watching TV with Monica. During the last few hours, they had been able to work through whatever damage his stupid prank had done to their relationship. By talking and laughing, they had been able to get back to where they were as a couple, before they boarded the large ship. This was something that Nico was very relieved about.

As he pulled his good jacket over his shoulders, his hand fell into his pocket and felt the velvet box. He reached in and lifted it out, and then wondered when he would get to propose to Monica.

Monica was still glowing from her wonderful day. She had spent part of it splashing around with Oliver and his dad, and she was very grateful that she had gotten the chance to get to know them better. The next three hours were consumed by Nico. After they had worked through 'that little stunt', the rest of the afternoon was relaxing and fun. They even hugged when Nico left to go to his room to get ready for dinner, but Monica noticed that something was different.

Monica was careful to dress in a way that attracted the right kind of attention, but it wasn't for Nico; tonight she was dressing for Walter. Her hair was fluffed and curled to perfection, her make-up had been applied so that her eyes and lips stood out, and her perfume was delicate and seemed to linger modestly in the air, every time she moved. When she stood back and it made her smile, she knew she was ready.

Nico placed the exquisite ring back into his pocket, and decided that tonight just might be the night when he would pop the question. He was taking one last look at himself when he heard the knock on his door. With one final adjustment to his hair, he went to open it.

Seeing Monica like that, made him swoon. It was a weird emotion, for he had never done that before in his life. "Wow!" he gushed. He stood with his mouth hanging open, in total admiration of how truly beautiful she looked.

Monica blushed, for she had worked extra hard to look like this. "Well, thank you", she replied in a sweet tone. She suddenly became nervous, but she wasn't sure why. "Shall we go?"

Nico closed his door and reached his elbow out for her to take. "It would be my pleasure to escort you, lovely lady." He was being 100% charming on purpose, for if everything went as planned, he hoped that the night would end with them becoming engaged.

It had been a couple of hours since the two of them had seen each other, and Walter had hoped to soften the aftereffects of their last conversation. He swallowed hard and hesitated, before he knocked on Penny's door. It was 5pm, he didn't want her to be alone, and he was hoping that they could have supper together.

"Penny?" he called. He knocked three times with his knuckle, and then he leaned his head close to the door. He could hear her moving inside of her room. "Penny? Are you going to the restaurant?"

"Yes, I am." Penny had been dressed and ready to go for almost 20 minutes.

"Do you want some company?"

"That would be nice, thank you." Penny had spent a great deal of the afternoon wallowing in sorrow over what Walter had said. However, she had spent the rest of the day praying that they could spend a little time together. She was more than delighted when she heard his familiar rap of three short knocks on her door, and her heart jumped with joy when she heard his voice asking her if she wanted to have supper with him.

Penny looked into the mirror and quietly gave herself a little pep talk. "I'm not sure why he thinks he fell out of love with you, but I'm going to bring him back to your arms, and fast", she mumbled to herself.

"I'm ready!" she called, as she placed her hand on the door knob. By the time the door had opened, Penny had plastered a huge smile on her face. "Hi", she said shyly.

Walter was impressed by how she looked. "Hi", he shot back. "I thought it wouldn't hurt if we went for supper together. That is, if you don't have any other plans."

Penny's smile grew bigger, as she wrapped her hand around his elbow. "I don't have anywhere else that I'd rather be", she sighed with sincerity. The touch of his arm brought her back to a place of comfort. She was nervous and played her part with caution, for these next few hours could make or break any idea of a relationship with Walter ... forever. Penny squared her shoulders and stood tall, as she began to walk towards the elevator. She suddenly noticed that Oliver wasn't with them. She turned to Walter and was about to ask him where his son was, but turned away again, as she didn't want to break the mood. Secretly, she was quite pleased that it would be just the two of them.

Without her knowledge, Oliver had been accepted to sleep over with a little boy named Harlin, who he'd met after Monica had rushed off to go to her room. The two boys got along very well, and because both Harlin and Oliver were the only children in their families, both sets of parents were pleased that the boys had someone to play with.

Nico and Monica had arrived at the 'Manhatten Dining Room', and they couldn't help but be astonished by all that they were seeing. The outstanding display of magnificent lights were hanging everywhere, showering everyone in the dining room with soft lighting. The embellished table cloths and napkins adorned every setting, and highlighted the glittering dishes and glasses, which were resting in front of every chair. The place was simply breathtaking, and looked far too elegant or expensive for a normal person to eat in.

"Monica Bellam and Nicholas Kostas?"

The guests were ushered in by their last name, and escorted to their tables by a well-dressed attendant. The charming employee pulled out the chairs for all the women, and tipped his invisible hat to all the gentlemen. He then bowed as he left their tables, and went to the front desk to escort someone else.

"Walter Ryng and Penny Haberdash?"

Walter raised his hand as he shouted, "Here!"

"Hello and good evening." An attendant bowed and smiled, and then, as the well-dressed man offered his elbow to Penny, he asked Walter to 'come this way'.

Nico and Monica had already been seated for two minutes when Walter and Penny entered the very large and elegant area.

They walked up the narrow path towards their table, which was situated near the many windows at the front of the ship. After Penny and Walter were seated, the employee of the ship bowed and told them to enjoy their meal.

Walter looked out at the vastness of the rippling water, while Penny scanned the faces of the many people in the restaurant. When she saw Nico, her heart jumped up and into her throat. He was obviously attractive, and she felt a connection with him that she couldn't explain.

Monica had seen Walter go by, but she didn't call out. He looked so handsome all dressed up, but she remembered how nervous Nico had been earlier in the day, and she didn't want to stir up any trouble.

Nico spotted Penny as soon as she sat down. He wanted to go and talk with her, in order to explain what had happened earlier with the spying and the rushing away and all, but he couldn't. Nico was already in trouble for getting an announcement made over the loud speakers, and he couldn't afford to screw up anymore. But just because he couldn't talk with her, didn't mean he couldn't take a few peeks in her direction.

When Walter took his turn to look around the restaurant, his eyes soon noticed Monica. He marveled at how devastatingly beautiful she looked in this particular setting.

When she felt someone staring at her, Monica searched the room until their eyes locked. The electricity that shot across the room had both of them smiling - from the memories of their pleasant hours in and out of the pool, and from their mutual attraction for one another.

When Walter nodded to Monica, he wanted to get up and tell her how truly beautiful she looked. He knew he couldn't, so he smiled his approval, and was grateful when she lifted her glass in appreciation.

The succulent cuisine was served, but the attention was not on the food, or on the other person at the table. It was being divided by everything all at once – the background music, the gentle swaying of the ship, the ambience, the loud roar of the motor, and the smells of the food which was being prepared not far from where they were all dining. But most of all, the attention was on the person that they were truly attracted to.

Their two tables were only a short distance apart, and all of them wanted the view of the occupants at the other table. Because that was impossible, napkins and cutlery accidently landed on the floor, in order to sneak a peek at the individual of desire. Faces lit up when the smiles were returned, and hearts were fluttering from appreciation.

When the meal was over, all four people seemed to head to the door at the same exact moment. Introductions were made quickly, and as awkward as anyone could imagine, Walter spoke up and invited Monica and her date to go out on the deck for an after-dinner drink.

"That would be great!" Monica shouted with acceptance.

"Then let's go!" Walter placed his hand on Penny's back, and led everyone outside.

Nico was both shocked and enticed at the invitation, for he had wanted a chance to get better acquainted with Walter's lady friend. He just wasn't sure how to avoid the possibility, that Walter might recognize him and begin to talk about their past. The fact that Walter didn't react when they shook hands was amazing by itself, but if Nico had to sit across from him and they got to talking, he was afraid that who he was, might become more obvious.

Nico grabbed Monica's hand and inhaled slowly and deeply. He then closed his eyes as he prayed for a miracle.

Walter had become totally enthralled with Nico's date, and he had no other thoughts but to be close to her. He had hoped to spend more time with Monica, but he didn't imagine that it would have happened so soon.

Monica was worried that Nico would be able to tell how she felt about Walter, but even she wasn't totally sure how to define her emotions. Monica truly liked Walter; she thought he was handsome and very kind, and she loved how he interacted with his son.

Monica's whole thought process suddenly zeroed in on the little boy. She turned this way and that, and then realized that she hadn't seen him all evening. She turned towards Walter, and as if she had the right, she asked,

"Where's Oliver?" She now had a look of real concern written all over her face.

Walter couldn't help but giggle, as he diverted his eyes towards what he was fidgeting with in his lap. Penny had not been the least bit interested in where his son was, and here was this woman, who had totally captured his heart, and she thought enough to ask about Oliver.

Walter raised his eyes to meet hers, and he told her all about the other family by the pool. "…..and then they asked Oliver to spend the night." When he was done, Walter gazed over at Penny, and saw that she had not even heard the explanation. If he was truthful, he was almost positive that she would not have cared where Oliver was. Without giving her another thought, Walter changed the subject and asked Monica where she had gotten the lovely necklace.

Monica tried to give him explicit details about the little shop where she had purchased her gorgeous piece of jewelry, but her thoughts were on the little boy; Oliver was amazing in every way possible. And the connection that she had with him, was enormous. 'What was it about him that grabbed so much of her attention?' she wondered. The way he crinkled his nose when he laughed, the small gap between his two bottom teeth, or how much he loved being in the water? She also thought it was odd that both he and Monica had the same birth mark, right behind their left ear.

Monica instantly lowered her head and smiled, for she had just described some of the attributes that both she and Cayson share with Oliver. If Monica were to put two-and-two together, she would have to say that Oliver could have been a product of their love.

"I should go and see what else they sell there", Walter stated. He was holding her necklace in the palm of his hand, while it was still hanging from her neck. "It's truly beautiful", he said, as he looked up. His eyes met hers, and it was like the rest of the people on the ship disappeared.

Because Penny now believed that Walter was no longer interested in her, she decided that she would take everything that he was willing to give her, and then she would try to build another life with someone else.

As if on cue, Nico called out her name. "Penny, is it?"

Penny turned her head to look in Nico's direction, and the world stood still. 'What was it about this man', she wondered. Was it his broad shoulders that curved his suit jacket to perfection? The shadow of a beard on his face, that seemed to give him a manly aura? What about his lips that were firm and sensual, or his face that was naturally bronzed by the wind and the sun? All of his features were divine and easy to look at, but it was his sexy smile that made her knees go weak.

He leaned in and tilted his face towards her, as he reached out his hand. "I'm Nico", he breathed, making sure to ooze as much charm as he could push out. His kissed the back of her hand, just like they do in the movies.

She bit her bottom lip as she shook his hand, and her eyes stayed fixed on his. There was a spark of energy when their hands met, and that's when she decided that he might be worth chasing; he was well-dressed, tall, very handsome, and it didn't look like there was much going on between him and Monica. "I'm Penny."

Nico couldn't help but chuckle, for that had already been established. "It's very nice to meet you, Penny." His laugh was light, and it wasn't meant to be unkind. "So, you come here often?" he joked.

It was now Penny's turn to laugh, and she could feel her cheeks becoming warm. As new interests and information came spilling out, the foursome's uneasiness became less awkward. And then, as if they had all suggested it at the same time, everyone agreed to go to the 'The Docking Station' for a quick drink.

For the first ten minutes, they had only spoken to their own partners. Once they were more comfortable, they began to fly questions to the other people at their table. It didn't take long before Monica and Walter had turned their chairs and were speaking only to each other. When Nico saw what had happened, he took full advantage of the opportunity, and spoke exclusively with Penny.

The four adults were enjoying their time together - much more than they had planned. At 12:00, they decided to call it a night. "It was nice to meet you", was shouted over the music and other people talking.

Monica had been polite and outgoing since leaving the 'Manhatten Dining Room', but she had not spoken a full sentence with Penny.

Penny was hurt after watching how chummy Walter had been with Monica, so she decided to steal Nico away from her.

Meanwhile, Walter and Nico had practically avoided each other. They had barely spoken two words together all night, but they had returned a few nods back and forth.

In the end, as everyone walked away, they all believed that the evening had been a huge success.

Walter winked in Monica's direction as they said goodnight, but it was not for the rest of the world to see. He watched her smile and then lower her eyes, and then he knew that it had been taken as he had meant it to be delivered. He also felt that his sentiments had been returned.

Nico had formed a new friendship with Penny, after learning that they had many of the same interests. Each one had confessed their need to have more than what they had in their current relationships, and each one disclosed in great detail, how they could help the other. Of course, they promised to be discreet, and then they made plans to meet up around 11am the next morning - not with their partners, but in a dark secluded place where no-one would find them.

"Night, Nico!" she called loudly, as she walked away.

"Night, Penny!" He smiled as he thought about all that was going to happen in the morning.

Walter hoped to share a cup of coffee with Monica at some point before the cruise was over, but he didn't know how to ask - they were definitely caught in an awkward situation. "If only things were different", he sighed softly to himself.

The men walked their women back to their rooms and said good-night, and then delivered the ever-popular, proverbial kiss on the cheek. All four adults then went inside of their own cabins, feeling quite content to be alone with their thoughts.

Nico said good-night to Monica, and then he had gone to his room like everyone else. But around 2am, just when he had finished a good 10-minutes of stroking, he heard a knock on his door. It was faint and he would have missed it, had he not been in the bathroom cleaning off his still-stiff member. He walked closer and peeked through the small hole, and let out a small gasp when he saw Penny standing in the hallway.

She was full of worry about how it looked, her standing there with barely anything on, but she couldn't help herself; she hadn't been able to stop thinking about him since they said good-night. Now she was waiting for him to open the door, and she hoped that she wasn't embarrassing herself.

Nico opened the door quietly, and in a low voice, he asked Penny to come inside. "What are you doing here?" He was delighted to see her, and he loved that her attire was almost non-existent.

Without speaking, Penny leaped into his arms and wrapped herself tightly around his body.

As Nico held her close, he very badly wanted to enjoy everything that she had to offer - but not in his room. Not next door to Monica, who might hear something that she shouldn't. "No", he whispered, as he tried to push her away. "Not here."

Penny's face showed fear and confusion, but she didn't want to go back to her own room. She stretched the two sides of her robe together, but before she could tie the belt, she felt herself being pulled out of Nico's cabin.

"Sh-h-h-h!" he cautioned. Nico grabbed her hand and led her down the long hallway. He quickly searched his mind for places that they could go. When a spot came to him, he walked her there.

Neither one of them could have understood how erotic the slight breeze blowing against their near-naked skin could feel. And it was quite sensuous to have forbidden sex in plain view, when you know that everyone else in the world was sleeping. The strangers had nothing but miles and miles of water around them. And there was no sound other than the loud engine on the large ship, which was pushing its cargo towards its final destination. It felt like they were the only two people on the earth, so when they stood within a foot apart of each other, there was nothing to stop them from bringing their bodies even closer together.

Because they had both started off with barely anything under their robes, it was easy to remove what little they were wearing. They threw their articles of clothing on the bare wooden planks of the deck, and then, with an unbelievable urgency, they got down to business.

Both Nico and Penny have had sex before, but neither had experienced the height of the sensations which they were feeling in those two hours of untainted passion. What went where was the same, but everything else felt different, and nothing was off-limits.

Neither Nico nor Penny uttered a coherent word, while they moved from one eager position to another orgasm; it was as if they already knew each other's needs and lustful requests. Once they were thoroughly covered in sweat, and they had totally satisfied all aspects of their desires, they went back to their own cabins and slept more peacefully than they had ever slept before.

The next morning, Monica woke up filled with confusion. She got dressed and went to the nearest deck, to process the thoughts which had kept her from sleeping straight through the night.

Walter woke up from a wonderful sleep, and then went to pick his son up. "I missed you", the man confessed, as he wrapped his arms around his little boy's body.

"I missed you, too", Oliver announced happily. "But I loved that I got to stay and play with Harlin."

Walter looked up and into Harlin's parents' eyes when he spoke. "Thank you very much for letting my son stay the night."

"It was our pleasure", they confirmed. "Bye, Oliver!"

"Bye, and thank you!" Oliver called.

As they began to walk away from Harlin's cabin, Oliver asked if they could go to the playground area before breakfast.

"Okay", Walter agreed. He patted down his pants and then blurted out, "It seems that I forgot my wallet, so you go straight there and wait for me. I'll only be a few minutes behind you."

Oliver nodded and ran ahead. A minute later, his world lit up. "Monica!"

The sound of someone calling her name startled her, and caused her to stop walking. She automatically brought her hand up to her chest as she turned around. She couldn't believe her eyes, when she saw Oliver running towards her with a great deal of speed. She smiled as she bent down to catch him, and she gave him the warmest, sweetest hug in the whole wide world. For whatever reason, she had truly missed him. "Where were you last night?" she asked, when their embrace ended.

"I made a friend when I was playing on the other side of the pool, and was asked if I could spend the night." He then cocked his head to the side and opened his eyes really wide, and he spoke with genuine concern. "Why? Did you miss me?" He batted his beautiful long lashes as he waited for her answer.

Monica couldn't help but swoon at how cute he was. "I did!" she shouted. She clapped her hands together to show that she meant it, and then giggled.

Oliver moved his head back to an upright position, and his face broke out into a wide smile. "I missed you, too." He gave her another hug, and then his lips landed on the small area between her eye and her ear.

This gentle touch put butterflies in her tummy, for nobody but Cayson had ever done that before. The memory of the first time he had done that, suddenly came back to her mind, strong and hard.

They were on their fifth date and they were talking. He had stretched his arm across her shoulders, and then he kissed her skin between her eye and her ear. She remembered the sensation of love which it brought to body, and now she felt it again.

Monica took Oliver's hand and led him to the nearest table. As Oliver sat across from her, Monica took a really good look at him. She bent forward with a terribly wild question in her mind, and swallowed hard before it came out of her mouth. "When's your birthday?" She held her breath until he answered.

"May 12. When's yours?" The way he looked at her, made her want to eat him up – he was so cute.

"August 29", she replied. It had barely been a full minute before another question slipped through her lips. "How old are you, Oliver?" There were too many things adding up to the fact that he might be her son, and she felt like she couldn't contain herself.

"I'm going to be seven next year. How old are you?"

"How old do you think I am?"

The little boy giggled and became shy, because he would guess her to about 20 years old – too old for him to marry, but young enough for them to be friends. Instead of telling her what number he thought she was, Oliver took over the conversation by telling her about all the toys he had, the places that he had gone to with his dad or his friends from school, what his room looked like, and what he liked to watch on TV. "Mostly cartoons, but I also like to watch ......." He talked non-stop for quite a few minutes, but he was never aware that Monica had suddenly zoned out.

As if she was looking into a crystal ball, the whole thing suddenly became clear to her. His name is Oliver Ryng - the same as the name her son was given, when he was handed to his adoptive parents. This little boy in front of her was born on the same day that her son was born on. He had a small gap in his teeth, he crinkled his nose, and he loved all aspects of being in the water – these were the same traits that Cayson had. And what about the same exact birth mark, in the same exact place where she has hers? Was that also a coincidence? And how about where he had planted that sweet kiss – it was magical, as if Oliver had been guided to do so, by someone who wanted Monica to know that he wasn't too far away.

Tears began to flow from her eyes, and she didn't want to stop them from pouring out. She had no idea if this was her body's way of expressing the love which she carried from her life with Cayson, or if it was from bringing their baby into the world. She now honestly believed that this was her child – the boy that she had given birth to.

Monica stared at Oliver with an alarming expression on her face, because she honestly didn't know what to do with the information.

Because she had been quiet for a while now, Oliver looked into her face and noticed that she appeared to be sad. He leaned forward and touched his tiny round nose against hers. "Are you alright?" he whispered. He placed his little hands at the back of her head, until their foreheads touched, and then he waited for her to reply.

There was no question that his hug made her feel better, but how could she possibly tell him that she might be his mother? Instead, she bought her own hands up to cover his ears, and gently pulled him away a tiny little bit. She then kissed his nose, and pulled his entire body back towards hers. And in that moment of sheer joy, she squeezed him a little harder than she probably should have.

"Hey!" Oliver laughed. He loved it, but it was a little tight.

"Oops, sorry!" Monica reluctantly released herself from their hug, and let him go back to sit on his own chair.

Walter left his cabin and made his way to the pool area. As he walked towards them, he saw Oliver and Monica talking within an inch of each other's faces. Inside his body, his soul was dancing with happiness, but he hoped that nobody would notice.

"So", he began. Walter's voice had a strange accent and it looked like he was deforming his body on purpose. "Do you come here often?"

Monica looked towards Oliver and he looked towards her, and then they all broke out laughing. Not because it was hilarious, but because Walter looked weird while he was doing his little performance.

Walter rolled his eyes as he sat down, and knew he was headed for trouble. "Everyone's a critic!" he stated jokingly.

He pouted his lips in Oliver's direction, which brought the little boy to his feet.

Oliver rushed over to his dad and gave him a huge hug. "We don't live here Daddy, so how can we come here often?"

Walter understood that his 6-year old son was serious, but the expression on his face made both him and Monica laugh again; the boy was dangerously cute.

To change the dynamics of the moment, Walter offered to get everyone breakfast. "You like your coffee with one sugar and two milk, right?" He was asking Oliver, which made the little boy burst out laughing.

"No-o-o-o-o-o!" Oliver hollered. "I don't drink coffee!" He wasn't sure if it was a joke or not, but he seemed genuinely insulted by the question.

Walter turned and now looked at Monica. "Oh, so it's you who drinks the coffee!"

Oliver was really enjoying the funny banter, and he wished that it could be like this all the time. His dad was happier than he'd been in a long time, Monica's smile was bigger than it had been since they first met, and Oliver was very happy overall. He liked how it all felt – like home.

Monica raised her hand and answered. "Guilty!" she said. "Can I also get some toast and jam?" She then pretended to duck, in case she had asked for too much.

Walter's eyes bugged out as he bent forward. He was hoping to make Oliver believe that he was upset that Monica would want more than just a coffee. And as soon as he heard his son's gorgeous laughter, he couldn't help but burst out laughing.

Monica was having such a good time, that she had completely forgotten about Nico, or the fact that Oliver might be her son. That next hour had her eating and drinking, and laughing and talking, and she had enjoyed every single second of it. When she looked at the time, she decided to go and see where Nico was. She thanked Walter and Oliver for breakfast, and after a few whines and a couple of nice hugs, she began to walk away.

Neither Nico nor Penny emerged from their rooms before 10:45, but each sought out the other, until their eyes met again.

"Was that a fluke?" Nico asked. His heart was racing, just from standing so close to her.

Penny had been with many men before, but she had never experienced anything like what had happened in the dark of the night. "I don't know, but just to be sure, we should probably try that again." She brought her index finger up to her mouth and dragged it slowly across her bottom lip. Her eyes screamed that she longed for his body, and she was hoping that he was only too willing to give it.

Nico's mouth went dry, and he could feel something hardening in the front of his pants. He knew he wouldn't be able to walk back to his cabin for a while, so he asked her to sit down at the nearest table. "Why are you doing this to me?"

"Me?" she stated softly and innocently. Penny actually knew damn well what she was doing. "What am I doing?" She parted her mouth and then slid her tongue out to wet both her top and bottom lip.

"You are driving me crazy, that's what you're doing!" Nico was trying to stay calm, but his body was about to give him quite the orgasm. He looked around as if he was trying to hide from someone, and then he devised a plan for how they could be together. He drew a map on a napkin and pushed it towards her. "Meet me here in ten minutes!" He then got up, pushed his hands into his front pockets, and he rushed away.

Penny knew exactly where this location was, so she stuffed the napkin into her bra strap and waited impatiently for the ten minutes to be over.

Monica was walking back to her cabin to check on Nico, when she spotted Walter's friend. "Hi, Penny", she said in a quiet voice. They were not friends now, nor will they ever be, but she was Walter's friend. That's the only reason that Monica was being polite to her.

Penny became startled when she heard someone say her name. She looked up to see Monica, and she was suddenly filled with fear. "Oh, Hi." With panic coursing through her body, Penny immediately turned her head to see if Walter or Oliver were also nearby. When she saw that they weren't, it eased her guilty mind.

Monica noticed that Penny seemed to be nervous. She took the seat beside her, even before being asked. "Are you ok?" she asked with real concern.

Penny's mind went into overdrive, as she searched for an answer. "I have an upset tummy and thought the fresh air would calm it down." Penny thought her answer was brilliant, and now she waited to see if Monica believed it.

Monica could see that something was troubling her, and because she didn't want to interrupt Penny from trying to feel better, she got off the seat and decided to walk away. "Oh, I'm terribly sorry. I'm won't disturb you, then." While Monica's feet took steps away from the table, she called out, "I hope you feel better soon!"

Penny decided that daytime might be too dangerous for her to have a rendezvous with Nico, so she rushed to her cabin and hoped that he would find her there. But before she had gotten too far, she could hear Walter calling her name.

"Penny!"

Penny turned her head and saw Walter and Oliver racing to catch up with her. "I'm not feeling well!" she shouted, and kept running. Thinking that Walter would follow her to her room, she headed straight to the spot where Nico was waiting, and hoped that the rest of the world would leave her alone.

Walter felt concern about Penny dashing away from them like that, but he understood if she wasn't feeling well. He placed his attention on his son, and they decided to go and see a movie on the 2$^{nd}$ floor.

Monica knocked on Nico's door, but she wasn't surprised when he didn't answer; he had said something last night about going to play pool in the afternoon. Monica went to her own cabin, wrote him a note, and slid it under his door.

*Hi Nico, from Monica. Did you want to meet up for supper at 6? I'll be in my room until then. Ox*

It was a short note, but Monica wanted to make sure that she had a chance to talk with him about Oliver; she now had more information that could prove that he might be her son.

Monica knew that Nico didn't want to have that conversation again, but now that she had more proof, maybe he might want to hear what she had to say. She closed her eyes and prayed that he would, for she had no-one else to talk to about this.

Nico was already there waiting, breathless and filled with desire, when Penny arrived. No words were needed, as she pushed her body against his, for their minds were in perfect harmony.

Because Nico wasn't in his cabin, Monica laid down on her bed and rested until suppertime. Once she had fallen into a deep sleep, her mind showed her an image of Cayson. He was kneeling down and having a conversation with Oliver. Their faces were at equal levels, their eyes were staring directly into the other person's, and Monica actually thought she could feel the affection dancing between them. And not just a little, for it filled every one of her senses. Monica honestly believed that there was more love in that one moment, than she had ever felt in her entire life.

She wasn't sure if she was dreaming or if this was real, because it didn't seem to have any boundaries. Monica moved her hands in the air, and she could feel the thickness of it against her skin. It felt real, but it couldn't be…right? Cayson had died in the street before their child was born. And how could Cayson know Oliver, unless ….

As Penny felt her breasts crush against the hardness of his chest, the last few minutes of her recent misery, disappeared. She wrapped her arms tightly around his neck and held him as close as possible.

Nico's lips kissed her neck, her ear, and then her mouth.

While Penny was kissing Nico, she felt his left hand caress the inner part of her upper thigh. It then slowly moved up to the edge of her panties. His warm breath was now against her neck, as one of his fingers slipped under the silky, white garment, and was heading for someplace warm and very wet.

Monica's body suddenly jerked her into a sitting up position. Her eyes were wide with wonder, her heart was pounding inside of her chest, and her mind was bouncing with questions about what was happening. Is it possible that Oliver really was her son? If so, she would have to find out for sure. She wasn't sure how, and then it came to her. She would ask Walter a question or two about his wife, and how he had enjoyed Oliver as a baby.

Nico was more than delighted that Penny had found the secluded place that he had drawn on the napkin, and now he was going to reward her. As his fingers found what they had been looking for, he felt her legs move apart for easier access. He brought his mouth down on top of hers, and suddenly he became very eager to enter her. Nico's hunger got the better of him, and he pushed the fabric aside with a little more aggression than he had intended.

Penny's eyes were closed, her head was tilted back, and her lips had parted, as she drank in all the wonderful sensations. She was now at the point where she was powerless to resist, and the motion of her hips invited him to have his way with her.

Nico positioned his hard member to where it needed to go, and then he forced it inside of her body with one quick thrust. She let out a soft moan, and it made his heart leap with extreme desire.

Ten minutes later, a delightful shiver of pleasure bathed them from head to toe, while their pulses quickened, and then slowly subsided.

Monica jumped out of bed with a renewed amount of energy, and got ready for supper. While she was getting dressed, she was excited to find Walter and learn the answers to her questions.

The nearness of Nico gave her a great deal of comfort, and Penny never wanted to let him go. But because she could feel the stickiness begin to run down her legs, she needed to leave him in order to clean herself up.

Nico looked into her eyes, and he could detect a delicate thread of love building between them. She was young and very beautiful, but she was also sexy and sweet, and she filled him with a yearning that left him wanting more of what she had to offer.

"I don't want to go, but you know I have to", she whispered. Her eyes studied his, and then she began to memorize all of the fine details on his handsome face, as if she would never see him again.

Nico gathered her into his arms, and when he pressed his body against hers, he could feel the heat that emanated from where their skin was making contact. Not just because they had just had sex, but because there was a definite chemistry between them. "I know", he said softly.

People were walking by, and someone had spotted them hugging and shouted for them to 'get a room'. The sweaty couple laughed it off, and agreed that it was time to go and get cleaned up.

"I'll see you for supper?" Penny asked. She sounded anxious as she gazed into his eyes, but she was desperate for him to say yes.

Nico lovingly removed a loose curl that was leaning against her right eyebrow, and pushed it back behind her ear. He then whispered as he nodded the answer that she was hoping for. "Yes, my darling. You will see me in a little while." Nico bent his head forward and placed his warm mouth against her bruised lips.

Penny swooned under his talented tongue, and when the kiss was over, she was left dizzy and completely under his spell.

Nico released himself from their embrace, and slapped her behind with a playful swat. "Go get cleaned up", he ordered softly.

"Aye, aye, sir!" she laughed. She pushed two fingers against her forehead and saluted him, and then she walked away.

Nico couldn't help but giggle at her awkward attempt to salute. And as she made her way to the nearest exit, he smiled, for she was beginning to grow on him. When she was completely gone from his sight, Nico lowered his head, and wondered how he would be able to see her after they got off the ship.

Monica was sitting at a table, anxiously waiting for Walter to arrive. She had gone over and over the questions that she wanted to ask him, but she wasn't sure how to broach the subject. Once she saw him, she decided to tread lightly.

"Hi", he stated in a velvety voice. Walter was pleasantly surprised that she had gotten there before him. "Didn't we say that we'd meet up around 6pm?" Walter checked his watch for the time. "It's barely 5:45 – you're early." He took the seat opposite Monica, and sat himself down. "But I don't mind, because it gives us more time to be together." Walter's expression went blank as he looked around the room. "Where's your friend? Is he not joining us?" he asked in a curious manner. He was secretly hoping that they could spend this time alone, and quite pleased that it was happening.

"I knocked on his door but he didn't answer. I guess he'll show up when he's hungry", she laughed. Monica placed her unfolded lace napkin across her lap, and focused all of her attention on her dinner guest. "Speaking of which..." It was now her turn to look around the room. "Where's Oliver?"

Walter turned his head to the left before he spoke. "He's over there, having dinner with the boy that he met two days ago."

Monica's eyes followed where Walter was pointing. In a gentle and soft voice she remarked, "He looks so content."

Walter was surprised by the genuine love that Monica seemed to have for his son; it was endearing and melted his heart, for she honestly acted like she was a mom to him.

Monica brought her hands together under her chin, while she gazed into Walter's face. *She had just found the opening that she was looking for.* "You're such a great dad", she sighed. "Have you ever thought about having another child?"

Their conversation was interrupted by the waiter who was bringing them their food. "Enjoy", he expressed happily.

Walter lowered his eyes towards his plate. He wasn't sure how to tell this beautiful woman that he wasn't able to father a child himself, but that he had always prayed to have more children. By chewing his food quite thoroughly, it gave him a moment to come up with the perfect response. When he had formed the reply in his head, he allowed it to flow from his lips.

"I would have loved to have more children, but it just wasn't in the cards", he began. "You see, my wife became ill and our first priority was to make her as comfortable as possible. We had no idea that she could die, and once she was gone and it was only Oliver and myself, I just never entertained the idea of having another child."

Monica's eyes glistened with sadness, for she had not expected to hear anything like what he had just delivered.

Walter turned his head to look in his son's direction. "He's my whole life – the reason I get up in the morning and my motivation to do anything. My goal is to keep him happy, because when he's happy, I'm happy." Walter turned and looked Monica in the eyes. "He's everything to me."

Monica could definitely see how emotional this was for her new friend, and she decided not to continue to grill him any further. She had felt an undying amount of love from Walter to his little boy, and she didn't want to break the mood with anymore unnecessary questions. For the rest of their night together, she would leave this topic alone, but she hoped to pick it up again sometime down the road.

Nico had eaten his meal in his room, for he had a lot to think about. He now knew that he needed to make some decisions about Monica and Penny, but it was important that he make the right ones. He and Monica had a long history together, but there has never been a love life between them. At best, they had always maintained a wonderful friendship. He and Penny had just met, but not only do they have a lot in common, they have great chemistry, and they've also had amazing sex.

Nico could see that he might never attain the love from Monica that he had hoped to get, and after meeting Penny, he no longer had the determination to keep trying. After so many years of being with Monica, doing things for her and waiting for something that might never happen, he was done. The money part was important, but he was tired of chasing her, and now he couldn't care less about pursuing her for anything more than a simple friendship.

Penny was soft and willing, and she was a tiger when it came to sex. He hasn't asked her about her money situation yet, but he didn't feel like it was all that important. She was giving him so much more than a dollar amount in his bank account; she was making him feel manly, strong, and very desirable. He felt ten feet tall when she was near him, and just the thought of her flooded his soul with love.

Penny had also eaten her meal in her room, and was just beginning to pack her things into the suitcase. It didn't take long though, before she remembered Nico's full and eager lips on hers, how her back arched when he touched any part of her, and how he made her tingle from head to toe. Her right fist rushed flat against her mouth as she suddenly remembered another tiny detail – she had never made those small groaning sounds before in her entire life. The skin on her cheeks was beginning to blush and tears were now springing from her eyes, for she was already missing the man who had brought her such joy.

As an empty ache settled into the pit of her stomach, Penny wondered if every memory of him would cause her to weep. Her chest exhaled as a heavy sigh left her slightly-parted lips. She then scolded herself for dwelling on something that might not ever happen again, but she had to agree that it was easy to get lost in the memories. Her mind suddenly rushed to the pictures of their last encounter. No details were left out, and the sight of his gorgeous, firm body, left her sad and weak.

Penny had never been able to give herself completely to a man before, but Nico was special – he had been able to melt the cold part of her personality that she had molded in order to survive. She now felt an incredible warmth for another living soul, and she realized that she couldn't let him walk out of her life.

Monica and Walter were talking nonchalantly about the lovely view and other things, as they strolled along the wooden planks of the 3rd deck. When he reached for her hand, she was barely able to control her gasp of surprise. His hand was larger than hers, strong but soft, and the moment that their skin touched, there was a faint glimmer of electricity which shot between them.

Walter was not surprised, for he had expected that to happen. The depth of his love for her was strange, for it wasn't a desire to get her into bed; it was about how much of his heart she had taken. He had developed a need to grow old with her, on whatever level that she was willing to let him. And because she had squeezed his hand after it had slipped around hers, he sensed that she felt the same way.

A cold shiver ran through Monica's entire body, but it was not because of the breeze coming in off the water. It was because of an enormous feeling of home that had grown in her heart, whenever she looked into his eyes. Being with Walter made her feel safe and loved, and as if she had no cares in the world. Her long lashes swept down towards her cheekbones, as the corners of her mouth rose up. She was smiling with happiness, while truly enjoying the final moments of a most enjoyable cruise.

Walter walked tall and proud for the first time in years. He loved how he felt when he was with Monica, and he loved how much Oliver adored her. As they continued to wander to the other end of the ship, dozens of sentences flooded his mind, all asking if he could stay in touch with her after they dropped anchor. None would come out though, until the moment when he stood at her cabin door.

They were standing face-to-face, his gaze imitating hers, and both of them were filled with worry that from tomorrow on, this moment will be but a lovely memory. They both believed that they might have been joined together by a force that was greater than themselves, and yet, neither one could verbally express how they felt.

In a brave movement, Monica moved her hands and locked them behind his back. The entire front of her body was touching his, and she could feel his muscles quivering, even though he usually carried himself with a commanding air of self-confidence. 'Was he nervous?' she wondered.

Walter's face lit up, showing his approval for what she had just done. The handsome man, who stood a good 5 inches taller than Monica, pulled her closer and kissed the top of her head. He then kissed her forehead, both of her eyes, each cheek, and was heading for her mouth.

Monica's tummy flipped a few times before their lips actually touched, and then she felt the warmth of his mouth cover hers. Their kiss was sensuous and strong, tender and captivating, and she gave herself freely to the passion of the moment. It took her breath away, and she didn't care; it felt so right and she never wanted it to end, and then it did.

As their lips parted, they stood back and stared at what could be their future. For in that brief moment, the clarity was deafening, and they both knew what they wanted.

Walter bent down and kissed her cheek, while he gently stroked her upper arm with his hand. "Have a good sleep, Monica", he whispered, his eyes were still locked with hers. His tone was simmering with hope that they would have many more moments like this, but he couldn't get his voice to confirm it.

Monica inhaled sharply from the way he touched her skin, and sighed from the manner in which he spoke. She wanted to add something back, but she was frozen in awe at how the evening had ended. As she watched him walk down the long hallway towards the elevators, she wanted to run after him, but it felt like her feet had been cemented to the floor. Monica heard the loud familiar ding and she wanted to cry, for now she might never see him again.

As she prepared herself to go to sleep, Penny refused to let any tears fall from her unhappy eyes. Her sadness came from the uncertainty of ever seeing Nico again. He swore that they'd keep in touch, but people say things like that all the time and never mean them. Penny needed to be strong, for she felt that Nico did want to see her again. "You can do this!" she stressed. With everything in her body, she wanted to rush to his room. But because he said they'd see each other in two days, she needed to wait. Penny didn't think she could wait.

The young woman attempted to talk herself into staying in her room for the night, by making promises that she could wake up early and sneak down to Nico's room to say good-bye. "Just try!" she urged herself. She closed her eyes and made an effort to go to sleep, but she struggled to get even an hour's nap.

At 5am, just as Penny was tapping lightly on Nico's door, he was about to open it to go to her. The instant they saw each other, their only emotion was relief, and they immediately rushed towards each other arms. This time, most of their clothes stayed on, and with every kiss, their love intensified. An hour later, with definite promises to see each other soon, Penny and Nico stepped back into their old lives, with their original partners.

Walter and Oliver walked off the ship at 8am with Penny, while Nico and Monica lingered around a little longer, hoping to catch a glimpse of the person that they would rather be with.

At 10am, on that bright and warm Sunday morning, the captain was making his final announcements through the loud speakers. At the end of his short speech, he asked for all passengers to please leave the ship. "And thank you for cruising with Holland America", he concluded.

Nico and Monica picked up their luggage and walked to the taxi stand. After hailing two cabs, they said good-bye, and went to their separate homes.

# Chapter 13

Emotionally, nothing seemed the same, but physically, it was exactly the same as how it was before they all left to go on the cruise.

That first night at home felt empty, for the ambience of being on the ship was now gone. The glorious meals which they had eaten, the maid service, and being in the company of someone new, were now all wonderful moments to remember.

The morning after they had gotten home, Oliver went back to school while everyone else went back to work. The excitement of being at sea was drifting away into memories, and by mid-afternoon, all discussions about their trip had ended.

During the next three days, Monica unpacked her clothes and souvenirs, and washed what was dirty. Nico had called her on Tuesday night, but it was evident that the attraction was no longer there. They spoke about mindless things and hung up mere minutes later, without any promises to see each other soon.

The click at the end of their call was surprisingly loud, and it suddenly made Monica feel awfully lonely. While she sat and stared at the receiver in the cradle, she wondered if she could call Walter. They had kissed, they had had fun, but then she remembered that he was with Penny. That concept made Monica sigh, and she wasn't sure how to mask her inner turmoil.

Nico was surprised by how indifferent he now felt about Monica. He had chased her for longer than he cared to admit, and he had ended up with nothing more than a friend. He then remembered his encounters with Penny. His eyes lit up and he suddenly jumped to attention. His energy soared as his heart raced, and then he rummaged through his luggage to find her number.

Walter and Penny went back to the home that they had shared before leaving for the cruise, and both agreed to sit down for a serious talk. It was harder than either of them had thought it would be, but Walter got his words out first. "I know that I'm no longer in love with you", he said sadly. "During the past week, I saw how unattached Oliver is to you, and he has to be my first priority; if he is not happy, I can't be happy either."

Penny tried to absorb all that he was saying, and while she secretly agreed that she didn't have a connection with Oliver, she wasn't willing to walk away from all that Walter could give her. "But maybe in time, we could build something where he and I could be closer", she suggested. She was struggling and she knew she was losing, but she didn't want to give up without a fight. "Can we give it a week or so, to see if things might change? I mean, now that we're back home again, maybe things will transform back to how they were before?" Her eyes were pleading with him to say yes, but flashes of sexual encounters with Nico were playing through her mind, and her body language was not in sync with what she was saying.

Walter was not one to continue with something when it wasn't working, so he made Penny an offer. "How about if you move out, I'll give you some money, and I'll find you a place to live. How does that sound?" He leaned forward, brought his hands together, and intertwined his fingers as he waited for her to answer.

Penny had to think. If she had gotten to marry him, she would be leaving with a bundle of money and possessions. Because it seemed like he was kicking her out, she believed that she was entitled to something more than 'a little money to tide her over'.

Penny's thoughts were all over the place while her body went into panic mode; she didn't know what to do. With the word 'perhaps' pounding inside of her head, she got down on all fours and shuffled her body towards his. She touched his hands with her own, and gently freed his locked fingers. She then moved herself in between his knees, as if she was going to give him a blow job.

Walter stopped her before she could undo the fastenings on his pants. "That is not going to work, Penny!" he stated sternly. "Sex between us is great, but I need Oliver to have someone who he can love, and who can love him back. I just don't think that you are that someone."

Penny wanted to cry, but she fought against it. With anger welling in every cell of her body, she stood up and raced towards the master bedroom. With a fury of hate enveloping her very being, she threw everything she owned into suitcases, bags, and boxes, and brought them to the front entrance. As she released her grip and let everything drop to the floor, she suddenly realized that she had nowhere to go. And because she had depended on Walter for most of her food, clothing, and all her other necessities, she didn't have much money in her bank account, either.

Walter had been on the phone while Penny was upstairs. What she didn't know, was that he had gotten things prepared for the beginning of her new life. He walked over to her and gave her a hug, even though she pretended to push him away. He then took something out of his pocket and presented it to her. "Here are the keys to the yellow Pinto – I know how much you really like that car."

Penny's face went from sad to happy and pale to flush, when she saw what he was putting into her hand. "Really?" she gasped. This made her very happy, indeed.

*The Pinto had belonged to Evelyn, but it hadn't been used in a very long time. Walter hoped that his wife could see how much joy it had brought to Penny, and maybe she would forgive him for giving it away.*

"And here is $3,000 dollars to help you get started in your new life." He handed the thick, white envelope towards her and continued, "You can count it, if you want."

"No, no, that's fine." She was pleased by what he was giving her, but she believed that it wasn't nearly enough for all that she had done to him and for him, and for his son. "Thank you", she said politely.

"And now", he added. "I just called a friend of mine, and he has a room at the Ritz-Carlton Hotel that you can use. It's only for the next month, until you find your own accommodations, but he assured me that it's really nice."

Penny was startled by all that Walter had given her, and she wasn't able to offer any kind of objection. "Thank you", she said with sincerity.

"We're going to miss you, Penny, and I hope you understand why we can't continue with our relationship." Instead of waiting for her to respond, he reached past her to open the door. "Bye, Penny."

Without saying a word, she carried all of her belongings out to the car and drove away.

As Walter watched his vehicle drive out of sight, he was relieved. There was no sense of sadness associated with Penny's departure, for he realized that he had never really been in love with her. Walter took a second to listen to the silence in the air around him, and then he decided to begin his new life.

After he closed the heavy door, Walter reached into his pocket and pulled out a piece of paper. He dialed the number, and waited for her to answer. There was a click, and then he heard her voice.

"Hello?"

"Hi." Walter was emotional and could hardly lift his voice above a whisper.

"Hi!" A smile of recognition appeared on her face, as she leaned forward and pushed the receiver even closer to her ear. "How are you?"

A second later, the memory of their kiss and the burning desire of wanting more, sparked tingles all over their bodies. Monica and Walter spoke for a little more than two hours before saying good-night, and they had set a day and time to see each other again.

Their first real date went amazingly well, and ended with a lingering kiss at her front door. Their next outing included Oliver, and an instant family was created. It was a full month before Monica and Walter had slept together, and it was different than either of them could have guessed.

Monica had experienced a familiarity that she had not shared with anyone before, and she knew that she would not share with anyone ever again. Nothing they did was rushed, for they took their time to explore, arouse, and to learn what gave the other person pleasure.

For Walter, it was exactly what he had hoped for – tender, loving, and very romantic. He had experienced the wild and adventurous sexcapades with Penny, but he was past middle-age and more than glad to tone it down a bit.

As she closed her eyes to go to sleep, Monica could now see that what she had with Cayson was puppy love – it was a combination of the adrenal of newness and the thrill of their life together. They were both young and in their first real relationships. Monica had so much more with Walter – the warmth and wisdom of being an adult, a sense of home and family, and it was all extremely relaxed and passionate.

The lovebirds slept in each other's arms that night, and it bound their bodies and minds together forever.

In the months since their cruise to Alaska had ended, Nico slowly slipped away from Monica's life – there were no more visits, and soon, even their phone calls had stopped.

Monica didn't notice when Nico had totally disappeared, because her mind was busy with new and wonderful distractions. She was happy in her relationship with Walter and she loved acting like a mom to Oliver. More importantly, she had no desire to change or add to the life that she now had.

Penny and Nico had been seeing a lot of each other, and when the time came for Penny to move out of the hotel, Nico suggested that she move in with him. "That way, we would never have to be apart again."

Penny was deliriously happy by the offer, and accepted right away. Not surprisingly, their money ran out by the end of the year; it was contributed to too much partying and unnecessary heavy-spending, but neither person wanted to admit that. Penny called Walter and asked him for a loan, but he refused to give it to her.

"You'll need to go to work, or find some other way to earn it", he told her. Walter didn't want to be so harsh with his ex-girlfriend, but also he didn't want her to lean on him forever.

Penny sold the Pinto to spite him, but she didn't get as much as she had hoped for.

"Don't worry", Nico mumbled in a low tone. "I'll figure something out." He turned away from her to think, and the tensing of his jaw revealed his deep frustration of the situation.

Monica had been a great source of income for Nico in the past, but they were hardly speaking anymore. She would usually pay for things outright, or at least split the cost of whatever they were doing or eating. She said it was her way of thanking him for all that he had done for her. To Nico, it was another way for him to keep the money in his own pockets.

Because he had lost contact with Monica, it wouldn't be right to ask her for anything, so Nico decided to find another way to buy food and pay bills. The attractive man prided himself at being able to seek out financial opportunities, and he turned back around to convince Penny that they would be okay.

"Something will come up", he promised. A smile suddenly found its way through the mask of their uncertain future.

"I hope so", she replied in a soft tormented voice. She lowered her head as a look of anguish appeared on her face.

Nico placed an index finger under her chin and lifted it up. He then caressed her lips with his own, until he felt her body relax.

One week later, Nico was in a bar and spotted a man who he had known from his days in prison. The two men recognized each other right away, and then they got to talking. They were having a great time over the last hour, and then a third man joined their table. Nico was introduced to him, and then Hunter and Grant began to talk in whispers.

Nico was suddenly the odd man out, and he hated that feeling. With a scowl on his handsome face, he leaned back in his chair and waited for Grant to leave. As soon as he heard the word 'heist' used in a sentence, his ears perked up and he invited himself into their conversation.

"Hey!" he said a little too loudly. "Can I get in on that?" Nico leaned in and quieted his voice. "I really need some serious cash, and I'm willing to do whatever you need me to do."

Hunter was not surprised to hear that Nico was broke, but this gave him an idea. He had worked with Nico on two other projects and he knew what his former cell-mate was capable of. Hunter turned to Grant and tried to assure him that three guys would be better than two. "Nico's okay, trust me. He won't let us down."

Grant looked into Nico's face, and then he couldn't break the stare. Hunter's friend suddenly looked very familiar to him, but he didn't know why. "Don't I know you, man?" he asked, as confusion wrinkled the corners of his eyes and pushed his eyebrows together.

Nico lowered his head in denial. "No, no you don't." He brought his right hand up and repositioned his hair, from the top of his head down to the middle of his face.

"Yah, yah!" Grant confirmed loudly. "Oh, my God! You're that guy who kills women for money. I saw you on the news!" He spoke a little too loud, and he began to chuckle with admiration at how great a gig that must be. "Okay, you're in."

Hunter smacked Nico on the back and laughed. "See? You're in!" he repeated.

Nico smiled and breathed a sigh of relief, for he desperately needed the money. "Thanks, guys. You won't be sorry."

The three men leaned in good and close, so that Nico could learn all the details about the robbery. When Nico heard that they would be splitting upwards of $2 million dollars, he totally agreed to all the terms.

With beers in their hands, they toasted good luck to themselves, and sealed the deal with a firm handshake.

A week later, Nico asked Penny to drive him to an address which he had written down on a piece of paper. As he got out of the car, he went over the instructions again. "Move the car three blocks away, but keep the motor running. Come back here in fifteen minutes, and after I get into the car, I need you to drive away like a bat out of hell."

Nico's voice was stern, and now he waited for Penny to nod in agreement.

Penny didn't fully understand what was going on, but she loved the idea that they would end up fairly wealthy - all she had to do was listen and obey to everything that Nico told her.

Because this was very important and Penny hadn't acknowledged that she had heard him, Nico stressed his point again. "You are driving me, Nicole is driving Hunter, and Matt is driving Grant. If you screw this up, I can't run fast enough to get to another car. Okay, so far?"

"Yes." She was nervous and wet her dry lips.

Nico continued. "I'll be inside the house, but once the timer goes off, we need to get out of there as quickly as possible." He paused to make his point stronger. "I'll need you to be right here when I come out. Do you understand?"

Penny had fear written all over her face, but she nodded, as it all sounded perfectly clear. "I hear you", she said with confidence. She loved him and she couldn't wait for the money to come into her hands. "I won't let you down", she promised.

Nico swallowed hard as he watched her nod. When he reached for the long handle, his mental state showed both relief and panic. He opened and then shut the car door, and stood completely still while looking up towards the sky. He made the sign of the cross on his chest, and then prayed to God that this will work as well as they had planned.

Penny drove the car a few blocks forward, just as she had been told to do. She marked the time on the car's clock, and began to count down.

The three men were inside the house, robbing the owner blind, with no-one knowing that they were even there. After breaking into the safe, they inspected every element of worth throughout the house, and even peeked inside the drawers and on the shelves for other valuable items. Everything was going as planned, until...

Someone had stopped and asked Penny for directions. "Can you help me?" an elderly man asked. He seemed confused and disoriented. "I'm looking for Webber Street."

The last time Penny looked at the clock, she still had four minutes to go before she had to turn the car around and park across the street from where Nico had gotten out. She opened the window and pointed, while trying to guide the man to where he needed to go.

The stranger was becoming frustrated because he couldn't hear well, and he did not understand what she was telling him. The man had now taken Penny's attention for far longer than she had wanted, which ultimately foiled Nico's plan to escape.

"Now!" Hunter shouted, when the timer began to beep. It was a firm order – one which had no other option. The three men grabbed their bags of loot and scattered to the exit doors as quickly as possible. Hunter and Grant ran out to their cars and were driven away to safety. When Nico ran outside to put everything into his car, he was shocked to find that Penny was nowhere in sight.

"Where the fuck are you?" he growled through clenched teeth. He thought he could see the car up the road, but it was too far away for him to run to. He couldn't shout her name, for fear that someone would hear him. "Damn!" he cursed. He couldn't remember the last time when he had been so angry, but he had no time to panic. With seconds to spare, he desperately needed to find a place to hide. His bulging wide eyes were scanning everything that was close to him. He was pissed that nothing seemed to be big enough for his own body, plus the bags which were holding the many items which he had taken from the house.

Nico could feel his hands begin to shake, and because his throat was closing up, it felt like he was suffocating. His head was swimming with too many thoughts, and because he was becoming worried and he wasn't thinking straight, his little world was suddenly being filled with terror and anxiety.

When he heard the many sirens racing to get to the expensive house, Nico had no choice but to duck into a bush which was sitting on the very edge of the property. He didn't know that it might be a little small until it was too late, but he was rushing and had run out of options.

Nico's heart was pounding, as his body was slowly covering itself with nervous sweat. He tucked his feet in and he sunk down as flat as he could go, onto the small bunch of crispy leaves on the ground. Summer was turning into autumn, which meant that the modest-sized bush was losing its fullness, and Nico wasn't hidden as well as he thought he was.

A police car came to a halt mere feet from the bush, and when Nico saw it, he held his breath. His eyes were open as wide as they could go, as he peered through the antler-like branches, which had begun to lose its leaves. Nico knew that he needed to wait until the coast was clear before he could make his escape, so he stayed as still as a rock. As luck would have it, a daddy long legs spider began to walk on Nico's cheek. Nico thought it was something tiny and brushed it away with his fingertips, but when he felt that it was much larger than a small bug on his skin, he screamed and squirmed to get away from it. With unexplained fear in soul, Nico bolted up while brushing the spider off of his head and upper body. Unfortunately, his foot got caught on a low branch as he was trying to escape from being bitten. He was panicking and confused, and Nico ended up tripping, as he moved from the inside of the bush to the outside.

Officer Jerry Greening was talking on the two-way radio, announcing that he and his partner had arrived at the location. He was describing the activity onsite to the dispatcher, when all of a sudden, someone was screaming and bounding out of the nearby bush. As the officer jumped from sheer fright, he let out a high-pitched, shrieking cry, which lasted for 5 seconds.

Officer Lawrence Cornacchia turned around when he heard his fellow officer scream, and ran back to see what was going on.

Before Officer Greening could catch his breath, Officer Cornacchia noticed the large bags in the bush, and reached for them. After opening one up, his eyes grew wide with surprised by the amount of valuable items that it contained. "I'm going to venture a guess and say that this is not yours, right?" he asked with suspicion in his voice. His head was tilted to the side as he spoke to the disheveled man on the ground.

Nico was mortified at being caught, and didn't say a word.

"You're under arrest", Officer Greening stated, as he grabbed Nico by the scruff of the neck. He motioned for

Officer Cornacchia to tell the other officers that one of
the suspects has been captured. "And I'll need them to
continue to find clues, in case there were more people
involved in the robbery", he added.

*Officer Lawrence Cornacchia was thrilled to be out
from behind a steel desk, after being seriously shot and
wounded a year ago. His wife would have loved to have him
off the streets for good, but Suzanna knew how much her
husband's job meant to him. Because there was nothing else
she could do, she prayed for him every morning when he left
the house, and said thanks to God when she saw him come
home every night. She wanted Lawrence to be happy, and if
that meant letting him be a cop on active duty, then so be it.*

Officer Cornacchia gave a thumbs-up as he nodded
his head in compliance, and did exactly what he was told
to do. "Listen up!" he called loudly, as he ran to the other
officers in the area.

Officer Greening turned back to Nico, and handcuffed
him as he recited the Miranda Warning. "You have the
right to remain silent ...", he began. His sultry voice was
filled with conviction, as he continued to list the many
points which the prisoner needed to hear.

"For the record, do you understand your rights as I have
explained them to you?" the officer asked as he led Nico to
the city-owned vehicle.

"Yes", Nico replied, as a look of rejection came over his
face.

"Good", the officer stated. Nico's answer had been recorded in the officer's notes.

The instant Nico was put into the back of the police car, he glanced down the road and saw his getaway car, which was still sitting three blocks away. Curiosity, confusion, anger, frustration, and several other emotions ran through his brain, one right after the other, and it was all for the same question – 'why was Penny still sitting there?'

The arresting officer had turned the key to start the motor, and as his vehicle began to roll towards downtown, Nico took one more look at the car he had hoped to drive away in, and he cursed under his breath.

"This is Four Two Nine Twenty-Six", Officer Greening called into the two-way radio.

"Dispatch, go ahead."

"We have one suspect in custody, but have no idea how many more are involved. Please standby for more details."

"Your ETA?"

"15 minutes."

"10-4"

Nico suddenly became very aware of a tightening feeling around his throat, and as he swallowed hard to remove it, he realized that it might be anxiety.

*Nico knew all too well what lay ahead of him, and with this arrest, there was a very good chance that he might be in prison for a lot longer than he would want to be.*

Penny had not heard or concerned herself with the blaring sound of the sirens off in the distance, for she didn't know that they were racing to get to the house that had just been robbed. Her entire attention had been on giving directions to the elderly stranger, who said he was lost and needed to get back home.

Penny hadn't meant to take so much time with the old, almost skeletal man, but she felt sorry for him. The wispy white hair on the top of his head was a mess, he was wearing tattered clothes and one shoe, and he looked like he might have some sort of mental problem.

Penny tried to give the confused man some very clear instructions on how to get where he needed to be, and without a doubt, had she had more time, she would have taken him to Webber Street, herself.

Once Penny was satisfied that the old guy was heading in the right direction, she smiled with pride.

"Thank you!" the elderly man said, in a soft and gentle voice.

"You're welcome!" Penny called to the stranger. Her eyes glanced to the clock on the dashboard in her car, and she gasped loudly. "Oh my gosh!" she called out. She was very late and now had to hurry. With no time to spare, she put the car into drive, made a U-turn, and raced to get to the pick-up spot as quickly as possible.

Before Penny could get within a block of the house, she saw a bunch of policemen and many colored, flashing lights in the area. "Shit!" she cursed, and kept driving as if she had another destination to go to. As she passed the property where Nico had gotten out of the car, Penny drove slower so she could scan the area. She also hoped that if Nico saw the car, that he would run to it and they could escape without being caught.

A large police officer noticed that she was driving excessively slow, and demanded that she 'move along'. "Let's go!" he ordered with his voice and animated hand gestures.

"Yes, officer", she replied politely. "I was just looking." She put her foot down harder on the gas pedal and smiled, but inside, Penny was scared and tried not to freak out. She desperately wanted to know where Nico was, but who should she ask? If she went to the police, they might question her motives for why she was asking. And she knew that she shouldn't go back to Nico's home – wasn't that the first place that the police would go?

Penny realized that it was her fault that they were not together, and she hoped that Nico was alright. Being alone and scared, caused her emotions to get the better of her. She pulled out her wallet and saw that she didn't have a lot of money, but it was obvious to her, that she would need to stay in hiding until the coast was clear.

As a few tears fell down her cheeks, she drove to the nearest McDonald's and ordered some food. She then sat in the car while she nibbled mindlessly on the greasy protein and potatoes. When she was done eating, the crying woman stared out of the front window and wondered what she should do.

In the meantime, Nico had been taken to the police station. After he had been finger printed and his I.D. had been checked, someone remarked that they recognized his name from somewhere.

"Anybody know anything about a Nicholas Kostas?" the officer asked to the people around him. As Officer Kyle Zip revolved his head to survey the crowd, he watched as some officers shook their heads, and two others walked to the file cabinets. "That name does sound familiar", one of them muttered. "I just don't know why." Within minutes, that same man shouted that he had found something.

"Says here that we have housed Mr. Kostas more than a few times already", the senior officer stated. Officer Danny Esford delivered his statement, as if his comment was almost humorous. "According to his file, our friend has been awarded life insurance payouts from quite a few dearly departed women."

"I think I remember hearing about that!" Officer Zip added. Without completing his thought, he ran to another room to get the newspapers articles that could possibly fill in the blanks.

As Officer Esford continued to study the details in Nico's folder, the young officer hurried back into the room.

"You've gotta check this out!" Officer Zip shouted. He was intentionally waving a bunch of papers in the air so that everyone would notice.

The captain, who had heard bits and pieces of the commotion, was in his office writing up a brief. After hearing the young officer claim that he had found more information about Nicolas Kostas, the captain stormed into the room. "Let me see that!" he ordered.

Officer Zip, who had just come back to work after a glorious 2-week honeymoon, passed all of what he had in his hand to the taller man. He then took two steps back, and watched while his fellow officer absorbed the lengthy details under the headlines.

Captain Brynn lowered his eyes, and flipped through the shocking information with disbelief written all over his face. "Geez!" he shouted before he was done. "How could he have gotten away with this for so long?"

A moment later, he looked up and congratulated his young officer. "Good job, Officer Zip."

"Thank you, sir!" A proud grin softened his already handsome features, and he couldn't wait to get to a phone and tell his wife.

When the captain had read enough, he slammed the folder shut. He then turned and made an announcement to his group. "Ok, listen up. Because it's highly unusual to be the beneficiary of that many spouses or girlfriends, we have no choice but to launch an investigation", he began.

"Stand here!" someone ordered, after a few loud movements.

Captain Brynn's head spun around with great speed, when two police officers walked into the room and rudely interrupted his speech. He was angry, but when he noticed that they were each holding an arm of Mr. Nicholas Kostas, this soured his already scornful expression. Without any warning, the captain used his loud gruff voice to bark, "Lock him up!"

"Yes, sir!" one of the officers replied.

As the prisoner was walking out of the room, the captain turned back to his men and continued his speech. Moments later, he praised his wonderful group. "Fine job, everyone. Now, let's get back to work."

As Nico was being led to the elevator, his head was bent forward and his entire body became submissive; he hated that he was going to have to spend more time behind bars. No more was he a smug individual who could scam hundreds of thousands of dollars from unsuspecting females. Jail was now his home, and he would be known by a number, rather than a name, from here on out.

Since he met Monica, Nico had screwed around with many women without getting caught, but he hadn't purposely gained any wealth from someone's death. But since facts were facts, and his past was being written about in newspaper articles for everyone in the world to see, he couldn't fight what he had done so long ago. With sorrow and regret filling every pore in his body, Nico resolved that he might not ever be in the free world again.

# 'CLINK'

The iron bar to his 6' x 8' jail cell, closed and locked louder than he had remembered, and now Nico was totally alone with his thoughts. He wondered what had happened to Penny, and hoped that she had not been caught. He had no way to get hold of her, and with a heavy heart, he knew there was nothing he could do to find her.

Nico honestly did love her, but his conscience now convinced him that she was better off without him. As he pressed his face tightly into the palms of his hands, he wished that he knew where she was, and if she was okay.

Because she was petrified that she would also be implicated in the robbery, Penny took the money which she had in her wallet, and ran scared for the next two days. She drove past Nico's home three or four times every 24 hours, and when she thought it was safe, she snuck in through the back door, and grabbed her belongings. She also took anything that she could pawn, and then drove to a town that was four hours away.

The town was beautiful, but it wasn't home. After finding a shop where she could exchange material possessions for money, she went in search of a motel room. Penny paid for one week up front, and then she drove up and down the picturesque streets of Aisley Sound, in hopes of finding a job.

It had been a few hours since she began her mission, and Penny was beginning to worry. She couldn't believe it when she saw a 'help wanted' sign, in the front window of a bar. Penny let out a short scream of delight, much like that of a little girl on her birthday, who had gotten the one gift that she had asked for.

'Waitress Needed As Soon As Possible'
'No Experience Necessary'

A smile trembled over her soft lips, when she sensed a faint bit of hope on the horizon. Penny parked the car and got out. She tried to compose herself, then fluffed her hair and straightened her posture. When she felt that she was ready, she went inside to talk with the manager.

"You ever been a waitress before?" he asked. His voice was deep and loud, but not intimidating.

"Oh, sure!" she lied. Her hands moved wildly in the air in front of her, as she fibbed her way through the entire interview. Whatever he asked, she had done it. And for added measure, she played with her hair and acted overly friendly, in case that would help her get the job.

The manager wasn't sure how to interpret her body language, but he had no interest in anything else but hiring a waitress. "Well, I see no reason why you can't start tomorrow." He held out his hand to shake hers and continued. "Be here at 3pm. If you do a good job, we'll give you more shifts."

Penny's heart jumped with enthusiasm. "3pm, I'll be here!" She knew that she sounded a little too eager, but she really needed the money. "Thank you", she said in a very happy tone, but she tried not to be too loud. Her spirits were now lifting, and the excitement added shine to her eyes as well as a red glow to her cheeks. "You won't be sorry."

The manager was amused by her young energy and charm, and he hoped that he had done the right thing by hiring her; he needed help in the bar, but he didn't have time to babysit anyone.

At the police station, almost 4 hours away, another decision was being made. Without having to delve too far, the two detectives who were assigned to the case, had uncovered enough evidence to put Nico away for a very long time.

'Conspiracy to Murder' was the charge that they had hoped to pin on Nico. But because they couldn't find any substantial evidence to indicate that he had planned or caused any of the women's deaths, Nico would not be charged with attempted murder. But, because he had collected money from all of their life insurance policies, bank accounts, personal possessions, etc…, he was going to be charged with numerous counts of fraud, which equaled somewhere in the neighbourhood of 4 million dollars. While that's a lot of money, the lawyers on both sides of this case, felt that the lawsuit was loaded with suspicions of even more that Nico should be found guilty of.

A trial date was set for 6 months down the road, and jury selection would begin in 6 weeks. The attorneys for both sides, and their very qualified teams, were going over their notes with a fine toothed comb, to ensure that their strategies would end in victory. Behind the scenes, a certain magistrate was being pursued to preside over this particular case.

Judge Bradford was well-known for his many high profile verdicts. He didn't care if a TV camera was in his court room or not, and he made sure to umpire each case as a standalone incident. Even though the magistrate in question had semi-retired last year to write a book, the 62-year old, grey-haired man was itching to end his career on a high note. Because the accusations against Nicholas Kostas involved murder and mystery, just like in his story, the judge took great pleasure in accepting the offer to get back on the bench. He gladly pushed everything else aside for that 3-month time period, and he felt truly honored to be part of the final ruling.

The Honorable Josh Bradford had heard bits and pieces of the many facts that were being thrown around in regards to this trial, but because he wanted to be totally impartial, the judge would not listen to or read anything pertaining to this case, until it was presented in his courtroom.

Meanwhile, the rest of society, as well as all forms of media, were having a field day with this impending trial. Because Nico was single and very attractive, many women had fallen in love with him and began to write him letters. They wanted to show him their support, and to offer him their hands in marriage. A small handful of men cheered him on, for trying to make a living off of unsuspecting women. But most citizens were furious with all that he had done, and protested in marches, with hopes that he would be made to stay in jail indefinitely.

In the voting sectors, large amounts of money were illegally laid out on whether Nico was going to be found guilty or innocent. In the end, the odds were 80-1 that Nico would never be a free man again.

When that terrifying statement reached his ears, it hit Nico harder than he had expected, and he was left momentarily speechless. The handsome man gasped loudly at how final it all sounded, and lowered his head in sorrow. Mere moments later, a single tear escaped from the outside corner of his right eye, which was soon followed by a thousand more salty drops. It was the first time in his entire life that Nico had cried - not for the women who had lost their lives because of his greed, but for the loss of his own freedom.

Penny loved being a waitress and she genuinely appreciated where she worked; it was dark and loud, the other employees were patient and helpful, the customers liked her, and she felt hidden from the rest of the world.

And it didn't take long before the pretty young woman felt like her old self again - flirty and funny.

Among the many people who came in to 'Uncle Bob's Bar' for the daily lunch specials, a few of the regular customers came back in the evening, but only if they knew that Penny was working. She loved it when they began to say Hi to her by name, and she never got tired of them asking her how she liked working there.

But it was the manager who Penny really looked forward to seeing, for he made her feel like she was the most important person on the planet.

Austin Barnes was a very good man – slightly older, slightly grey, he loved cooking, and he had a fondness for beer. While the burly man looked like a large ex-biker, he was really a teddy bear with a soft heart. Austin had never married and hadn't had many girlfriends, for he said, "I've never found the one that made my heart flutter."

From the first moment he laid eyes on her, he knew that she was different. Austin saw something in Penny that she probably hadn't ever seen in herself. It soon became his mission to protect her, and to get her to know how truly wonderful she was. But as much as Austin tried to keep her safe, he soon found out that he couldn't shield her from everything.

Three weeks and two days after becoming a waitress, Penny saw Nico's face, and that's when she learned what had happened to him.

Penny was not one for watching game shows or ½ hour sitcoms, but one day, while she was bringing some dirty dishes back to the kitchen, she caught a glance at the TV hanging off the wall. There, in full color, and taking up the entire screen, was a picture of a man who she knew as Nico. His dark eyes were staring straight at her, and she suddenly couldn't catch her breath. Her muscles stiffened and she felt cold, but she couldn't turn her eyes away from the TV set.

Nico's picture disappeared, and it was replaced by a handsome, middle-aged reporter sitting at a long desk. He was revealing the troubled past of Nicolas Kostas to the world, and providing everyone with the juicy details of his current trial – nothing was being omitted.

Penny held her breath while the reporter listed all of the women who Nico had been with, and she was thankful that her name had not been among them. She sighed with relief that she was not going to be implicated in anything pertaining to Nico, and then she listened to the rest of the story.

"It was said that Mr. Kostas was not given the right to have bail, on the hunch from the bench that he would flee. That means that Mr. Kostas will have to stay in jail until his hearing", the reporter stated. After two more sentences about Nico's trial, the man concluded this story, and began a new one from a different camera angle.

'How could he do that?' her inner voice asked. Penny couldn't believe that she had once been in love with that deceitful man, and it made her want to cry.

"Order up!" Austin called loudly from the kitchen – it was his favorite place on earth. He shared the cooking duties as often as possible, and played bartender the rest of the time.

Penny walked towards the kitchen, put the dirty dishes down onto the counter, and then raced to grab the new order. As she was bringing the fresh food to the customers out front, her body cringed from all that she had heard. As she set the food down in front of the four individuals, she forced a fake smile to spread across her beautiful face, but inside she was dying. "There you go", she said softly, and then she moved herself away from the table.

Penny had been filled with worry for the man who she had met on the cruise, and now hasn't seen since the day he helped rob that house. She had come up with dozens of guesses as to what could have happened to him, but after hearing what he had done, she had to agree with the rest of the world, that Nico is right where he belongs. As she walked back to the kitchen, Penny scolded herself for being such a fool.

*Up until these last few moments, whenever Penny reminisced about their time together, it was flawless, like a romantic fantasy. She had adored Nico and constantly ached for his touch, and now she despised him with every fiber in her body.*

"How could I have known?" she moaned softly, as her eyelids dropped.

Austin saw the expression on her face and wondered what had happened to bring about the faint, rose colored flush to her cheekbones. "Are you ok?" he asked with real concern. He could feel his temper climbing, and he was getting mentally prepared to fight with the customer who was responsible for her pain. All he needed was the name of the person and where they were sitting.

When she heard his voice, Penny raised her chin, and after throwing a cool stare in his direction, she rushed into his arms without thinking. The embrace was unexpected and only lasted a few seconds, but it was well received by both Penny and Austin.

Austin had not hugged a woman in a very long time, and he loved how powerful it felt to be able to give this kind of comfort to someone who really needed it. He reached around her with both of his arms, and held her even tighter against his body.

Austin's musky aroma wafted through all of Penny's senses, leaving a lasting memory that distinguished him from every other man she had ever met. His frame was larger than most of her boyfriends, and she loved how protected she felt in his arms.

Suddenly, the idea that they were hugging felt very wrong. "S-sorry", Penny stated. Her voice was fragile and soft. "I shouldn't have done that." With embarrassment in her soul, she cast her eyes downward, and then walked to the other side of the kitchen. "I had a bad moment, but I'm okay now."

Austin's eyes followed her as she moved around the square room. He was now very worried about her, for when their bodies were so close, Austin could feel that she was trembling. He trusted that whatever had caused her to be upset, would not keep her sad for too long. "Are you sure?" he asked with genuine concern; her pain was now his pain.

She nodded slowly, and then turned her face away from his.

Austin's heart was breaking. He wanted to rush into her arms again, but he chose to keep their relationship on a professional level. "I hope so", he said, after he saw her signal that she was ok. Reluctantly, he moved himself back to the stove and left her alone to work through her pain.

Penny appreciated how well he understood her feelings, and she made a mental note to return the favor on another day. For now, she had customers to serve and tables to clean.

Penny finished her shift at 2am, and she was proud that she had worked the whole day, while pretending that everything was okay. The reporter's words had echoed in her ears all evening, and now it was time to take Nico out of her mind forever.

As soon as she got to her motel room, Penny gathered up all the photos and other memorabilia that she had of him, and she threw them into the large garbage bin at the main gate. While she was walking back to her room, she slapped her hands together as if she was cleansing her soul. "Good riddance", she called to the air around her.

Penny cried herself to sleep that night, and dreamed that Nico had apologized for all that he had done. He also forgave her for not coming back with the car. But this was not the same man who she had had great times with; she remembered him being taller, sexier, standing proud, and walking with a strut of confidence. This man in her dreams was small, hunched over, weak, and he had admitted to doing some terrible things.

With tears in their eyes, they said good-bye to each other, and when Penny woke up the next morning, she realized that her heart was now free of him.

Austin went to bed that night, worrying about Penny. They hadn't known each other for very long, but he hoped that she was going to be okay. Because he didn't want to cross over the lines of employee/employer relations, he had no other option but to wait. And the next time he saw her, Austin couldn't believe his eyes.

"Morning!" she called, as she walked cheerfully from the front door of the bar to the kitchen. Penny looked refreshed and was beaming from ear-to-ear.

Austin's mouth hung open in sheer awe. Penny appeared to be emotionally stronger, and she was in a cheerful mood. Because they didn't know each other that well, Austin didn't feel he had the right to ask for any information. She seemed truly happy and that's all that he cared about. "Morning!" he replied, as he reached for a clean apron. And while the corners of his eyes crinkled and a smile grew across his 5 o'clock shadowed face, he prepared the stove for the lunch time rush.

Nico's trial had become a world-wide phenomenon, and the countless details of his torrid past were now spilling out of every reporter's mouth. Nico's name had suddenly become so famous, that it was being used as a reference for when mother's cautioned their daughters about men. "You don't want to go out with someone like Nico", they warned.

Thankfully, Penny's name had not been mentioned in any form of media. She felt blessed and continued to breathe small sighs of relief, while hoping that it never would. She continued working at "Uncle Bob's Bar' – not for the money, or for the fact that she believed it was a good place to hide, but because she truly liked the atmosphere and the people.

That night after closing, Penny told Austin that she was thinking of moving out of her small motel room. Austin was more than happy to help her, and they talked about it over a quick cup of coffee.

It took a week before Austin found a small apartment for her to move into, and after that, their business relationship leaned more on the verge of friendship. Both were aware that their protective walls were slowly tumbling down, but they were still trying to keep things on a professional level.

Three weeks later, Austin was short-staffed and asked her to help out in the kitchen. After 6 hours of working side-by-side in the hot, 13' x 13' squared room, the dynamics of their friendship changed again. They found themselves bumping into each other, or grabbing for the same item at the same time. Because it had happened so often, it was hard to say if it was done by accident or on purpose. Before the end of the shift, it caused them both to re-evaluate the reasons behind their overwhelming need to be close.

In the weeks that followed, their happiness and laughter turned into small displays of affection; his hand gently landed on her forearm, or her head leaned against his chest or shoulder. While these intimate seconds eventually exposed their real feelings to each other, they tried their best to keep things business-like.

# Chapter 14

Six months after they met, Austin arrived at work all dressed up, and he was holding a bouquet of flowers in his hand. He stood right in front of Penny and cleared his throat. "Would you like to go for dinner and to a movie with me?" The look on his face was priceless; it seemed like he was about to throw up, but trying really hard not to.

Penny couldn't contain her excitement and said yes by jumping into his arms.

Everything about their date was wonderful - from beginning to end. And when their lips made contact for the very first time, it confirmed what they already knew; they had fallen in love. Because they saw no reason to wait, Penny married Austin one month later, in the same spot where they had first met - in the office at the bar. From that day forward, she was officially known as Penelope Barnes – her new legal name.

Nico's trial lasted 5 weeks, and it had been sensationalized to the max. It had triggered a backlash of emotion and anger, and dozens of lawsuits from the families of the many women who he had been involved with. Everyone had their hand out, but unfortunately, nobody was going to get any money; there wasn't enough to go around.

Nico's name and picture were now everywhere, including on the front page of the local paper in Monica's town.

It had been a full year since they had all gotten back from their cruise, but each time Monica saw Nico's face on the news, she flinched with fear that he would reach out to her.

Monica's heart pumped faster than normal, as she gazed into the face of a man who she had almost spent the rest of her life with. Like everyone else, she had heard fragments of details about him and his past from the papers and TV, but she wanted to believe that it was all gossip. Because she had not seen him in a very long time, it was easy enough to ignore what everyone was saying.

"Morning, honey!" Walter called as he came into the room.

"Have you seen this?" Monica asked. She held the page out so that Walter could see what she was talking about.

Walter had tried to avoid every avenue of publicity which Monica's friend was receiving. He could care less about the man who he had shared a brief few days with on the cruise, and he tried to keep the details of Nico's past and his trial away from Oliver. Walter wanted his home to be filled with happiness, and the destruction of someone as evil as Monica's former friend, was not welcome.

"Look!" she demanded when she saw that he was avoiding her request.

Walter took one look at the picture and his mind exploded. The look on Nico's face had instantly triggered the memory of when he and Walter had shared a jail cell together. Right away, all the specifics of the corruption that had followed after their release, shot past his eyes. Everything came flooding back, all the grim details of their escapades, and it made him sick.

'Why didn't I recognize this man when we were on the ship?' Walter wondered. He then turned to face Monica, and there was the answer.

Walter had already fallen in love with her, and he couldn't see past the end of his nose. The instant he saw her and Oliver in the pool, he felt his heart skip a beat and he somehow knew that he would spend the rest of his life with her.

Nico was never a formidable part of the cruise to Walter, and until this very moment, Walter hadn't put all the pieces of the puzzle together.

"How could he have done that?" she stated, not knowing if it was out loud or in her head. Monica had just read some of the details that were written in the large article, and her mind was spinning before it went completely blank.

"I don't know", Walter stated, in a voice that was a little louder than a whisper. Because he did not have a blemish-free past, Walter realized that he needed to change the subject. He took the newspaper from her in a rather aggressive manner, and folded it in half. He then tucked it into his briefcase and made himself promise to throw it away when he got to work. "Will you be okay if I take it with me?"

Monica snapped out of her short trance when she heard his caring question. She wrapped her arms around Walter's waist, and stared up and into his handsome face. She loved his compelling blue eyes, the wrinkles which appeared when he smiled, his confident set of shoulders, and how his firm mouth curled just seconds before he laughed.

"Honey?" Walter's lips remained slightly parted after he tried to catch her attention, displaying a dazzling example of straight, white teeth.

"I'm just drinking in your beauty", she sighed. She spoke in a soft tone, which reflected her love and respect for him.

Walter smiled at her loving gesture. "Thank you." He kissed the tip of her nose and then tenderly released himself from their embrace. He bent down and grabbed his briefcase and lunch, and then told her to have a good day. "Oh, and maybe you'd consider marrying me in the near future." He began to walk away, but stopped when he heard her scream.

"WHA-A-AT?" Monica had been caught off guard, but she couldn't have been any happier. She shouted yes a thousand times while jumping in the air, and then she asked where Oliver was, so she could tell him.

Oliver had been in his room, but he dashed down the stairs when he heard the commotion. "What's happening?" He was spooked because of the screaming, but confused when he saw her smiling.

"We're getting married!" Walter replied happily.

"WHA-A-AT?" Oliver screamed. He was very loud, and also very excited. The little boy regarded Monica as a mom, but after they got married, he could legally call her mom. This made him extremely happy, and he was jumping up and down along with Monica.

"Like mother, like son", Walter joked to himself as he watched them.

While it was hard to resume the stance of a normal work and school day, they all tried their best. That night, the three of them celebrated by going out for supper, and then they talked about where and when the ceremony should be held.

The next couple of months went by quickly, for their days were full of decisions and ideas, and planning and buying. Invitations were sent out, the honeymoon was paid for, and time was booked off. Their special moment was approaching quickly, and all three of them were getting more and more excited.

On the day before their wedding, Walter had a lot on his mind. Without realizing what he had done, he asked his bride-to-be to grab his blue tie from the bottom drawer of his dresser. "I want to see how it matches with this suit", he confessed. He was wearing a jacket and pants with a white shirt, but he wasn't sure which tie he should add to his ensemble.

Monica was only too glad to get it, as she was already going upstairs for something else. She went into the bedroom and opened the bottom drawer. She stuck her hand in to grab a few ties, and hit something stiff and sharp. "Huh?" A melancholy frown flew across her pretty features.

Monica was surprised that her skin had been grazed in a clothing drawer, so she moved everything out of the way in order to see what had scratched her. It was a large brown envelope, and because the flap wasn't sealed shut, she could see that there was a stiff piece of cardboard and official papers inside.

Monica wasn't sure that she should snoop, but in case it was something important, she thought she should take a look. She found many important documents that she assumed, Walter must have tucked away for safekeeping. With her finger tips, she moved each one forward, until she found one of interest. "Oh, we'll need this", she stated, when she saw his birth certificate. As she riffled through the rest of the documents, she stumbled across something that looked like adoption papers. She pulled the pages out to examine them more closely.

Monica's eyes shot wide open, when she realized what she had in her hands. She was in complete shock, and it felt like the whole room would shatter, like delicate crystal falling to the ground. She wanted to run and ask Walter what this was all about, but instead, her legs folded beneath her and she was now sitting on the floor, her eyes devouring every word for the second time.

M. Bellam and C. Ross were listed as the birth parents, and W. Ryng and E. Ryng were listed as the adoptive parents. The document also exposed the date of the delivery, the name of the hospital, her room number, the time of Oliver's birth, and the names of the nurses and doctor who had delivered the beautiful baby boy.

Monica noticed that the letterhead did not appear to be genuine. She also noticed that there was no official red seal on the bottom of the page, and that there was no lawyer's signature or name, anywhere on the 8x11.5" pieces of paper. It did have Walter and Evelyn's names and address printed in bold letters at the top, and their names were also written in the first line of the certificate. As well, Monica could see their signatures down at the bottom, right beside the fee of $1,000 a month. Her eyes bugged out of her head as she examined that number a second time. "What?" she whispered in disbelief. Monica was crushed when she realized that she had gotten a smaller portion of the amount which was stated in this certificate.

"Could this be a legal document?" she questioned with mistrust and concern. Monica held it closer to her face in order to see every single word. She then noticed another cause to be uneasy; because of how many spelling mistakes the document had, it looked like someone had typed it up far too quickly.

Monica couldn't believe it, and leaned back until her body was touching the bed. As she sat there wondering what to do, she was shocked and filled with anger.

Monica suddenly remembered how forceful Nico had been during her pregnancy – insisting that he could find suitable parents for her child, and convincing her that he would take care of everything. He made her believe that all she had to do was deliver her child, and then she could carry on with the rest of her life.

Monica wanted to cry, for she had been such a fool. It was becoming clear to her now, that Nico had devised this plan as a way for him to make money.

Monica remembered how he swore that he had checked out the background of these adoptive parents, to make sure that they were honest, kind, and able to raise her little boy with love and the best of intentions. She then remembered how often Nico had tried to keep her away from Walter and Oliver, when they were all on the ship together.

Her mind was suddenly simmering with a million questions, but the first one she wanted to ask is, 'Does Walter know that she is Oliver's mother?'

Monica lowered her head in amazement, at how many questions she didn't know the answers to. She realized now that many things had gone on behind her back, while to her face, Nico was claiming that he loved her and wanted to be with her.

As Monica stared down at the phony adoption papers again, she wondered if she would ever know the truth. 'Do Nico and Walter know each other? How did Walter end up with her baby?' She wanted to ask these questions and others, but to who?

Monica was suddenly drained of all emotions, and she wanted to cry. Her memories drifted once again, to when they were all on the ship together. In her mind's eye, it didn't look as if they had known each other, but then, the two men didn't talk much when they were in the same place at the same time. She couldn't even remember them making odd facial expressions whenever the other man's name was mentioned. 'Were they just playing it cool?' she wondered.

Because everyone on the planet knew that Nico was in jail, she couldn't ask him about the adoption, for fear of being associated with him. Her name had not been mentioned in any report or article so far, and she wanted to keep it that way. And even if she was able to ask him any questions, who knows if he would tell her the truth?

The whole time that Monica had known Walter, he never brought up Nico's name - except to repeat a few words that he'd heard about the trial. And as much as she could recall, Walter had never asked her to leave Nico, or gave her any reasons to. With this in mind, Monica was suddenly feeling foolish; Walter had given her a plausible story about why he only had one child, and never once did he try to run away when Nico was near him or his son.

As if she was in a dream-like state, Monica wondered if she had become overly paranoid. Somehow, Nico had gotten Walter to adopt her son. Years later, fate stepped in and brought mother and child together again.

Monica couldn't help but smile at the mere thought of her gorgeous little boy. And because Oliver was very happy and Walter did a great job in raising him, Monica decided to push the adoption papers back into the envelope, and never bring up the subject again. However, she would openly appear grateful to both Nico and Walter, for keeping her son safe.

Without a warning, Oliver ran into the bedroom with a copious amount of energy. "Daddy wants to know where his tie is", he stated. The little boy dropped himself onto her lap with a thud, and then placed one leg on each side of her body. He stared at her face and watched her expression change.

Monica had become startled by the loud noise, and suddenly lost her train of thought. The instant the boy plumped his body down onto hers, she placed all of her emotions on what her child was about to show her. "What have you got in your hands?" she asked. She was suddenly feeling much better about everything.

"I made something for you and my dad for tomorrow", he shouted with a child's delight. The features on his tiny face showed pure joy, and then he held it up for her to see.

Monica's tears welled up in her eyes, as she studied the crayoned picture of the three of them getting married. She couldn't speak as she continued to focus on the image; she absolutely loved what he had drawn. "We're going to keep this forever", she whispered. Her tears were now flowing down her face, and her voice was all but cracking under the emotional strain of the moment.

"Yah!" he shouted. He then pressed his nose against hers as he cheered his approval.

"Let's get daddy that tie, shall we?" She moved her little boy off of her lap, grabbed the tie, and put the envelope back into its hiding place. She then grabbed Oliver's hand and walked him down the stairs.

"What have you guys been doing up there?" Walter asked when his family finally stood before him.

Monica looked at Oliver, who in turn looked at her. "Oh, nothing", they said as one voice. Both of them laughed at their private joke.

Monica married Walter the next day, in a simple, outdoor wedding. As she was walking up the aisle towards him, she decided that it didn't matter if Walter was the adopted dad to her son – this was her family. And whether Oliver was her biological son or not, they would always be mother and child.

Twenty minutes later, Walter had become Monica's husband, and then a second ceremony had to be done. The minister asked Oliver to join them, and after a five-minute ceremony, he announced that Oliver was now the son of both Monica and Walter Ryng. Oliver proudly called her mom from that day forward.

They honeymooned in San Jose, Costa Rica, and very much enjoyed the warm weather and the beautiful landscape. Because the newlyweds had the great foresight to bring a babysitter along, Oliver was entertained whenever Walter and Monica wanted to slip away for some time alone.

Two years later, just after Oliver had celebrated his 9th birthday, he was rushed to the hospital by ambulance. In an examining room, hours after he'd been brought in, the doctor told his parents that Oliver had experienced an allergic reaction to a medicine that he was on, because of his infected tonsils. Walter reached for his son's hand and squeezed it in a loving manner.

Monica was stunned to learn that Oliver was hypersensitive to the same medication that she was allergic to. "How long does he have to stay in the hospital?" Monica asked.

Let's keep him overnight, shall we?" the Registered Nurse asked, but it wasn't a question.

Monica turned to her husband. "Because you have to get up early in the morning, why don't I stay here and you go home and get some rest. I'll call you in the morning with the updates." In a gesture that spoke volumes about how much she loved him, Monica laid her hand gently on top of her husband's. She then watched as Walter nodded.

Walter kissed his son on the forehead, whispered some encouraging words to get him through the night, and then promised that he would be there to drive them home the next day. Walter turned to his wife and kissed her lips. "Thank you for staying here tonight", he began. "Call me if anything changes", he ordered, in a parent's caring manner.

"I will." Monica smiled adoringly in her husband's direction, and when he was out of sight, she placed all of her attention and concerns to Oliver.

"We're going to draw some blood to see what other allergies he might have", the new nurse said as she entered the room. The family's own doctor pushed the curtain aside and stepped into the small area. "How is he?" he asked the nurse.

While they were talking, Monica listened, and her mind went into over-drive. She spoke before she thought it all out, but if they were going to take Oliver's blood, Monica asked if they could take her blood, too. "That way he won't be so scared", she stated, to back-up her plan. She held her breath and her eyes went wide, as she waited for them to answer.

The doctor thought it was a great idea, and he agreed. He nodded to the nurse, who complied with his wishes.

Monica exhaled and turned to Oliver, as she began to roll up her sleeve. "Look, mommy's going to do it, too." Monica was proud that her hidden agenda had worked, and now she couldn't wait to get the results from her doctor.

After drawing some blood into tiny test tubes, the staff did the ELISA test (this measures the amount of allergen-specific antibodies in the blood in order to identify a person's allergy triggers).

Oliver was released from the hospital the next day as planned, and driven home by Walter and Monica. He was given a new medicine to try, and told to come to the doctor's office in a few days. "We'll call you when we receive the results."

"Thank you!" they called.

When the anticipated phone call came, it rang loudly throughout the entire house. "Are you available to come in this morning?" the nurse asked. "The doctor would like to see you as soon as possible."

"Yes, of course", she replied. After packing Oliver into the car, Monica rushed to the clinic where she knew she would be told the answer to her question. She was on pins and needles while entering the building, and wasn't sure if she would be able to wait the 5 minutes that were needed, for the doctor to bring her into his office.

"Mrs. Ryng?" the nurse called. "The doctor will see you now."

Monica inhaled a very large amount of air into her lungs, before she began the short walk down the hallway. Oliver was holding her hand and agonized if they were going to give him another needle.

"Have a seat. He'll be right in." The nurse closed the door and left, leaving Monica to remain anxious about what the tests had found out.

"Hello", the doctor announced, as he walked into the room. He touched Oliver's throat, felt his forehead, and checked his eyes before he went to his side of the desk and sat down. "How do you feel, Oliver?"

"My throat's still sore, but I'm okay." He looked up at his mother to see if she had approved of his answer.

Monica smiled and then placed her focus back to the doctor.

"I think I have some news that will brighten your day", he began. The doctor flipped through the perfect bundle of papers on his desk, until he found the last page. "The tests determined what I've already told you, that your son will need to have his tonsils taken out." He let what he had in his hands drop onto the desk, and then he looked into at Monica's eyes. "When do you want to have the surgery?"

Monica's heart was pounding in her chest, for that was not the conversation she was expecting to have. "He's got a school break coming up, soon. Why don't we plan it for then?" She moved her bum a little closer to the edge of the seat, and swallowed whatever saliva she had in her mouth. "And what about the other test?" she asked shyly.

The doctor looked puzzled and grabbed the short stack of papers again. "Which test are you referring to?" His eyes inspected every line in the papers, from page one to page 5.

Monica was barely able to sit still while he scanned through the lot.

"Oh!" he shouted a minute later. The sound of his voice was now a bit higher, and full of absent-minded recognition. "I know what you're talking about."

Suddenly, Monica couldn't breathe. Her eyes were not blinking, she had moved up even closer to the edge of the chair, and she couldn't wait to hear what he had to say.

"You will be pleased to learn that your son has all of the same allergy triggers as you do. In fact, your DNA matched

92%, which means, you could be twins." He laughed at his own joke, not really knowing if that was true or not.

"Twins!" Oliver roared. "We're not twins – she's a girl!"

The doctor laughed at the little boy's sense of humor, but Monica's first reaction was to gasp with astonishment and pure joy. She was happily stunned beyond belief, because this answered all of her questions. "Thank you", she said with sincerity. Love and relief were pouring out from every cell in her body. She stood up to shake the doctor's hand, but she wanted to hug him and give him a million dollars. "Thank you."

"Well, you're welcome", he replied, as he reached his hand out to shake hers. He wasn't sure what he had said to make her so happy, but he didn't really care. "I have another patient to see, so you can make the appointment with my secretary." He rushed to open the door for her and her son, and smiled as she thanked him again. "You have a good day", he called, and he dashed across the hall. As Monica ambled her way to the front desk, the doctor was already in another room, and about to begin his next appointment.

"Have you decided on a date, Mrs. Ryng?" the admitting clerk asked.

Monica was still dazed about the news, and had to force herself to be in the moment. "Oliver has a break coming, so we can do it then."

"Okay, let me check the school's schedule."

Oliver had let go of Monica's hand, and was running to the waiting room to play with the toys. In the meantime, Monica's mind was playing back the doctor's words.

"Yep, that sounds fine", she confirmed. "And I've got you booked in." She typed the details up and printed it off. "Here you go. It tells you all you need to know."

Monica reached for it, thanked her, and in a moment of braveness, she asked for something else. "Is it possible for me to have a copy of the results from our tests? The doctor has already given them to me, but I'd like to show them to my husband."

"Oh, certainly!" And in no time at all, the paper was handed to Monica, who tucked it away into the bottom of her purse.

"Thank you", she said quietly. But now that she had it, Monica wasn't sure what she should do with it. "Come on, Oliver", she called. As they walked outside, Monica wondered if she should tell Walter. Would that change things between them or with them as a family? She put Oliver into the car seat, as if on autopilot. "Buckle up, please."

As Monica drove home, she focused on the road ahead of her. Every time she glanced in the rear view mirror and saw her son's reflection, she grew to love him that much more. As she drove, Monica slowly came to realize that this information would only concern her; they were already a family, and they would stay a family for the rest of their lives. Having a piece of paper that proved that Oliver was her biological son, would not change anything.

By the time she had parked the car in her driveway, she had decided to tuck the paper away.

"Mom?" Oliver called when he jumped out of the car. "I'm hungry."

Monica turned and looked into Oliver's gorgeous face, and the word totally melted her heart; she really was his mother. She was the woman who had given up her child, so that Walter and Evelyn could raise it. However it happened, Monica was back in his life, and that's where she intended to stay.

"Come on, little man. I'm going to fix you something to eat." She laid her right hand gently on the back of his neck, and guided him towards the house.

"Fish and chips?" Oliver asked, almost pleading. "I love fish and chips!"

Monica laughed at his pleasant personality. "Yes, you can have fish and chips."

"Oh, boy!" Oliver raced to the TV room and picked up the remote. "I'll be in here until it's ready", he called.

As Monica began to make their supper, she couldn't help but smile; the entire situation brought a tear of joy to her eyes, for she truly appreciated that she had been given a second chance to raise her very own child.

In the past couple of years, the three of them had become a family in every sense of the word, so why would she want to change the dynamics of what they already had, by telling anyone the details about what she had found out? Monica was now falling into a slight depression, as she thought about what would happen if and when Walter found out about Oliver's true patronage.

Monica put the food into the oven and went to find her son. She didn't know if she had the right to keep this secret hidden or not, but for now, she was pushing it deep into a special spot in her heart.

But every once in a while, over the next several years, she tried to tell her son how he had come to be on this earth. The words would fail her or get caught in her throat, and then she would lower her head with embarrassment.

"Mom?" Oliver would ask, when she would go quiet.

"I just wanted to remind you of how much I love you", she'd say so he wouldn't worry.

"I love you, too." Because he had grown used to these strange little chats, he shrugged it off and walked away.

# Chapter 15

In 1987, the family got together to celebrate Oliver's 21st birthday. Monica and Walter had carefully put decorations up all over their house, they invited friends to come over, and they had the pleasure of offering their one and only child his first alcoholic drink. "Cheers, and Happy Birthday!" his parents sang. The large group raised their glasses in a toast, and then chugged back the one ounce of whiskey, which had been handed out in decorative shot glasses. "Happy Birthday, Oliver!" everyone shouted.

After enjoying the cake and ice cream, the large group split up and each went to different areas. While Oliver took his friends into the basement, Monica and Walter brought their friends out to the backyard. The merriment for the older group, lasted for another two hours before they called it a night. The festivities of the younger crowd, lasted well into the early morning hours.

Three months after Oliver had turned 21, Walter Ryng celebrated his 56th birthday. He made it look like he was having an amazing time, but he hadn't been feeling well for most of that day. Walter had tried his best to hide his pain, because he didn't want his wife or anyone else to worry. But sadly, because he'd had such a miserable time that night, the ailing man was put into the hospital first thing the next morning.

The doctors were quick to detect that Walter had developed pneumonia. He died a week later.

"He seemed fine right up until his birthday", Monica cried to her friends, on the night of his passing. "I thought he'd been suffering from a chest cold, and now he's gone."

*Because the moment was much too large to comprehend anything other than the fact that her husband was no longer here, it didn't occur to Monica that she had been standing in that very same hospital, on the very same floor, almost 22 years ago, when she was told that Cayson had died.*

They were sitting and having a cup of tea before going to bed, when Monica and Oliver each confessed how terribly heartbroken they were by Walter's death.

"We've got a long and rough week ahead of us, mom", Oliver stated slowly. His voice was filled with sadness, love, and exhaustion. "And I've already made plans to be here with you, until next week-end." He placed his hand lovingly on top of hers, to let her know that she would not be alone.

She turned to look into his beautiful eyes, and thanked him. The love she had for him was intense and peaceful, and filled every thought in her soul. "I'm glad that you'll be here with me", she sighed. "Thank you."

Oliver had never felt the awful feeling that one experiences when a loved one dies, and he wasn't totally sure how to navigate through it. From his own prospective, a colossal part of him was now gone; the overwhelming feeling of his dad's death was crippling, and it touched every part of his soul. And as much as he was suffering, Oliver could see that his mom was suffering even more.

An empty tumbling sensation suddenly took hold of him, and he couldn't turn it off. He classified it as a taunting ache – 1,000 times stronger than love, and it could bring you to your knees in a heartbeat. And it didn't just pertain to physical pain, but emotional as well. Oliver understood that there would be many levels of grief that he would need to sift through, in order to get past this very sad period of time. And he would, but he could see that it would take a great deal of effort. For now, his main focus was on his mom and how she was coping.

Oliver looked over at her, and he felt sorry for her. He watched as she was trying so hard to be brave, and he knew that she was trying to stay strong for him. Oliver had a feeling that she would sob violently once she was alone, and there was nothing that he could do to prevent that from happening. In fact, he might also have a moment such as that one, as soon as he was alone and assured that no-one could hear him.

"I think you're right, but I don't know where to start", Monica added softly. She was already feeling very lonely for the man who she had loved for most of her life.

"We'll begin the process tomorrow, mom. Tonight, let's just go to bed and try to sleep."

Monica nodded. She felt weak, she couldn't stop crying, and she was full of desperation and despair. She was also afraid to go into the bedroom, for she knew that her husband would not be there. Monica wasn't sure how she would get through the night, let alone the next few days, but she was thankful that her son was nearby.

Unbeknownst to Monica, Penny was also going to bed that night with a broken heart, and with thousands of tears being soaked into her pillow. Both women, living miles apart from one another, were again living parallel lives - other than being moms and having once been in love with Nico, they were now both widows.

Austin and Penny had celebrated 14 glorious years of wedding bliss last Wednesday, and he died on Friday. Austin had been laid to rest on the same morning when Walter had died. Like Monica, Penny had been crushed by her husband's sudden death, and she wasn't sure how she would be able to carry on. "I didn't get enough time to be with him!" she sobbed uncontrollably, when the doctor confirmed that Austin was gone. "I need him to be here with me, to love, and to help me raise our children!" she commanded loudly. In her mind, her words were being delivered as an order. In reality, they were heard as a desperate woman's pleas. "Don't tell me that that part of my life is over – it can't be! Not yet!" she screamed. She was slowly slipping into hysteria.

Without warning, Penny's body had descended to the floor. She was now down on her knees, and loudly renouncing the fact that her husband was dead. She was praying that it wasn't true, but knew in her heart that her world would never be the same again. "I can't live without him!" she cried. "Why is nobody listening?" She was sobbing was so loud, that she could hardly hear her own words being spoken.

A friend of hers from the bar helped Penny get home, and then arranged for Austin's wife and children to have someone with them day and night. Everyone else rallied together to plan out the funeral, and the small gathering afterwards.

"We think Austin would've been quite pleased", Dorothy said, when she showed Penny the rough details.

After a quick glance, she nodded her approval. She then turned her head and sunk into her own world again.

Dorothy watched her nod, and she could see that this seemed to bring more reality and heartache to what was already happening. "We can talk later", she whispered. Penny's friend packed up all that she had brought with her, and walked away.

Penny was rude and she recognized it, but she was drowning in her own sorrow. She had given birth to two beautiful little girls during the course of her marriage, and she never regretted one single day of her life with Austin Barnes. Now that he was gone, she knew that she would have to be both mother and father to her charming little angels – Layla 7 and Kalysta 10 – but it wasn't going to be easy.

Fortunately, she had dozens of people gathering around her; to keep her company, to be godparents, and to take turns playing with the girls when Penny went to work or needed to rest. She wasn't prepared to move forward with her everyday life, and she didn't know if she could do it without Austin beside her, but she realized that it had to be done.

Penny struggled a great deal through the week of Austin's funeral, and the first week of life after burying her husband. She stayed in bed and cried for the most part, except for when she knew the girls needed her attention.

Layla and Kalysta were worried for their mom, just like everyone else, because they didn't quite understand everything that was going on. With their papa gone, they still needed their mom, and it turns out, she needed them more now than she ever did before. They all leaned on each other, and tried to move forward as best they could.

'Uncle Bob's Bar' was shut down from the day Austin went into the hospital, until the week after his funeral.

And because Penny understood her husband's heart, it was time to re-open it.

Penny knew that Austin would not want her to mourn for too long, and she knew that folks depended on the bar to be open. "There are people to feed and money to make", Austin used to recite every morning. 'Another day, another two dollars', was his little speech at closing time.

All of Austin's all-time, favorite phrases were going to be truly missed, by his steady customers as well as his dear friends.

On her first morning back to work, Penny asked her best waitresses to line up, and then she handed out their schedules. "We can do this", she stated with conviction, after a short inspirational speech. "I know it won't be the same, but let's do our best to keep going."

Effie, Mechelle, Susan, and Ellen agreed to work as as if Austin was still there, and overseeing everything. The long-time waitresses made a pact to honor him, for Austin Barnes was a wonderful man who was loved by all.

Penny promised that the bar would remain the same, and in that way, Austin's spirit would always be there with them.

Monica had a terrible time making the arrangements for Walter's funeral, and then she had to see him in a coffin - it was one of the worst things that she could've imagined. He appeared to be was sleeping, and while he looked the same as he always had, he seemed very different.

Monica spent a lot of time sitting beside her husband in the casket, holding his hand and telling him everything that was on her mind. She wept uncontrollably through the entire funeral service, and she didn't hear anything that was being said. And when it was time to bury him, she placed a kiss on his cheek before they closed the lid. In that second, with unbearable agony ripping through every part of her being, she fell apart with the notion that she'd never see him again.

The gravesite service was short and sweet, but Monica's mind was still having trouble digesting all that was happening. Thirty minutes later, she drove away from the cemetery, but left a huge part of herself in the cold dirt.

It was a week later when Oliver announced that he needed to go back to college to continue his studies.

It's so far away", she stated sadly. Monica then rushed into his arms, with hopes of never letting him go. "I wish you didn't have to leave", she said, trying not to cry.

"I know, but I will call regularly and I will visit as often as I can", he promised. He also hated leaving her alone, but he couldn't just walk away from his classes when he was so close to graduating. Oliver hugged her hard and long, and told his mom over and over again, how much he loved her. "I will always be a breath away from you", he whispered. "So please, never think that you are ever truly alone."

But without Walter and Oliver in her home, she was. "Thank you, dear", she sighed reluctantly. Her heart was heavy with the thought of living in her strange new life, but she respected that he was doing the right thing. She placed her hand against his cheek as she spoke. "Ok, you go." Despite her protests, Monica was proud that her son wanted to keep studying in order to fulfill his dream.

When Oliver was ready to leave, Monica struggled with the concept of telling Oliver that she was his birth mother. Walter's sudden death had revealed how very precious our time on earth was; it could be taken away so quickly, and sometimes without any warning.

With Walter gone, Monica suddenly felt that it was more important than ever, to tell Oliver who she was. They'd always been very close and have been able to talk about most anything, but no matter how often she tried to tell him, her little speech just couldn't come out of her mouth. Not that it mattered after all these years, but Monica really wanted him to see her for who she really was – his mother. Not just the lady who married his dad, but the woman who had given birth to him.

As each hour ticked away, Monica watched Oliver gather his things together, and her anxiety grew.

Oliver had packed everything into his car and was now coming back to the porch to give her a hug. "Bye, mom. I love you." He kissed her cheek and then walked away.

Monica felt lonely for him already, and she felt disappointed that she hadn't told him the words which had been hidden in her heart. "Bye, son!" she called, as he got into his car.

As Monica stepped inside of her empty home, she felt a chill and a loneliness that she didn't know how to cope with. She wrapped her arms across her chest and closed her eyes. Immediately, she saw her dear husband in her mind, and she cried out to him. "Walter, my love. Please help me learn how to get through the next few weeks without you. I don't know why you had to leave so soon, and with Oliver at school, I know that I will be lost."

Monica needed to pause in order to collect her thoughts, and to keep the tears from spilling down her already flushed cheeks. "I miss you like crazy, and I promise to love you for the rest of my life." Monica couldn't go on; tears poured out of her eyes like a fountain, her knees buckled, and her body sank to the carpeted floor. She cried like she'd never cried before, and when her throat was raw and there were no more tears in her body, that's when she stopped – too weak to get up, but not caring about moving.

As the months flew by, her son eventually graduated, and he got hired by a very distinguished organization. Oliver was now busy and very happy, and he was beginning to come home less and less.

It had been almost a year since Walter's death, when Monica recognized how isolated she had become. With encouragement from her son and help from her dear neighbours, Monica searched for reasons to get out of the house. In the next 12 months, she began to go to church again, took a sewing class and a cooking class, and joined a Red Hatter's group that met once every three weeks. She was now keeping busy, making new friends, and learning to adjust to her new life, all of which made Oliver happy.

With his demanding work schedule, Oliver relied on his mom's friends and neighbours to keep her busy. Sadly, that caused him to not need to come home as often as he should have. It took almost two years for their usual visits of an entire week-end twice a month, to be whittled down to a couple of hours once a month. While Monica would have liked to see her son more often, this unspoken arrangement suited him quite well.

During that time period, Monica learned how to navigate through her new life. While it took a lot to get used to, because she was confused and sad at times, she congratulated herself at the end of every day.

On Valentine's Day in 2002, a group of mature women were enjoying their Red Hat Luncheon. They were gathered in the meeting room on the main floor of a fancy hotel, and the place was spruced up to perfection. Everyone adored the food, the red and pink festive decorations, and they were laughing at the funny things that were being told at their tables and throughout the rest of the room. An hour after beginning their Valentine's Day luncheon, no-one could remember ever having a better time.

And then, just like that, it all changed. For in the blink of an eye, one of their own had dropped to the floor.

"Monica!" a few ladies screamed at the same time. Several members of the Red Hatter's group began to cry, and some become panic-stricken. People from the lobby and other areas of the hotel, came running in with questions, and to see what was going on. "Help!" yelled someone with no medical knowledge. "I think she fainted!"

"Call 9-1-1!" a female voice shouted. Her voice was filled with fright, and she was trying not to fall to pieces by what was going on.

An ambulance arrived on the scene less than 5 minutes later, followed by the police and a fire truck. Uniformed personnel carried their equipment and a stretcher into the building, and this caused the festivities to shut down completely. Everyone was asked to move aside, or go home or to their rooms, while the lifeless body was being checked out.

"What's her name?" A police officer asked loudly to the people around him. He watched as a little old lady moved her way through the small crowd.

"Monica Ryng", Gail Traverse stated loudly. At 81 years old, she was still sharp and spry, and thought of herself as quite a catch. She stood all of 4'10", but by the way she carried herself, she appeared to be much taller.

"Thank you", the officer replied. "We'll need someone to call her next of kin. Can you do that?"

"Yes!" Gail replied happily. "I just have to find her son's phone number." While most of the onlookers stood frozen with fear, Gail grabbed Monica's purse and then made her way to the front desk to place the call.

The color was draining on Monica's face and the paramedics couldn't find a pulse. The experienced personnel were concerned, and gave her every method of CPR that they could. After many minutes of giving her all they had, they were able to get a reading, and then rushed her to the nearest hospital.

Gail looked through Monica's handbag, and eventually found what she had been looking for. She dialed the number on Oliver's business card, and pushed the receiver against her ear. As she listened to the lines connect, the fear of delivering this news, suddenly caused her to panic.

After the receptionist had recited her usual greeting, it was Gail's turn to talk. "Can I please speak with Oliver Ryng?"

"Certainly. One moment, please." Gail listened as her call was re-directed to Oliver's office.

# Chapter 16

Oliver was busy at work when his phone rang. On the display it showed that the call was coming from the 'Second Avenue Hotel', and he almost didn't pick it up. Then he remembered that his mom was going to celebrate Valentine's Day in a hotel restaurant, and his hand lifted up the receiver. "Hi, mom", he said in a composed office tone.

"Hello, Oliver?" Gail began. "You don't know me, but ...." The elderly woman introduced herself, and then, in a sweet but tearful voice, she told him what had happened to his mom.

The words brought shudders to his entire body, and emotionally choked his very soul. He couldn't think, he was now shaking, he had trouble breathing, and he needed to get to his mother as quickly as possible. He was so terribly distraught that he couldn't remember the woman's name, but he was grateful that she had called. "Thank you", he announced into the phone before he hung up. "I'll be there soon."

Without a hint of hesitation, he ran down the hallway to the large corner office. After briefly explaining the situation to his boss, Oliver dashed out of the building towards his car.

Oliver lived in a town not far from where his mom lived, and as he shifted the gears into 'drive', his mind did the math – the distance to the hospital times the speed that he needed to travel, equaled the estimated time of his arrival.

The grief-stricken man was driving much too quickly, but he didn't care; his whole intention was to be with his mother as soon as he could. As he focused on the road before him, his mother's face suddenly splashed through his mind in pictures. The way her smile lit up a room, the way her eyes sparkled when she laughed, and the way she sang and whispered, were all memories that he had kept in his heart for whenever he felt lonely for her. The scent of her perfume was imbedded in his brain, and how she insisted on wearing her hair down, despite of her age, are things that he would hold onto for the rest of his life.

Oliver suddenly reminisced about their last phone call. He was only half-listening, he had groaned a few times when she began her long-winded stories, and he had answered her questions in one-syllable sounds when it was needed. He now regretted not giving her his 100% attention. "If only I could do that phone call over", he moaned in sincere sorrow. "If she dies, I'll never get to hear her voice again."

As Oliver drove, he had to wipe a tear or two away from his blurry eyes so he could see the road ahead of him. His mother meant the world to him and he wasn't sure how he would cope without her. "My mother", he whispered out loud, as if he had heard those words for the very first time. Oliver's eyebrows suddenly drew together in an agonizing expression, when a vivid moment flickered through his mind.

When he was 9 years old, he had to have his tonsils taken out and that required him to stay in the hospital for a week. On his first day back home again, he had a very interesting conversation with his father – one that stuck in his mind from then until now. Why? Because it changed how he looked at the woman who he and his father had met on the cruise.

*Monica had gone to the store to get all the things that her son would need while he was recuperating, and left Walter and Oliver to fend for themselves for the next hour or so.*

*"Daddy?" the little boy began, once they were alone. He worshipped his dad like crazy, and loved that he had taken time off work that week, just to be with him.*

*"Yes?" Walter brought his hand up and ruffled the hair on the top of Oliver's head.*

*"Could I be twins with mom?" Oliver was looking into his father's face with a blank expression, hoping for a good answer.*

*Walter's eyebrows had pushed together, and a look of confusion was now written all over his face. "Oliver, why are you asking me such a silly question?"*

*Oliver told his dad everything that the doctor has said to them that day in his office, including the part where the DNA matched so well, that 'they could be twins'.*

*Walter didn't know what to say, as he was more than surprised by this information. His eyebrows lifted up very close to his hairline, while his eyes looked like they were about to pop out of his head. His mouth was open and ready to speak, but he wasn't sure what to say. He knew that Oliver had to have blood taken when he was rushed to the hospital, and he knew that Monica had suggested that she get some taken as well. But it was his impression that her blood was taken so that Oliver wouldn't be afraid to get it done. Walter had no idea that their blood samples would be compared, and that they would match! He was completely blown away by all of this, and his mind couldn't wrap itself around this stirring bit of information.*

*Walter's thoughts were now running around in circles, while the air around him was becoming thick with curiosity.*

*"Daddy?" Oliver questioned after the long pause.*

*"Yah?" Walter's eyes blinked rapidly, and then he was back in the moment. "Oh, sorry. Listen, I'm going to go and check on something and then I'll be right back." Walter spoke firm, but on the quiet side.*

"Okay." Oliver watched his dad get up and leave, and then passed the time by clicking through the channels on the TV.

Walter rushed upstairs, and headed straight to the drawer that contained the envelope. He pulled it out and inspected the adoption letter, and read each and every single word. He noted Nico's signature on the bottom of the page, the lack of an authentic letter head on the top, and then he began to put two-and-two together.

Years ago, when Nico had presented the idea of adoption, Walter and his wife agreed to it with only slight moments of hesitation. When the paperwork was laid down in front of the happy couple, their minds were blurred with the notion that they were going to be parents – an idea which they thought would never happen.

Looking back on it now, Walter could see that he and his wife had not asked enough questions, nor had they suspected that it was not a legal adoption. It should have been understood, that with Nico taking care of things, that it might be one of his famous get-rich-quick schemes; it all sounded too good to be true, and it was something which Walter should have watched out for. Sadly, he had been so excited to become a father, that he wasn't as careful as he should have been.

Walter sat back, and because he was getting angry at himself, his mind couldn't fathom all the information that was rushing at him at the same time. He decided to sort it out slowly, by dissecting one item at a time.

*Nico and Monica had come on the ship together. He never saw them kissing, but it did seem like they were a couple. Nico and Walter didn't spend much time in each other's company, but the one thing they had in common was Monica.*

*Monica and Oliver got along surprisingly well, while Penny didn't want to bond with Oliver at all. Skipping ahead to today, Nico was in jail and Monica was helping Walter raise Oliver.*

*Had Nico and Monica planned the adoption together? Why did she give her baby away in the first place? Why did they pick Walter and Evelyn to raise the baby?*

*Walter's mind was racing with questions, and he was on the verge of becoming panicky, when something significant stuck out. Was Oliver Monica's son? Is that possible? Does she know?*

*Walter was shocked by the allegations and decided that he needed to know for sure. He reached for the phone and called the clinic to speak with their family doctor. The doctor wasn't in, but the nurse was only too happy to give Walter the results from the most recent tests.*

*"Yep, I see that your wife and your son have an almost identical match to the ELISA test. That means that they would have very close to the same allergies and reactions to things", she stated with certainty.*

*Walter was trying to sound calm, but he felt that he needed to know more. "Could someone use that test to, like, match a child to a parent?" He hated to ask, but the words rushed out of his mouth before he could stop himself from speaking.*

*"Most definitely", she replied. "But he is your son, right? That's what it shows on Mrs. Ryng's tests. They are definitely mother and child."*

*Walter was stunned beyond belief, but said thank you and hung up. His mind then went crazy with hundreds of different thoughts and questions. He wasn't sure how to answer them on his own, nor was he sure what he should do with this information. He felt his body slide down towards the carpet, while his eyes stared off into the distance at nothing at all. 'What do I do?' he wondered.*

*Walter suddenly remembered that Monica must know the results from the tests, for she was in the room when the doctor shared them with her and Oliver. 'Why hasn't she said anything?' he wondered. And as if his mind had split between a good cop and bad cop, he answered his own question. 'Maybe she didn't want me to know, but why?'*

*Several more questions and different emotions were coming at him much too quickly, and he was having trouble coping. The moment felt too surreal, and he wished for it to be a dream so he could wake up.*

"Dad?" Oliver called. He had been eagerly waiting for his dad to return, but now he was becoming impatient. "Are you coming back?"

Walter had been blind-sided by the last 15 minutes of his life, and felt sorry for leaving his little boy alone for so long. After placing the paperwork back to where it had always been, he raced downstairs to be with his son. "I'm here", he stated when he sat down, but the words of the clerk in the clinic were still ringing in his ears.

Walter turned and now studied his little boy's face. A second later, his lungs involuntarily gulped in a bit of air, as Walter noticed a few features that clearly reminded him of Monica. "Yup, you guys could be twins", he snickered lightly. He was still trying to absorb the news that Monica was Oliver's mom, and this left him a little more than confused by the whole situation. "Would that be okay?"

"Yah, but we're not really twins, because I'm a boy and she's a girl", he responded in a serious tone.

Obviously, Oliver had no concept on the meaning of twins, and that made Walter laugh. "You're right, but when someone says you could be twins, it just means that you guys are almost the same."

Right there and then, Walter decided that if Monica had just found out that she was Oliver's mom, then he truly doubted that their relationship had been some kind of a ploy.

*Walter now assumed that Nico had been the middleman, and it was possible that Monica had no idea that it had all been a scheme. Perhaps she found herself in a predicament where she had no other choice but to give her baby up for adoption, and Nico took advantage of her situation. And now that she knew that Oliver was her baby boy, maybe Monica didn't want to tell anyone the truth, for fear of being sent away.*

*As that information sunk into his brain, Walter concluded that meeting Monica was a happy coincidence. Because of that notion, Walter felt his body begin to relax, and he exhaled a long sigh of relief. After his next breath, his dark set of lashes flew up as he looked towards the ceiling, and he prayed to God that the three of them would always remain together.*

*Walter loved Monica, and he wanted to continue being her husband. Oliver also loved her, and the three of them were a family – biological or not. He realized that if he didn't want their situation to change, then he should probably do something to protect it.*

*"Oliver", Walter began, as he looked into his son's face. Walter was going to do a little back-pedaling, in order to ensure the future happiness of his little family.*

*"Yah?" he answered, without looking towards his father's face.*

*"Maybe it's best if we wait for mommy to tell me what happened in the doctor's office", he suggested. Walter was a*

*little worried that if he broached the subject first, that the whole thing might turn awkward. But, if at any time Monica wanted to talk to him about it, he would not only listen, he would welcome the discussion; there were questions that he wanted answers to.*

*"Okay", the little boy replied. He was only half-listening, but he honestly didn't care to talk about it anymore.*

*Walter smiled at his son with an abundance of love, and silently thanked Monica for giving life to this precious little boy. "Oliver, you truly are 'our son', and together we will raise you to be a fine young man."*

'Our son'. The words lingered in the air like a giant balloon. Oliver could hear his father's voice saying those words, and then another image jumped into his mind.

*When Oliver was 17 years old, he had his father help him find information about his first mom – Evelyn. It was an elaborate school project that he was doing, where each student had to see how far back they could go on their family tree. Walter was only too happy to help, and guided his son to the drawer that contained all of his important paperwork.*

*Oliver was going through the papers in the envelope, and accidently came across the adoption papers, which were sitting in amongst the other documents. In disbelief he studied them, and then brought the whole envelope to his father's attention.*

*Right away, Walter's skin went pale and his mouth dried up, and then he decided that it was probably time to tell his son the truth. Walter took every second of the next 20 minutes, to explain the adoption in a very delicate and loving manner. He began by letting Oliver know that Monica had given birth to him, but that she had given her baby to Walter and Evelyn to raise. "Not that she didn't love you or want you, because she did – always know that!" Walter waited for Oliver to digest the words.*

*Oliver was paying attention, but his heart was racing and he was becoming terribly confused. Hearing the hypnotic details of his past was hard, but he tried to listen as his dad continued to speak.*

*"After your mom passed away, we made friends with Penny. I don't know what happened, but when we went on the cruise and we met Monica, everything changed – Penny left and Monica stayed. Because you and I liked her, I asked her to be a part of our life."*

*"Why did she give me away?" he asked. Tears of sadness were forming, but had not yet decided whether to fall down his cheeks or stay where they were. Oliver was a strong and healthy, 17-year old man, but in that moment and in that light, he looked like a worried, 10-year old child.*

*"I honestly don't think she was able to give you what you needed", he replied. Walter had no idea the real reasoning behind why Monica had given her child up for adoption, because he and Monica have never had that conversation.*

*"But she knew that your mom and I could, so she gave you to us to love and take care of." He was making it up as he went along, and hoped that his son would accept what he was saying.*

*"Why did she come back?" Oliver had a look of concern written all over his face, as he waited for the answer.*

*"I strongly believe that we met her by accident", Walter began, and he meant every word. "I don't think she knew who you were, but I believe she fell in love with you right away. When I asked her to marry me, she said yes, because she wanted to come into our home to help me raise you."*

*Walter watched his son try to soak up the information, and while he knew it would be hard to understand, it looked like Oliver seemed to be handling it well. "And now that she's here, she doesn't ever want to leave us."*

*As he listened to all the facts in the story, Oliver had his eyes cast downward. He was trying very hard to figure it all out, and he could feel himself becoming emotional.*

*"She's your mom, Oliver – no matter what." Walter was trying to be compelling, even though he didn't know the backstory. "She didn't marry me because you might be her child. She married me to be with both of us, because she loves us very much."*

*It was a lot of information, and it was very hard to process it all at once. After Oliver thought about it, and he realized that it didn't really matter if Monica was his real mom or a stepmom, he was okay. He had had the benefit of having two fabulous mothers in his life, and he knew that both of them loved him very much. He smiled with that knowledge, and then hugged his dad very hard. "Thank you for telling me", he said. Oliver was sincere in his delivery. "I'm sure that must have been very hard for you."*

*"You have no idea." Walter welcomed the hug, and pulled his son close to his body. When the embrace ended, he asked Oliver not to mention their conversation to his mother, until the subject got brought up by her. "I think she's embarrassed to tell you that she's your mom", Walter guessed. "I think she wants you to love her no matter what."*

*Oliver lifted the left corner of his mouth in agreement, as he nodded. "I promise."*

*"Thank you." Walter was pleased that this crisis was over, and hoped that they could keep this a secret for as long as possible.*

*"I'm home!" she called loudly. Her foot was dangling in the air, in hopes of trying to catch something solid. After touching what she was searching for, she was finally able to slam the front door shut.*

*Oliver ran down the stairs and right into Monica's arms. "Hi mom", he cooed lovingly. He helped her put her bags down, and then hugged her long and hard, which drew suspicion from his mother's maternal instincts.*

*"What is this for?" she asked, surprised by the unexpected embrace.*

*"Oh, nothing", he laughed. But he knew, and he loved her for it.*

*When Oliver had stepped aside, it was Walter's turn to run into her arms. He also gave her a very affectionate hug, followed by, "I love you."*

*"I should go out more often", she laughed. "What a welcome."*

*Walter and Oliver turned to each other and they also laughed, but because of the secret that they had vowed to keep between them. They never spoke about it again, and that's why it was almost forgotten from his memory.*

Oliver arrived at the hospital and parked the car. He raced through the sliding glass doors, told them who he was, and then demanded to see Monica Ryng.

"I'm sorry, but her body has been taken to the morgue, and it won't be released to the funeral home until tomorrow or the next day", the admitting clerk stated with complete authority.

"She died?" His eyebrows drew together in a tormented expression, as his tear-smothered voice remained quiet.

"I'm sorry, I thought you knew." She nodded as she spoke, to confirm what he was now finding out.

Oliver was a little baffled, because he had driven so fast to get there. He was hoping to see her, and now he wasn't allowed to be with her at all.

"I'm terribly sorry for your loss." The nurse posed all of her attention to Oliver, and spoke slow and soft. "We have a chapel around the corner, if you would like to go and sit for a while."

Oliver shook his head, no. "Thanks", he uttered quietly, but the word got stuck in his throat. He tapped the long desk with two fingers, and then he moved his body back to his car. As he sat there, he felt helpless, and he wasn't sure what he should do. Tears were now flowing from his eyes, even though he fought them with everything he had. His vision was blurry as he fidgeted with his key chain, and then he realized that he had a key to his mother's home. After using the back of his hands to remove the water that had thoroughly moistened his cheeks, that's where he decided to go.

As he drove towards the 2-storey, 4-bedroom house on Bernard Drive, he couldn't help but think of all the things that he would need to do in the next few days – arrange the funeral, find a casket, find a funeral home, look through her closet for an outfit for her to be buried in, etc....

Suddenly the reality of her dying, really hit him. The more he thought about it, the more he hated what was happening. A single tear slid slowly down his cheek, and touched each hair and every crevice on his skin. This time, he didn't wipe it away.

Forty minutes later, the 35-year old man parked his car in front of the place that he'd always called home, and he was surprised to find two cars parked in the driveway and another one on the street. He was confused, and feeling emotionally drained and quite nervous as he walked up to the porch. He noticed that the front door was slightly ajar, so he grabbed the handle and stepped inside. Right away he could hear people talking and things being moved around. "Hello?" he called, with trepidation in his voice.

"He's here!" Because they were expecting him, and they had recognized him from the many pictures that were strewn enthusiastically around the house, they ran towards him as if he was a close family member.

As Oliver moved himself into the front hall, he was greeted by people from the neighbourhood, from the church, and from the Red Hatter's club.

*Sadly, Gail had taken ill and couldn't be there, but she did leave him a very nice sympathy card.*

One-by-one, they introduced themselves, and then stepped aside. After everyone had said hello and 'sorry for your loss', they talked all at once, so it was hard for Oliver to hear a lot of what they were saying.

He remained polite and nodded constantly, but it felt like he was walking in a tunnel that seemed to have no end.

Oliver decided to go further into the room, and then he noticed all the boxes which were neatly closed and lined up in the living room area. "What are these?" he asked with suspicion in his voice.

His question suddenly brought a quiet murmur into the room that wasn't there before, and then things became a little awkward.

"We packed everything up for you", someone in the crowd called out.

"We thought we were helping", someone else announced.

Mrs. Sylvia Ruiz, the elderly lady from next door, suddenly took control of the situation. "Ladies!" she called in a loud and stern voice. She patted the air with her hands, as she motioned for everyone to settle down. "I think we should go now." She could see that Oliver was upset, and thought it best that he have some time alone with his thoughts and his mother's things.

Everyone agreed and began to collect their own belongings.

Mrs. Ruiz walked up to him and spoke softly. "If you need anything at all, please don't hesitate to call any one of us." She handed him a long piece of paper and continued, "All of our names and phone numbers are on that list."

"Thank you, but you don't have to leave." Oliver's voice had cracked when he spoke, and he could feel himself falling apart; he was thoroughly amazed by how this day had progressed. From when he woke up until now, seemed like many days all rolled into one; so many things have happened, and his life had completely changed since breakfast.

"Oh, I think it's better if we leave." Mrs. Ruiz gave Oliver a quick hug, and then she rushed everyone out of the house. "Bye, dear!" she called behind her.

He nodded and shouted, "Thank you, to all of you." Once he was alone, he turned to face the sealed boxes. He clearly wasn't prepared to go through a lifetime of memories and feelings in that moment, but he knew it had to be done at some point. He then wondered how long this heart-breaking ordeal was going to take.

After releasing a long puff of air into the well-decorated room, he brushed his hand through the thick strands of hair on his head. He then walked further into the living room, sat down, and began the intimidating task.

While going through the first two large boxes by the end of the long couch, Oliver had found many things that had belonged to his father, and most of them, he had forgotten about – some suits, 2 hats, a small bunch of important papers, his pipe, his favorite hankie for the lapel in his jacket, a half bag of menthol hard candy, and a framed picture of himself and his dad on a fishing trip. While the many treasures he had looked at made him a little sad, it also made Oliver want to continue to open more boxes.

The grieving man turned to his right and saw a box which was boldly marked with the name, Monica, on the front. Suddenly, dozens of questions flooded his brain. His eyes blinked more than a few times, as this was very odd; all the other boxes had 'mom' written on them, but this one did not. He bent his body forward and proceeded to drag the large cardboard container closer to his feet. He then began to pry it open.

To his surprise, it was secured very tightly. And even by using strong scissors and a long, sharp knife, he had an awful lot of trouble breaking through the many ribbons of strong tape. As each second ticked away, Oliver was growing ever more curious about why the hidden contents were being so overly protected from enquiring eyes. This whole ordeal made him even more persistent to find out.

After several drawn-out minutes of grunting and brutal physical labor, he was finally able to rip open the first flap. Oliver looked inside, and with absolute amazement, he couldn't help but gasp loudly. For there before him, lay many of his mother's precious belongings – some of which he'd never seen before, and some that had been strewn around the house as nick knacks. "My, gosh", he whispered softly, while his eyes scanned the tops of each and every item.

As the neatly-groomed, slim-but-fit man, carefully sifted through the many delightful possessions, he became extremely interested with one item in particular, that he'd never seen before. He picked it up with both hands and placed it gently on his lap, making sure that the entire book stayed perfectly intact. As he examined the colors and the intricate details on the front cover, his eyes grew wide with total appreciation of all the time and work that must have gone into making this very handsome album.

Oliver was in complete awe. He wasn't sure what he would find in between the covers of this 3" mysterious scrapbook, but he half-expected to find pages filled with pictures and precious memories of his childhood.

The grown man understood that going through it was not going to be a short trip down memory lane, so he decided to make himself more comfortable. He removed the autumn-colored, $400 dollar tweed jacket off of his pleasantly-sculpted body, and prudently folded it over the back of the couch. He then sat back down on the over-sized recliner, and raised the foot rest up for optimum comfort. Oliver then placed the heavy photo album back onto his lap, and emotionally prepared himself for whatever he was about to discover.

He was apprehensive as he let out a heavy sigh of amazement, and then he slowly lifted the sturdy front cover of Monica's spectacular photo album. He moved it gently to the left, and was now staring, with complete fascination, at the first page.

*Whenever he had heard anyone talking about Monica's exquisite album, he thought it was something that his mother was keeping safe for him, until he grew up. Instead, he was surprised to be looking at what he now determined, was a secret diary-of-sorts.*

His highly educated mind was feeling terribly cautious, for he already knew that Monica had given birth to him, and now, he hoped to fill in the blanks. As his anxiety was building, Oliver was developing a bad feeling in the pit of his stomach. Should he read this, he wondered? His heart was now racing with fear of what this collection of words and pictures might reveal. His mind was confused and his thoughts were spinning, and all at the same time.

In order to calm himself down, Oliver closed his perfectly-symmetrical eyes and gulped a long breath of air into his lungs. He knew that he needed to soothe his jumbled nerves, before his brain got the wrong idea about what might be hidden within these pages. He tried to make his mind go blank, but it wasn't working; curiosity was getting the better of him. He tilted his head from side-to-side, as if to relax his shoulders and slow down his thoughts. He then rolled his head to the left and then to the right, and ended up sitting perfectly still for the next dozen or so breaths.

When he was ready, he opened his eyes and found that they were beginning to well up, as he looked down at the mysterious album. The second he recognized her familiar hand-writing, his once imprisoned tears, fell proudly down his rosy cheeks.

Oliver moved his fingers very methodically across the delicate page before him, with the intention to lightly caress the slightly-slanted, blue ink in her sentences. In doing so, it was as if he thought he could touch or connect with her spirit. "These were her private thoughts and words", he confessed sadly. "I know I shouldn't be snooping, but I have to."

The first thing he saw, was a quote from Charles Dickens. It came from the story, 'A Tale Of Two Cities', and it read;

> 'I wish you to know, that you were the
> last dream and thought of my life.'

His mom had obviously paraphrased the words to make it her own language, and it touched Oliver's very soul; he could feel the meaning behind the lovely sentence, and it made him want to read even more.

As he quickly skimmed the first few days of entries, his mind went into a state of admiration. It was written like a book – a biography that someone else had written about her and her life. After peaking at a few more pages, Oliver had learned things about himself and his mother that he had never known before. There were things that had shocked him, events that made him quite sad, and words that told him the story leading up to his birth. His eyes were glistening and his expression was that of sorrow, as he suddenly felt very sorry for the woman who he had called mom.

Oliver was fighting back the tears, as he carefully flipped through the next two discolored pages. His mind was racing as he was connecting with the words, and he had gotten distracted and intrigued by the many photos and newspaper clippings in the large book.

In the first four pages, there were a few pictures of his mother with another man. They were smiling and seemed awfully happy, and it caused Oliver to wonder who the man was. He tilted the book on its side and could see that the name in the caption said, 'Cayson Ross'. Was this his birth father? He leaned his face in closer, in order to examine the man's features. Oliver wasn't surprised when he recognized a few similarities between him and the man with the big smile. After another moment of consideration, Oliver's eyes moved to another section of the page. There he saw a newspaper article, with a large black and white picture of chaos in a busy intersection. The caption read; 'Man Dies, Due To Bad Weather.' The article described how much rain had fallen, it explained all the destruction which the water had caused, and then it listed all those who had been injured.

Oliver saw that Cayson Ross was the name of the man who had died that day. Many people had given their accounts as to what had happened, and the article ended with, '...he died at the scene.' Oliver looked up at the picture where Monica and Cayson were smiling, and he vowed to keep that image in his heart forever.

Oliver breezed through a few more pages of his mother's hand-written notes, and then glanced lovingly at a ton of black & white photos which she had so carefully glued into place. He then saw two photos of his mom with another man, who Oliver thought looked very familiar. There was no mention made as to who they were to each other, or a name to put to the man's face, so Oliver moved on.

After turning the page, Oliver could see that there were plenty of pictures and hand-written notes about him while he was growing up. These were dated from 6 years old to now, with him standing alone in a photo, and others where he was with Monica and Walter. There were also dozens of recipes stuck haphazardly all over the place - foods that he remembers eating, and others that he does not.

In the countless passages that he had skimmed over in the diary part, Oliver suddenly took notice, that there were many examples where it showed him exactly how much this woman had truly loved him. Sadly, a part of him wished that he had known that she was his mother all along. 'Or would it have really mattered that much?' he argued.

Oliver's eyes looked around until they stumbled upon a tender half-page passage, which she had obviously written a few days prior to her wedding to Walter, and Oliver's heart sank. He started reading it, and followed each gentle word by sliding his index finger underneath. His soul tried to guess what she must have been feeling in those awkward moments, but he truly couldn't begin to understand her pain.

My Dearest Cayson,

My biggest hurdle is living without you. My biggest regret, is giving away our beautiful son. I now have a chance to raise him and love him, as I should have since he was born. How? I'm about to marry the lovely man who has been caring for our child, all of his life. While I wish it was you that

I will be pledging my heart and soul to, I believe that you put Walter in my life. He's helped me to heal, he's given me great happiness, and he's letting me be part of his family. Thank you and God for making this possible, for it has truly brought me more happiness than I can tell you. Raising Oliver will be a joy like no other, and being married to Walter will bring me the love and peace that I should have had all along.

I miss you terribly, Cayson, and I will always love you. While you will always have a piece of my heart, my life is here with Walter and our son. Thank you for giving me what I now have, and I promise to treasure it always.

Monica oxoxo

When Oliver finally arrived at the last word in the last line on the page, he suddenly realized who this woman really was, and why she had not told him the truth – she was scared of losing the family that she had been given.

Oliver still had many more pages to go, but he couldn't go any further; his eyes were blurry and his tears were falling in a steady stream. When Oliver wiped the salty water away from his eyes, he noticed that he was mentally and emotionally exhausted; the day had already been quite long, and he had now learned a truck load of things that he'd never known before.

Oliver leaned back in the chair for a much-needed moment of clarity, as he stared out the front window before him. In his mind, he could see that Monica did indeed have regrets about giving her child away, and he had no doubt that it was probably the hardest decision she ever had to make.

Suddenly, the name 'Nicholas Kostas' rang a bell, and the weary man wondered if he was the same man who was on the cruise with them, so many years ago. Because Oliver was only 6 years old at the time, his memory was a bit distorted, but he would bet that Nico and Nicholas was the same person.

Oliver got up and ran to grab one of his mom's older Time Magazines, and sure enough, there was a story all about Nico. Oliver's finger touched the rather long article which detailed Nico's trial. Monica's name wasn't mentioned, but there were two pictures in the album of the two of them together. That proved that they at least knew each other.

Oliver didn't know why his mother had been spared, but he decided that she must have had an angel on her shoulder. That same angel could have been the one who brought her back into his life. 'Thank you', Oliver said in his head. He then looked down at the article again. The things that they said he had done were inconceivable, and Oliver was glad that Nico would be in jail for the rest of his life.

Oliver pushed the magazine away and sat down again. He wondered what his mother's life would have been like, had Cayson lived and Nico not interfered. She had obviously been confused – her fiancé had just died and she was pregnant. She most likely felt pressure from society, if not from Nico, and hoped that she was doing the right thing by giving her child up for adoption.

Oliver was becoming overwhelmed by the amount of information that he had had to absorb in the past few hours. As he closed his eyes, he was suddenly seeing flashbacks of his life in pictures, that were not found in the beautiful album. These were moments that he could recall, in a glowing tribute to how he grew up and with whom.

As he sat there contemplating the last 35 years of his life, Oliver could suddenly detect that there was something nonconforming in the cool air around him. It was compelling him to push past his opinions, and to engage in the words which were written in the book. It was calling him to really embrace the feelings, which were captured and then written down on the pages before him. It was an overpowering sensation, that enveloped his entire body with a great deal of love, and left him with goose bumps all over his skin.

Oliver's eyes were now wide open, and every muscle in his body was on full alert. He rushed to sit up, but he couldn't explain what was happening. He knew that nobody would ever believe him, but there was definitely a presence or an aura in the room, which was enticing him to continue reading what was on his lap. The urgency was strong, and it seemed to be begging him to see more of how their life together had begun.

The nervous individual moved his eyes from side-to-side but barely moved his head, and now closely regarded everything in the oblong room. He was sure that he could feel something, but he wasn't sure that he wanted to see what or who it was. Oliver didn't believe in ghost or spirits, but he was becoming more than intrigued by how things were shaping up.

Was there a plea of forgiveness in the air? He didn't know, but because of the powerful push for him to learn more, Oliver decided to keep going. And by doing so, he hoped to understand what his mother had been trying so desperately, to keep so safeguarded.

The very instant when he made this decision, the ambience in the room and within himself, changed. Quite strangely, the air around him suddenly felt lighter and happier. Because of this, Oliver's handsome face presented a smile; he predicted that the rest of the curious story would be of great interest to him, and now he couldn't wait to dive in.

Hours later, as he closed the back cover of the beautiful photo album, he inhaled a great deal of air; he could now put the pieces of his life together, complete with pictures. Evelyn was his first mom and Monica was his birth mom. Evelyn had been there from the beginning, and Monica had been there for him when he was sick, sad, happy, and as a teenager. She was also there when he got his heart broken, when he graduated from high school, and when he announced that he had gotten his dream job.

Oliver suddenly felt like the luckiest man alive. For he not only got to have these two special ladies in his life, he also had a devoted, loving, and very attentive father to look up to.

As Oliver removed the album from his lap and put it in a safe place, he believed that he understood things much better. He could now see why Monica had tried to keep that piece of information hidden from the world, and it only made him love her more.

Oliver took the next four days to sort through the rest of the boxes – keeping some things and throwing other things away. He then helped to prepare things pertaining to the funeral, and the gathering afterwards. On the fifth day, Oliver was an emotional mess. And as much as he would have liked to sit and rest, today was his mother's funeral.

Oliver parked the car in the freshly-paved parking lot, and then took a lot of air into his lungs. It was released slowly, as he stepped out and stood up, and then he made his way up to the large, elegantly-engraved, front doors. The building was pristine, mostly white, but certainly not a place that one enjoys going to.

A well-dressed man held the door opened and offered, "Good morning, sir. Welcome to the Aramis Funeral Home."

"Morning." Oliver mirrored the man's tone of voice when he spoke, but certainly not his cheerful personality.

The employee of the funeral home stepped aside to make the entrance easier. There was only one event happening that day, so he stretched out the palm of his hand to show Oliver where to go.

Oliver nodded his thanks. He proceeded to walk towards where he heard the sounds of the many people talking. It soon became apparent, that they were commenting on how much they loved the person who had been laid out so nicely in the coffin. Oliver's face was becoming warm, and he was now fighting back the tears.

Oliver said his hello's in a low and mono-toned voice, and then walked over to his mom to pay his respects. As he approached the rich-looking, shiny, dark wooden casket, his tears were begging to be released. He hated what was happening and wished that he could turn back time, but he knew that was not possible. Still, had he known that his mother would die before the year was out, he would have come back home sooner.

As Oliver looked down at his beautiful mom, he heard small groups of people shuffling behind him. When he turned to see where they were all going, the minister whispered that the funeral service was about to begin.

Oliver didn't want to walk away from the woman who had raised him, but someone had a hold of his arm, and they were guiding him to sit in the front row.

Minutes later, the minister was at the front of the room, and he began to speak about the life of the individual in the coffin.

"Good afternoon", he began in a strong and loud voice. "We are gathered here today, to say good-bye to Mrs. Monica Ryng."

As the eulogy unfolded, Oliver looked over to study the 11 x 14" picture of the beautiful woman he had known as 'mom'. He could recall each and every exciting event that they had shared together, but his mind couldn't distinguish if the recollection was what he knew on his own, or what had been regaled to him on more than a thousand occasions. He quickly decided that it didn't matter, as all of those memories were very precious. It took his breath away to look at her, for she was even more beautiful than he had remembered.

Her hair was dark and flowing, and she liked to wear it loose. Her smile was infectious, and her personality was warm and inviting. She was easy to talk to, and she always made everyone around her feel safe and happy. And when she hugged him, there was a definite difference in their heights and body sizes; she was short and tiny, and she claimed that she loved that he was bigger.

Oliver's head bent forward in an automatic response to his grief, and he tried not to cry out loud. In his mind, he asked God why she had been taken from him. In an almost inaudible method, an answer was provided. Somewhere, from deep down in his soul, he heard the following message.

"Remove the veil of darkness, my son, so that it does not block the light which I will provide you, in order to cast warmth and healing upon your wounded heart. God has a specific purpose for all souls on Earth, and your mother's time had come to be with Him, again. Try to remember that she is but a moment away, and the instant you think about her, she will be right by your side. She is well, my son, and has always been very proud of you. She wants you to carry on with your life, just as you have been doing. Please move forward now, and do not lose your faith in God; He did not take your mother away from this Earth – He brought her back home."

Oliver's eyes popped open with fear, and he immediately looked to all sides of where he was sitting. He could see that everyone else in the room was facing forward, and listening intently to the end of the hour-long service.

Oliver had to wonder if he had dreamed the message that he had just heard. He couldn't be certain, but perhaps the minister had delivered something similar, and his brain had interpreted it to make it more personal.

Oliver's right hand came up to the top of his head, while confusion invaded his very soul. With his fingers spread apart, they found their way through his hair, and eventually slid from his forehead to the back of his neck. With anguish written all over his face, he couldn't dispute the fact that the message felt real, like someone had been talking directly to him.

"Oliver Ryng?"

Oliver jumped when he heard his name being called, and he could feel his flesh crawl from sheer fright. He looked up and then noticed that the minister was looking in his direction.

"Would you like to say a few words?" The minister was beckoning him to come up, by using hand gestures.

Oliver suddenly remembered that he had been asked to speak. Absolute panic rushed through his body as he rose from his seat. He reached into his pocket for his notes, while he made his way up the two wooden steps. He flattened out his paper on the podium, and hoped that his anxiety would shrink - even a little bit. "Hi and thank you for coming", he began.

Oliver Everette Ryng felt faint and ill, as he delivered the 7-minute eulogy. His toes were sweating inside of his polished, black shoes, and his voice was quivering as he breathed the carefully-selected words. He felt embarrassed when he had inadvertently lost his place – not once but twice, in the two-page speech. He truly hated that he was there, in front of approximately 80 people, and saying

good-bye to one of the most important people in his life –
his mother.

Oliver finished his eloquent homily with a simple,
'Thank you'. He then bowed and rushed back to his seat.

"Let us stand!" the minister commanded in a booming
voice.

Oliver got to his feet along with everyone else. He
then saw the minister spread his arms wide open, as the
church music began to play softly in the background. It all
felt so powerful, and he made a mental note to thank all
of those who were responsible for helping him plan this
magnificent event.

"As you leave here today, keep Monica in your heart",
the minister instructed. "God will watch over her, as he
will continue to do with all of you. Now, let us bow our
heads and recite The Lord's Prayer."

Everyone did as they were told, and four minutes later,
the funeral service was over. The minister exited down
the narrow aisle first, followed by Oliver and everyone
else.

Outside of the church, on a small patch of grass, is
where they stopped and waited for the rest of the group.
The minister was the first person to extend his hand to
Oliver, in order to express his deepest condolences.

"May God bless you and send you his best angel, in order to give you the comfort and strength that you will need."

"Thank you, sir." Oliver found the minister's words to be very comforting.

Everyone else who had been in attendance that day, said thanks to the minister for a lovely service, and also offered their sincerest sympathies to Oliver.

"I'm so sorry for your loss, dear", whispered one of his mother's neighbours.

"I'm so sorry for you. I realize how tough this is, but because she talked about you all the time, I know that she loved you very much", a woman from the church stated.

"She was an amazing woman", Iba Boda, another neighbour, claimed with pride.

"Hello, dear", a little old lady stated. "Your mother was such a wonderful woman, and I'm very sorry that she's gone."

"Thank you", Oliver replied softly. She was old and looked fragile, and he treated her more gently than anyone else he had seen that day.

Gail Traverse was not surprised or hurt that Oliver didn't remember her voice, for their brief conversation had broken his heart. Gail moved out of the way to let the next

person in line give him their love, without ever letting on
who she was.

Oliver made sure to thank them all for coming, while
trying desperately not to let his tears escape from their safe
spot, behind his puffy wet eyes. He had been listening to
all of their well-wishes, and there were a few times where
one or two of the salty liquid drops had fallen down his
cheeks. He made sure to wipe them away quickly, and he
hoped that no-one had noticed. He tried to remember to
keep a smile on his slightly flushed face, but it didn't always
work; he had been numb for days now, and he couldn't
remember when he had a thought that didn't pertain to
his mother and her funeral.

Oliver was the last person to get into his car, but he
didn't know how to drive away. The hearse had come to
collect his mother's body, and Oliver was frozen with fear
of her leaving and him never seeing her again. He watched
them load the coffin inside the long vehicle, then they shut
the doors and they were gone.

Oliver had to meet a bunch of people at the restaurant,
even though he knew that he wouldn't be the best company
on the planet. Still, it was the right thing to do.

Two hours later, he said thank you and good-bye
to everyone again. As he was driving away, he wasn't
sure where he was going, and then he decided to go
to her gravesite. His heart was pounding in his chest,
while fear of the unknown was building apprehension
throughout his body. His father's service had been

quite simple, for that's how the older man wanted it to be. His mother's service was much more elaborate, for that's how her friends wanted it to be. And while both services were nice, both were quite heartbreaking for Oliver to bear.

He drove his car through the front gates, and he had forgotten how large and beautiful the cemetery was. Oliver parked the car on the side of the dirt hill, a minute's walk from where his mother had just been buried. He got out and stood at her burial place, and looked down at the large mound of fresh dirt before him. With tears spilling from his eyes, he got down on one knee, and sifted some of the loose soot through the fingers in his right hand. As he tucked a piece of paper into the fresh mound, he spoke straight from his heart.

"I'm not sure why you didn't tell me who you really were. Maybe because you thought I was too young, and maybe you didn't want to be judged – I don't know. I do know that I love you for you, and not for any other reason. You were my mother on the day you married my father, but I've learned that you were my mother even before then."

Oliver unconsciously smoothed the ruffled soil that was surrounding the edges of his right shoe. When he had patted it all down, he stood up. He did not feel embarrassed for crying like a lost little boy; he knew that his mother would understand. But she would not want him to continue to mourn for too long.

As he looked down at the messy pile of dirt, Oliver wished for his mother to have a peaceful sleep, and he hoped to see her in his dreams.

The realization that he had once been inside of her body, suddenly draped his soul with high admiration of the person she was. Hundreds of goose bumps popped up on his arms and legs, as a cold chill travelled up his back. Oliver was not frightened, for he sensed that it was his mom. It was like she was telling him that she was ok, and thanking him for being in her life.

"Your journey of finding answers is now complete; you now know how you came to be on this earth, and that you are very loved."

What Oliver just heard wasn't a voice as such, but a clear thought that seemed to speak to him from somewhere faraway.

Oliver nodded and smiled, for he could almost feel her urging him to go on with his life. He tapped the tip of his right shoe against the ground, and he was now mentally ready to walk away. But before he could go, he gave a quick wave to his father, whose gravesite was on Monica's right, and to his first mother, Evelyn, who was in the plot on the other side of Walter.

"I love you, guys", he declared, as he began to move his feet towards the car. The wind suddenly picked up its pace, caressing his entire body, and making a whispering-like noise as it rustled through the leaves of the nearby trees and bushes.

As he walked away, Oliver could feel their love all around him.

His parents were now at peace, and so was he, although he would carry their secrets with him, for the rest of his life.

**The note in the dirt said;**


You may have left this earth today
But you'll never leave my heart
For you have laced your love within
A very tender part


A peace of you is what I'll carry
Today, tomorrow, and forever
For you're my mom and I'm your son
And someday we'll be together


Bye for now, but not for long
I'll see you in the stars
And every day until that day
That secret will be ours.


**From Oliver Ryng, to his mom oxox**

CPSIA information can be obtained
at www.ICGtesting.com
Printed in the USA
LVOW11s2228070817
544170LV00001BA/1/P